CEREMONY
OF
SEDUCTION

CEREMONY OF SEDUCTION

CASSIE RYAN

𝒜

APHRODISIA

KENSINGTON BOOKS

http://www.kensingtonbooks.com

APHRODISIA BOOKS are published by

Kensington Publishing Corp.
850 Third Avenue
New York, NY 10022

All Kensington titles, imprints and distributed lines are available at special quantity discounts for bulk purchases for sales promotion, premiums, fund-raising, educational or institutional use.

Special book excerpts or customized printings can also be created to fit specific needs. For details, write or phone the office of the Kensington Special Sales Manager: Kensington Publishing Corp., 850 Third Avenue, New York, NY 10022. Attn. Special Sales Department. Phone: 1-800-221-2647.

Aphrodisia and the A logo Reg. U.S. Pat. & TM Off.

ISBN-13: 978-0-7582-2065-3
ISBN-10: 0-7582-2065-0

First Kensington Trade Paperback Printing: August 2007
10 9 8 7 6 5 4 3 2 1

Printed in the United States of America

For those who keep me inspired on this lifelong writing journey—my critique group, The Butterscotch Martini Girls: Judi Thoman, Beverly Petrone, Isabella Clayton, Kayce Lassiter, Carol Webb, and Samantha Storm.

Special Thanks

To Audrey LaFehr for pulling my manuscript out of the slush pile and for seeing the possibility of a trilogy in my little story.

To my agent, Paige Wheeler, for all the support and encouragement.

To everyone at Kensington for a terrific HOT cover, and giving this series a home with the Aphrodisia line.

To my husband, Jon, for being my happily ever after.

Chapter 1

Alyssa Moss floated into her recurring erotic dream with a sense of keen anticipation. "Stone?" The vibrations of her words echoed as if she were in a long tunnel. Misty fog drifted around her ankles, as she searched for the man who came to her each night.

Even though she knew he would appear, she was startled when strong hands captured each of her arms from behind. She inhaled the wild scent of sandalwood, woodsy and natural, with a masculine essence completely Stone. With just his touch, her body came alive. Her breasts grew heavy and moisture dampened the inside of her thighs. "Touch me," she whispered, leaning back against him, waiting for the moment his large hands would caress her full breasts. Anticipation in the form of white-hot electricity stung her nipples. "I thought you wouldn't come tonight. I've waited—"

He spun her around and silenced her with a kiss. His hands were everywhere, his tongue mating with hers, dipping and tasting her lips, her teeth, every part of her mouth. Her T-shirt swept along her skin, up over her head. He smiled that sinfully wicked grin that always made her toes curl as he flung the discarded shirt aside. His eyes darkened with desire and a feral growl rumbled deep inside his throat. Before claiming her mouth again, he laid her back on the feather bed. Her senses swirled and the bed dipped as he followed her down, anchoring his fully clothed weight on top of her.

"I'll always come for you, Princess. One of these days I'll find you and we can be together." His lavender eyes smoldered with lust as he stared down at her. "Will you tell me where you are, Alyssandra?"

She threaded her fingers through his silky mahogany hair and sighed. "I tell you every night. I'm in Phoenix, waiting for you." His hard cock dug into her stomach. She arched, wrapping her legs around his narrow hips, pressing against him, enjoying the way his rough jeans stroked and teased her wet pussy.

He shook his head. "I know not of this 'Phoenix', but I shall find it and when I do, we will be together at last." He stole her senses in a soul-searing kiss that hardened her nipples to taut beads beneath the touch of his callused hands.

She arched against him, offering herself, begging for his touch. He chuckled and she captured the sound in her mouth. "My greedy princess." His hips thrust against her hot core, mimicking what she wished he would do in reality. She moved with him, each movement rubbing against her aching clit just the way she liked. He gently rolled her nipple between his thumb and forefinger and she gasped. When his mouth replaced his hand, she released a moan. Moist heat closed over her sensitive peak and lava burned from the tip of her breast straight to her pussy, liquid heat pooling between her legs.

Stone turned his attention to her other breast. She ran a hand over his hard cock and he shuddered and groaned. She cupped the hot length of him, stroking him through his jeans as he suckled her breast harder, teeth scraping over her nipple until she thought she would explode. She traced her fingers along the waistband of his pants and slowly dipped her fingers inside to feel the silky head of his cock, already moistened with pre come.

Stone's breath hissed out as he captured her hands in his, stretching her arms high over her head, her breasts thrusting upward. "You know I cannot let you touch me like that, Alyssandra. Not yet. You are not strong enough to give sustenance, only take. But soon, very soon."

As it happened every night, her hands were magically bound. She could neither see nor feel her bindings, which only served to heighten her arousal. Another rush of excitement dampened the juncture between her thighs and she squirmed against her restraints.

"I want to feel your naked skin against me, Stone. I want to take your cock deep into my mouth before you bury yourself inside my pussy, your balls slapping against my ass while we fuck." She smiled as Stone's features suddenly appeared strained. She hoped someday, she would break his control and he'd do all of the things she longed for.

"You are a witch." He smiled down at her, his features softening, obvious affection in his gaze. "And someday I will fuck you until you can no longer stand for teasing me so wickedly." His tongue traced a slow path down to her aching mound and she bucked against him, wanting him to taste her, to suck her clit until her world shattered.

Maddeningly, he took his time, tracing her thighs, calves and feet with his rough fingers and then following with open-mouthed kisses, nips and well-placed licks. Then, he pushed her thighs wide and settled between them, placing a pillow under her ass, opening her fully to him.

"You have the most beautiful pussy, Princess." He gently separated her folds and pressed a single finger inside her slit. "Slick and wet, as always." His moistened finger traced a path downward to tease around her tight rosebud and her breath caught in her throat at the forbidden sensation. When he slowly inserted one blunt finger, a long moan ripped from her throat. "One day, I will stretch this beautiful tight ass with my cock." Before she could reply, he dropped his head and laved her clit with his tongue, erasing all her thoughts.

"Stone, yes," she managed as he began to finger-fuck her ass hard while he caressed the sensitive underside of her clit with his tongue. Her inner walls tightened, ever tighter until she teetered on the precipice, and then he pulled back. "No," she screamed in frustration. "Please, Stone. Make me come. Don't leave me like this again. I can't stand it."

He only smiled and shook his head. "You need sustenance not completion. However, I will stay with you a little longer tonight. Not to worry, Alyssandra, we will not be apart much longer. I can't stand it either."

She thrashed on the bed against her invisible bonds. She couldn't go through another night of this frustration. Every day she spent with her entire body buzzing and ready, her breasts sensitive to every movement against even her softest bras and her clit and pussy lips so swollen with need, she could only wear skirts and not pants that rubbed against her sensitive flesh. Not to mention her daydreaming about the next time she could feel Stone's touch. "Please . . ." she begged. "You can't keep leaving me like this."

"Shhh . . ." he said before dipping his head to trace the swollen folds of her pussy. She willingly gave herself up to the waves of pleasure that coursed through her body at every swipe of his talented tongue. Then Stone did something he'd never done before, surprising her. He continued to lave her slit, plunging his tongue deep inside then carrying her moisture on his tongue to stroke her clit. Then he gently probed into her ass with two fingers, stretching her slowly.

Her eyes widened and she gasped as the new sensation

zinged through her body, her nipples tightening painfully. She took a moment to allow her body to adjust to this new invasion, but then she bucked against him wanting more. He only continued the slow torture on both fronts. Each time she neared the edge, he would stop and whisper soothing words to her until the feeling would recede, just enough to keep her from coming.

Finally, after what seemed like hours, using his other hand, he inserted two fingers into her aching slit, filling her equally from both sides. She loved the sensations, but wished he would replace one of them with his hard cock. Sounds of his hands slapping against her flesh as he pumped his fingers into her filled the air, causing her breath to catch and come in choppy pants.

Suddenly, he removed his fingers, leaving her bereft and empty. Then he sucked her clit between his lips in long pulls, scraping it lightly with his teeth. Her arousal wound tighter and tighter and just before she found her peak, he dissolved away.

Her alarm clock began its relentless drone.

Alyssa opened her eyes to see her own room. "Damn him!" He had left her once again unfulfilled. She pounded the covers in frustration. Stripping off her T-shirt, the soft cloth scraping across her engorged nipples like sandpaper, she hissed against the sensation and headed to the shower. "Another wonderful morning, with a nice hard shower spray to get me off," she grumbled. "Whoever invented the handheld showerhead should receive sainthood."

Stepping under the hot spray, she wet her hair and reached for the soap. The scent of honeysuckle filled her nostrils when the soap lathered between her fingers. As steam drifted around her, she imagined Stone's large hands touching her body, caressing her as he had in her dream. She closed her eyes and spread the lather onto her sensitive breasts. She'd dreamed the touch of his calloused fingers on her body so many times, she knew how each caress would affect her. Tossing the soap back into the dish, she propped her left leg up on the side of the tub and took down the showerhead, adjusting the water to high pulse— her favorite.

She took a deep breath and in her mind's eye saw Stone's dark head between her thighs, his tongue buried deep, his thick fingers fucking her ass. Then she aimed the spray toward her aching clit. As arousal arrowed through her, she pictured his golden body naked and glistening with water. His massive cock driving deep inside her until she screamed his name. The thought sent her spiraling into an orgasm, which seemed to last forever. Energy zinged through her body, and then drained away as if it flowed down the drain with the water.

When the spasms finally eased, she sat down hard on the edge of the tub, exhausted, the showerhead still hanging limply from her hand. The sound of someone banging on the bathroom door startled her. She braced a hand against the wall as she lost her balance and fell forward in the tub. She caught herself just before tumbling headfirst.

"Alyssa! If you want a ride to work, then move your ass and quit masturbating in there. You're screaming loud enough to wake the dead!"

Her cheeks burned. "How fucking embarrassing. If Debbie keeps catching me masturbating, she's going to start checking my vision. Maybe I shouldn't have listened to my father when he said I wasn't smart enough for the driving test. If I studied hard enough and passed, I wouldn't be dependent on rides from Debbie anymore."

Chiding herself, Alyssa quickly finished her shower and dressed in her usual baggy oversized shirt, long jeans skirt, her favorite cowboy boots and a ponytail. She looked into the mirror and sighed at the sight of her pale freckles and plain face. "As usual, this is as good as it's going to get."

When she entered the kitchen twenty minutes later, Debbie was eating corn flakes and reading the morning paper. Alyssa studied her roommate and wished for the millionth time she could look more like her.

Debbie's silvery blond hair hung in a satin waterfall to her shoulders, her wispy bangs giving her a trendy look. Her perfect makeup, designer jeans and sandals showcased a tight athletic body, which would look equally at home on the pages of *Playboy* or in a modeling session.

Alyssa shook her head. She was pudgy instead of sleek and no matter how much weight she lost, she'd never look like Debbie. She had hips and breasts where Debbie had a tight trim body. That was probably why Debbie's room was a revolving door for all of the hottest guys in Phoenix. Alyssa had joked about installing a take-a-number machine on her roomie's bedroom door. Surely, she could steal one from the post office. But Debbie would just grin and say it would cost too much to keep replacing the numbers.

"Hey, you gonna eat before we go?" Debbie looked up from her cereal. "I'm sure all that whacking off helped work up an appetite." Her perfectly lined lips curved up in a smirk.

Alyssa ignored her and sighed. "I'll grab something at the bar. I'm training a new bartender this morning, so I have to be there early." She opened the side cabinet, which held all her medicine and took out the appropriate doses for the day. Ever since she'd turned sixteen, she'd been sickly and the doctors could find no cause. Instead, they treated her symptoms with no less than twenty different meds she had to take at various times throughout the day. Her adoptive parents often remarked that her real parents must not have been very healthy to pass on so many problems to their daughter. A familiar wave of pain spiked through her as she wished for parents who looked like her, acted like her, and understood her.

"Earth to Lyssa." Debbie waved a hand in front of Alyssa's

face, breaking her out of her thoughts. "Do you have your fucking pharmacy ready? We're going to be late."

Alyssa snapped her purse closed and stifled a yawn. It didn't feel like she'd slept at all last night. *Damned erotic dreams.* "Yeah, I'm ready. You're going to be able to pick me up at closing, right? I don't want to have to walk home that late."

"No sweat. I don't have a date tonight, so I'll cut out of work early and come get you. We can grab drive-through on the way home or something."

"Or something." She sighed. Debbie knew she wasn't supposed to have take-out. The doctors had kept her on a strict diet to try to minimize her symptoms. And even though nothing had helped, she did feel better when she didn't eat a constant stream of grease and french fries.

Alyssa looked up as a sly look crossed Debbie's face before she hid it. *Uh-oh, here it comes.* "What is it, Deb? You only get that look when you want something."

Debbie shrugged, trying and failing for nonchalant. "How 'bout you leave work early on Friday? I have someone you should meet."

Her mouth dropped open in shock and she turned to stare at her roommate. "You mean a guy?" Debbie always told Alyssa she wasn't attractive enough to have a relationship. And when guys did look at her, they were just staring because she looked like she needed a mercy fuck. So, why was Debbie suddenly trying to fix her up?

"Not a guy, a *man,*" Debbie clarified. "Your twenty-fourth birthday is coming up, and I know this guy who is perfect for you." She stopped and looked Alyssa up and down. "He doesn't mind body types like yours. And since he has dark hair too, he probably won't mind your muddy brown."

Disappointment and hurt arrowed through her, tears burned at the back of her eyes and she blinked rapidly to clear them. She'd known her entire life she wasn't very attractive. If her family and best friend didn't even think so, then there was no use thinking anyone else would. *The only time I feel attractive is with Stone. I just don't fit in anywhere else.* She suddenly longed to call in sick and return to bed and to the comfort of Stone's arms—even if they were only in her dreams.

"About eight o'clock, okay?" Debbie continued, either not noticing Alyssa's reaction or not caring. She bet it was the latter. "And try to wear something that hides your weight. I want him to like you."

Alyssa swallowed her embarrassment and slid into the passenger's seat. *Maybe I can get sick before Friday.*

"If I'm raped and murdered tonight, so help me, I'm going to haunt Debbie until her dying day!" Alyssa quickened her steps as the shadowed stranger behind her loomed closer. She searched the darkened street and closed shops in front of her for some sign of life, to no avail. The stifling Phoenix night closed around her like a shroud, heat still radiated off the cement and her footsteps clicked in time to her beating heart. The smell of stale grease from the Chinese restaurant permeated the air. *Why the hell can't something still be open?*

"Damn you, Debbie!" she growled under her breath, and glanced over her shoulder to see the menacing shape of the man who still followed her. Debbie was probably off fucking some pretty-boy and forgot all about her promise to pick her up after work. *If I live through tonight, I'm taking that fucking driver's test. Even if I have to study for the rest of my life to pass it, it will be worth not having to wait on Debbie.*

Quickening her steps, she rummaged in her purse for her switchblade. Luckily, an extremely drunk Hell's Angel had run short on money and made a tip of the switchblade a few months ago. Now if she could just figure out how to use it.

A strong hand gripped her shoulder, startling her and causing her to drop the knife, which skittered away over the hot cement. Time slowed and her self-defense training took over. *Thank God I didn't listen to my family and took the class anyway!* She stomped down hard on his instep, the heel of her cowboy boot hopefully leaving a permanent imprint. Then she drove her elbow back into the attacker's midsection. A surprised "oof" of pain sounded behind her and she bolted forward out of his reach.

Before she'd taken two steps, he grabbed her around the waist, and all her air whooshed out in a painful rush. When she recovered, she realized he hadn't even broken stride and she hung over his arm like a sack of dog food. If she weren't so scared, she'd have to admire the man's muscle and strength. She screamed, but no sound came out. She took a breath and tried again, but it was as if she screamed inside a soundproof room.

"Calm down, witch," he said and slapped her on the bottom. "I haven't searched for you for ten years to have you feed me my own bollocks." The voice, which held a note of amusement, was so deep she felt the rumbling through his arms wrapped beneath her ass. There was something familiar about it she couldn't quite place.

"Put me down, you bastard!" Alyssa was surprised to hear her voice this time, although muted. She kicked and flailed to no avail. She started to bite him, but some deep internal instinct warned her not to push her luck. She could sense the aura of power that surrounded him without ever seeing his face. And she'd learned long ago not to ignore her gut.

"In good time, witch. You're almost home." He punctuated his remarks with another slap on her ass.

He knows where I live? Oh, God, I'm going to raped and murdered in my own shabby apartment!

She raised her head and was shocked to see her apartment steps come into view. Metallic panic rose in the back of her throat, and she renewed her struggles. As a single woman, she knew better than to let her attacker get her inside the apartment. Better to take a stand outside where someone could happen along or she had a hope of escape. But just as she took a breath to scream, he set her down in front of her apartment door, sliding her down his firm body until her feet touched the concrete. She startled when something about the sensation tickled her memory.

The scream died in her throat as she looked into the face of a familiar stranger.

Stone.

She'd know him anywhere since she'd dreamt of him so often over the past ten years, she hadn't ever bothered to find a flesh-and-blood man. To find him here now, standing in front of her, sent an erotic thrill racing through her body.

She shook her head, convinced she was dreaming again, but none of her dreams of him had ever taken place anywhere but in an ethereal bedroom. She took a moment to study him and compare him to her dream memory. He towered over her five-nine frame so much he would have to duck to walk through her apartment door. Broad shoulders stretched his black T-shirt taut across a well-defined chest, and his face resembled chiseled granite. When he smiled, the small dimple next to his mouth softened him, making him seem approachable. Unruly mahogany hair gave him a rakish air and liquid lavender eyes, the same color as her own, stared back at her.

His deep rumbling chuckle shook her from her reverie and she realized she'd been staring. "Do you see anything you like, witch?" His tone held a teasing warmth as he gestured to himself from head to toe. Following his hand all the way down, she noticed an extremely large bulge that tightened the front of his jeans.

She swallowed hard as she recalled her dream with him last night and liquid heat pooled between her legs and dampened her panties. Then fear and the remaining adrenaline brought her back to reality. How could a flesh and blood man invade her dreams? Could this man really be Stone?

"Who are you?" she demanded, ignoring his question.

"You already know who I am. The more appropriate question is who are you and why have I come to find you." He crossed muscular arms over his chest and grinned while he waited for her to ask.

An overwhelming curiosity had her inviting him in before she could think better of it. Her intuition was blissfully silent and she took that as a good sign. But her pussy screamed to be introduced more intimately.

Thankfully, her roommate wasn't fucking an entire football team in the living room, like she was last time Alyssa came home. She tossed her purse on the counter and grabbed two bottled waters from the fridge. She handed one to Stone who had already made himself comfortable on her couch. "So who am I?" she asked, as her fingers itched to trace the strong lines of his body. "Why did you come to find me? And who the hell are you?" Alyssa settled herself on the opposite end of the couch where she could watch him, and waited for him to dissolve at any instant.

He took his time studying her as she had him. Finally, he twisted the cap off the bottle of water and swallowed half in two large gulps. "You," he pointed toward her, "are Alyssandra de Klatch, First Princess of the Klatch. And I've told you for years, one day I'd find you and we could finally be together."

Shock traveled all the way to her gut. When she dreamed of him, he'd always called her Alyssandra or Princess. That was one of the reasons she'd always assumed he was purely a product of her overactive imagination. All of this was crazy, but something inside her knew he wasn't lying. But a princess? Not likely.

"Stone," she whispered. *I might be losing my mind, but if I get to be insane with him for the rest of my life, I'll take that over what I've lived for the past twenty-three years.*

He nodded, his lopsided smile making his dimple more pronounced. "Yes, you remember me." He looked pleased. "If you'd taken better care of yourself, witch, then you wouldn't have had to subsist on dreams. Since I'm here now, we can rectify that situation."

She blushed as she realized exactly what his definition of "rectify" was. "Stop calling me witch and just answer the rest of my questions!" *Or throw me on the floor now, and we can talk later . . .*

He shook his head. "Your heritage is very strong." He rubbed his stomach and chuckled. "As well as the rest of you. But you are a witch. A *Klatch* witch."

She narrowed her eyes at him. "You said my name was Alyssandra de Klatch. But that still doesn't make me a witch. And I was born Alyssa Moss."

"No, actually you were stolen from your true family by Cunts."

"Excuse me?" she demanded, shocked he would use the offensive term in front of her. "I'm far from prudish, but I *hate* that word."

"As you should." He laughed, the warm sexy sound, which had melted her in her dreams, even now caused her nipples to tighten against her thin cotton top. His eyes zeroed in on her shirt as if he knew. She blushed and looked away. "My apologies. You have lived among the humans for far too long to understand my reference. Long ago, the Klatch had a civil war and split into two factions, the original Klatch and a new faction who called themselves Cunts."

Alyssa snorted in disbelief. "You've got to be fucking kidding me."

"As much as I'd like to fuck you . . . no. I do not joke about our history." He took another long pull of the water and she was fascinated by the way his throat worked as he swallowed. She resisted a sudden urge to run her tongue over the dip in his throat where his Adam's apple bobbed. His eyes glinted with mirth and she was afraid he knew what she'd been thinking.

Mercifully, he continued without mentioning it. In one fluid movement, he stood and pulled her to him, pressing her against the long line of his body. Her breath caught in her throat and every inch of her body screamed for her to rub herself shamelessly against him—or maybe just throw him on the floor and impale herself on his cock.

The sudden urge slapped her back to reality and she bolted from his grasp, putting the couch between them. He merely chuckled and continued. "The word 'cunt' is used as a slur because witches interact with humans and they pick up on our language. 'Cunt' has become synonymous with 'traitor' and 'outcast' to any witch. Although the humans use it in a slightly different way. Now come and kiss me, Alyssandra, I want to finally feel your lips in the physical world."

When he started around the couch after her, she held up a hand. "Wait." She gave her traitorous body a firm talking to, *this can't be real so work with me here,* and pierced him with her most skeptical stare. "What do witches have to do with this? You mean like Wiccans?"

He leaned forward resting his forearms on the back of the couch, causing the already tight black T-shirt to mold over the best shoulders she'd ever seen. Shoulders she knew she'd seen before—and felt before. She licked her lips at the sudden urge to trace each inch of his muscular shoulders with her tongue.

He continued, breaking her out of her thoughts. "Wiccans are humans who choose to practice a set of beliefs. Being Klatch is what you are." He shook his head and sighed. "I can see the Cunts withheld from you your heritage. This must be remedied." His hand snaked out to grab her arm and he pulled her to him across the back of the couch. When he cradled her in his lap on the couch, his strong arms bracketed around her, a sexual thrill zinged straight to her pussy. The fact that a very large bulge swelled against her hip only served to scramble her thoughts further.

He smiled, his eyes darkened dangerously. But a dangerous she knew from ten years of dreams that meant wonderful sexual things, not anything to harm her. Every erogenous zone in her body rejoiced, drowning her in a sea of sexual energy.

She put her fingers against his lips when he lowered his face to hers. "Please, tell me about the Klatch." Anything to keep him talking until she could figure out how he evoked these feelings inside her.

"A Klatch witch is a being who needs sexual energy to survive. We also eat and drink, but in order to thrive, we must imbibe sexual energy." He kissed the fingers still resting lightly against his lips and then pulled one into his mouth. He sucked on the tip and swirled his tongue in a familiar pattern she remembered him using on the soft underside of her clit—which throbbed in response. She pulled her finger away, her breathing coming in short gasps.

His voice was a low rumble when he spoke. "Intercourse is the best and easiest, but any kind of sexual energy will do: masturbation, voyeurism, or even sexual dreams."

Alyssa found herself laughing despite the sexually charged atmosphere. "You're trying to tell me I'm some kind of sexual vampire?"

"Good God, no." He looked horrified at the suggestion. "You are no succubus, Princess. You are my betrothed and a full-blooded Princess of Klatch."

"Betrothed?" She gasped, and her mouth fell open. "As in engaged to be married?"

He nodded. "Yes, most Klatch never marry. They will either

have half-breed children with humans or just feed from humans sexually their whole lives. But the full-blooded Klatch are betrothed at birth to another of full blood to retain the line and our heritage." He lowered his mouth to hers, but at the first jolting and very familiar touch of his lips, she squirmed out of his grasp and put half the room's distance between them.

Alyssa's mind whirled. When he was near her, it felt like all her circuits were on overload. She looked up into his darkened lavender eyes. The hunk of testosterone who sat across from her thought he was her fiancé? How lucky could she get? Her body immediately wanted to claim its conjugal rights. But then her overly logical mind weighed in and ruined everything.

"Look, I don't even know you. You follow me home from work, scare me half to death and now you're trying to tell me I'm some sort of witch who feeds off sex?" She paced back and forth in front of the coffee table. A large ball of lead settled in her gut and she knew at least some of what Stone said was true. She could feel it deep inside her. "Why did you wait until now to find me?"

"Alyssandra, I have searched for you for ten years. You were well hidden among the humans. When the civil war ended, they stole you as a bargaining tool so the king and queen would not hunt down the remaining Cunts. Then they slithered away to the human world to hide." He stood and laid a comforting hand on her shoulder. "I know you believe and I also know you don't want to. But tell me this. Did you fit in growing up? Are you like your parents or your siblings or even your friends?"

The awful truth hit her like a sledgehammer. She squeezed her eyes shut as tears burned at the back of her eyes. He was right. She'd never fit in and she never had any true friends. Her mother and father had fair hair and she had dark. Her pale lavender eyes had always been a topic of fascination or outright teasing and her early development of full hips and breasts had set her apart from her model-thin mother and sisters. She figured that's why she'd dreamt of a handsome man who made her feel as if she belonged. But now, with him standing so close she could smell the woodsy musk of pure man, she knew better. "Are my adoptive parents . . ." She struggled with the word, "Cunts?"

He nodded and gestured to a family picture hanging on her wall. "The civil war came partially because of physical differences. The offspring of Klatch and humans who called themselves Cunts are fair of hair and skin and usually have thin bodies. The remaining faction of Klatch are dark haired, olive skinned and blessed with curves." He stared down at her body as if he could see through the baggy clothes. She thought he would devour her whole.

"The Cunts thought themselves more attractive, superior and better breeding stock, so they tried to overthrow the king . . . and failed."

Alyssa thought back over her life. Her family had always treated her more as a pet who wasn't very smart than a part of the family. College was never an option. Her father convinced her she just couldn't handle the higher learning and it wouldn't be worth wasting the money. The same thing happened when she wanted to get a driver's license.

So, she'd gone to bartending school. The pay was decent and she enjoyed interacting with the customers—most of the time. As for her personal life, her sisters still teased her about being fat and her long dark hair was always downplayed as less attractive than their lighter tresses. If everything Stone said was true, it made a lot of things more clear. *Go with your gut!*

"What exactly do you want me to do?" Her mind whirled.

"Your twenty-fourth birthday grows near and you will be coming of age. Because of your heritage, you'll be an extremely powerful witch in her own right. Come with me and meet your real parents and then you can decide."

She closed her eyes and searched inside herself for answers. Should she trust Stone? This entire situation was too crazy for words. She went with her gut. "Prove to me you are who you say you are, and I'll go."

Chapter 2

Stone's desire reached a fevered pitch and he reined it in hard. He very much wished he could reenact their joint dream last night—*then* she would be a true believer. However, he needed to get her back to Klatch as soon as possible before the Cunts found her. "As you wish, Princess." He'd waited for years to touch and possess his betrothed, but he could not slide his aching cock inside her until her coming-of-age ceremony. She needed the sustenance of many strong Klatch men to fully attain her powers. Before that, emptying his seed inside her would be dangerous and most likely fatal.

That didn't mean he couldn't prove to her now that she already trusted him with her heart and body. Her heart-shaped face tipped up to him in a silent plea, her ripe lips softly parted, waiting. He threaded his fingers through her long mahogany ponytail. The hair flowed through his fingers like silk, the scent of honeysuckle scenting the air. He longed to see the cascade of hair surround her like a halo.

Her pale lavender eyes watched warily as he slipped the elastic band from her hair and let it fall to the floor. Freed from its prison, her hair fell in dark waves to her shapely waist. Pulling her tight against him, he ground his hard cock against her, enjoying the way her lips rounded in a surprised "o." He feathered kisses over her face until she melted against him. "I told you I'd always come for you, Princess," he whispered against her forehead. "And that we would be together." She gasped. He knew she recognized the words he'd said in their dream last night. He swallowed the sounds of her surprise as he captured her mouth with his.

She tasted stronger in person, like honey and exotic spices, and his energy flowed into her with every touch and caress. She twined her arms around his neck and he pulled up the back of her skirt so he could touch the beautiful skin of her bottom through her thin panties. He hardened further as he remembered his two fingers buried deep inside her sweet ass in their dream joining last night. How much more intense would it be when he buried his cock inside her slit, taking her virginity?

He steeled himself against the urge to throw her to the ground and take her now. *You are a Prince of Klatch, you have control over your urges.* He just hoped it was true. Reluctantly, he pulled away and steadied her as she swayed on her feet, her eyes still closed in ecstasy. "Princess?" he asked softly.

Alyssa slowly opened her eyes, a large smile bloomed over her face. "It is you." She traced his face tentatively with her fingers. "I've waited for you a long time. I'm ready for wherever you're going to take me."

"Leave now and I won't kill you!" came a voice from the back of the apartment.

Alyssandra whirled in his arms to face the intruder. "Debbie, what are you doing?"

Stone stepped in front of his betrothed, protecting her from this Cunt bent on harming her. She may not be familiar with the ways of the witching world yet, but he was. He could feel the princess's energy draining into this intruder witch's aura.

No wonder his beloved appeared drawn and exhausted. "I've come to reclaim the princess. You'll have to find another victim to feed from, Cunt."

"Debbie's not—" Alyssa began.

"She is ours, Klatch. Step away from her, and I won't kill you." Debbie turned her attention to Alyssandra, her voice cajoling. "Come on, Lyssa. Are you going to believe some man over your best friend?"

Stone held his breath as shock clouded the princess's lovely features. He couldn't force her to come with him—that would only drain her powers further, and she was weak enough now that she might have complications from the trip *between*. She reached up to touch his face and he sent a jolt of his own energy flowing into her body. She moaned and stiffened from the contact and his cock throbbed.

"Lyssa, step away from him and go into your room. Now." Debbie gestured toward the princess, increasing her drain spell, causing Alyssandra to sway.

He steadied her against him, then brought his hand down in a chopping motion across the field of draining energy, cutting the connection. Immediately, the Cunt's legs buckled under her and she fell to her knees as her own spell rebounded toward its creator.

The princess straightened and whirled to face him. "What just happened?" She stared down at her pale roommate.

"She's been draining your energy. The Cunts like to use the Klatch as a food supply of sorts. That's why you're always exhausted and tired." Several emotions including hurt and shock flowed across her face one after another until finally, realization and then anger prevailed.

She stalked across the room where Debbie, still on her knees, knelt dazed and weak. "All this time, you've watched me take numerous medications and endure all those painful tests at the doctor every month and you continued to feed on me like . . .

like a damned parasite? I trusted you. . . I wanted so much to be like you . . ."

Debbie raised a hand and as it connected with Alyssa's ankle, she swayed again. Before Stone could raise his hand to hit the Cunt with another spell, Debbie's hair began to stand on end and small sparks of static electricity popped and crackled along her skin. Suddenly the Cunt's head snapped back, her eyes rolling upward until only the whites showed before she slumped to the floor.

Pride swelled in Stone's chest. Alyssandra may not know how to use her Klatch powers yet, but she just proved to herself she had them.

She turned to him, her eyes sparkling, her cheeks flushed, her mouth open with disbelief. "What did I do to her?"

"She tried to drain your energy and make you black out. You reversed the spell and took her energy instead."

"How the hell . . ." She stared down at the still, pale form of the Cunt for several moments before turning to him. "I'm ready, Stone. There's nothing here for me now. Show me who I really am."

He concentrated, waved his hand in the air in front of him and opened a portal to the Klatch world. The air shimmered and expanded until it was an oval large enough for them to walk through. He raised the princess's hand to his lips and brushed a kiss against the silky skin. "Come with me to your new life."

Alyssa took a deep breath and stepped through the portal. The air around her sizzled, raising hairs all over her body. She shivered as the dark still air surrounded her, making it difficult to breathe, the tang of mold strong on the back of her tongue. Her only link to reality was his warm fingers twined with hers. Anxiety and doubts assailed her. What was this place? "Stone?" Her voice quivered. She hated the note of panic she heard.

"It is called *between* because it links the human world with our own." His voice sounded distant and tinny. She squeezed his hand to reassure herself he stood right beside her. Each step became harder than the last, like walking through thick molasses. Her limbs, suddenly heavy, drug her down, her energy draining away. But just when she was about to ask Stone to stop and let her rest, a shimmering oval appeared in front of her, illuminating the blackness.

The oval grew until it was large enough for them to step through. The shimmering faded and a lush landscape appeared beyond the opening. A gasp sounded in her ears, echoing around her, and only when Stone chuckled did she realize the sound had come from her.

She stepped through the opening after him, unable to take her eyes off the sights before her. Dappled sunshine kissed green rolling hills that reminded her of pictures she'd seen of Ireland. Lush trees and plants of every color imaginable dotted the landscape in blues, greens, lavenders and reds. Birds and wildlife chirped and rustled, giving the impression that she'd stepped into a pristine rainforest. A crisp fresh breeze brushed the strands of her hair against her cheek and carried the sweet scent of flowers. Turning in a circle, she tried to take in every sight at once.

"Welcome home."

His voice, dark and low, broke her out of her perusal and made her think of dark sweaty nights in his arms. Her nipples tightened to hard nubs and heat coiled in her stomach causing a new rush of moisture to dampen her thighs. She turned to Stone, and her heart swelled with hope and excitement for the first time in her life. The dream world she looked forward to every night had now become her reality. She was here with Stone in this amazing place. Even though the betrayal from the people she'd always thought of as her family still stung, she wasn't ready to deal with those emotions yet. Instead, she concentrated on the here and now, a luxury she'd never let herself enjoy before. "Is this Klatch? And why is it daytime here, but night at home?"

"Actually, our world is called Tador. And the human world and ours are always on opposite schedules." He pulled her into his arms and pressed the long line of his hard body against hers, his hard cock digging against her stomach. "You need more nourishment before we make the trek into the city."

Thousands of questions flowed through her mind, but when Stone fused his mouth with hers, they all dissolved like dust on the wind. His tongue traced her lips before he dipped inside as if he sampled a delicacy. He tasted spicy and masculine, as if he'd drunk rum earlier. Kissing him greedily, she slid her fingers into his hair, and pulled him closer. Rough stubble scratched against her cheeks reminding her of how that same stubble felt against her swollen slit last night in her dreams. The thought immediately triggered another rush of moisture between her thighs. If her clit swelled any more, she thought it might explode.

Still kissing her, he pulled her down to lie on the soft grass beside him, in between two large trees, the leaves casting dappled light over their bodies. She wriggled closer, and pressed her breasts against his chest. A sense of power shot through her as he moaned into her mouth.

Her whole life she'd been timid and afraid, but with Stone, she could be confident and sexy. She planned to take full advantage of it. She ground her hips against the large erection straining at the front of his pants and ran a finger just under the waistband of his jeans to stroke the velvety tip of his cock. His surprised intake of breath made her smile.

"Alyssandra, you mustn't tease me. I've waited too long for you."

She tangled her tongue with his, gently pulled open the top button of his jeans, slowly unzipping them. She'd expected him to grab her hand as he'd done in her dreams. When he didn't stop her, she reached inside his pants and finding no boxers or underwear of any kind, she wrapped her fingers around his large cock. He gasped, and his head dropped back onto the grass as if the sensation was too much for him.

She stroked the length of him, enjoying the silky feel of his skin against her palm, and the firm hardness when she squeezed him. He was long, thick and hot in her hand and she longed to trace him with her tongue or even better yet, impale herself and fuck him until they were both exhausted. Stone arched into her touch, and suddenly braver, she leaned down until she could trace a tentative line over the head of his cock with her tongue.

His breath hissed out, but when he didn't push her away, she wrapped her lips around the engorged head, and caressed it with her tongue. She loved the silky texture of his cock inside her mouth. The taste of his pre come, tangy and sweet, burst across her tongue and she made an "mmm" sound deep in her throat. A surge of energy flowed through her body, traveling along every nerve ending until she was ready to burst.

When she slid her lips down over Stone's shaft, taking him as deep as her throat would allow, a sudden orgasm burst over her and a kaleidoscope of colors flashed before her eyes. Then suddenly, the world began to spin until darkness swallowed her.

When her mind finally cleared, she was lying on her back, the soft grass tickling her arms and neck. Stone kneeled over her, his magnificent cock still hard and proud against his belly, protruding from the open fly of his jeans. She thought back over the last few minutes and gasped. *How embarrassing! I finally get his cock in my mouth and I come . . . I must have bitten him or something!*

Stone laughed. "You did not bite me, little one. My essence was too strong for you before your coming-of-age ritual. Only then will we be able to fully enjoy one another."

She bolted upright and her head swam with the sudden

movement. "How did you know what I was thinking?" Fear and embarrassment warred inside her.

He reached out to steady her. "Don't worry, I can't read your mind—not yet. The look on your face made it clear what horrible thing you thought you had done." He brushed a wayward strand of hair out of her face. "You blacked out when my pre come overloaded your system. But on a bright note, you have enough energy now to make it into the city."

Looking between them, she nodded toward his cock, still hard against his stomach. She reached up to smooth away the line of strain between his brows. "I have lots of questions about this coming-of-age ceremony, and everything else. But right now, you need some energy of your own." She wrapped her fingers around him. After everything he'd done for her—even if most of it was in her dreams—she refused to leave him unsatisfied.

He placed a hand over hers, stopping her motions. "You can't let my essence touch you, not yet. As you've already seen, it would be too dangerous."

"I agree." She pulled away from him before kicking off her boots. Then she stood to remove her jean skirt.

"What are you doing?" He sounded almost panicked.

Enjoying his discomfort, she continued to strip, dropping her clothes in a small pile beside her. "You obviously need energy, and from what I understand so far, anything sexual will do, right?"

Stone's brows knit with confusion, but he nodded slowly. "Yes, anything sexual. But—"

Alyssa dropped her bra into the pile of clothes and stood bare before him. She took a deep breath and let it out slowly. *You've come this far, you might as well go all the way. This has been one of your fantasies for years, so why not make it come true?* "Then let me see you, all of you. You can . . . take care of yourself, while I do the same." When he only continued to stare at her, she continued quickly as if to ward off his impending rejection. "I just thought we would still be able to share sexual energy that way."

A slow smile spread across his rugged face and he jumped to his feet, kicking off his boots while pulling his shirt over his head. "I love your creative thinking, Princess."

Within seconds, he stood before her naked. His sculpted muscles were just as she'd imagined, his olive skin lightly dusted with dark hair. Following the line of his tapered waist, and the intriguing line of dark hair that arrowed down toward his groin, she studied his cock, now freed from his clothes and nestled in a patch of mahogany hair. His balls hung tight against his body and she wished she could feel their texture with both her mouth and her fingers.

She'd never touched a man's balls before, in fact before a few minutes ago, she'd never held a cock in her hand, or tasted come. It was a day for firsts and she didn't want to waste one minute.

Taking Stone's offered hand, they knelt in the grass facing each other, their legs open, bent at the knees and tangled around each other. She giggled as the lush greenery tickled her bare ass and she leaned back against a large boulder, the stone cool against her bare back.

Stone grasped his cock and slowly stroked its impressive length. "Fuck yourself for me, Alyssandra. Let me see you."

Reaching down tentatively, she rubbed her first two fingers against her aching clit. Sensations and energy flowed through her as her own juices coated her fingers, lubricating her movements. Stone continued to stroke himself, and she imagined his cock filling her, stretching her, his hot come spilling inside her. "I've always wanted to watch you pleasure yourself while I masturbate." The flower-scented breeze played across her ripe nipples heightening her arousal.

Stone relaxed against the tree trunk, one hand cupped his

balls, stroking his cock faster. Noticing pre come that glistened on the tip, she licked her lips and couldn't wait to taste him again—hopefully when she could do it without blacking out. She rubbed her clit faster and with her other hand, rolled her nipple between her thumb and forefinger and then pulled on the ripe bud, enjoying the fresh spurt of energy that surged through her. Her arousal continued to tighten inside her, energy flowing through her veins like lava. He stroked faster now, his breathing labored and uneven, matching her own.

"Come for me, Stone. Let me see you come, push me over the edge. Please . . ."

As if triggered by her words, Stone's body shuttered and creamy fluid spurted from his cock. At the sight, her own orgasm broke over her in a rolling wave. Almost peripherally, she noticed he aimed to the side, so his essence wouldn't touch her, and kept pumping, milking his cock until every last drop escaped.

Her head swam as the energy flowing through her threatened to overwhelm her. She slumped sideways, lying flat on the grass, and closed her eyes. Her nipples and her pussy still tingled with delicious little aftershocks and her bare skin prickled with goose bumps as the gentle breeze teased her already sensitized system. *God help me, he didn't even touch me and that's the most intense orgasm I've ever had.*

Stone pulled his T-shirt on over his head and turned to see Alyssandra pulling up her jeans skirt. "Well, witch," he said with affection and smiled when she blushed. "It seems you've given us both enough energy to make it to the city and back ten times over, even with those orgasms."

Her eyes widened with shock, but then her face softened and a smile blossomed across her face. "Anything I can do to help. And what do you mean, even with the orgasms?"

Stone knew she didn't have much experience with compliments or praise. He planned to change that. "The sex helps you build your energy, but until you can harness it—until your coming-of-age ceremony, the orgasm drains some of it away again."

"At least now I know why you left me hot and bothered every night and dissolved away." She sat on a nearby boulder and pulled on her cowboy boots.

"Believe me, I would've liked nothing better than to finish what I started. I too was left 'hot and bothered' as you put it. But don't worry, your ceremony will take care of that problem." A mental picture of him sliding his aching cock inside her hot core sent a sudden flood of arousal straight toward his groin and he had to adjust himself inside the tight jeans more comfortably.

"How am I supposed to remember all this stuff? I feel very out of my element."

The vulnerability in her eyes made him ache. This woman should have been raised as royalty, not treated like a pet for the Cunts. He fisted his hands at his sides, containing his anger. "You'll learn, give yourself time."

She nodded slowly and combed her fingers through her hair, smoothing the mahogany locks into a ponytail. Before she could slip the elastic band in place, he snatched it from her hand, pulling her into his arms and fused his mouth with hers. Threading his fingers through the silky waterfall of her hair, the scent of honeysuckle surrounded him and he inhaled, trying to imprint her smell into his memory.

Pulling back reluctantly, he leaned his forehead against hers. "This is your world, Alyssandra—yours and mine. We will rule together and the world will prosper." He took a deep breath and then said with obvious strain in his voice, "And don't bind your hair. There's not a bigger crime against nature than hiding your beautiful crowning glory." He kissed her forehead and took her hand as he resisted the urge to undress her again and spend the entire day discovering every secret her curvy body held. "Ready for the walk into the city?"

She nodded and bent to pick a small blue flower, bringing it to her nose to inhale the musky vanilla fragrance she knew it held. "Tell me about the city. What's it like?"

They walked hand in hand, picking a path through the trees, the wind whistling through the leaves and branches high above them. The path before them dappled with sunlight. "It's beautiful, built from *balda,* the white stone which is native to Tador. Throughout the city, there are waterfalls and fountains that feed into bathing pools and several large grassy areas dotted with trees and flowers." He pulled a branch back, allowing her to pass before letting it spring back into place.

"It sounds lovely. And a bathing pool sounds great about now."

Trying not to think about all the wonderful things he wanted to do to her inside a bathing pool, he swallowed hard and willed his erection to relax. "Soon enough. But for now, I think we should discuss your parents."

She stopped walking and turned to face him, all the blood draining from her face, leaving her pale and drawn. "My parents?" Pulling her hand from his grasp, she slumped down against a large boulder. "I've thought about it a few times since I found out about my parents—my real parents. But I think I was afraid to ask."

"Why?" He knelt in front of her and placed a finger under her chin, raising it until she met his gaze. "They have been looking for you for twenty-three years. It was extremely hard for them to wait until I reached maturity and could psychically connect with you. Until that day when I turned sixteen, they didn't know if you were dead or alive."

She sighed, the sound sad and vulnerable. "How much worse for them. I spent my entire life not even knowing they existed." Her eyes sparkled with tears and a lone drop slid down her cheek.

He caught the tear on the end of his finger before he placed the salty liquid on his tongue, her energy and her grief surging through him from the contact.

"What do I say to them? How do I know they won't be disappointed with who I am?"

He pulled her against his chest and buried her head against his shoulder, as Alyssa let the sobs come. "Shhh, beloved. They will love you as I do." She stiffened in his arms at his words. She would have to come to terms with his feelings for her, but not now. He knew she hadn't thought him real all those years, but he had always known one day they would be together.

He'd lost his heart to her over the course of the first several months of their dream contacts. Meeting the real woman all these years later only assured him of his love. "They are your parents and would gladly have traded places with me all these years. I got to connect with you each night and they were forced to wait until I came into my powers and was able to search for you in the human realm."

Gently rocking her, he let her sob. He knew years of frustration and loneliness had finally caught up to her as well as the betrayal of those she thought were her family. Through her dreams, he'd learned enough to know that the Cunts had eroded her self-confidence and sense of worth from infancy. She'd spent her life hiding behind baggy clothes and developed an uncanny ability to blend into the background. He'd done his best inside her dreams to show her how special a woman she was, but each dream connection took so much energy, he often didn't have time to do anything but give her sustenance and retreat before having to recharge himself.

She pulled away far enough to raise her tear-stained face to his. "Do they look like me?" She looked so hopeful and fragile, he was glad to reassure her.

Wiping away her tears with his thumb, he nodded. "Your mother looks just like you, except her hair is longer. King

Darius looks much like me—all the Klatch do. Dark hair and lavender eyes are the easiest ways to identify the Klatch."

"Darius . . ." She looked up at him, her teary eyes sad. "I can't believe I don't even know their names. What's my mother's name?"

He swallowed hard. How would she react when she learned of her mother's illness? "Annalecia," he said softly and kissed her forehead. He knew he'd have to face it and tell her eventually, but not while she was still so fragile. She took a deep breath and smiled, hoping to lighten her mood. "If you continue to cry, all your energy will be drained before we even get into the city. And if that happens, we'll be extremely late getting back."

She laughed, as he'd hoped. The sound twisted around his heart, warming him.

"I suppose I should pull myself together so I can meet them." Wiping her eyes on the tail of her oversized shirt, she straightened and stood. Will I have a chance to get a shower before I meet them? I don't want them to see me like this." She gestured down at her rumpled clothes and looked so beautiful, he was tempted to get her out of them again.

"Earth to Stone," she said, and waved a hand in front of his face.

He laughed as he realized he'd been staring. "Yes, you'll have a chance to get cleaned up before your parents see you. I just wish I could help." He pictured her naked and glistening with water in the bubbling baths, surrounded by dozens of other voluptuous Klatch women.

Turning to him with desire smoldering in her lavender eyes, she asked, "Why can't you?"

"Because there is too much of a risk that some of my essence would reach you within the waters. Women who have not yet gone through the coming-of-age bathe together in all-female baths. It's not a matter of modesty for them to bathe apart from the men, but necessity."

Her beautiful brow creased and she chewed her full bottom lip. He already knew from their short time together that this meant she was pondering something. "So, all Klatch women have that issue, not just me?

Smoothing the crease from her brow with his fingers, he took her hand and they began to walk again. "Every Klatch has a coming-of-age, both men and women. But you are a princess and have more tolerance. What you experienced from just a small taste of essence is nothing compared to what effects a nonroyal would have."

"What about the men, do they have a bad reaction to 'female essence'?"

"Actually, they do. Female juices are just as dangerous for males before that time, but fortunately, males have their coming-of-age at sixteen, not twenty-four."

She whistled and he stared fascinated with the way her lips worked together to make the sound. "Another sexist society." She smiled, removing the sting from her comment, and stopped walking, turning to face him. "You said once the ceremony is performed we'll be able to . . . finish what we started. We'll be able to do anything without worrying about me blacking out. Right?"

Stone smiled at her enthusiasm and took both her hands in his, placing a gentle kiss on the back of each. "You are exactly right, Princess. And I can't wait." He just hoped she'd still be so enthusiastic once he explained the ritual to her.

Chapter 3

Alyssa's first view of the city literally stole the breath from her lungs. It was more beautiful than she'd ever imagined. And she *knew* this place. Her entire life, she'd thrived inside her own imagination and this had been her dream world. Only now, it was real.

Her gaze traced the gleaming white towers and parapets, which elegantly sliced into the cerulean blue sky. Deep purple flags, emblazoned with a curved sword crisscrossed with a red rose, flew from each turret, flapping in the gentle breeze. Almost eclipsed by the castle's beauty, smaller white stone buildings spread in a pleasing arrangement between large waterfalls and lush green parks. The gurgling of gently falling water sounded all around her and she breathed deep, enjoying the clean crisp air.

Stone stepped behind her, and pulled her back against him. "Wait until you see it at night, Princess. The view from your room is spectacular." His breath feathered against her neck, making her shiver.

Smiling, she closed her eyes and pictured the room from her

dreams. It had a large four-poster bed with purple sheets and spreads, with several fluffy pillows. There was a white stone dressing table with pink crystal seams running through it, a large sitting area with floor to ceiling bookshelves, overflowing with books, a bathroom bigger than her apartment, and a veranda, which overlooked the main bathing pools. She would wait and see if reality again matched her dreams. She turned in his arms and twined her arms around his neck before brushing a kiss over his lips. "I'm ready to see more."

They walked hand in hand and within minutes, began to see people. People who looked very much like she and Stone. All of them with dark wavy hair and lavender eyes—the women voluptuous and the men muscular. Even though each was individual, she'd never felt more like she stuck out. Everyone dressed scantily in comfortable-looking light cotton clothes and all were barefoot, while she was wrapped in oversized denim and a baggy T-shirt. Alyssa cringed at the thought of showing as much of herself as these people did in public.

When they reached the main grassy pathway, she heard a gasp and turned to see a young woman staring at her wide eyed. "Princess Alyssandra!" The woman bowed her head and dipped into a curtsy before raising her gaze.

"Stone," she whispered, feeling very much like an imposter about to be unmasked. "How do they know who I am?"

He raised her hand to his lips, and brushed a kiss on the back before answering. "You look very much like your mother. And of course, you're with me. The entire kingdom knows I've been looking for you. They've all eagerly awaited the return of the First Princess of Klatch."

Before Alyssa could reply, several other people caught sight of her. A loud chatter rose around her, her name murmured through the crowd like a living thing. Dozens of men and women bowed and then studied her with friendly and open curiosity.

Stone placed a protective hand on her shoulder and borrowed energy flowed through her body as his deep voice rang out over the noise of the crowd. "The princess must rest and recover before meeting the king and queen. There will be time enough for everyone to meet her later." As if by magic, the crowd bowed again toward Stone and then parted, allowing them to pass.

"Wow," she murmured. "I didn't really buy the whole princess thing until just now."

His rich laugh flowed over her body like an erotic caress. "I have a feeling all your doubts will be erased very soon." He chuckled as he led her toward the largest of the white buildings that sat at the foot of the castle.

She swallowed her disappointment—after all, didn't the princess live at the castle? Her childhood fantasies always revolved around her own room just across the hall from parents who loved her and would comfort her when she had nightmares. So far, this world was everything she'd always hoped, so why did that one difference make her sad? She was a grown woman now, who didn't need such things as comfort from bad dreams. She squared her shoulders and lifted her chin. "Is this where my room is?" she asked tentatively.

"This is where your *bath* is." He squeezed her hand as they stepped through the doors into a large open area with corridors leading off to each side and a large fountain in the middle. "Don't worry, after we take our baths, I'll meet you at the dressing room and take you up to the castle."

Maybe her dream room at the castle *was* a reality. For some reason, that made her feel better, like the parents part of her dreams would come true too. She smiled at the thought. "You'd better not forget to come back. I don't know anyone here but you." She looked around at the smooth white walls. They resembled the creamy marble she'd only seen at museums, but these had lines of soft pink crystals running through them— like the dressing table she'd imagined inside her room. She stepped close to the wall to run her hand over them. When her fingers brushed against the pink vein, warmth pulsed against her skin, where the white parts of the wall were cool as she expected.

"I could never forget about you, Princess. I've waited far too long to have you by my side. Just wait, by the end of the day, your pretty head will be swimming with the names of people you've met. All of them, happy to see you safe and finally home." He brushed his lips across hers and energy flowed through their connection, zinging down to each of her nipples then making a beeline for her pussy. Moaning, she melted against him, pulling him closer and tracing his lips with her tongue until he opened for her so she could delve inside. Heat sizzled between them and flashed as she ground her body against his erection.

Stone pulled her away, firmly holding her at arm's length, his breath coming in labored pants. "I think we both need a bath before I endanger you by fucking you here on the floor and pumping my seed deep inside you."

Smiling, she enjoyed the pure feminine power of being able to push him beyond the limits of his control. But after her earlier blackout from just a taste of his pre come, she would trust his judgment that tempting him too far would be dangerous. Exciting and erotic as hell, but still dangerous. "How soon is this ceremony?" She couldn't wait to have all restrictions gone between them.

He smiled and leaned his forehead against hers as if still fighting his urges. "It is on the eve of your birthday."

A rush of relief flowed through her. Surely she could survive one week. She hoped.

Alyssa stepped through the archway on the left and followed the corridor toward the sound of a waterfall. The sharp click of her cowboy boots against the stone floor echoed around her. Erotic paintings of couples and even groups in varying stages of copulation graced the walls on both sides. All were naked and uninhibited. Totally unlike the world she knew. *I wonder how different I would be if I'd grown up here, around these people.* There was even a painting of several naked women in a pool, pleasuring each other.

It had always been a deep dark fantasy of hers to have sex with another woman, but not one she'd ever admit aloud. She'd never been tempted by Debbie or any of the other Cunts she knew. Her fantasy had always revolved around curvy voluptuous women with dark hair and full lips, not the too thin and trim body of her roommate. She stepped closer to study the painting. Women with full breasts, rounded hips, curvy stomachs and lush thighs open and waiting taunted her from the wall causing her clit to swell and ache.

"Welcome, Princess," a sultry feminine voice said from behind her.

Alyssa jumped, her cheeks burning at being caught studying the erotic painting. She whirled to see a young woman about her own age with hair so long, it brushed the ground. Her dark hair cascaded around her with small braids sprinkled throughout, each adorned with multi-colored beads. She wore nothing but a white gauzy half top and string bikini underwear. Her coral nipples poked against the thin cloth and the creamy bottom curve of her breasts were visible just underneath the short top. Alyssa couldn't help but stare. The woman stood the same height as Alyssa and had the same full hips, rounded stomach and thighs that she looked at in the mirror every day. Yet, this exotic woman looked sexy, enticing and comfortable with her body. Something Alyssa had wished for all her life.

There was more. The woman's aura was electrifying and drew Alyssa in like a moth. A breath caught in her throat. She wanted this woman to touch her. Wanted to feel her petite hands on her body. Wanted to try out every fantasy.

Must be the effect of that damned painting!

"I'm Sasha, your lady's maid. I've waited a long time to be able to fulfill my duties." She bowed and then stepped forward to link her arm with Alyssa's as if they were lifelong friends. "Come this way and I'll show you the pool. I'm sure you're exhausted and in need of some energy before meeting your parents."

Alyssa walked with her willingly, instantly comfortable with this beautiful woman, even despite the sudden attraction. "I'm actually a little hungry," she admitted, noticing her growling stomach for the first time all day.

Sasha frowned. "The prince knows to take better care of you than that. You are precious to all the Klatch." She led Alyssa into an open room with only a chair and dressing table. Its gleaming white stone surface was covered with brushes, beads, combs, perfumes and assorted makeup.

"Stone took very good care of me," she said, suddenly defensive. She wanted to defend the man who'd saved her from her previous life.

Sasha laughed. "Believe me, I know the prince would not be able to keep his hands off you after all this time. But if you are hungry, he let you orgasm, which means you lost energy. Until the ceremony, he'll have to exercise more restraint."

Alyssa's mouth dropped open and her cheeks burned. Did everyone know she and Stone had been fooling around?

"Don't mistake my meaning, Princess. I know from personal experience what a good man Prince Stone is, and how honorable his intentions. But until the ascension, he needs to have a care with you."

Sasha's words caused a trickle of ice down her spine as jealousy spurted through her. The exotic woman obviously knew Stone quite well. Alyssa couldn't help but wonder *how* well. She tried to keep her voice nonchalant as she studied the maid, ready for her reaction. "What type of personal experience . . . if you don't mind me asking?" She held her breath while she waited for an answer.

Laughter filled the room and Sasha's eyes danced with amusement. "Oh, Princess. I'm sorry, I didn't mean to imply anything like that." Sasha's features suddenly seemed strained as if she were thinking of unhappy memories. "When I was but twelve years old, my mother and I had gone to an outlying village while the queen was there visiting. I wandered away chasing a kitten, as young children do."

A sudden flash of pain filled her eyes before she masked it. "Several Cunt warriors came through a portal in front of me and well . . . They would've raped me if Prince Stone hadn't stopped them. As it was, I was merely bruised and frightened. He was severely injured from the encounter, and could have died. The fact that he was willing to risk his life for mine, a mere daughter of a lady's maid, has always stayed with me. He will always have my complete trust and loyalty."

Alyssa could picture a younger version of Sasha, frightened and alone until Stone put himself at risk to save her. It explained why Stone was so bitter toward the Cunts and also why he was so protective of her. This new insight about Stone gave Alyssa a greater understanding of the man she'd only known through dreams for the past decade. She promised herself it wouldn't be the last she found out about her mysterious betrothed. "Thank you for telling me, Sasha. I'm sure it's something Stone would never tell me, but I'm glad you did. I still don't know very much about him."

Sasha's gaze softened and a small smile tugged at her lips. "Don't worry, Princess. Now that you are back where you belong, the two of you have a lifetime to get to know one another. I know it's difficult to put your trust in new people after what you've been through, but Prince Stone won't let you down."

Alyssa returned her mind to their previous conversation and curiosity pushed her to ask, "You said that Stone let me orgasm and it made me lose energy. You don't mean that all Klatch women have to forego orgasm before their coming-of-age ceremony?"

Sasha turned to face Alyssa with a sexy half smile that made her pulse jump. "Not at all. It just means they must eat more to maintain their sustenance. Think of sexual energy as another food group, but the most important one for our people. While we need water and food, sex can cover for both of them for a time." Her kohl-lined lavender eyes sparked with amusement. "I have a feeling many of our human sisters wish it were the same way for them."

Alyssa thought about all the women she knew who either complained about not getting enough sex or went without it altogether. "I think you have a very good point." She smiled at Sasha, who grinned in return. "I feel completely out of my element here, so you'll have to tell me what I'm supposed to do."

"As your lady's maid, I'm here to be your companion, your confidant and your friend. Not to mention, I've always been curious about the human world. How about you answer my questions and I'll answer yours?" She smiled, her pink tongue darting out to moisten her bottom lip.

Alyssa found herself fascinated with the small action and longed to feel the woman's pink tongue exploring inside her mouth.

"Let's get you out of these clothes and into a bath." She pulled Alyssa's shirt up and after a moment of shock, Alyssa raised her arms, so the shirt could continue its path over her head.

She opened her eyes in time to see Sasha fold it carefully and lay it on the chair. She raised each leg dutifully as Sasha pulled off her boots and placed them on the floor next to the chair.

"I understand humans are modest. But here on Tador, where sex is a needed staple, modesty only gets in the way of your well-being. I will try to keep your discomfort in mind and explain what's happening, since I know this is all new to you." Sasha stood and faced her. "How did you keep up your sexual energy among the humans—besides your dreams with the prince?"

Alyssa swallowed hard. She'd spent her whole life trying to hide her body, and now it looked like it was expected that she show it freely. Resisting the sudden urge to grab for her shirt, she balled her hands at her sides. *This is my real home. I need to get used to who I am supposed to be.* "I didn't know I needed the sexual energy, but I did, uh, take care of things myself quite a bit."

"You're a Klatch. That's perfectly normal." Sasha stepped forward and reached both arms around Alyssa's waist to unfasten the button and zipper of her jean skirt, their full breasts brushing against each other. Heat coiled in her stomach and she wondered how it would feel to have this woman's soft breasts pressed against hers with nothing between them but skin. At the thought, a rush of energy flowed through Alyssa's body and she bit back a moan.

Now that she was paying attention to it, she could see the energy as a direct result of the sexual stimulation. *No wonder I always felt as if my energy drained away when I had my sessions with the showerhead!*

Sasha slowly unzipped the skirt, her breath feathering against the side of Alyssa's neck, causing her to gasp as another shudder of pure lust and energy flowed through her veins.

The maid turned her face into Alyssa's neck and whispered, "Remember, Princess, sexual energy is like food here. There are very few things forbidden." Before Alyssa could react, Sasha hooked her thumbs into the waistband of the skirt and slid it down over her hips, until it fell to the floor in a puddle of material. The maid's hard nipples teased against her own. Only then did she step back and offer her hand, so Alyssa could step out of the skirt.

Alyssa's heart pounded in her chest and her brain scrambled

for something intelligible to say. "What sorts of things are forbidden?" she croaked and then cleared her throat.

Sasha's lips curved as if she knew exactly what effect her proximity had. "Anything is permissible that is consensual between adults who have completed their ceremony. It is death to force anyone, especially those uninitiated with the ceremony, or to copulate with the dead or animals. Beyond that, Klatch is a very open society. Even those who have yet to undergo the ceremony are permitted to indulge where they please without putting themselves in danger."

"Well, that sounds pretty straightforward." Alyssa mentally kicked herself for the lame comment. "Since there are certain dangers in indulging with the opposite sex before a coming-of-age, are there lots of same sex . . . uh . . ."

Sasha shrugged. The motion caused the exposed bottom curves of her full breasts to jiggle enticingly, mesmerizing Alyssa. "As I said, Princess, Klatch is a very open society. Sex is a part of our nature, there is nothing shameful about it. People may choose to indulge wherever the arousal takes them, as long as they are not married. Then both partners must consent to activities involving others."

"So monogamy is prized here inside a marriage?" Somehow, it made Alyssa feel better to know that she wouldn't have to worry about Stone fucking other women.

"Not in the same way humans term it, but yes. However, there are married couples who consent to group activities quite often and have no barriers beyond that as long as both parties are in full agreement."

The implications flashed through Alyssa's mind and she shoved them away to study later. Worrying about Stone wanting to have orgies after their marriage seemed a little premature, although she made a mental note to talk to Stone about his preferences *before* the ceremony.

"Would you like to bathe in the public pool, where there

will be several dozen young women at any one time, or would you like this first bath to be private until you are more . . . comfortable with our ways?" Sasha's voice held no note of censure, only a real desire to put Alyssa at ease. She appreciated it.

"Will . . . will the bath involve . . . sustenance?" she asked hesitantly. Her pussy and breasts throbbed at the thought of this woman giving her sexual energy as Stone had. She could admit, if only to herself, that the thought of several women at the same time turned her on too. But she didn't think she was *that* comfortable yet. Better to start slow. *Tackle one thing at a time. Or one woman, in this case . . .*

She'd seen women kiss in a few movies and was curious how different it would feel to have a woman touch her the way Stone's wonderfully callused hands had.

Sasha nodded and stepped forward again, reaching around her to unhook her bra. Again, her full breasts pressed against Sasha's and her warm breath danced across the side of Alyssa's neck as she spoke. "Sexual energy giving and taking is very much a part of our bathing rituals."

The bra loosened and Sasha stepped back, pulling the straps off Alyssa's shoulders before she set it aside on the chair. Then the maid dropped to her knees in front of Alyssa, her gaze hungry as she took in Alyssa's gently rounded stomach and very full breasts. Alyssa squirmed under the frank scrutiny and covered her chest with her hands.

"There is no need for that, Princess. You are most beautiful. In fact, you look so much like your mother, the queen, it surprises me."

A lump formed in Alyssa's throat. The thought of looking like her mother both excited and confused her. Would she find her mother beautiful when she met her, or would she be disappointed that she looked like Alyssa did?

Sasha interrupted her musings by pulling down Alyssa's white cotton granny panties. Alyssa's cheeks burned and she wished she'd worn some better underwear—not that she owned any other kind. Debbie had always reminded her that sexy lingerie was for attractive women—not fat ones. She squeezed her eyes shut against the tears that threatened.

The betrayal of her "family" and her roommate burned through her. She promised herself she'd never be so foolish again. But she had given her trust to Stone and to Sasha. Was she headed for more betrayal?

Nimble fingers sifted through her pubic hair causing her to jump. Looking down, she saw Sasha grinning up at her. Alyssa's heart pounded in her chest as her blood flooded her pussy causing it to tingle and throb.

"My apologies, Princess. The women of Klatch stay clean-shaven, so I've never seen a mound with full hair. I just wanted to see what it felt like. It almost reminds me of men's crispy chest hair."

Alyssa's clit throbbed with the proximity of the hand that still rested lightly against her, just a hairsbreadth away from her swollen nub. She knew she should be shocked or push Sasha's hand away, but she'd spent so many years convincing herself to be something she was not. It was time she made her own decisions. As hard as it was to admit—she wanted Sasha to touch her, to show her how those petite hands felt against her sensitive skin.

She swallowed hard before she could speak. "If the culture here is shaved, I'd like to do that too." It was another thing she'd thought about doing back home, but Debbie had talked her out of it, saying that the upkeep wasn't worth it if no one was going to be looking.

Sasha grinned and sifted her fingers through the curly dark hair again, the side of her hand brushed against the swollen tip of her clit and caused Alyssa to gasp. "Your wish is my command, Princess."

The maid stood and stripped off her own gauzy half shirt,

her rounded breasts bounced invitingly with the motion. Then she hooked her thumbs in the sides of her string bikini underwear, sliding them off until she stood naked as well. "Shall we head out to the bathing pool?" Not waiting for an answer, she hooked her arm with Alyssa's and led the way, the silky skin of her breast rubbed teasingly against Alyssa's bare arm.

Alyssa took a deep breath and let it out slowly. Her own breasts were heavy and sensitive, her slit slick and ready. If she didn't come soon, she was going to lose her mind. This was almost worse than when Stone left her horny and wanting every night for ten years!

They stepped through a curtain and entered a semidark alcove, lit only by flickering candles, which painted red and gold designs on the shadows of the walls. There was a large pool inset in the middle of the floor with seats and raised platforms visible just under the water in the shallow end. The water churned and gurgled and a small waterfall fell into the pool against the side, so people could enjoy it both from the shallow and deep ends.

Grabbing a small basket from an inset ledge along the wall, Sasha led her toward the pool. "We'll get you shaved first," she said as she started down the steps leading into the water.

Alyssa followed her, enjoying the way the warm water swirled and fizzed around her already heated skin. Several jets of water shot currents out from the walls, which kept the water in constant motion. She was tempted to lean her clit against one and end her torment. But even as much as she masturbated at home, she couldn't do it in front of someone she'd just met. Doing it with Stone had been a first. Besides, having erotic dreams with the man for ten years surely put him in the category of nonstranger.

Allowing herself to be led to one of the raised platforms, she couldn't help but notice how Sasha's breasts bobbed just on top of the water, the ripe tips cutting a current as she moved. She resisted a sudden urge to pull one of the ripe nipples between her lips and explore the texture with her tongue.

"Lie back," Sasha said, her voice husky and low. "And relax. I promise to be gentle."

To Alyssa's surprise, the platforms were soft, like lying on a gel mattress and the head was raised and cushioned enough that it was as if a pillow cradled her. She pulled her hair out from under her shoulders, letting it flow around the platform into the swirling water. An inch of water lapped against her body, leaving most of her exposed, but since the cavern was warm, she didn't shiver as she'd expected. The motion and sound of the water relaxed her, making her feel as if she were at one of the day spas her mother and sisters frequented.

Warm fingers gripped under her knees, raising them so her legs were bent, her thighs spread wide to give the maid better access. At the first tentative touch against her mound, she jumped and Sasha's musical laughter echoed around her like an intimate caress. "Relax and hold very still, Princess. I'll have you smooth and perfect for the prince in no time."

Gripping the sides of the platform, Alyssa willed herself to relax, or at the very least hold still. When the warm fingers touched her again and then traced through her pubic hair, she didn't jump, but had to bite back a moan. This felt forbidden, wicked . . . naughty, and she wanted to enjoy every minute. She heard the "snip-snip" of scissors, and decided talking would keep her from embarrassing herself further.

"How did you become a lady's maid?" she asked, trying to both enjoy and ignore the slender fingers touching her mound.

"Being a lady's maid is in my line. My mother, mother's mother and so on, were all maids to the royal family. It is an honored position."

Glancing down, she saw Sasha take a small purple fruit from the basket and peel off the skin. The scent of musky lavender rose around her. The purple flesh of the fruit looked fluffy like whipped cream. Scooping some of the flesh with her fingers, Sasha slathered it onto Alyssa's throbbing mound.

Alyssa's skin immediately began to tingle and she fought the urge to buck her hips against the wonderful new sensation. Clearing her throat, she said, "What if you didn't want to be a lady's maid? Do you have a choice?" Her voice sounded breathy and low.

The maid's laugh bubbled around her, causing heat to coil in her stomach and she looked down to see a long straight blade pulled across her mound, shaving off a perfect line of dark hair. Then Sasha rinsed it in a small basin floating next to her.

The sight of Sasha standing naked between her open thighs made her release a shaky breath. And the cold pull of the blade across her skin sent lava and energy spiraling throughout her entire body.

"I could have chosen another path, but I'm proud of my family's tradition. I'm a strong supporter of the royal family." She rinsed the blade in the basin again and closed her hand around Alyssa's ankle, raising her leg to rest on top of her shoulder. "I need to be able to reach everything, to fully shave you," she explained as she spread on more purple fruit flesh and then drew the blade gently across Alyssa's swollen pussy lips.

Sasha's smooth fingers rubbing over her already-engorged flesh sent a series of small energy tremors through her thighs and tightened her arousal. Despite her best efforts, a gasp followed by a low moan ripped from her throat. Realizing what she'd done, heat blazed into her face and she screwed her eyes shut, wishing she could disappear.

"Do not be embarrassed," Sasha whispered. "The *ponga* fruit enhances arousal. It helps with shaving and brings sexual energy, which you are much in need of. Not to mention, it has a sweet fluffy taste and is often used in foreplay."

Alyssa slitted open her eyes to see Sasha's smiling face. "What does it taste like?" she asked softly. She gasped as Sasha stepped forward between her legs, leaning her own smooth mound against Alyssa's swollen folds, and reached up to rub some of the *ponga* flesh across her lips and then down across both her nipples. Alyssa licked her bottom lip, and a sweet nutty flavor spread over her tongue. Immediately, her lips, nipples and even the inside of her mouth tingled, sending shockwaves of energy through her body, causing a rush of liquid heat to her aching pussy.

Sasha stepped back to finish shaving her and then splashed water against her mound to fully rinse her. "The *ponga* is never used in nonsexual meals because of its unique properties. But is always associated with summoning energy." The maid reached into the basket again and pulled out a bar of soap, which she dipped into the water and began to lather between her hands.

"Does that have some sort of aphrodisiac powers as well?" Alyssa asked nodding toward the soap.

The maid's lavender eyes darkened with desire and Alyssa's breath caught in her throat. "Not by itself. But soap is used both before and after lovemaking, so it does come in several pleasing scents." Her last words fell away to whispers as she reached down to spread her soapy hands over Alyssa's stomach and then farther up, to cover her aching breasts.

Sensations, erotic and compelling, washed through her. Sasha's hands were soft and gentle and her touch felt much different than Stone's. His touches were rougher and more demanding, even when he was being gentle. Where Sasha's touch was nurturing and sensual, probably how she herself liked to be touched.

Alyssa sat up and faced the woman, taking the soap from her and dipping it into the swirling water, lathering it between her hands. She reached out slowly to run her soapy hand over Sasha's coral tipped breasts. When the nipples pebbled to hard peaks beneath her hand, her pussy tightened and throbbed.

Sasha arched into her touch, so Alyssa became braver and cupped and kneaded the full breast in her hands, enjoying the feel of the silky smooth skin and the moans and gasps coming from Sasha. Her lips were parted, her gaze boring into Alyssa. Before she could think about it, she allowed her body free reign and she leaned forward to brush her lips across Sasha's. A sound of approval spilled from the back of Sasha's throat as she ran a wet line across Alyssa's bottom lip with her tongue, causing a new wave of energy as Alyssa's nipples ripened further.

Throwing aside her caution, she dipped her tongue inside the maid's mouth and reveled in the soft, lush taste of her. The *ponga* on her tongue tingled as tongue met tongue and the sweet nutty flavor sharpened inside her mouth. Pulling Sasha closer, so the hardened peaks of their breasts rubbed deliciously against each other, she explored and plundered the woman's mouth. Their tongues tangled, but whereas with Stone, it had been rough and exciting, with Sasha, it was silky smooth and erotic—a slow burn that would incinerate them both.

Tracing a path between them with her fingers, she found Sasha's mound partly submerged in the water. When her finger caressed the seam of the swollen lips, the maid moaned into her mouth and widened her stance to allow better access. Alyssa swallowed the sound and dipped her fingers between the hot petals to find the swollen nub beneath.

She'd never touched another woman's body and she found the sensations so soft and so vastly different than when she'd touched Stone. She wondered briefly what it would feel like to have both Stone and Sasha giving her sustenance at the same time. She bit back a moan as her fingers traced Sasha's clit.

I want to make her come against my fingers while I watch. She dipped her finger deep inside Sasha's pussy to pull some of the creamy juices up to caress the swollen clit. When her finger feathered a slow path along the silky underside of Sasha's clit, the maid arched against her hand and thrust her tongue against

Alyssa's with more urgency. She wound her arms around Alyssa's neck, burying her fingers in her hair, their mouths still fused, their tongues dueling and mating, while Sasha's hips ground against Alyssa's hand.

"Please, Princess," Sasha begged in an urgent whisper against her lips. "Make me come . . ."

Energy poured into Alyssa like she had become the vacuum focal point. She pulled Sasha's body full against hers before rolling Sasha's clit between her thumb and forefinger and allowing the built up power to flow through their connection straight into Sasha's most sensitive erogenous zone. The maid shuddered against her and immediately screamed out her release. Enjoying the way Sasha's nipples pulsed with her orgasm, Alyssa ground her mound against the maid's until all her spasms stopped.

When she finally pulled back and spoke, Sasha's voice was deep and breathy. "You are starting to gain your powers, my lady."

Trapped power still zoomed through Alyssa like gunshots infinitely ricocheting through her system. "I've got to get rid of some of this power." Her words sounded distant as she whispered through the tightest arousal she'd ever experienced.

"It is my turn to help you. Lie back, Princess, and allow me to attend you."

Her maid stepped between her raised knees and ground her mound against Alyssa's. She slathered more fruit flesh on Alyssa's nipples and leaned over to take one of the *ponga*-covered tips deep into her mouth. Alyssa's moan echoed around them as sensations assaulted her. Sasha's skin was soft as silk against her own and the smooth rub of smooth pelvis against hers was unlike anything she'd ever felt. She reached down to trace her fingers down the maid's arms and then around to cup her breasts. They were warm and full, the nipples ripening again under her touch.

When Sasha had laved all of the *ponga* from one breast, she turned her attention to the other, being just as thorough as with the first. Then finally, she traced a wet line down Alyssa's stomach to her mound and then down to her aching clit. Alyssa widened her legs, offering herself. "Please, Sasha. I have to come now."

Sasha parted the swollen folds with her fingers and Alyssa shuddered as warm breath feathered against her slit. When a silky tongue traced her nub before soft lips closed around it, sucking it inside a delicious heat, she moaned and bucked against Sasha's face.

Sasha sucked hard, while still feathering her tongue against the tip. Alyssa found her own nipples with her fingers, and pinched and pulled as heat coiled tighter and tighter inside her. When Sasha gently scraped her teeth against the swollen bud, Alyssa's world shattered. Her pussy clenched and convulsed while ripples of energy flowed around her like a maelstrom. Bright colors danced in front of her eyes and small static shocks of electricity danced along her skin.

After what seemed like an eternity, Alyssa's body and mind settled back together. She took stock and was surprised to find herself refreshed and alert. Sitting up, she faced Sasha. "That's the best I've ever felt after an orgasm."

Sasha smiled, her hands still resting on Alyssa's thighs. "You tapped energy from Tador as a true queen would. It is the renewable energy source that all share. That was but a small preview of your power. It will be infinitely stronger once your ceremony is complete." Sasha smiled. "We need to get you cleaned up and dressed before you are presented to your parents."

"Presented? I feel like a package."

"You're the First Princess of Klatch and heir to the throne." She handed Alyssa a bumpy yellow fruit that smelled like almonds. "Of course you'll need to be presented." She nodded toward the fruit. "Bite into it, it's good. Even though you have plenty of energy, not even Klatch can live on sex alone." She winked.

Alyssa bit into the soft yellow fruit and closed her eyes in ecstasy as the sweet juices slid across her tongue and down her chin. "Wow, I was never big on fruit, but what is this?"

"It's called *salda*." Sasha reached for the basket of fruit, taking her own snack.

Tentatively, Alyssa rubbed Sasha's braid between her thumb and first two fingers, the multicolored beads glinting in the candlelight. The hair felt like velvet silk under her touch. *Who would I be and what would I look like if I weren't stolen?* "Do you think you could do something like this in my hair?" she asked, her voice sounding sad and distant in her own ears.

A smile bloomed across Sasha's face. "I'll make you look every inch the stunning Klatch Princess."

For the first time, Alyssa actually felt like a princess. She might as well go all the way. "I'm all yours, Sasha. Turn me into the Klatch I should've been."

Chapter 4

Debbie slouched in her chair in front of the Cunt council and tried to think of a way out of her current situation—before the council decided her fate. She'd had to befriend that Klatch bitch from an early age and make her feel included and needed so the council could keep an eye on her. Now that the ungrateful cow had run off with that bastard prince, the council wanted answers. Answers Debbie knew they wouldn't like.

She glanced at the row of five women and four men who stared at her with contempt. All of them were the epitome of the Cunt people—silvery blond hair, clear blue eyes and athletic thin bodies that all the humans envied. She still didn't understand what twist of fate had made a princess out of that fat olive-skinned, mousy bitch she'd lived with for the past few years. Just more evidence that life wasn't fair.

"How did he find her?" Sela, the Queen of the Cunts and council head demanded.

Debbie winced at the cutting tone, but took a deep breath and let it out slowly before she answered. "I have no idea. When I dropped her off at work this morning, everything was in place. I'd even mentioned to her that I wanted to introduce her to Shawn." She gestured to the dark haired Klatch bastard in the corner.

"She was subdued as usual. Then, when I went to pick her up, her boss told me she'd left early." *Okay, so I lost track of time while I was fucking my human boss in an elevator, but the council doesn't have to know that!*

"When I got home, the Klatch Prince was already there with her. We fought for several minutes, and I'm sure I injured him, but then he slashed through my draining spell and zapped me, knocking me out." She still had the energy hangover to prove it. It would be a cold day in hell before she'd admit that mealy mouthed little Alyssa had been the one who'd given it to her. Besides, if the council knew she was already coming into her powers, things might be even harder for Debbie to wriggle free of.

The energy level in the room skyrocketed, causing the hairs on Debbie's arms to prickle. In the next instant, an invisible blow landed hard against her jaw and she suddenly flew across the room to slam into the far wall and land in a heap. Small silver bursts swam in front of her eyes and she shook her head tying to clear her vision.

At least human hits you can see coming. Damn. She swiped the back of her hand across her mouth wiping away the blood and looked up to see Queen Sela looming over her. Even in her fury, Sela was beautiful, and Debbie's pussy clenched at the thought of the queen using her as one of her sex slaves. Everyone knew the queen's tastes ran to the exotic and kinky—even for the Cunts, and Debbie had always skirted that line herself.

The queen's silver-blond hair flowed around her shoulders in a shimmery waterfall and her blue eyes glinted with icy danger. "Your *only* job was to watch her, to keep her out of trouble. I spent twenty-three years raising the little bitch with my own family, and now everything may be ruined because you were off fucking some human." She spat the last word as if it was something distasteful and then kicked Debbie in the side, knocking all her air out in a painful rush.

Debbie bit back a moan as one of her ribs cracked, the sound echoing through the room like a gunshot. Showing Sela that pain affected you was a surefire way to invite more. *How the hell does Sela know I was fucking the human?*

"We allowed you to drain her energy to keep her docile and to free you from having to constantly feed on the humans so you'd always be around to watch her." The queen reached down grabbing a handful of Debbie's hair and pulled her face close. "You find her and somehow make this right or I'll enjoy finding the longest and most agonizing way for you to die that I've devised to date."

The queen's spittle splashed in angry droplets against Debbie's face and she shuddered. The Queen of the Cunts was infamous for her cruelty when she was crossed. Debbie swallowed the lump of fear lodged in her throat before answering. "Yes, my lady. I'll find her. I swear it on my life."

"Your life isn't worth enough to even swear on." The queen yanked hard, ripping some of Debbie's hair out by the roots and tearing a scream from her parched throat. "And if you don't find her, there will be nowhere on either planet that you can hide from me."

"What of our bargain?" Shawn asked from the side of the chamber. "I've held up my end all these years. I've waited patiently and bided my time. It's through Cunt incompetence that this happened. It shouldn't negatively affect me."

Debbie stayed as still as possible, not daring to move, hoping the queen would turn her wrath elsewhere.

Shawn had been cultivated for his role since birth. When Alyssa was kidnapped, her nanny, Natasha, had been taken too. No one knew Natasha was pregnant until she was already through the *between*. Everyone was surprised the baby even survived the trip. From there it was easy enough to take the child and raise him to believe he was to be the father of an entire race—especially since he'd been taught an amended version of history.

Sela wanted to breed a race of subservient sex slaves, starting with the princess and Shawn, and ending with Alyssa luring the royal family of Klatch over to the human world for the slaughter they deserved so the Cunts could return to Tador, where they rightfully belonged. And it all hinged on one fat, dark haired worthless princess.

Sela rounded on Shawn as if offended he would address her directly. "Debbie will find her and you will still mate with the little bitch." Sela kicked Debbie again without even looking down at her. She curled into a tight ball on the floor and tried to disappear.

"We still have another week," Sela continued. "Stone won't risk mating with her until the ceremony because he knows it could kill her."

Shawn nodded but looked unconvinced. "If you don't find her, what then?"

The queen scowled at his impertinence. Hatred burned in her eyes and she raised her hand to strike him, but stopped only inches from his face. A quick flicker of fear ran through Sela's eyes before she masked it and then slowly lowered her hand. "I won't waste my time striking you. I've never broken my word to you. Your destiny is an important one to our people. And I won't deprive you of your chance to make up for the dishonor among your people." She straightened her skintight leopard print dress and glanced back at him. "If Debbie fails in her journey, you can have *her*."

Shawn took a hostile step toward Sela and she took two hasty steps back. But then, as if realizing what she'd done, she raised her chin in a defiant gesture. Shawn's deep voice reverberated through the room. "You promised me a virgin to make my own. To share energy with. Not a common whore. How can I fulfill the prophesy of being the father of a mighty race with this—" he gestured to Debbie, contempt plain in his voice, "—in my bed? So many men have had her, I'd probably fall inside her overused pussy and never again be found."

The queen nodded once and then glared down at Debbie. "She will not fail, or I'll let you kill her, however you choose." Returning her attention to Shawn, she said, "Remember, if you take the princess on the day of her birth, she won't die, but you will conceive a full Klatch child. I'll have twenty of our best Cunt men ready to complete the ritual when Debbie finds her. Just be ready to do your part."

Stone bowed low before the king and queen. "Your Majesties," he said before rising to face them. They sat in the throne room in high backed, purple velvet chairs. Both were dressed in the gauzy revealing clothing of the Klatch, but instead of pastels or white, they wore the colors of royalty—hues of deep purple and blue. The king in breeches and a tunic and the queen in a simple top and skirt.

Queen Annalecia coughed before asking, "Where is she?"

Stone met the queen's gaze and his forehead creased in concern. She was more drawn and frail than when he'd last seen her. Her skin pale, her long mahogany hair dull and lifeless, dark circles marring the skin under her eyes, and her cheeks sunken from the weight she'd lost. Lines of illness creased her face, but he could see remnants of the beautiful woman he'd known all his life. Her frequent coughs now rumbled inside her chest and made her gasp for each breath.

Pushing his concerns for her from his mind, he tore his gaze from the queen's face and forced his lips to curve. "I went to fetch her, but Alyssandra and her maid told me to wait here, that she wanted to be presented at her very best. Sasha advised she would bring her to the castle when she was ready."

King Darius held his wife's hand tenderly. When she coughed again, concern and love etched deep into his expression as he brought her hand to his lips before turning his attention back to Stone. "Tell us how you found her. Where has she been all this time? Has she been mistreated?"

"For heaven's sake, Darius, at least invite the boy to sit before you grill him." The queen gestured to a servant who immediately brought a comfortable chair and wine for all.

After settling himself and accepting the wine, Stone cleared his throat, not wanting to inflict pain on his godparents. "She has been sickly her entire life with the Cunts. When I found her, the woman she lived with had a drain spell in place."

Anger flowed across Darius's features, his jaw clenched and his eyes narrowed before he gestured for Stone to continue.

"As far as I can tell, she hasn't been mated, but I have not asked her. It is not my place. But she is very self-conscious about her body and thinks herself to be unattractive and undesirable . . . despite my best efforts." With the last, his lips curved as memories of all his best efforts flowed through his mind.

The queen's laughter rang out across the large throne room echoing around them. For a moment, it was like having Annalecia back healthy and whole. She squeezed the king's hand. "I'm sure you've done your very best, Stone. I know you've waited a long time for her. I'm proud of you for having such iron restraint."

She turned toward her husband. "Calm down, my love. She is home now and nothing has been done that is not reversible. She will need all our love and understanding, not our anger. Save that for when we find the Cunts who stole her."

Darius sighed and shook his head, frustration evident in the stiff gesture. "You're right, but I've spent over twenty years helpless, not knowing what was happening to her, and being unable to protect her. When I find the traitors who took her from us, I will show no mercy." He turned his attention once again to Stone. "How long will it take her to ready herself? I want to see my daughter."

"As do I, Your Majesty, but Sasha gave me no chance to ask, and closed the door in my face." Stone's lips curved. Sasha's job was to do the princess's bidding, not his, and apparently, the princess had her own timetable.

"She is still getting used to our very different culture. Remember, she was treated as an outcast among the humans as well as the Cunts." He took a sip of the wine, savoring the fruity flavor, thoughts of licking it off Alyssandra's writhing body making him instantly hard. "I think if we let her take things at a pace she's comfortable with, she'll recover from this faster."

The majordomo cleared his throat, interrupting their conversation. All of them turned their attention toward the large ornately carved double doors in the back of the room. "Your Majesties and Prince Stone, may I present the First Princess of Klach, Alyssandra de Klatch." Wrapping his fingers around the round door ring, he pulled and the heavy doors slowly slid open.

Interminable seconds later, they revealed the most breathtaking woman Stone had ever seen, let alone imagined. It took him a moment to reconcile her with the girl he'd visited in dreams for the last ten years. She smiled at him and he realized his mouth hung open. Snapping it closed, he looked his fill.

She wore the gauzy half top of the Klatch women, dyed a medium lavender color that reminded him of the *ponga* fruit. The bottom curves of her ripe breasts were just visible underneath the hem of the top. On the bottom, she wore a pair of half shorts in the same material. They hung low on her hips, showing her full figure and gently rounded stomach to perfection. Her hair tumbled around her shoulders the way he loved it best, but small braids with purple beads were scattered throughout. Her eyes were kohl lined, her lips full and ripe, glistening with color.

From behind him, he heard the king and queen stand and step forward. But they must have been just as stunned as he, for neither spoke. Finally, Alyssandra lifted her chin in a stubborn gesture he'd come to know well before she walked toward them, her back straight, her gaze guarded. He shook his head in an attempt to regain his senses, but most of his blood now resided firmly in his groin. "Alyssandra," he said, his voice a strained rumble. "You take my breath away."

When her face blossomed into a beaming smile, he knew the stubborn display of a moment before was because she thought he hadn't approved. She'd taken his silence for something other than total amazement.

The king and queen brushed past him in their haste to get to their daughter. Darius's voice was thick with emotion as he stopped an arm's length from the princess, his hand still firmly holding his wife's. "Alyssandra, you are even more lovely than I'd imagined." A shocked expression played over the princess's face before she was buried in a crushing hug by her father and then her mother.

When she pulled back to look at them, tears glistened, unshed in her lavender eyes. He'd brought her home to all of them at last. Now if they could successfully complete the coming-of-age ritual and allow Alyssandra to ascend the throne, the Klatch might still yet be saved.

Alyssa couldn't believe what was happening. It all felt like a surreal dream and she was terrified that at any moment, her alarm would sound and she'd be back inside her dingy apartment hearing Debbie across the hall fucking someone.

The tight grasp of her father—her real father—enveloped her and she wallowed in the sensation as if she might never get this chance again. "Father," she whispered, hoping to cement this reality before it disappeared. She refused to call him "Dad," because that's what she'd called her imposter father all her life.

Pulling back just far enough to look into her face, the king smiled down at her. "Alyssandra, I thought this day would never come."

She blinked furiously to keep the unshed tears burning in her eyes from falling. This was one of the happiest days of her life, she wouldn't ruin it with tears.

"Step aside, Darius. You've hogged her long enough." Alyssa turned at the sound of her mother's voice. Annalecia's face was lined and drawn, as if she'd been very ill. But her voice was strong, her eyes clear and loving. Without hesitation, the queen stepped forward and enveloped her in a hug even more crushing than the king's. Alyssa hugged her back, burying her face against her mother's shoulder. How often growing up had she longed for an embrace such as this from parents who loved and approved of her?

When she released her mother, Stone cleared his throat behind them. She turned to face him, still holding her mother's hand and noted the mist in his eyes as well.

"Beloved." He stepped forward to capture her free hand and bring it to his lips. "I can see you are comfortable enough with your parents. I think you need some time alone with them. And my parents would like news of you, as well. I'll be back for you after dinner to show you to your room."

Almost before realizing she was going to, she jumped into Stone's arms, fusing her lips with his. She poured all her gratitude for her new life into the kiss, and for the first time, their kiss held tenderness rather than only lust and sexual energy. When she pulled back, Stone's expression was stunned—his eyes wide, his mouth parted. "Thank you. For bringing me home and for being the only thing I looked forward to for all those long years. Before you, my life was dreary and lonely."

Color flashed into Stone's cheeks and she smiled as she realized she'd made him blush. "The pleasure is all mine, Princess." He turned her hand over and placed a hot kiss just inside her palm, then curled her fingers inward as if to allow her to hold onto his kiss until he saw her again. "Until later."

She watched until he disappeared through the double doors and then turned back to her parents.

"Are you hungry?" Her mother linked her arm with Alyssa's, leading her toward a large table in the back already heavy with a wide assortment of strange looking foods.

Her stomach grumbled in response and her parents laughed. Her father walked on her other side laying his hand lightly on the small of her back, as if he was afraid she'd disappear if he let go. "I think it's time you ate. You need to keep your energy up for the upcoming coming-of-age ceremony. Being queen is hard work."

She stopped dead in her tracks to stare at her father. "Queen? I don't understand, I just found out I'm a princess and now I need to learn to be queen? What's the rush?"

Annalecia guided her to a cushioned high backed chair. "I'm sorry, I know all of this is strange to you. Maybe we'd better start by answering your questions, so you feel more comfortable." She ran a gentle hand over Alyssa's hair causing at least some of the panic to recede. "But why don't we eat first and just get to know each other again. After all, the last time we saw you, you were in diapers."

Alyssa pushed aside her fears and questions and grinned across the table at her parents. "I'd like that."

A servant poured wine for them and Alyssa blindly took food and chewed, not tasting much of anything. She was too intent on listening to the timbre of her mother's voice and studying her father's smile and the way he often ran his fingers through his thick dark hair, mussing it. It was almost as if she memorized everything about them, she could never lose either of them again.

They asked her about her life with the Cunts and she tried to give an honest picture while still shielding them from the worst of it. Hurt swam in their eyes even as they heard the damped-down version. The feeling of belonging was so strong, she tried to imprint every detail firmly in her mind to replay later.

Finally, she pushed her plate away and looked from one to the other. "I'm glad for the chance to finally get to know you. You've only existed in my wishful fancies for so long. But for now, maybe you'd better explain to me exactly what this coming-of-age ceremony entails."

King Darius looked decidedly uncomfortable. The queen smiled a knowing smile and reached out to lay a gentle hand on his arm. "Why don't you go and help the cook decide on what dessert to serve our lovely daughter on her first night home, darling?"

Did I say something wrong?

He cleared his throat, never meeting Alyssa's eyes and beat a hasty retreat to the sounds of the queen's soft chuckles. Annalecia placed a hand on Alyssa's arm. "Why don't we walk in the water gardens while we talk?" They rose and Alyssa followed her mother outside, their arms linked at the elbows again—both women afraid to let go of the other for any long period.

The water gardens turned out to be a large open garden with thousands of exotic looking plants interspersed among breath-taking waterfalls. The falls emptied into small ponds teeming with brightly colored fish and frogs. The scents of fertile earth competed with the mist of water and the aroma of flowers. The gentle gurgling sound of the water, accompanied by soft frog croaks and other sounds of the night blended around them. The moon shone down on them, bathing everything in silver light and a gentle breeze teased Alyssa's hair.

"Did I ask something I shouldn't? About the ceremony, I mean?"

Her mother chuckled and led her to a cushioned bench in front of a large pond. "We may be a society that must have sex or at least sexual energy to survive, but no father is comfortable talking about his own daughter having it. It is much like a human father not wanting to talk about the feminine cycle."

Understanding dawned as well as dread. She'd accepted that most everything with the Klatch centered around sex, but she hadn't thought the ceremony would too. Although she probably should have known. Stone had kept his comments vague, probably to keep from scaring her.

Taking Alyssa's hands in her own, the queen turned to meet her gaze. "I'll be as forthcoming as I can about the ceremony and any questions you may have. I know you haven't known me as your mother for long, but I went through the ceremony as well and I know knowledge can make it easier." Annalecia squeezed her hands. "Have you been mated?"

Alyssa had never had a talk with her mom growing up about anything. She'd found out about her period from listening to her sisters talk, and anything else she'd wanted to know from books or the Internet. But having this open, wonderful woman who genuinely seemed to care about her offer to give her information felt wonderful and different. "Mated?" she asked. "I'm not sure what you mean. Is that a Klatch term?"

Her mother's brows knit together for a second and she seemed to be searching for the correct term. "I believe the human equivalent is losing your virginity?" her mother said, sounding not quite certain.

Understanding dawned, as did a hot blush that crept up her neck and cheeks. She couldn't convince herself to meet her mother's eyes as she shook her head from side to side.

Annalecia let out a breath of relief. "Good, then at least there's no irreparable damage. I'm not sure how much Stone told you, but having the essence of a Klatch man touch you before your coming-of-age can be deadly. A human's essence can make a full-blooded Klatch royal sterile, or just weaken your system permanently."

She stared open-mouthed at her mother. "But my roommate, Debbie, she fu . . . I mean, she had sex all the time and she's apparently a Cunt. Aren't they just another faction of Klatch?"

"The Cunts are a product of a Klatch and human mating. They have different constitutions. They aren't as sensitive to human essence, but are even more sensitive to Klatch essence. Another tradeoff is that we are more powerful."

"In what way?" Alyssa's curiosity peaked. "Back at my apartment, I zapped Debbie unconscious. I'm not sure how I did it, or even what powers Klatch have." She blushed again as she remembered the episode in the baths where she'd used her powers to make Sasha come.

"From what Stone told us, you defended yourself admirably." Her mother squeezed her hand in reassurance. "Powers vary from witch to witch, but you should be able to control energy, cause instant arousal, and once mated with Stone, you will share an empathic bond."

I'll be able to experience Stone's feelings while he's fucking me? Her sex clenched at the thought. Then she remembered her mother's presence and pushed the erotic thoughts from her mind. "About the ceremony—maybe you'd better start at the beginning and assume I don't know anything." She swallowed hard. "Exactly what's involved, what I'm expected to do. Those types of things."

Her mother nodded and smiled. "All Klatch women come of age at their twenty-fourth year and the men in their sixteenth. But those of royal blood must marry another of royal blood."

Ewwww! "You mean Stone is my brother or cousin or something?" she demanded in horror.

The queen laughed aloud, the sound easing Alyssa's fears about Klatch incest. "No, Stone is the product of another royal family. There are sixteen royal families. We are the first, so therefore, you are the First Princess of Klatch. We hold the same mores about incestuous relationships as the humans, I assure you."

The soft breeze latticed her hair over her face and the queen brushed it back with her fingers. "Unfortunately, the Cunts don't share our concern. They inter-mate quite often, which was one of the many reasons for the civil war."

At Alyssa's audible sigh of relief, her mother continued. "Stone is the Fourth Prince of Klatch, but since we are a matriarchal society, everything is determined by the needs of the woman."

"Wow, too bad they don't have *that* mindset on earth." She reached down to pet a neon blue frog that had wandered close and laughed as he hopped into her hand. "Okay, so no incest. What exactly does the coming-of-age ceremony entail?"

Annalecia pursed her lips and studied her for a long moment. "How comfortable are you with your sexuality, Alyssandra? The Klatch ways are probably taboo by human standards of sex."

"Not very," she admitted. "I mean, I . . . have the urges and I've . . . masturbated." She stared hard at the little frog, not comfortable with this discussion. "But until Stone . . . I really didn't feel very attractive or comfortable with my body. And he was a dream!"

The events of the last day suddenly caught up with her in a rush. She stood, startling the frog, which jumped back into the pond with a plop. She stood rubbing her hands up and down her arms, trying to smooth away the conflicting emotions that invaded her. "And now, he's suddenly real . . . I'm not sure exactly who I am or how I feel."

She let her mother smooth a comforting hand over her hair. "I'll tell you of the need for the ceremony first, that way you'll understand why the mechanics are the way they are."

A shudder ran through Alyssa and she wanted to stop her mother's words. Somehow, she knew she wasn't going to like what she heard. "Tell me," she said simply and sat again.

Her mother continued to stand and trailed her fingers in the nearest waterfall, watching the water spill around her hand rather than looking at Alyssa while she talked. "When a First Princess comes of age, she must come into her powers fully to assume the throne. And assuming the throne isn't just in title as it is with human royalty, it's in function. As queen, it will be your responsibility to feed the nation of Klatch with your energy."

Alyssa bolted to her feet. "You don't mean I have to supply *everyone* with sexual energy?" A sudden picture of her having to go from person to person sharing energy every day flashed through her mind and she shoved it aside. Dread flowed through her as she waited for her mother's answer.

"I don't mean the nation as in the people, I mean the land." Her mother turned to face her. "Usually, as the First Princess grows older, her powers increase and she begins to help the queen with the nourishment of the land. It flows from you in a give and take with the world. And in turn, once you marry, your husband keeps you supplied with energy to share."

Alyssa looked at her mother, the pale skin, the etched lines in her face and then she knew, somewhere deep in her soul. "And since I was stolen, the full burden fell on you to give this world its energy, didn't it?" Nausea roiled inside her stomach and she swallowed against the acidic taste of bile on the back of her tongue. It wasn't her fault she'd been abducted, but that didn't stop guilt from flowing through her.

Annalecia stroked a thumb across Alyssa's cheek. "Sometimes that is the way of life. But you are here now. The land has begun to sicken and die, but no affects are visible inside the city. The edges of the wilderness are showing the first signs. Hunts and harvests are not what they were. Once you assume the throne, my energy will no longer be needed. You'll be strong enough to maintain the world until you have a daughter to help you."

"And what if I have a son?" she asked, picturing a miniature Stone.

"All of the first-born of the ruling family are female. It has always been so."

"Then why didn't you just have another child when I was taken?" she asked and then instantly regretted it when jealousy at the thought ran through her.

"All of my energy went into the world and my grief. I knew you were not dead, for I would have felt it, even though I know the council believed me foolish." Her brows knitted and her fists clenched for a moment before she relaxed and turned back to Alyssa. "You and I are connected as the world and I are connected. And even now, since you've returned, some of my burden eases."

Alyssa knew she must complete the coming-of-age-ceremony and assume the throne. If it would help her mother, she would do anything. She couldn't bear to lose her again. The rest would reveal itself in time. "So give me the bad news—what exactly is involved in this ceremony? No one seems to want to talk about it, so it's got to be bad."

Annalecia sat next to her and took her hands in her own once more. "It's far from bad. It's a very erotic ceremony, and rather enjoyable. However, you need more energy than just Stone can provide. The good news is that you and Stone will finally be able to consummate your relationship fully. You two will become mated during the ceremony."

So far, this doesn't sound bad. What's the catch? "Wait," she said as her mother's words sank in. "More energy than Stone can provide—exactly who all do I have to sleep with?"

"Stone will be the only one to invade your body—in all three of the usual ways. He is your betrothed. But in order for you to gain enough energy to survive the ascension, to wield power and fully bear the weight of being queen, you must ingest the essence of twenty of the strongest Klatch men."

"In . . . ingest? As in swallow? No way!" Her mind whirled with the possibilities. Her traitorous pussy clenched at the thought of tasting several of Klatch's "strongest," but her morality balked at something so intimate with others on the same night she bonded with Stone.

"No, Alyssandra." The edges of her mother's lips twitched as if she was trying not to smile. "Not swallow. Their essence will be ingested through your skin while Stone claims you as his bride."

Alyssa's mind tried and failed to picture exactly how that would be done, but she pushed the thought aside. She'd had too much to digest for one night already. *Thank God it wasn't "ingest."* She didn't think she'd ever think of that word the same way again.

Chapter 5

Stone took the steps to his family's rooms two at a time and pushed open the large double doors before the majordomo could announce him. The heels of his soft leather boots clicked against the stone floor, and his mother and father turned from their meal, both faces blooming into smiles as they saw him.

His mother had rounded a bit over the years and now tended to wear less revealing clothes than she had in her youth, but the extra weight made her no less beautiful. Her almond shaped eyes and quick wit make any room sparkle. His father remained muscular and tall, with just a touch of gray dusting his dark hair at the temples. His easy smile and gentle nature made him approachable by all. The fourth house of Klatch was always filled with visitors both because of its excellent array of wines and his parents love of gatherings.

"Stone!" His mother rushed forward to envelop him in a quick hug. The top of her head barely reached his chest and he leaned down to let her kiss his cheek. "Did you find her? Is she here? When do we get to meet her?" He smiled at the rapid-fire questions his mother loved to use during conversations.

"Take a breath, Darla. Stone can't tell us his news if you don't give him a chance." Stone's father clapped him on the back and gestured to an open seat at the table. For the first time, Stone noticed the fine lines around his father's eyes, caused from many years of laughter. He knew Alyssandra's childhood wasn't filled with the same happiness as his, so he hoped to spend the rest of his life making sure to erase the damage her past had inflicted.

"Have some dinner and tell us your news, before you mother starts her questions again." The older man winked at his wife, softening his words.

Stone smiled at the familiar banter. His parents had a much different relationship than the king and queen's. No less loving and committed, but they didn't have the added strain of ruling, which also allowed Darius and Annalecia to share an empathic connection. He smiled at the thought of his father and mother having to listen to each other's internal thoughts after all these years. Some things were better off left as they were.

Stone nodded thanks to the servant who filled his goblet and took a healthy sip. "I did find her, and she's meeting with the king and queen as we speak."

His mother opened her mouth, no doubt to ask more questions, but his father placed a hand on top of hers and she smiled sheepishly and closed her mouth, allowing Stone to continue.

"She's been raised without knowledge of her heritage, but no permanent harm has been done." Both his parents would know he meant she was still virginal without him having to explain further. "Her roommate was a Cunt who had been continually draining her. No wonder she needed so much sustenance through our dream liaisons." His fist clenched around his goblet as he thought about closing his hands around the throat of the skinny Cunt who had fed from his beloved.

The double doors banged open to admit Grayson and Ryan, both princes from other royal houses, and Stone's two best friends growing up. His mother had always said where there was trouble to be found, the three princes would be right in the middle of it—and more often than not, she'd been right.

Stone stood, and shook hands with each as they pulled chairs up to the table and helped themselves to the wine without being invited.

"Don't you two have any manners at all? Stone is about to tell us how he found the princess." Stone's mother shot each of them a reproving look softened by a smile as she tapped her cheek for her expected kiss of greeting. Both men had been frequent guests of the household since they could walk, and Stone's mother had given up on all formalities with them long ago. There were only two unforgivable sins in the Fourth House of Klatch—deceit and not greeting Darla with her customary kiss on the cheek.

Grayson, the taller of the two men, grinned, and snatched a piece of bread from the middle of the table before leaning over to kiss her cheek. "Forgive us, my lady. That's why we're here, we wanted to hear about the princess firsthand. I've heard about nothing but this goddess from Stone for the last decade. We're here to see if his dreams were accurate."

Darla shot the second man a mock glare and lifted her brows expectantly. "Well, Ryan?"

He hesitated a moment as if had to think about it and then laughed before leaning over and providing the requested kiss. "You know I could never deny you, my lady." He picked up a *salda* fruit off a platter in the middle of the table and took a large bite.

Stone's father cleared his throat loudly before signaling for more wine. "If everyone is settled, I'd like to hear what Stone has to say."

Grayson and Ryan grinned, unrepentant, but they sat quietly, waiting for Stone to speak.

"As I told my parents, I found her and she's meeting with

the king and queen now. She's unharmed and easily the most stunning woman I've ever laid eyes on."

Ryan leaned back in his chair, the angry red scar that ran from his right temple down his cheek stretching a bit as he smiled. "From the look on your face, I'd say she's everything you hoped for. I'm amazed after all this time you haven't soiled your breeches twenty times just getting her back here." He smirked at Stone. "Or did you?"

Stone ignored his friend and took another sip of wine, savoring the taste while he chose his words. "I'd seen her in my dreams for all those years dressed in baggy clothes with her hair pulled back, but when I saw her a few minutes ago in full Klatch dress, she took my breath away." *Not to mention caused a sudden evacuation of blood from my brain.* He laughed at the awed note in his own voice when he spoke of her. "She's coming into her powers already and I know she'll make an excellent queen . . ." His voice trailed off as he remembered another woman who had wanted to be queen. *Alyssa will be successful. She has to be. I'll not watch another woman die trying to ascend the throne—especially not this one.*

Grayson leaned forward and pierced Stone with an intense gaze. "Lianna's death was not your fault, Stone. It was her decision to make."

Familiar pain spiked through Stone and he took a deep breath against its intensity. "She wasn't strong enough to ascend. I knew it, and didn't try hard enough to make her listen. And I kept my promise to not mention my doubts to her betrothed." He gripped his goblet so tight, he was surprised it didn't crumple in his hand. "I could've prevented both their deaths, and instead I kept quiet." He looked up to meet everyone's uneasy gaze. "I have no such doubts about Alyssandra, or I'd never let her even try—regardless of the fate of the planet."

His mother sighed and leaned back in her chair. "Grayson's

right, Stone. Lianna wasn't strong enough and she knew it, but wouldn't admit it. Nothing you said would've stopped her. But Alyssandra will be different." She picked up her fork and gestured around the table with it. "Annalecia's daughter was born to sit on the throne. I knew she would be perfect for you. She has to be much like the queen—blood will always win true. Her return should also help Annalecia. Her condition is worsening, and I fear she won't last much longer."

"She only has to last a week." Stone pictured how drawn and pale the queen was when he'd left her. Even her elation at seeing her daughter hadn't erased the damage done. "Now that Alyssandra is safe and sound, some of the burden from the queen will ease."

Grayson held his goblet up for the servant to fill. "When do we get to meet her? If she's that gorgeous, then she obviously has the wrong Prince of Klatch." He allowed his lips to form a knowing smirk. "An oversight I'm sure she'll recognize as soon as she has a choice of more than just you."

Jealousy spurted through Stone, stiffening his shoulders and clenching his jaw. He knew his friend was joking, but the thought of anyone touching Alyssandra besides him made thick hot anger course through his veins. The princess was his.

Ryan shot Grayson a warning look. "It's too close to the ascension to bait him, Gray. You know the future queen's pheromones are high. One too many jokes and he'll rip your heart out with his bare hands, friend or not." The open amusement in Ryan's eyes showed that he thought it would be entertaining to watch.

Stone forced himself to relax. "I doubt either one of you could handle her—she's quite a handful, and besides, she can well take care of herself." He winced as he remembered his bruised instep and stomach where she'd attacked him outside her apartment.

Laughter from around the table caused Stone's lips to curve into a smile. "Let's just say I pity the man who sneaks up on her unawares."

"I definitely have to meet her then." Ryan absently rubbed at the bottom end of his scar with his thumb. "If she's a spitfire, then she's absolutely perfect for you. I'm almost jealous of you having a woman like that all to yourself."

Since several of the Klatch princesses and their respective princes had died trying to ascend the throne in Alyssandra's absence, the selection of royal females in Ryan and Grayson's age range were all but gone. They would have to wait until some of them came of age, marry a princess easily twenty years their senior or dilute the Royal line, none of which held much appeal.

Stone cleared his throat. "You two are very creative. I'm sure you'll come up with something that your families will approve of."

"That doesn't necessarily mean those are choices *we* approve of," Grayson said around a mouthful of bread.

Silence reigned until Stone's father held up his goblet and the others followed suit. "To the future king and queen, who will save us all."

Stone stood to the side, letting Alyssandra explore her room. It had been updated over the years to meet her current age so it would be ready at any time the princess was recovered. Now it was the room of a young and vibrant woman—natural woods, deep purple cloth and the snow-white *balda* stone. She'd seemed happy enough to find it as she said she'd always dreamed it would be. But Stone could tell something bothered her. Ever since he'd met her after the dinner with her parents, she'd been quiet and withdrawn.

He sighed. Once they completed the coming-of-age ceremony, they would share an empathic link. He wished they already did, since his last several attempts to find out what was amiss had resulted in her averting her eyes and saying she was "fine." He knew enough about women to know that wasn't a good sign.

After completing a circuit of the room, opening every drawer and cabinet, and thumbing through several books, she opened the French patio doors and stepped out on to the veranda. Stone followed her, admiring the sway of her hips and the halo of mahogany hair that flowed around her. When she leaned her arms on the stone wall railing, he stepped close behind her.

"Isn't it beautiful?" He looked up at the dark sky, the stars twinkling silver overhead, the moon bathing Alyssandra's smooth skin in a silver glow. "I've often stood here wondering where you were and what you were doing." He placed his hands on her shoulders, unsure what kind of reception he would receive.

She sighed, the soft sound echoing off the stone of the veranda. "Why did it take so long for you to find me?" Her voice so low, he had to strain to hear her words. She sounded like a lost child.

He hesitated until she placed one of her hands over his. Stepping close behind her and enveloping her in his arms, he kissed her hair before answering. "I could see you and you only. We were meant from birth, so therefore we have been linked since puberty. But only our minds were linked, not our locations. I searched for you since the first day I came to you in your dreams."

She nodded and leaned back against him as if basking in his warmth. "Do men have a coming-of-age ceremony?"

He smiled to himself. So that's what this was about. Her mother must have discussed the ceremony with her. "Yes, but men have theirs at sixteen, not twenty-four."

Turning in his arms, she studied his face. "What does the male ceremony consist of? How many Klatch women did you have to bed?"

Stone's mouth dropped open, but all that came out was, "Uh . . ." How could he discuss *that* with his betrothed? Not only was it not a good idea to talk about any other woman than Alyssandra meeting his sexual needs, he knew it would end up hurting her in the long run. He knew how the female mind worked and like it or not—no matter how he answered, this was a recipe for disaster.

"Well?" she prompted. "This is a sexual society and you already said you had a coming-of-age ceremony." She pierced him with a stare that pinned him in place. "So, explain what was involved in yours. You obviously already know what happens in mine." Her tone was clipped and she crossed her arms in front of her, placing a barrier between them. Stone refused to step back, but instead kept his arms loosely around her.

Leaning forward, he kissed the crease of her brow and pulled her toward his chest until she gave up her crossed arms and threaded them around his waist. "I would never wish to hurt you in any way, Alyssandra. If you wish to know of my ceremony, I'll tell you. But I think your question has more to do with your fears over your own. Does it not?"

A warm wetness touched his skin through his shirt and he realized she was crying. He held her, rocking her gently while the moon slowly sailed across the sky the span of his outstretched hand. He knew she was reacting to more than just the ceremony—she grieved for her lost childhood and heritage. Those years she could never reclaim. He regretted that so much responsibility fell squarely on her shoulders. It didn't give her much time to come to terms with her new circumstances.

Finally, she sniffled and pulled back enough to raise her watery gaze to his. "I'm sorry. I think something inside me finally broke." She blinked and a few more fat tears carved a slow path down her cheeks. "I'm scared. I don't know if I can handle the ceremony. But if I don't—my mother will die . . . won't she?"

For the first time, Stone wished he could lie to her. Anything to remove the pain from her eyes. A quick flash of memory reminded him of the night Lianna died. She hadn't been able to contain the energy of the planet and her body, overloaded with energy, had just stopped functioning. The backlash of the energy had flowed down through her intimate connection with her betrothed and electrocuted him. He'd been one of the twenty Klatch men, there to give his essence, and the sight of Lianna's lifeless eyes staring up at him still haunted his nightmares.

He tightened his grip around Alyssandra. "Annalecia has been weakening for some time. If you do not assume the throne, both your mother and Tador will slowly die."

She shook her head against the words, as if her denial could change the circumstances. "But what about the Second Princess or the Third or any of the sixteen?" A tinge of desperation darkened her voice.

He swallowed hard against his pain. "Unfortunately, others have tried to take the burden from Annalecia, but so far every mating has failed." He shook his head to remove Lianna's sightless eyes from his mind. "She has allowed her hope to dwindle to the point that no one but her blood daughter could take over from her without dire consequences."

The Princess stiffened within his embrace. "What kind of dire consequences?"

"She would die as would Tador." Brushing a beaded braid out of her face, he continued. "She held out hope for too long, as did we all. By the time the other mated royal couples were tried, none of the princesses and some of the princes . . ."

She wrenched out of his grasp and wrapped her arms around herself in a protective gesture. "None of the princesses and some of the princes what, Stone?" She pierced him with a stare that would brook no argument.

He knew if he told her, she might refuse to take the risk of the ceremony, but he also knew he couldn't keep it from her.

She was strong enough to undergo the ascension—he would bet his life on it, and in fact, he was, as he knew firsthand from witnessing Lianna's attempt to ascend. "None of them survived the ascension."

Expressions chased across her features until she scrubbed her hands over her face, slightly smearing the kohl lining her eyes. "What makes everyone so sure *I'll* survive?"

Stone reached for her, but stopped before touching her. He needed to let her assimilate this in her own way. "You are the blood descendent of the true queen and you have already begun to come into your powers. None of the others' powers appeared until the ascension began. Please believe me, Alyssandra. I would never allow you to go into the ceremony tent if I had any doubts about your ability to successfully complete the ascension."

Her expression turned tender and she reached up to cup his cheek in her palm. "I'm sorry, Stone. I just realized, the royal couples who died were all friends of yours. It must've been difficult for you. Were you there when they . . ."

Stone closed his eyes and took a deep breath before blowing it out slowly. When he opened his eyes, the understanding in her soft lavender gaze almost broke him. "I knew all of them, but I only participated in one of the ceremonies—I was one of the twenty Klatch that would lend their essence. Lianna was a close friend, and I saw her die, along with her betrothed. I knew she wasn't strong enough for the ascension, but I didn't try hard enough to dissuade her."

"Did she have a choice? I mean, could she have said no?"

His brow furrowed. "Of course. No one is forced to ascend. It is always a conscious choice to accept both the risk and the responsibility involved."

"Then Lianna could've said no. You can't be responsible for the world, Stone. Everyone has to make their own choices—

including me." She dropped her arms to her sides and stepped back. "When do I have to decide?"

His heart squeezed inside his chest. Not only would Tador perish, but he would lose Alyssandra if she chose not to go through with the ceremony. He was the only prince powerful enough to supply the new queen with energy. Yet, he couldn't imagine sharing his life or his bed with anyone but the woman standing before him. Taking a deep breath, he told her the truth, although his heart begged him to lie. "You can choose to decline at any time before our mating inside the ceremony tent." His voice sounded distant and flat.

Alyssandra nodded. "Thank you for telling me. Even though it's not what you want. I have to decide this on my own—I don't want to be pushed into it and then resent you later. And Stone," she placed a tentative hand on his arm. "Any risk I willingly choose to take is my responsibility, not yours."

He pulled her back into his arms and laid a simple kiss on her forehead. "I would never wish to force you into anything, beloved. You must embrace this choice willingly or not at all. You must be true to yourself." *Even if it rips me to shreds.*

She raised a tentative hand to trace his face with her fingers. A slow exploration, as if she saw him for the first time.

As her fingers left a feathery hot path across his face, his heart squeezed inside his chest. He'd spent so many years with the sole purpose of finding her, now that she was here, he felt like an awkward teenager. Just like he did before his own coming-of-age ceremony.

The smell of the ceremony tent from all those years ago still blazed inside his memory. He remembered the twenty Klatch women who had instructed him in the ways of pleasuring a woman. He remembered the hours spent buried between lush thighs and lips and the pungent scent of sex that had clung to him for weeks.

At the time, he thought he'd died and gone to heaven, but now, looking back, he knew the pleasures of the flesh were nothing compared with the act with a true lover. Looking into Alyssandra's misty eyes, he wanted nothing more than to make slow love to her and join their bodies as one. His cock stiffened against her stomach and she smiled up at him.

"He's just as impatient as I am." She laughed and wiped her eyes with the back of her hand before pressing herself against him.

"Witch." He growled low in his throat before touching his lips to her shy smile. He traced his tongue over her full bottom lip, seeking entrance. When she opened for him, he delved inside, his tongue mimicking driving his hard cock into her waiting warmth. Energy sparked and flowed between them like a circuit opened wide and looping back on itself. She responded eagerly, her small hands dipping beneath his shirt to trace and explore him. The scent of her arousal rose around him, filling his nostrils and hardening him further.

When she moaned against his mouth, he traced the exposed bottom curve of her breasts and slipped his hands under her shirt to cup the ripe globes in his palms. She arched into him, offering herself, her mound pressed tight against him. He rolled her nipples between the thumb and forefinger of each hand. The aroma of her juices rose stronger around him and it was his turn to moan. As if their minds were one, he lifted her and she wrapped her legs around his waist, rubbing her slick slit against his aching cock through their clothes while he anchored her back against the stone railing of the veranda. Their mouths still fused together, he pumped against her, driving both of them closer to the release they sought.

When her breathing reached a choppy fevered pitch, he reached between them and into the leg of her half shorts to thumb her clit, sending her over the edge. When his hand encountered not a wiry thatch of curls, but a smoothly shaven mound, slick with her juices, his control shattered as well. Hot seed spurted from his cock, soaking his breeches. He had just enough control left to lift her higher, so her exposed pussy would not accidentally touch any of his essence that seeped through the cloth.

"Mmmm," she hummed against his neck. "Come to bed with me, Stone. Let me fall asleep in your arms."

He hugged her tighter, turned and walked toward the bed, gently lowering her until she sat on its edge. "I have to change my breeches. And I'm not sure it's such a good idea to open ourselves to such blatant temptation."

Her lavender gaze locked with his. "Please, Stone . . ." she whispered. "I don't want to be alone tonight. And I know you'd never do anything to hurt me."

Looking down at her, disheveled and sexy, her lips still swollen from his kisses, he couldn't deny her anything. He nodded and stepped toward the door. After murmuring some instructions to the servant standing watch outside, he received a pair of replacement breeches and donned them before joining her.

Her lips curved and mischief danced in her eyes as she stripped off her shirt and shorts to stand before him naked. His eyes were immediately drawn to her smooth mound and his cock surged to life once more. "With such a sexual society, I thought everyone here would sleep naked." Her last word was obscured by a large yawn.

She needed rest more than he needed to soak another pair of breeches. He bit back a scowl as he remembered Grayson's earlier comment. His cock must've understood because it softened slightly against the confines of his breeches.

"We do," he said as he pulled back the covers allowing her to slip underneath. "But until we don't have to worry about my essence harming you, I think it's wise to keep a barrier between us."

Patting the bed beside her, she said, "I see your point, he

does tend to have a mind of his own." She gave a pointed look toward Stone's crotch.

Taking a tight reign on his control, he slid next to her, pulling her against him, spoon-style, and closed his eyes as contentment settled around him. She placed his arm close against her chest, so he cupped her breast. When he heard her happy sigh, he kissed her hair and let sleep take him.

Sela paced in front of the small cell where she'd kept Shawn's mother, Natasha, incarcerated for the past twenty-three years. The simple room had been made in the corner of a basement and consisted of bars placed diagonally across one corner. It contained only a bed, a chair, a small shower stall and toilet and a small bookshelf stacked tight with books—the only thing Sela had allowed her. *How has she survived like this for so long?*

Natasha closed the book she'd been reading and looked up. "What can I do for you, Sela?" she said as if she were the one with all the control. The calm tone of her voice irritated Sela, as it always did.

"Why haven't you died yet, bitch?" Sela ground her teeth and paced back and forth in front of the cell, her high heel clicks echoing around the basement.

"Because I have a duty to the princess and to my son." Her open, assessing gaze burned through Sela and she berated herself when she looked away. This woman had infuriated her for over two decades and now her damned son was starting to do the same.

"Your son doesn't even know you exist," she snapped. She stopped pacing and grasped two of the cell bars in her hands, Natasha's calm gaze sparking her temper higher. "We have always told him his Klatch mother abandoned him. And that the Klatch are a sect good for nothing but extermination. We're going to have him mate with the princess so we can breed a race of slaves we can siphon energy from. Then we're going to overthrow the imposter king and queen and take Tador back. What do you think of that?" Sela studied her, hoping for some sign of fear or better yet, hopelessness. But as usual, there was none. Only a serene calmness.

Sela'd made sure she had just enough food to survive, and she knew the woman masturbated to keep up her sexual energy. Despite her best efforts to break the princess's nanny, she'd been unsuccessful. Instead of sunken cheeks and drawn skin, the woman looked healthy and fit, her long dark hair flowing around her in a cascade of sable, her annoying lavender eyes cool and assessing. The same damned eyes as the little bitch she'd raised from an infant. The same ungrateful bitch who'd escaped with the prince.

Natasha shrugged as if she hadn't a care in the world. "The Princess's betrothed will come for her. As for Shawn, he'll eventually realize his true path. It's in his blood." She placed the book back on the bookshelf and stood, stretching as if just waking up from a relaxing nap. "Besides, once he comes into his full powers and realizes he is more powerful than the Cunts, he will not have to work hard to overthrow your hold."

Sela ground her teeth. She would never admit to Natasha that the prince had already rescued Alyssa. If Natasha thought the princess was safe, she'd turn her powers on Sela in an instant. The only insurance Sela had was the threat of harming Shawn or Alyssa. "Your son has already attained all the powers he'll ever get. All your hopes and optimism are for nothing. The only future you have is being a food supply for our Cunt warriors."

"We shall see, Sela. You may have denied Shawn a coming-of-age ceremony, but the Klatch blood in him will prevail. And be careful what you wish for. I don't think your so-called warriors could handle me." A smile curved the corners of her lips and she began to do stretching exercises, ignoring Sela completely.

Chapter 6

When Natasha heard the door slam behind Sela, she stopped stretching and looked to make sure the Cunt was gone. *There has to be some reason why she's suddenly so upset right before her supposed victory! Now we will see, Sela.*

Natasha sat on her cot cross-legged and closed her eyes, allowing her mind to relax. When all thoughts were gone, her mind at peace, she allowed herself to reach out, seeking, until she brushed against Alyssandra's thoughts.

She could tell from the distant connection and the contentment of the young woman's thoughts while she slept, that the princess had been recovered. Natasha forced her lips not to curve in triumph. It wouldn't do to have the guards report her actions and warn Sela.

Next, she reached out her thoughts to Shawn. She'd kept in touch mentally for twenty-three years. Shawn thought of her as his voice of conscience, not his mother, but it had been enough to keep a watchful eye on him.

I know you think you'll be fathering a new nation, my son. But the Klatch were not made to be cattle for the vampire

Cunts. Soon, very soon, I will show you the world of your heritage.

A short knock sounded on her door and Alyssa opened it to find her parents standing in the doorway smiling at her.

"Good morning." She blinked, afraid she'd imagined them and they would disappear at any moment. But when she opened her eyes again, they were still there. She fidgeted with the doorknob still held in her hand as silence fell between them.

Both Annalecia and Darius seemed nervous, as if they wanted to reach out and touch her, but weren't sure if it was welcome. For a long uncomfortable moment, they all just stared at each other. Finally, Alyssa laughed, pushing aside her hesitance and hugged each of her parents in turn—each holding her tight as if they expected someone to try and take her from them again. "I hope you both don't mind, but I've lived without true parents long enough. I plan on taking every opportunity I can to make up for lost time."

"What did I tell you, Darius? She's very straightforward, just like you. There was no reason to be nervous."

The king laughed. "No doubt she's also a beautiful charmer like her mother. I'll have to be extra careful or you'll both have me wrapped around your fingers soon enough."

Now that the ice was broken, Darius yanked playfully on one of the Klatch braids scattered throughout her hair. "Alyssandra, we thought you might like to have some breakfast with us before your mother begins your lessons."

Alyssa's stomach growled and they all laughed. "Breakfast sounds great, I'm obviously starving." She followed them down the hall, her father leading her with a gentle hand on her lower back. "You mentioned lessons. What lessons?"

"Well, I suppose you'd call them 'queen lessons.' There are several things you need to learn before the ascension. Things you would've learned as you grew up if . . ." Annalecia trailed off, her lips thinning into a tight line as if she were afraid to say the words.

"If I hadn't been taken?" Alyssa smiled to assure her parents she hadn't taken any offense.

"Yes, exactly." The queen smiled gratefully and grabbed Alyssa's hand.

They entered the dining room and sat around the table, which was already laden with food, only some of which Alyssa recognized from her previous meal with her parents. She took a seat in between them. "Do you think my first lesson could be on what the heck all these foods are? I was so excited to meet you both yesterday that I don't think I tasted a thing."

Darius laughed and picked up his glass. "Of course. I'd forgotten that several Tador foods aren't available on earth. You're in for a real treat, daughter. Even though Klatch tend to stay trim due to the way we use energy, we really know how to eat." He raised his glass in a toast. "To my beautiful daughter and her growling stomach."

Alyssandra spent the next two hours laughing and talking with her parents while she sampled and tried to remember the names of several native Tador foods. In fact, she'd instantly decided to have some of the fleshy blue *ool* at every meal. With a texture like a plum, and a taste like a vanilla milkshake all rolled up in a healthy good-for-her fruit, she couldn't resist. This was much better than the greasy burgers and fries Debbie always picked up for them on the way home.

Throughout the meal, she began to recognize her parent's mannerisms and realize where she'd gotten some of her own. Her mother consistently bit her bottom lip when she was embarrassed or thinking and her father shared her same sarcastic sense of humor. Her sense of belonging became stronger as the minutes ticked by. Maybe with enough time, the past twenty-three years would melt away as if they were nothing more than a bad dream.

"Well, ladies. I have to meet with the Klatch Council about surveying the damaged outlying areas. So, I'll leave you to your lessons." Darius stood and kissed Alyssa on the cheek and squeezed her shoulder. "It's so nice to finally have you home where you belong, Alyssandra." His eyes misted and he turned toward his wife, brushing a gentle kiss over her lips. "Promise me you'll lie down if you grow tired. There are still a few days until the ascension and you must conserve your energy."

"Good luck with the council, Darius. Don't worry, I'll be fine." Annalecia squeezed his hand and a look of vulnerability and love passed between them, making Alyssa smile. She hoped she and Stone still looked at each other like that after thirty years together.

Stone professed his love for her freely, while she was still getting used to having a man all to herself. She hoped over time, she could return his feelings and have a relationship like the one she saw before her in her parents.

The king held his wife's hand for a long moment before stepping away and flashing her a devastating smile that reminded Alyssa of Stone.

She sighed as the dining room door closed behind him. "You can tell how in love you both are. It's obvious, and wonderful." Her heart squeezed in her chest and she blinked back tears at witnessing such an intimate moment.

The queen placed a comforting hand on hers. "Your father is stubborn, overbearing, insufferable and he grinds his teeth until I'm tempted to kill him in his sleep." Her lips quirked up, and amusement danced in her lavender eyes. "But he's also my best friend and I love him with my entire being. Besides, he overlooks all my annoying habits and loves me anyway." She shrugged. "I know you and Stone have only known each other for a short time, but there's already a connection between you. It's obvious . . . and wonderful to see the two of you together. Give it time to blossom into something more. I've known

Stone since he was born—he's grown into a very good man. One I trust to take care of my only child."

Alyssa's cheeks heated and she grinned up at her mother. "Stone sounds a lot like Father—especially the stubborn, over-bearing and insufferable part. I don't think I've noticed any teeth grinding yet, though, but I'll keep watch."

The women shared a knowing laugh.

"All right." Alyssa nibbled on another piece of *ool*. "So, tell me everything I need to know to be queen."

"I think it will take more than a conversation over the re-mains of breakfast." Annalecia took her napkin off her lap and laid it on the table next to her plate. "Stone will have to teach you how to control energy, and he and Darius have had many discussions on how to coach you through it. I can tell you how I do it, but I won't be there when . . . you have the excess en-ergy to distribute." The queen took a sip of wine and set the goblet back on the table before continuing. "There's not really a checklist of things you have to know to become queen—it's more of an on the job training opportunity. And since you haven't been around to watch me do the job, I'll make sure I'm around to answer your questions while *you're* doing the job." The queen grinned over at her.

Alyssa thought back to her last energy sharing with Stone and her clit tingled in response and she clenched her thighs to-gether to try and make it stop. Somehow having an erotic reac-tion while talking to her mother just didn't go well together.

Annalecia, oblivious to Alyssa's discomfort, sipped at her coffee—a definite earth import—and studied her daughter. "Let's see, beyond your symbiosis with the planet, there are several duties that the queen performs, but the symbiosis and the sharing of energy definitely takes most of your time and en-ergy. Things such as meeting with the Klatch Council, helping solve disputes that the council can't, and making appearances at balls, ceremonies and other events. Of course, the king handles many of those same duties, so there's nothing you have to do alone. However, since we are a matriarchal society, the people will look to you for strong leadership and vision. Sometimes I think that's the most difficult part."

Panic fluttered deep in her belly. "I don't know anything about solving disputes, or how to act at fancy events. Even with Stone at my side, I'm terrified I'll make a complete ass of myself. And how do I suddenly develop strong leadership and vision? I don't think my work history as a bartender exactly prepared me for the throne."

"Don't worry, Alyssandra. Some of it is already in your blood. You were born to be queen, and the universe wouldn't create you without the needed skills. The rest you can learn as you go—some by learning from your mistakes and some by taking good advice or studying the history of Klatch." She leaned her elbows on the table and steepled her fingers in front of her lips. "I wanted to bring up appearances because you'll be expected to attend the presentation ball so we can introduce you to your people, and there is a ceremony involved."

Alyssa swallowed the lump that formed inside her throat. The thought of being on display in front of all of the Klatch terrified her. What if she disappointed not only her parents and Stone, but all the Klatch people as well? Then another thought occurred to her, arrowing a keep sense of panic through her. "This ceremony, it's not a sexual ceremony I hope. I don't think I can do anything sexual in front of a group just yet. I'm having enough trouble adjusting as it is."

Annalecia laughed. "No, my daughter. For once, believe it or not, it's not sexual."

An hour into their "queen lessons," her mother began to look pale and drawn and had to excuse herself so she could lie down.

After Alyssa made sure the queen was comfortably resting, and a guard dispatched to inform her father, Alyssa took the opportunity to explore the grounds around the castle.

When she stepped outside and into the sunshine, she sighed as the warm rays caressed her skin. A gentle breeze kept the day from being too hot and carried the fresh scent of the gardens and the sound of the fountains. The lush grass tickled between her bare toes and she stopped to wiggle them and enjoy the sensation.

Immediately in front of her was the main fountain, which was as big around as a single-family home back on earth. Several Klatch splashed and played in the sparkling blue water, some naked and some dressed, their traditional white Klatch clothes nearly transparent. Off to her right were the baths where she'd met Sasha, and to her left, the gardens.

Sasha had explained the gardens were a large maze made from trees, shrubs, flowers, waterfalls and fountains that contained several intimate alcoves and gazebos. People would use the gardens for solitary walks, a quiet place to read or reflect, and even for rendezvous. The gardens were also home to several species of animal life, some quite different from earth animals from what she'd heard. The description reminded her of a great Alice in Wonderland adventure and she had been dying to explore them ever since she'd learned about them.

Splashing from the main fountain caught her attention and she hesitated. As much as she'd have liked to go toward the main fountain and meet the seemingly friendly people, she wasn't comfortable joining in their water play. She might be starting to appreciate her sexuality, but she wasn't comfortable yet beyond Stone and Sasha. She knew no one would force her, but she would feel awkward opting out.

Decided, she turned left toward the gardens to take a relaxing stroll. She slipped inside the maze and past flowering rose bushes, carrying all colors of blooms, their petals opened wide to drink in the golden sunlight. She stopped to sniff and sighed as the sweet aroma filled her senses. She knelt to pick up a handful of multicolored rose petals that had fallen to the ground. She held them to her nose and took a deep breath before dropping them into her pocket.

Farther along, the canopy overhead thickened, filtering the sunlight and casting latticed shadows over the lush ground. Alyssa trailed her fingers over blue feathery leaves of a tree she didn't recognize and laughed as the scent of cinnamon filled the air. She plucked a blue leaf and added it to her collection before moving on.

The path in front of her forked and she veered to the right, following a small rabbit as it darted away toward the sound of rushing water. Her feet squeaked against the damp grass and her stride faltered when she stepped out onto soft sand. She glanced up and the sight before her stole her breath.

A twelve-foot waterfall flowed lazily over several large white boulders of *balda* to fall into a pool ripe with large koi fish and blue and purple frogs as big as her fist. Delighted, she stepped forward and sat down on large rock to dip her toes into the pond. The cool water lapped around her ankles and she swung her legs back and forth idly as the fish nibbled at her toes and the rich scent of flowering plants and flowing water suffused the air around her.

"Princess Alyssandra, I presume?"

The deep voice startled her and she pushed to standing, automatically assuming a defensive posture as water dripped down her calves to the tops of her feet. The man before her stood just as tall as Stone, his navy tunic loosely laced so crispy black chest hairs were clearly visible. The blue color of the tunic designated him as from one of the royal families.

He had the same wavy dark hair as Stone, but it was pulled

back into a ponytail and hung halfway down his back. His face appeared harsh and unforgiving except for his full lips, which almost seemed feminine. But when she looked him up and down, she knew no one would ever accuse him of being anything but a man. His broad shoulders and sculpted muscles were evident, as if he worked at a job where hard physical labor was required. She couldn't see a Prince of Klatch doing time in a gym.

His breeches clung to him like a second skin and she couldn't help but wonder what his tight muscular ass looked like. There was a definite sexuality that clung to him, and as a woman, Alyssa was definitely affected, but there was nothing deeper. His presence didn't make her stomach flutter and her heart skip as they did every time Stone was near.

Get a grip! You're betrothed to Stone. The other side of her mind answered quickly. *You're engaged, not dead. Not looking at this perfect male specimen would be like turning your back on a great work of art. Just a little perfectly normal lust.*

He held his hands out at his sides, palms open. "I apologize, I didn't mean to startle you. I'm Prince Grayson. Prince Stone is one of my closest friends and I've heard quite a bit about you—not to mention you look just like your mother."

Stone hadn't mentioned any of his close friends, but most of their time together hadn't exactly been spent talking. Alyssa made a mental note to change that.

Her gut told her this man wasn't a threat, but old habits died hard. She'd been assured it was safe to wander the maze alone, but it never hurt to be careful. She relaxed her stance and held out her hand to shake. "Nice to meet you, Grayson, I'm Alyssa," she said, purposely dropping the titles, which still made her uncomfortable.

He took her hand in his and pinned her with an intense stare while he slowly brought the back of her hand to his lips. "I think Stone's right, Alyssa doesn't suit you. It's not regal enough. You're definitely an Alyssandra." His warm lips against her skin sent a jolt of lust through her system, but nothing lingering or building as it always did with Stone.

He studied her intently until his gaze became almost creepy. Alyssa pulled her hand from his grasp and his brow furrowed in confusion. She crossed her arms under her chest to put distance between them. "Everyone on Earth called me Alyssa. I guess I've gotten used to it."

When he only continued to study her with his inscrutable expression, the only clue to his mood, his furrowed brows, she had to break the silence. "Is there something wrong?"

He laughed, his entire face blossoming into a boyish grin, softening him. "Forgive me, as this will sound rather conceited, but I'm just surprised I had no affect on you."

"Excuse me?" She wasn't quite sure what to say. Assuring him he'd had an affect didn't seem like the best way to go, and denying it reeked of lying, which she wasn't comfortable with either. What kind of man hoped to cause a reaction in his good friend's fiancé?

His grin turned sheepish and he gestured for her to return to her seat at the pond. Not sure what else to do, she sat and dipped her toes back in the cool water, while he sat beside her facing the opposite direction, his long legs stretched out in front of him away from the water. "I hadn't realized until just now how often I use my natural gifts. In my many years of meeting women, I've never experienced one who had absolutely no reaction to me whatsoever. It's refreshing actually."

Alyssa remembered hearing that each Klatch had their own natural ability, but she hadn't heard anyone talk about it yet. "What exactly are your natural gifts?"

"All Klatch have some ability to cause arousal in others. My ability is to cause an instant and intense sexual reaction—instant intense lust, if you will. It's just a new twist on an already common Klatch trait."

She turned her head to study his profile, the dappled light

through the tall trees making the hard line of his jaw appear to be carved from pure granite. Without thinking, she said, "That must make for a very lonely life."

His eyebrows rose slowly as he regarded her silently.

Her cheeks burned under his intense scrutiny and she searched for words to explain. "I mean, lust without anything else is sort of like masturbation, only another person is present. Doesn't having that intense lust up front keep you from getting to know the real person?" After years of watching Debbie have not only one-night stands, but five-minute stands, Alyssa had formed definite opinions on the subject. And although she and Stone had started out very much from lust, it was definitely different, and she would defend it.

He seemed to genuinely consider her words. "Forgive me for being too personal, but I think we've already gone past the point of delicate speaking. Do you and Stone have more than lust between you?"

She startled as he mirrored her recent thoughts. She searched his face for any signs of mockery or condescension, but found none. "I know it sounds strange, but even when we only met in dreams, there was a connection between us on a deeper level. Don't get me wrong, Grayson, you're an attractive man, no woman with eyes could deny the truth of that. But whenever Stone is near me, my reaction goes beyond lust. Butterflies flutter in my stomach, my heart squeezes in my chest, and the physical takes on a new meaning. Then when he's gone, there's an anticipation until I see him again."

She turned to see his full lips curved into a frown and his brows furrowed even further than before. A laugh escaped her at his confusion. "I'm sorry, I don't usually lecture people I've just met. Besides, I'm afraid I'm not explaining it very well. It's not something I've tried to put into words before."

He shook his head and smiled, his nonchalant expression suddenly back. "Not at all, Princess. You've given me a lot to think on. It's been a long time since a woman has intrigued me to think about anything. You're absolutely right—I don't bother to get to know many women outside my family, so the unrelated women I do meet, I guess I've never given them a chance to intrigue me beyond the physical. Stone is a lucky man. I have a feeling you will keep him very intrigued on many levels." He flashed a devilish grin. "Besides, he's been far too responsible for too long. I think you'll be good for him."

It was Alyssa's turn to furrow her brow. "What do you mean?"

He didn't pretend to mistake her meaning. "I'm sure you already know that several tried and failed to ascend the throne." At her nod, he continued. "Even before that, Stone took the weight of the world on his shoulders. He's so protective of everyone, the queen and king included because it makes him feel like he can actually control things and keep them together. When in reality, fate has more to do with the outcome than Stone. I fear the weight of the world will one day crush him if he's not careful. But you, my dear Alyssandra, will keep him on his toes and keep him honest."

He stood and brushed the grass from his form-fitting breeches and she purposely kept her eyes from tracing the movements of his hands. "Besides, you've restored my confidence. You admitted I had some affect on you at least, so my male ego is still intact." He flashed her a quick smile. "It was very nice to meet you, Princess. I'm sure we'll meet again." Before she could open her mouth to say anything, he'd disappeared through the dense foliage.

She shook her head, not quite sure what to make of Grayson. She'd have to ask Stone about him later.

Chapter 7

A muffled sound to the side of the waterfall caught Alyssa's attention and she stood, deciding to investigate. She ringed the pond, walking softly toward the sound and stepped through a gap in the trees that bracketed the waterfall on either side. She emerged into a small clearing surrounded by large leafy bushes. She stretched out her arms and her fingers just brushed both sides of the small clearing. Just large enough for the illusion of privacy for two people. She smiled as she imagined bringing Stone here for one of the rendezvouses Sasha had mentioned.

Another muffled sound just on the other side of her small clearing had her inching forward to peer through the leafy bush in front of her. Twenty feet away, a naked woman with lush curves stood in between two equally naked men almost as well endowed as Stone. Both men caressed her gently with lips and teeth and tongue while she moaned out her pleasure. Their engorged cocks rubbed against her stomach and her ass with their motions.

Heat pooled low in Alyssa's belly and traced a hot path down toward her pussy. She groaned as arousal fired to life and sudden need speared through her. It had been several hours since breakfast and her energy levels were waning. Taking a quick glance around her small clearing, she shrugged. Might as well take sustenance where she could find it. *Besides, I've always wanted to watch.*

She pushed her short top up over her breasts and pulled on her suddenly engorged nipples as she turned her attention back to the trio.

The man in the rear reached around to cup the woman's plush breasts in his large hands, and Alyssa bit back a moan as she imagined Stone's rough hands caressing her. The man plucked the woman's large dark nipples between his thumbs and forefingers and Alyssa followed suit. When the woman gasped against the sudden sensation, the man in front swallowed the sound as he captured her mouth and then trailed his fingers down her rounded stomach to slip two fingers between her slick folds.

The woman leaned back against the man caressing her breasts, allowing the first man more access to her juicy core. Alyssa gasped when a hand closed over her mouth and another grasped her around the waist before slipping down inside the front of her skirt.

"Shhh, you don't want to interrupt the show." Stone's breath feathered against her neck causing a rush of goose bumps to march over her. One blunt finger traced her wet slit slowly back and forth, shooting fresh jolts of pure arousal through her.

Stone removed his hand from her mouth and traced his fingers down to cup her aching breast. "Good morning, beloved. Don't worry, all who come to the garden to share energy know they may be watched. It's an unspoken agreement. Besides, I thought you might be in need of some sustenance. I had no idea you'd found your own. Do you mind if I help?"

She stiffened against him as the implications of his words hit her. "That means someone could be watching us right now . . ."

She wondered if Grayson was still lurking in the bushes somewhere watching them. Moisture pooled between her thighs at the thought.

Stone continued to trace her slit. "I see that thought excites you, my greedy Princess."

Wanting more, Alyssa bucked her hips against Stone's finger. She returned her gaze to the trio just as the woman locked her arms around the man in front of her and rubbed her breasts against his well-defined chest.

"Describe to me what you're seeing," Stone whispered against her ear, his hot breath causing a sudden zing of energy to shoot down every nerve ending in her body.

"What?" she squeaked before she remembered to whisper. Lowering her voice, she looked over her shoulder at Stone's amused expression. "You can see what they're doing as well as I can." Her breath came out in an urgent hiss.

He chuckled, the deep vibrations rumbling through her. "Actually, since you're peering through the foliage, I don't have a really good view." He pinched her nipple causing her to gasp. "So, tell me, witch. What do you see?"

Alyssa swallowed the sudden lump in her throat and turned her attention back toward the trio. "The man in front is lifting her so she can wrap her legs around his waist."

"And?"

Her clit throbbed as the woman reached down and positioned the man's engorged cock against her pussy lips. "He thrust his hard cock fully inside her." The woman's head lolled back as she moaned, her eyes closed, her full lips parted.

Stone traced her clit in small circles until Alyssa bucked her hips against him and her breath came in short choppy pants. Her release zoomed toward her, but then his hand stopped and she resisted the urge to scream in frustration.

"Don't stop, Princess. Tell me what they're doing now."

She opened her mouth to tell him he was the one who

shouldn't have stopped, but snapped it shut when she realized the quickest way to get him back to rubbing her clit like she wanted was to describe the scene. "The second man is smearing *ponga* onto his cock and into the crack of her ass." Realization hit her, and her pussy clenched at the thought of having two large cocks inside her at once. "Wow, he's going to fuck her up the ass while she rides the other guy. Two cocks inside her at once . . ." She trailed off and squirmed against Stone's finger as she tried to imagine what they would feel like inside her at the same time.

Stone's fingers resumed their ministrations, his other hand pinching one aching nipple. Power sizzled along her skin and flowed down her body and into the ground like lightening. "Does that excite you, witch?"

How could she admit that it did, when it would mean having someone else inside her body besides Stone? She'd meant what she'd told Grayson. A nameless man fucking her in the ass while she rode Stone did excite her, in fact it made her wet and panting with need. But the second man was just an additional sexual element, not an emotional one like she had with Stone. She opened her mouth to deny it, not sure Stone would understand, but he spoke before she had the chance.

"No lies between us, Princess, remember? There's no shame in what excites you. Very little is forbidden among the Klatch, and from what I know of you, I don't think your tastes run to anything that crosses the line."

The short list of forbidden things Sasha had told her flashed through her mind and she shuddered. She had no desire to do any of those. However, if everything else was fair game, that left a lot of territory to explore. Fresh moisture dampened between her thighs and Stone chuckled against her ear. She ignored the heat that flowed up her neck and into her cheeks and glued her gaze to the scene playing out before her. "He's positioning his cock against her ass and slowly pushing forward, stretching her." Her voice sounded strained and it was suddenly harder to pull air into her lungs.

"Imagine it, Alyssandra." He traced his fingers down her slit to tease her opening. She bucked her hips against his hand, silently begging him to finger fuck her, but he only continued his slow teasing. "Imagine my cock plunging inside your pussy, filling you, your long legs wrapped around my waist, while another thick long cock slowly pushes forward into your tight ass. Picture both cocks buried inside you to the hilt, the feeling of being sandwiched between two men while we fill you."

She moaned and he increased his pressure on her clit. With the vivid picture flashing inside her mind as she watched it played out in front of her, her ass and her pussy throbbed with sudden awareness. For a brief second she wondered if the men could feel the pressure of the other's cock head pounding against the woman's core.

Stone slid two fingers inside her pussy, curving his fingers against the front of her pelvis until they hit a spot that spiraled energy throughout her body. She moaned and arched back against him, so he could reach farther inside her.

The sound of flesh slapping against flesh filled the air, punctuated by moans and gasps as the trio's rhythm increased, pushing them all closer to release. The rhythmic flex of the men's muscled asses and the scent of sex permeating the air insinuated themselves into her fantasy, and Alyssa's orgasm hit her just as the woman moaned out her own release. The two men continued to pump into the woman, through her contractions, until they both stiffened as they spilled their essence inside her.

As Alyssa's awareness returned, she had a brief flash of sensation—two streams of thick hot liquid spilling deep inside her from both sides. Her knees buckled and Stone caught her easily, guiding her down to lie on the ground.

He pushed wisps of hair away from her face and leaned

down to brush a kiss over the newly bared skin. "Have you come back to me, Princess?"

A languid haze of liquid gold flowed through her veins and she sighed, contented. "Mmm hmm. How are you, my Prince?" She looked up into Stone's strained features and realized how much control her betrothed had employed.

"I'll be fine." He smiled down at her weakly.

She reached down to cup him, enjoying the way his cock jumped against her hand. "Liar."

Stone hissed through his teeth and bucked against her hand. Alyssa sat up, pushing Stone onto his back before he knew what she was about to do. She straddled his thighs and unlaced his breeches, freeing his cock to her hungry gaze.

"Alyssandra . . ."

"Don't worry, I'll be careful." She leaned forward to run her tongue up the length of him, careful to avoid the glistening pearl of pre come pooling in the eye of his swollen tip. Blacking out again wouldn't help either one of them. The silky skin under her tongue made her long to lick every engorged inch of him, but she knew when too much temptation would get her into trouble.

She pulled back and wrapped her fingers around him, stroking him slowly while she used the other hand to yank on his pants. She rose up on her knees to give him room. "Down."

Stone didn't need to be asked twice. He lifted his ass and wriggled his breeches down around his ankles. Alyssa spread his thighs and with her free hand gently rolled the soft sacs covering his balls in her fingers. Stone's cock hardened in her grip and his hips bucked against her hand. She lowered her face until she could trace a line between his balls with her tongue and then gently sucked one of the sacs into her mouth, caressing it with her tongue. Stone hissed against the sudden sensation and she couldn't help but smile. The ribbed texture of the soft skin fascinated her and she promised herself when she was no longer worried about the effects of his come, she'd make time to do a thorough exploration of Stone's entire body.

She continued to slowly stroke his engorged cock up and down, careful to avoid the growing dollop of pre come that tempted her to lean down and taste. Watching Stone's olive skin flush and his breathing become ragged, Alyssa's own arousal mounted again. Would there ever be a time when she was fully satisfied and didn't crave any more? She fervently hoped not.

Remembering her session with Sasha, she funneled her arousal down both arms and into her fingers, the energy flowing out into Stone's cock and balls. He stiffened and cried out her name as his cock pulsed rhythmically under her touch and his thick creamy come spurted out the tip. She licked her lips as it splashed against the grass and flowers next to him. A small drop fell against the smooth skin of his stomach and she had to forcibly restrain herself from leaning down to lick the salty liquid from his body. She continued to stroke him until the pulsing stopped and his cock softened a bit in her hand.

Unsure what to say, she allowed silence to fall between them. As Stone's breathing returned to normal, he huffed out a contented sigh. "I might not live through the several days until the ceremony at this rate, witch." He smiled up at her and then slowly stood, pulling up his breeches and tying them securely.

"I know what you mean," she muttered under her breath.

Stone's laughter rang out over the clearing and he pulled her into his arms. "Really? Am I not keeping my Princess satisfied, then?"

Her cheeks burned as she realized her comment had sounded like a complaint against Stone. "It's just . . . I . . ." She squared her shoulders and lifted her chin, which always helped bolster her confidence. She pierced him with a steady gaze and spoke her mind, not holding anything back. "I crave your cock inside me, and I think this constant foreplay is going to kill me too. I want to feel your hot come spill inside me as you fill me. I want you to fuck my ass until I scream out my orgasm. I want to taste your come on my tongue as you spill against the back of my throat. And then I want to start over and do it all again in every conceivable way we can both imagine."

Stone leaned his forehead against hers and closed his eyes, his features strained again, the outline of his now fully hard cock digging against her stomach. "You don't know how much control it takes not to throw you to the ground and slip inside you, Alyssandra. Your body calls to mine as I've never experienced before. Believe me, once the ceremony is complete, I'll be happy to fulfill every fantasy inside that creative mind of yours."

He pulled back to look at her, his hands on her shoulders. "But no one else will ever enter your beautiful pussy. That is mine and mine alone." His eyes burned into hers, not so much with command, but with a vulnerable plea. "There have been kings who have allowed such things, but the thought makes me want to crush *balda* with my bare hands."

Alyssa tried and failed to picture anyone else but Stone filling her pussy. Although the thought of another man filling her ass while Stone fucked her still made her clit throb with reaction. She looked up at Stone. "I agree completely. I think I also have some terms of my own."

His eyebrows rose and his sculpted lips curved upward, accentuating the deep dimple next to his mouth, and she had to remind herself to focus on the discussion at hand before she got lost tracing that adorable dent. "Name your terms, Princess."

"It doesn't seem fair, considering what you've just said. But I don't want you entering anyone else—ever. I'll just have to make sure to keep you satisfied enough that you never need to. The thought of you inside another woman, even if it was her ass—" She shook her head and closed her eyes trying to erase the picture from her mind. "I don't know how often it's done, but I probably wouldn't care if you . . . gave your essence. You know—like the twenty Klatch men will do for my ceremony. Or even if another woman sucked your cock." She swallowed hard and forced the next words past her lips, determined not to hold anything back from Stone. "But I would want to watch." Her pussy throbbed at the erotic thought and she rushed on before she lost her nerve. "And I suppose if we ever had any others join us—that outside of those parameters, it would turn me on very much to watch, or even to . . . participate, as you are comfortable."

He silenced her with a kiss that scattered all her thoughts and stiffened her nipples against the soft cotton of her shirt. When he slowly broke the kiss, he pulled back just far enough to look down at her. "I need no other woman but you, Alyssandra, and I accept your terms. Don't mistake my own terms. If you desired another cock to fill your ass, it would never be without me there and participating. You are mine and mine alone. No other woman has held my full attention as you have from the very first. And if we do decide to invite others, then we will discuss terms as we go."

Stone's words warmed her and she grabbed a handful of his tunic, pulling him down so she could capture his lips. He tasted spicy and masculine with a hint of the wine he'd had with breakfast. A sudden vision of licking wine off Stone's golden body made her moan against his lips.

In the next instant she found herself on her back against the cool grass, her hands bound over her head and her skirt pulled off and flung away leaving her bottom half bare. Excitement coursed through her at the thought of breaking Stone's control so he would finally fuck her senseless, but then she sobered. He would never endanger her, so he had to have something else in mind.

He pushed her thighs open wide and knelt between them, looking down at her as if she were an amazing piece of art to be studied and revered. "I want to tell you exactly what I plan to do to you, Princess, as soon as the ceremony is complete."

He traced a gentle finger along her slit, her female juices making his finger slide effortlessly. Each time his finger reached the middle, he would dip inside her as if gathering her juices and then trace her again front to back, front to back. Her hips slowly arched in rhythm with his gentle touch, her breasts thrust up against her cotton top, her sensitive nipples making the soft cloth feel like sandpaper against her tender skin.

Stone pushed her top up to free her breasts to the gentle breeze and she gasped at the sudden sensation. "As soon as the ceremony is done, and I have bathed you completely and thoroughly, I plan to bind you just like this and lick every inch of your body, Alyssandra."

She shuddered at his dark promise and her pussy lips throbbed with need.

"Does that excite you, Princess?"

"Yes . . ." She tried to say more, but too much energy zinged through her body and she couldn't form coherent thoughts.

Stone leaned down to pull one aching nipple between his lips. As the velvet heat closed over her breast, he sucked hard, each pull of his mouth causing a surge of energy straight between her thighs. She bucked against Stone's hand, but his touch remained gentle against her slit. He scraped his teeth lightly over her nipple as he pulled back and turned his attention to the other aching breast. This time when he sucked against her nipple, the energy flow hit her so hard, she arched up off the ground, her back bowing against the overwhelming sensation.

"Relax, Alyssandra," he said against her breast. "If you fight the energy, it only makes it worse. Let it flow through you."

She shook her head from side to side in denial. "Too much . . . can't . . ." It barreled through her in a rushing maelstrom followed quickly by fear. This rush of energy would tear her apart, there was no way her body could contain such a thing. She pulled against her invisible bonds and a whimper escaped as her pulse raced and she struggled to drag air into her lungs.

Stone bit down on her breast and the pain allowed her to swim past her fears and focus on his voice. "Concentrate, love. Breathe deep and relax, just let the sensations flow through you, don't stop them, just let them flow."

She swallowed hard as Stone dipped his finger inside her slit once more, carrying her juices back toward her ass. He spread her wider and then slipped one blunt finger slowly inside her ass. The sudden spurt of energy threatened to drown her again, but she focused on Stone's voice and tried to relax and let the energy flow as he'd said.

"That's better, Princess. Enjoy the sensations, but when the energy builds, don't fight it, just let it flow past you. I'll teach you to harness it later, now you just need to learn to co-exist with it."

As her body relaxed to accommodate his erotic invasion, he pushed another finger inside her, stretching her until the energy threatened to rip her apart. "Stone!"

"Relax, you can do this. Let it flow by you."

Her entire body trembled with the effort just to let the surging river of energy flow through her. It seemed that it would overwhelm her at any moment and she would be lost. She wondered if this was how Lianna died. Sweat trickled down her stomach and the gentle breeze did nothing to cool her skin as bubbling lava flowed through her veins churning the already rushing energy.

When Stone slowly pushed a third finger inside her ass, stretching her impossibly, she screamed as a sudden kaleidoscope of sensations buffeted her like a leaf in a hurricane. A sudden flash of pain against her inner thigh returned her to herself and she realized her hips still bucked against Stone's hand, wanting more. Apparently, her body didn't agree with her mind on this one.

"Please, Stone. I can't handle any more . . ." Tears streamed down the sides of her face and she whipped her hand back and forth begging him to end her torment.

Stone's dark head slowly dipped until he laved his tongue over her aching clit. She cried out and was surprised Stone didn't burn his tongue on her smoldering swollen flesh. His three fingers thrust into her ass faster and faster as he took her clit between his lips and sucked hard. The pull of his mouth seemed to concentrate the entire tsunami of energy through her clit and for a minute, she was afraid the fragile flesh would explode inside his mouth. Impossibly, the energy honed down to a laser's edge, burning through her and pushing her toward some high cliff that terrified her.

She clenched her hands into fists within her bonds and thrust her hips upward, pushing her aching slit harder against Stone's face. The entire world spiraled down until it centered around Stone's mouth sucking the energy through her body, dragging her closer and closer toward the cliff. For long moments, she hung suspended on the precipice, unthinkable power buffeting through her, her body only tethered to reality by the erotic pull of Stone's mouth against her core.

Finally, he scraped his teeth over her and she exploded, the energy blew outward in every direction like a bomb suddenly exploded and she was afraid she'd never be whole again.

Then the vibrations of Stone's deep chuckle against her stomach made her realize she was still alive and her body intact. She floated in a golden haze and she stretched like a contented cat, realizing her bonds had disappeared. "What the hell was that? Is that what it will be like when I'm queen?" Her ears still buzzed with energy aftershocks so she wasn't sure she'd spoken aloud until Stone answered her.

"Actually, my love. That's only a pale comparison of what it will be like when you're queen."

Her eyes popped open and she pushed up on her elbows to look down at him. "You've got to be fucking kidding. I didn't think I'd survive that!"

He shook his head, his hair tickling the inside of her thigh since he still lay slumped between her open thighs. "If being queen is taking the energy of the entire world, then what you experienced is on the same scale as taking the energy of only ten people."

After staring at him in open-mouthed disbelief, she slumped back against the ground and flung her arm over her eyes. "Holy fucking shit. What the hell have I gotten myself into now?"

Alyssa put her hand over her stomach, hoping she didn't embarrass herself and throw up on her future in-laws. Ever since Stone had asked her to come to this dinner to meet them, her stomach had roiled with nausea and her brain had manufactured several scenarios in which she would somehow embarrass herself and Stone would dump her unceremoniously back through the portal and onto a hot Phoenix sidewalk.

Stone placed a comforting hand on her lower back and leaned over to brush a tender kiss against her temple. "I've already told you, beloved, you are not meeting them to gain their approval, you already have mine and you are the blood heir to the throne. However, since they will soon be your family too, you can't avoid meeting them forever."

She tipped her head back to look up into his handsome smiling face and reached out a fingertip to trace his dimple. "I can't help being nervous, Stone, I truly want them to like me. I'll try not to throw up on anyone."

He laughed, amusement dancing in his eyes. "Alyssandra, as the future queen, you're fully entitled to vomit on anyone in the kingdom without them taking offense. Royalty has its privileges."

She tried unsuccessfully to hide her smile. "Are you teasing me?"

"Only a little." He tipped her chin up farther with his first two fingers and then lowered his head slowly to brush his lips over hers. When he pulled back, only a hairsbreadth separated them, his hot breath feathered over her lips as he spoke. "Let's go in before all the *ool* is gone and we can't feed your new addiction."

She poked him in the ribs with her elbow and he only laughed harder. "Let's not start hitting below the belt, or you'll regret the paybacks, mister."

The large double doors opened before them and the majordomo announced them before they walked inside. The Fourth House of Klatch took up one of the twenty wings of the castle, and it looked very similar to the wing that held her parents' and her own room. Although the ruling house's rooms were immediately behind the throne room and these were off toward the west side of the castle.

Before she'd taken more than a few steps, Alyssa found herself engulfed in a bear hug by a woman who only stood as high as her breasts. Plump arms bracketed Alyssa's waist and the woman kept up a constant dialogue of questions from the upward lilt at the end of each one, although Alyssa couldn't understand a thing she said since it was said into her boobs.

A man almost as tall as her father beamed at her bewildered expression and stepped forward to place a gentle hand on the short woman's shoulder. "Step away from there, Darla. The girl can't hear a thing you're saying that way." When the woman stepped back, he took Alyssa's hand and laid a chaste kiss on the back. "Welcome, Alyssandra. I haven't seen you since you were in diapers. I'm Stone Sr., Stone's father. You can call me whatever you like, I'll answer to almost anything. Saves confusion around the household if you know what I mean." He winked and she immediately liked him.

"It's nice to meet you both." The dynamics of this family were much different than with her own parents, and she felt a bit out of her element.

Two imposing Klatch men stepped forward. The taller of the two was Grayson, the man she'd met earlier in the garden. Stone's appearance in the garden had chased the meeting from her mind and she'd forgotten to mention it.

The second man was a half a head shorter than Grayson and an angry red scar ran from his temple down to the side of his mouth. It didn't distract from his male beauty, but made him look more dangerous and tough somehow. His body was compact and stocky, almost like a boxer, and he watched her intently as if cataloguing her every action.

"Alyssandra, I'd like you to meet my two best friends, Grayson, the Seventh Prince of Klatch." Grayson stepped forward and raised her hands to his lips, winking and flashing a smile that could melt a woman's ovaries at sixty paces before brushing his hot lips over the back of her hand, and if she wasn't mistaken, just a hint of tongue.

She shook her head at his mischievous grin. "We met earlier in the gardens."

Stone pinned his friend with a questioning look and Grayson held up his hand in front of him, clearly amused by Stone's reaction. "I met her by the waterfall and we spoke. She's quite intriguing and very outspoken. I apparently startled her, and for a moment, I was afraid she'd remove my manhood."

Stone chuckled beside her. "I did warn you that she could take care of herself."

"That you did."

Stone turned his attention to the second man. "Beloved, this is Ryan, the Tenth Prince of Klatch." The man with the scar stepped forward and kissed her hand as well, his inscrutable expression giving nothing away.

"It's nice to meet you, Ryan, and good to see you again, Grayson." She turned her head to look at Stone. "How do you keep track of who's with what number house? What do you do if there are several siblings in the same house?"

Ryan smiled, the movement stretching the scar that marred his face. "There are actually six princes of the tenth house, but then you get into semantics such as so and so is the third prince of the tenth house, and introductions become tedious. We try not to get that far into it."

"Wow, you mean there're more of you guys?" She blushed as she realized what she said and everyone in the room laughed.

When Stone laughed too, she let out the breath she'd been holding. He leaned close and mock whispered. "Way too many to keep track of. It makes me appreciate that I'm an only child."

Everyone sat and as the first course was served, Alyssa finally relaxed. Stone's parents were warm and unassuming. Their constant banter was laced with love and obvious affection. She could see why Stone had such a gentle and quiet countenance. He probably couldn't get that many words in growing up.

Grayson and Ryan were charming, gorgeous, and funny, and having all four Klatch males at the same table was something of a testosterone delight—better than any chocolate dessert she'd ever had back in Phoenix. By the end of the second course, they were openly flirting with her and constantly lacing the conversation with innuendo. Other than an occasional dark scowl from Stone, he seemed to laugh along with them, so she didn't worry about his reaction.

Her entire life, she'd never been the woman men flirted with, she'd always been the unattractive friend who blended into the background. The attention made her feel sexy, daring and attractive—and so horny for Stone, she was amazed she didn't jump him right here at the dinner table. Although the thought did spark a vivid fantasy or two she made a mental note to try out later.

"Princess, what are your plans for tomorrow?" Ryan poured her another glass of wine as he spoke.

"I'd actually like to go to one of the meetings of the Klatch Council. I should probably have a clue what they do before I'm expected to be queen and make any decisions. My father mentioned the meeting this morning at breakfast."

Stone nodded his approval and took her hand in his. "I didn't think you were ready to face that quite yet, but I trust your judgment. I'll take you after breakfast in the morning."

"Make sure you sit in the back, so you can slip out—it's boring as hell." This from Grayson who leaned back comfortably in his chair and studied her over his goblet of wine.

"Somehow I don't think they'll let me sit in the back. As much as I've tried to ease into things since I got here, everyone is always thrusting me in with both feet." She slid her gaze toward Stone as she remembered his energy lessons earlier in the garden.

Ryan snorted. "I think she's referring to you, Stone. You're right, she's a fiery handful and I think she's absolutely perfect for you."

At all the other nods and murmurs of agreement around the table, Alyssa's brow furrowed. It may have been the wine, or the comfort she felt with this group, but she couldn't stop herself from asking. "What else has Stone said about me?" She grinned, but pinned each person around the table with a steady stare.

Grayson leaned forward, evil amusement dancing in his lavender eyes. "I recall something about you being the most stunning woman he's ever seen. And even though I still think you picked the wrong Prince, I can't argue with facts. I think for an arranged marriage, Princess, you've already got a tight leash on Stone's . . . family jewels."

Stone glared at his friend and Alyssa couldn't help but laugh. "Really? I'll have to try out your theory later, Grayson, thanks. Does anyone know where the royal family keeps their . . . leashes?" The thought of tying Stone spread-eagled onto her bed flashed through her mind and her nipples pebbled into tight nubs against her soft half top.

Everyone laughed and Stone's eyes darkened with passion at her words and he cleared his throat while stroking a single finger over her palm under the table. Goose bumps rose all over her body from the sudden sensation and she bit back a moan.

Stone returned his attention to his two friends. "If you two would like to be useful tomorrow, you can come with us to the Klatch Council meeting and help answer Alyssandra's questions. Knowing her as I do, she'll have plenty. Besides, there will be so many people vying for her attention, she'd probably appreciate some friendly faces to keep the crowds and the council at bay—even if it is the two of you."

She hadn't thought of that, but was grateful Stone had. She wanted to learn, but the crowds still made her uncomfortable. At least she'd have a few people there she could be herself with. She grinned around the table. "Cool, three hot Klatch men all to myself. It's good to be the future queen."

Chapter 8

The Klatch Council chambers reminded Alyssa more of an intimate auditorium than a courtroom like the one she'd expected. There were seats for several thousand, but the circular layout allowed all the seats an up-close view of the dais. The walls and floor, just like every other building she'd seen on Tador, were made of the snowy white *balda* stone, the pink seams winking whenever the light hit them just right.

The council, five women and two men, sat on a raised dais behind a table laden with huge books and goblets no doubt filled with the wine that was consumed almost nonstop on Tador. In fact, they'd refined the wine so the alcohol content was low and the nutritional value high. Too bad earth hadn't figured out how to do that yet. When she was bartending, that kind of beverage would've made a big difference in several of her patrons' lives.

She wasn't sure what she'd pictured, but all seven of the council members appeared jaded and bored. Apparently, politicians were the same no matter the planet. Her gut intuition told her to be very wary of the council.

The Council Head would've been beautiful except for the cold hard eyes and the severe frown lines marring the skin around her mouth. She looked over everyone she met, refusing to debase herself by actually making eye contact and would then sneer behind their backs when they'd passed by. Alyssa instantly disliked her. The rest of the council were unremarkable and if she'd seen them in a crowd outside, wouldn't have been able to pick them out except for their red clothes that signified their place among the council. They all seemed to nod mindlessly and agree to whatever the Council Head said.

After the inevitable introductions, she found herself seated with Stone on her right and Grayson and Ryan on her left. Grayson had already whispered several sarcastic and suggestive comments about the proceedings in her ear and she had to bite her lip to keep from laughing aloud. But then, the subject of how many grazing animals a certain section of land could "succor" did leave it wide open for smart assed comments and innuendo. She elbowed him and he smiled, but didn't appear the least bit repentant.

The king and queen sat on one end of the dais in larger cushioned chairs. Now that the topic had turned to the health of the planet, her mother's pale features were set into a frown and her lovely brows furrowed as she listened to the council deliberate. Alyssa leaned forward, intently listening.

The Council Head sighed dramatically, not bothering to even look at Annalecia when she spoke. "My Queen, there is no need for panic or for the council to waste time looking for alternate options. The blood princess has returned and will ascend the throne in less than a week." Her voice continued, brisk and impatient. "A fresh pureblood queen will fully heal the planet and all will be as it was."

Annalecia opened her mouth to protest and King Darius laid a gentle hand against her arm and stood to address the council in her stead. "The damage to the planet may well be more than even a new pureblood queen can heal. Even one as powerful as Alyssandra has already shown herself to be."

All eyes swiveled toward her and she swallowed past a sudden urge to hide under her seat. The Council Head looked her up and down as if she were considering purchasing some horse-flesh and then returned her gaze in the general direction of the king, although still not meeting his gaze.

"We would be foolish not to explore other options. As we've seen from Annalecia's experiences, the current state of the planet is quite taxing on the reigning queen. Why stress the new queen's powers unduly, if there are things we can do to mitigate the strain? We also don't want to endanger the pregnancy with the future heir."

He turned to look back at the queen before sweeping his gaze through the crowd and then back toward the council. "When Annalecia ascended, the strain of her new duties almost caused us to lose Alyssandra. Do we want to take that chance again when so many of our royal princesses have died so recently in their attempts to ascend? I don't think we can afford to."

Fear tightened deep in Alyssa's belly. She'd heard all this of course, the information was nothing new, but hearing her father describe it brought home the gravity of the situation. The news that she'd almost died before she'd even been born shook her as well, but she pushed that aside to deal with later. One thing at a time. But what of her future daughter? She'd avoided thinking about that, but if she went through with the ascension, she'd be carrying the next heir to the throne. *No pressure there!*

She leaned forward to hear the council's response. They had to agree to look for alternatives. Her father's argument had been a good one.

"King Darius," the woman began, her tone seemingly gentle with a definite undercurrent of condescension. "We all understand the strain you and the queen have endured having your daughter taken from you. Not to mention not having anyone to ease the burden of your duties all these long years. However, Alyssandra is now safe and sound and will continue the tradition as it has always been. Your concerns are duly noted, but I think colored by the strains and stresses you've endured."

Anger welled up hot and explosive and Alyssa pushed to her feet gripping the seat in front of her until her knuckles turned white. All eyes turned toward her again and she raised her chin, as she fought to control the rising tide of her raging emotions.

"Do you have something to add, Princess?" The woman's voice wasn't exactly condescending, but neither was it welcoming. It reminded Alyssa of the way everyone in her "family" growing up had addressed her, as if her opinion didn't count.

Alyssa hadn't realized there was a power struggle between the throne and the council, but she saw it clearly now. They took their home world for granted, and for the first time she realized that being raised by the Cunts had allowed her a unique perspective that no one else in this room had.

"Yes, actually I do." The words came out clear and confident, surprising her. She took a deep breath as she searched for a diplomatic way to state her opinion. Alienating the council at this point would only muddy the waters. "I have to agree with my parents. The most important thing for Tador is to make sure the planet can be fully healed and keep it that way." She took a deep breath to continue and the Council Head cut her off with a dismissive wave.

"Obviously, that's the goal of all present." The woman's gesture encompassed the entire assembly. "Do you doubt your own powers already, Princess?"

Anger burned in the back of Alyssa's throat like bile and she swallowed it back and forced a smile. *I've dealt with bigger bitches than you on a daily basis, lady. You can't intimidate me with your bullshit!* Adrenaline coursed through her, giving her an almost eerie sense of calm. She allowed her lips to curve as she stared down the council leader. "I don't doubt my powers, but I doubt the leadership of any council who fails to look at all options when so much is at risk."

Gasps sounded from around the chamber and the woman's eyes narrowed as she glared at Alyssandra with barely concealed fury. Alyssa ignored her and turned her attention to those seated around the auditorium—her people. "I've spent the bulk of my life living among the Cunts, and even though they're cruel and ruthless, they never fail to consider every option available to them before acting. Shouldn't we be just as deliberate with our decisions?"

A realization hit her like a sledgehammer and she couldn't believe she hadn't thought about it before. A lead weight settled in her stomach and she swallowed past it before she continued. "If they waited patiently for twenty-three years to enact some sort of plan using me, I'm sure it had something to do with revenge for being cast out of Tador. I won't delude myself into thinking they're going to just sigh and let me walk away after investing that much time and planning. They *will* try again, and when they do, Tador must be at full strength, or we are at risk. Any and all options must be considered and fully utilized to save our home world and our way of life."

The murmurs of approval from the crowd around her grew and flowed around the room like a living thing. None of the seated council looked pleased with the development, but both her parents looked quite smug as they smiled at her.

The head of the council pounded a smooth white *balda* stone against the table and the noise died away leaving tension thrumming in the air. Alyssa refused to sit, but remained standing, watching the council leader expectantly.

"The council will take everyone's opinions under advisement and we will meet again after the ascension." She pounded the *balda* gavel again and turned her back on the entire assembly, effectively dismissing them.

Alyssa's fingers dug into the seat in front of her to keep her

CEREMONY OF SEDUCTION / 121

knees from buckling. Stone and Grayson stood on either side of her and she fought to keep from throwing up as she'd threatened last night.

"Alyssandra, you were wonderful." Stone gently pried her fingers from the seatback in front of her and kissed her fingers.

"Best council meeting I've ever been to," Grayson stage-whispered beside her. "Not boring at all."

Ryan's laugh drew her attention and she glanced over in time to see him giving her a thumbs up, an earth gesture she'd taught him last night at dinner.

"Well, I'm glad you three are still speaking to me. I think the council wants to march me to the guillotine and I'm not even queen yet."

Stone squeezed her shoulder and placed his hand on the small of her back, guiding her out of the row and toward her parents. "Come on, Marie Antoinette, let's make a break for it."

When they were all seated in the king and queen's reception area, reaction had set in and Alyssa shivered as all the adrenaline drained from her body. "I'm not sure where all that came from. I've never spoken in front of a group in my life, let alone disagreed with an authority figure. Who am I to speak to the council that way? I'm not even queen."

Sasha wrapped a quilt around her shoulders and handed her a cup of steaming cider, which turned out to be heavily laced with something that resembled whiskey. She sipped gratefully, letting the fiery liquid sooth her quaking nerves and then smiled her thanks toward her lady's maid.

"Well, my daughter," her father said, not trying to hide his chuckle, "I think you've declared your intentions to the council and they know the new queen will not be afraid to speak her mind." He winked at her. "We're very proud of you. You spoke very eloquently today, just as a queen would. It was a brave thing you did today and will help you in the future when the council tries to bully you."

"Thanks." She basked in the warm glow of the compliment for a few seconds before turning her mind back toward the meeting. "Do you think they'll actually listen?"

Annalecia shook her head. "No, I think they set the next meeting after the ascension because they think you'll be more malleable once you've ascended the throne and you are busy keeping the symbiosis with the planet. Not to mention your father and I will no longer have any say in the ruling of the country. They've forgotten that the council was formed to advise the queen, but that she has no obligation to take their advice."

She shook her head and sighed. "You had the people behind you today, Alyssandra. You spoke from your heart and they listened. You'll have to be ready to stand up to the council again and again. They will attempt to wear you down until you submit to their wills."

"Great. Sounds like fun. Ranks up there with having my toenails pulled out one by one." She took a healthy sip of cider, letting the hot flow of alcohol down her throat soothe her anger. "I don't see how they can live in this paradise and take it for granted. They should go live with the Cunts for a few years and then see how much they appreciate Tador."

Stone accepted a steaming cup of cider from Sasha and nodded his thanks. "At least you've kept your sense of humor. We'll both need it with that group of vipers. Don't worry, beloved, together, we can make them see reason."

She nodded and took a deep breath, inhaling the fruity scent of the cider, letting it infuse her senses. "I hadn't thought about the Cunt's reaction to me leaving, but I should have. The people who raised me are very proud and will take this as a personal insult. I put everyone on the planet in danger by coming back, and I'm not even sure what their plan for me was."

Stone sat down beside her. "You are going to save everyone on the planet by ascending the throne. If today didn't prove to you that you have the heart of a queen, then nothing will.

You're safe here, the royal guards are keeping a close watch on all the portal points."

Alyssa laughed, a cold bitter bark of a laugh. "I'm not even sure who that woman is who stood up and said all those things. She's certainly not me. What if she doesn't return when a strong queen is needed?"

Ryan spoke for the first time since the ceremony. "Oh, I have no doubt that she'll return. The council has a special knack for raising people's ire and that's what brought out that wonderful woman you claim not to know. In fact, I look forward to seeing a lot more of her."

He wiggled his eyebrows up and down and the double entendre made Alyssa laugh. "Don't forget the presentation ball is coming up and not only will we all get an eyeful, but the Klatch Council will see how powerful our new lioness of a future queen is first hand. I'm actually looking forward to it."

Alyssa shook her head and took a big gulp of the heavily laced cider, biting back the cough as it seared down her throat. "I'm glad someone's confident in my abilities. Because I'm sure the hell not."

Alyssa awoke to the comforting sensation of Stone's arms around her. Keeping her eyes closed, she savored the sensation and snuggled back against him. His cock instantly responded by hardening against the crevice of her ass. "Mmmm," she said with a sigh, as moisture pooled between her thighs.

"Good morning," Stone said into her neck, where his face burrowed against her hair. "I think you are in need of morning ablutions." At his husky words, her breast, still cradled in his palm from last night, tingled and her nipple hardened to a taut peak. "I see your body agrees." His deep chuckle reverberated through her body like lightening.

"And what about *your* ablutions?" She arched back against him, grinding her ass against his swollen cock.

"Witch," he growled playfully before he flipped her onto her back and anchored himself above her.

Reaching down between them, she rubbed the bulge straining at the front of his breeches. He pumped against her hand until his breathing became ragged and he grabbed her hand, lacing his fingers in hers and stretching her arms up high over her head. The movement caused her short top to ride up, the hem barely covering the tips of her hard nipples. The soft material grazing across her engorged flesh sent coils of hot lava flowing through her veins.

When Stone ran a line of open-mouthed kisses along the hollow of her throat, she gasped and heat pooled low in her belly, flowing steadily outward like a hot tide. When his hot mouth closed over her nipple through the soft cloth, she thought she would explode. Energy flowed through her body faster and faster until her vision blurred and white spots danced in front of her eyes. In the next instant, the energy broke out of her body and zigzagged outward toward every surface in the room. The *balda* stone of the walls sizzled around them and short bursts of electricity danced along the pink veins in the rock.

When Alyssa could breathe again, she looked up at Stone. "What just happened?" she asked, the wonder in her voice surprising her.

A slow smile spread across Stone's face as his gaze moved from her face up to the still-sizzling *balda* and back again. "You're coming into your powers, and you didn't fight the flow of energy. You're learning."

Her skin still tingled where the energy had escaped and she wondered why it hadn't done that in the gardens. "Does it always happen like that?"

He rolled off her and cradled her close to his side. "No, but because the ceremony draws near, your powers are gathering. Things will continue to increase in intensity right up until the ceremony."

At the mention of the ceremony, her breathing caught and her pussy drenched. Her vision blurred and for a moment she saw herself in a candlelit tent surrounded by naked, virile men stroking pale, long cocks. All of them staring at her hungrily as if she were the latest course on the dessert menu. A feeling of claustrophobia overtook her as the circle of men closed in around her, and power surged through her veins until she exploded inside her own skin. The orgasm exploded outward until her entire body zinged like one giant erogenous zone.

"Alyssandra!"

After Stone's frantic voice finally reached through the haze, which drifted over her mind, she opened her eyes to see his concerned expression looming over her.

"Alyssandra, speak to me!" His lavender eyes sparked with fear.

It took several attempts before she found her voice. "I'm fine. I think." She closed her eyes and took stock of herself. She floated in a sea of a languid afterglow of the power surge and orgasm she'd just experienced. But she had no idea what triggered it.

"Tell me what happened. I know none of my essence touched you." His hands roamed over her as if to ensure she was unharmed. His frantic touch against her oversensitized heated skin sent small aftershocks of power sizzling over her.

When she opened her eyes again, Stone looked ready to shake her. She licked her lips and gathered her thoughts. "When you mentioned the ceremony, a picture of what it might be like popped into my head. The next thing I knew, there was a power surge and a really big orgasm. I'm not sure what exactly happened."

Stone exhaled audibly, a broad smile spreading over his features, chasing away the fear in his eyes. "Thank heaven. You scared the hell out of me." He flopped down beside her on his back, a low chuckle escaping from his lips.

Irritation pricked her. He seemed relieved, but he still hadn't told her what happened. "I'm glad you feel better. Are you going to tell me what happened?" She propped herself up on her elbow to glare at him, still none too steady.

Stone pulled her on top of him so she straddled him, her still-sensitive pussy lips rubbing over his breeches as she moved. If she weren't so interested in his answer, this position could be very promising—even with their present restrictions.

"You had a vision of the ceremony to come. Again, it's another sign that your powers are growing, and another reason to know that you will succeed where so many others have failed." She wasn't sure if he said it for her benefit or to reassure himself.

She started as realization hit. *I saw the upcoming ceremony?* She closed her eyes, trying to recall the picture inside her mind. She saw the men surrounding her, their long pale cocks jutting out before them, straining out of their nests of stiff blond curls. She turned to see a man with dark hair and lavender eyes approach toward her open thighs. He didn't look like Stone, but his features were obscured.

Her eyes popped open as she thought about what she'd seen. *Wait! The men surrounding her had blond pubic hair! Klatch men all have dark hair...* "Are you sure I was seeing the future? I don't think some of the details are quite right."

Stone's arms cradled his head resting on the pillow. He gazed up at her. "Describe the scene to me."

She shifted on top of him to find a more comfortable position and smiled as he groaned. Placing her hands on his chest, she leaned over him, so she could study his face while they talked. "I saw myself in a room. There were lit candles everywhere and I was lying on my back naked on some sort of altar. There were a ring of naked men stroking themselves and closing in around me."

Stone's eyes darkened with the description and his cock hardened beneath her. His voice sounded husky when he finally spoke. "That sounds like the correct ceremony."

"I saw a man with dark hair and lavender eyes approaching me, but his face was obscured. But the men surrounding me . . ."

"What? Tell me." He sat up, with her still straddling him and shifted them both so he leaned back against the headboard.

"The men surrounding me had blond pubic hair."

Stone's eyes widened and he grabbed her by both shoulders, his fingers digging into her skin. "Are you sure?"

Alyssa closed her eyes, replaying the scene inside her head again. "Yes. And they were thin and pale like my Cunt family. What does it mean, Stone?"

When she studied his face, it was a mask. She could glean no emotions at all from him. Fear flowed through her veins, chilling her. "What does it mean?" she repeated in a strained whisper.

"It's probably nothing. After all, it's your first vision." He kissed her forehead before setting her gently off him and rising from the bed. "I'll send Sasha to you for breakfast and bathing. I have duties to attend to."

"Damn it, Stone. What the hell aren't you telling me?"

He turned back toward her and brushed a quick kiss over her forehead, but his face remained a passive mask. "It's nothing, beloved. I merely have duties to attend to."

Before she could protest, he'd disappeared through the doors to her room leaving her confused, angry, and scared. She crossed her arms under her breasts and huffed out a frustrated breath. "I'm not the only one who's a horrible liar around here. Damned infuriating man!"

Stone didn't bother to change or bathe before requesting an audience with the king and queen. The royal women's visions were always very accurate, and if Alyssandra had seen men with blond pubic hair surrounding her during an ascension ceremony, then it was an omen of the future.

Cold fear pricked along his spine at the thought of his beloved in the hands of the Cunts. Not to mention, she'd seen a Klatch man who would complete the ceremony. Jealousy burned hot, chasing away the fear and replacing it with cold determination. Alyssandra was his, no other man would enter her slick canal but him.

He knew of no Klatch who would align themselves with the Cunts—especially not after the atrocities committed during the civil war. However, Alyssandra's vision said otherwise, and they would all have to be on their guard if there was a traitor in their midst.

As soon as the majordomo announced his presence, he pushed past him, lengthening his stride until he stood next to the king and queen's breakfast table.

King Darius's smile faltered as it met Stone's concerned frown. "Come sit, Stone, and tell us what's wrong. Is Alyssandra all right?"

Stone ignored the invitation to sit and instead gripped the back of a wooden chair so hard he was surprised it didn't break off in his hands. "The princess has had her first vision, an omen of things to come."

Queen Annalecia's haggard face drained of color, but she lifted her chin in a stubborn gesture that Alyssandra shared. "Tell us."

Stone relayed the vision and when he reached the part about the blond pubic hair, Darius shot to his feet, his chair and silverware clattering to the floor.

"Guards!" His voice echoed off the walls causing the *balda* stone to vibrate and small pink sparks popped and fizzed throughout the room.

The king and queen's personal guards burst into the room.

Each of the dozen dressed in the dark purple livery of the royal family and each was a powerful witch and warrior in his own right. After assessing that there was no immediate threat, the leader, Gavin, bowed low before them, while the others followed suit. "How may I serve you, Your Majesties?"

"I need a special guard for the princess until her coming-of-age ceremony. She is in danger, and I'll not lose her again!" The king punctuated his words with a fist to the table, causing the dishes and food to jump and wobble precariously.

Annalecia rose and placed a gentle hand on the king's arm. "Calm yourself, my love. Her powers are gathering. The fact that she had this vision and trusted Stone with it speaks well of the outcome."

Stone turned to the king and queen. "The princess doesn't know that the royal women have visions. When she described the scene to me, I told her it was probably nothing. She has enough to worry about without adding to her fears."

"That's probably for the best, Stone, at least for now." Darius scrubbed his hand through his hair leaving unruly tufts behind.

"I disagree." The queen pierced Stone with a look that reminded him of the time he'd used one of her best skirts to catch frogs from the water gardens. "Keeping information from Alyssandra is not the best course. First, visions are one of her Klatch powers, and they usually only come to warn of great danger. She has every right to know. And second, the men of the royal families seem to think that by keeping information from us, that they are protecting us, when in fact, they are treating us like children." She shot first Darius and then Stone an arch look before she crossed her arms under her breasts and fell silent.

Stone sighed. "Annalecia. I have no desire to incur your wrath, but I must protect her. She's having a hard enough time dealing with her new circumstances without adding this."

The queen's lips curved. "Are you sure it's not you who is having the more difficult time?" She shook her head. "May the universe have pity on you, Stone, because my daughter is not stupid. I'll defer to your decision as her betrothed, but I wish her well in whatever punishment she devises for you when she finds out you've been keeping things from her."

Stone breathed a sigh of relief that the queen was going to accede to his wishes on this issue. He hadn't thought she would. "Thank you, my lady. I assure you, I only do what's best for the princess."

The unladylike snort that emanated from the queen surprised everyone in the room. "Just don't say I didn't warn you. All women, royalty or not, like to be treated with respect. Acting as if we aren't strong enough to grasp the gravity of a situation is *not* giving us the respect we deserve." She sat quietly, showing that she'd had her say on the matter and was now finished.

Gavin stepped forward, obviously impatient to understand the situation. "May I ask from what quarter you perceive this threat?"

Stone relayed the vision and by the time he was finished, the guards looked as angry as the king and queen.

Gavin's eyes narrowed, a sign Stone knew meant he was analyzing the situation. "We will immediately be on guard for a Klatch traitor. Where is the princess now?"

"She is with Sasha at either breakfast or in the bathing chamber."

"Good. Sasha is an expert warrior and will protect her well inside the bathing chamber. However, I'll speak with her to ensure they only use the private chamber until the ceremony." He nodded to Stone. "And I'll ensure Sasha keeps the details of this from the princess per your wishes, sire. However, if the princess does find out, we will let her know we were acting on your orders."

The man tried and failed to hide a smirk before he turned to the other eleven guards and motioned to four women, who stepped forward and nodded their heads in respect at the request. "Protect the princess at all costs. We have only a few days until the ceremony, so the Cunts will move soon if they mean to take her."

"It will be done," they said in unison before slipping out the door toward their new duty.

"Wait!" King Darius glowered over Gavin, who stood unflinching against his wrath. "I want every royal guard protecting my daughter. Do you hear me?"

Stone opened his mouth to protest, but Gavin beat him to it. "With all due respect, my king, I must decline."

Darius's face turned a mottled purple and he took a deep breath to retort until Annalecia stood and grabbed the front of his tunic and captured his attention. "I love her too, Darius, but Gavin is right. Hear him out."

"Thank you, my queen." He turned to Darius, his back stiff, his gaze direct. "My duties are to protect the queen, her husband, and the royal family. If we leave the queen and yourself unprotected and the princess fails to ascend to the throne, Tador is lost. We must protect all until we know the extent of the threat. You are welcome to dismiss me from my post, but I must warn you, every guard has taken the same oath."

Slowly, Darius's stance relaxed and he nodded to Gavin. "I'm sorry, you're right. I just can't bear the thought of losing her again."

"None of us can afford to lose her, my liege. We will protect her with our very lives."

Queen Annalecia turned to Stone. "I hesitate to ask this of you, Stone, as you have waited so very long for her and I know your control will only get worse as the ceremony nears and her natural pheromones increase."

Stone reached out and placed a comforting hand over the

queen's. "I will stay with her. I'll make some arrangements and then I'll stay with her in her rooms until the ascension. I've waited for this long, I think I can hold out a few more days."

"Good luck, Stone." Darius placed a firm hand on his shoulder. "I stayed apart from Annalecia until the ceremony and I almost didn't survive. You're a better man than I if you can hold out while sleeping in the same bed with a future queen scant days before the ascension."

Darius's words hit Stone like a punch to the gut. The past few days had been pure torture, he didn't know if he would survive if the temptation became even worse. But for Alyssandra, he would have to. He met Darius's gaze with the most confident expression he could muster. "For all our sakes, I hope I can become that better man in the next few hours."

Chapter 9

Alyssandra turned from the view off her balcony at the soft rap on the door to her room. "Come in." She welcomed the distraction since she'd been silently brooding over Stone's quick departure.

The door cracked open to admit Sasha, her bright smile immediately cheering Alyssandra. "Good morning, Sasha. I'm glad to see a friendly face." She stepped forward into her room to meet her maid.

The girl's brows furrowed for a moment as she closed the door behind her. "Has someone been unfriendly to you, Princess?"

She crossed her arms under her chest and scowled. "No . . . not exactly unfriendly. Just infuriatingly stubborn and overprotective. Not to mention pigheaded, and utterly and complete male." Thoughts of Stone's hasty exit this morning made her want to throw something—preferably him. She knew he was upset about her vision, but he refused to discuss it with her, instead protecting her like a child. If he thought she'd be the meek and malleable wife while he ran her life, he was sadly mistaken. She'd had people pushing her around all her life, but no more. Not even a future king.

Sasha's full lips curved and her eyes twinkled with amusement. "Ahh, you speak of Prince Stone. Yes, even though I've never had a man of my own, I'm familiar enough with the species, and they do seem to think we women will shatter into a million pieces at every turn."

"You've never been with a man? So you've never had a coming-of-age ceremony?"

Sasha shook her head. "My birthday is the same as yours, so I'm not yet twenty-four." She finished crossing the room and sat down. "However, since I'm not ascending the throne, my coming-of-age is a bit different than yours."

Alyssa plopped down on her bed, crossing her legs Indian style under her as she pulled a pillow into her lap. "Different how?"

"I will of course as your lady's maid, help with your ceremony. However, since I'm not royal, I have no need of a ceremony for myself. I will mate with the Klatch man of my choosing, and then I'm free to share sustenance with whomever I wish."

She burned to ask Sasha how she'd be helping with the ascension ceremony, but she wasn't sure she wanted to dwell too much on that at the moment. "Have you picked the man?"

Sasha blushed, intriguing her. The woman hadn't shown any type of embarrassment until now. "Yes, I think so." A look of uncertainty flowed across her face before she masked it. "Enough about me. Do you still have any questions about the ceremony? We can always stop by the queen's archives after our breakfast and bathing if needs be."

"The queen's archives?"

"Yes, that is where the knowledge of Tador is held. There are writings about the ascension ceremony, journals from the past and reigning queens, as well as a full history of Tador, including laws and rulings."

Alyssa's initial excitement was suddenly dampened by a flood of doubts. She had always longed to lose herself in a library with thousands of books at her disposal. But what if her Cunt parents were right and she wasn't smart enough to handle reading anything beyond magazines, let alone taking over as queen?

"What troubles you, princess?"

Alyssandra met Sasha's concerned gaze and squared her shoulders. "Just fighting some demons from my past."

"I heard of your treatment at the hands of the Cunts." Sasha placed a gentle hand over hers. "You're the crown princess and no one can tell you who you are or what you can do but you. You must remember that."

Alyssandra's lips curved on their own and she impulsively hugged her lady's maid. "Thank you, Sasha. I needed to hear that."

Sasha pulled back to smile at her. "That's settled then, once we are done with bathing and breakfast, we'll stop by the archives."

They decided on breakfast first since both of their stomachs growled loudly at the wondrous smells wafting from the kitchen below. Once in the grand breakfast room, Alyssandra met several of the other princes and princesses and their lady's maids and valets, as well as had some more time with her parents. Grayson and Ryan were off on some errand with Stone, and she ground her teeth once again at the arrogance of the male species.

After overcoming her initial bout of shyness, she found she truly enjoyed the conversations and camaraderie of these friendly people, who were her true extended family. She also reveled in having her parents close enough to reach out and touch. Several times throughout breakfast, she found them watching her and she reached out to grip their hands in hers. For the first time in her life, she truly belonged.

Annalecia smiled at her often, but the queen's face remained pale and drawn. Worry gnawed inside Alyssa, but she reminded herself that as soon as she completed the ceremony, her mother would be safe.

She would have gladly spent the entire day with her parents, but they still had duties to perform, so she reluctantly hugged each of them before turning to leave.

When she and Sasha finally reached the bathing chamber arm in arm, the familiar drag of fatigue slowed her steps. At least now she recognized it as a need for sexual sustenance and not illness.

She thought of the last "sustenance" session with the maid and her nipples hardened and a hot ache began between her thighs. It was hard to believe just a few short days ago she dressed in baggy clothes to hide her body and masturbated like a horny teenager at an all-girl's school.

She swallowed past her embarrassment and reminded herself that needing sexual energy in this world was just like asking for food and water. Squaring her shoulders, she turned to her maid. "Sasha . . ."

"Yes, Princess?"

Alyssa took a deep breath and plunged in. "I'm feeling very weak this morning. I think I need lots of . . . sustenance."

Sasha's smile brightened before she whipped off her top and stepped out of her string bikini underwear to stand nude before Alyssa. "Of course you do, Princess. As your ceremony draws near, you will require more and more energy. From what I understand from the queen, it is perfectly normal."

Another rush of moisture dampened the juncture between Alyssa's thighs as she appreciated the maid's lush body. Her fingers itched to touch and explore and she licked her lips in anticipation before something the maid said stopped her. "Wait— you said from what you understand from the queen. Didn't your mother help the queen through her ceremony? I thought she would've passed all the lady's maid knowledge onto you herself."

Shadows darkened Sasha's lavender eyes. "My mother died giving birth to me. The queen had grown up with her, so she grieved my mother and never took another lady's maid. King Darius has fulfilled all her needs since."

Alyssa pulled Sasha into her arms, the need to comfort overwhelming. "Oh, Sasha. I'm so sorry. I didn't know."

Sasha's arms tightened around her as she accepted the offered solace. "The other lady's maids raised me as their own, but I've missed having a mother all to myself." She pulled back to look into Alyssandra's eyes. "The queen has always been kind to me. It had to have been lonely all these years without a lady's maid of her own, and yet she always made time to talk to me even before I was old enough to assume my duties."

Alyssa thought of how much she appreciated having Sasha to talk to and explain things to her—especially when she was irritated at Stone for his overprotective ways. What must it have been like for her mother all those years to have no companion, no daughter and only King Darius to rely on to meet all her needs, not just sexually, but emotionally as well? Not to mention maintaining a symbiotic relationship with an entire planet. *No pressure there!*

"I'm glad you were here for her, Sasha. I'm sure you made it more bearable—especially since we are the same age. You allowed her to see what it was like to have a daughter even though I couldn't be here. Thank you." Alyssandra was surprised to realize she meant it. She had expected to be jealous of Sasha's relationship with her parents, but Alyssa was glad that her mother and Sasha didn't have to be alone. She knew first hand how difficult that was and would never wish it on anyone.

As silence descended inside the bathing chamber, she realized she still held a very naked Sasha in her arms and her body screamed for sustenance. The heated flesh between her legs began a slow throb and her breasts were suddenly heavy with need.

Sasha smiled as if she could smell Alyssa's arousal in the thick air around them. She stepped back just long enough to pull off Alyssa's top and skirt and lead her toward the steaming water. "Shaving first, I think. The *ponga* will help replenish you."

Alyssa reached into the basket first and pulled out one of the ripe purple fruits. The fuzzy skin tickled her palms, almost like a peach, but when she gently squeezed it between her fingers, it was soft instead of firm as she'd expected. She edged one fingernail under the peel where it had been broken from the stem of whatever bush or tree it grew from, and peeled it back to reveal the whipped cream-like meat of the fruit. "I think there's plenty of *ponga* for play *and* shaving."

She dipped two fingers in the fluffy fruit and smeared some on Sasha's left breast. Sasha giggled and grabbed a fruit of her own, retaliating as soon as she peeled back the fuzzy skin. Soon, both of them were nearly covered in fruit and laughing uncontrollably. Alyssa loved the playful atmosphere and when her mind's eye conjured the disapproving face of the woman she grew up thinking was her mother, she shoved it aside. *You stole my life from me, but I won't let you take anymore of it. From here on out, I get to choose who I am and what I do!*

The silent declaration lifted a giant weight from her shoulders and she sighed as her laughter subsided. Tingling all over, her body soon showed her the folly of overusing the fruit and a moan escaped from deep inside her throat. Arousal arrowed through her veins and it seemed like every nerve ending in her entire body had turned into a giant erogenous zone. Her nipples hardened to painful peaks and she shifted as her swollen clitoris scraped uncomfortably against her pussy lips.

A quick glance at her lady's maid showed her struggling

similarly. Sasha's skin was flushed, and her eyes wide with shock.

Alyssa grabbed Sasha's hand and led her to the platform that stood in the middle of the pool. "Sit," she commanded, her voice a strained squeak.

Sasha sat, biting back a gasp as her flesh touched the gel-like platform. "I'm sorry, princess. I didn't think . . . I've never used so much, and . . ."

Alyssandra silenced her by closing her lips around one of the maid's engorged nipples. The *ponga* dissolved on her tongue, the nutty flavor causing a new burst of tingles inside her mouth. She wished Stone was here to fuck her from behind while she pleasured the maid. The picture formed so vividly in her mind, she knew exactly what Stone's thick cock would feel like sliding into her as she suckled Sasha's breasts.

Sasha jerked and her eyes flew open. "Oh, princess . . . I can see your vision! You, me . . . and the prince."

Rather than embarrassment, a flow of heady power surged through her and a slow smile curved her lips. "We need to gain some sustenance, right? I can't think of anything better than a combination of voyeurism and actual touch, can you?" At Sasha's answering grin, she stepped forward pressing her bare breasts against the maid's.

The fluffy fruit made their skin slide against each other in a silky caress and Alyssa eagerly lowered her lips to Sasha's, gently licking away the *ponga* before dipping her tongue inside to explore the lush softness of the maid's mouth. As both their hands roamed and explored, Alyssa closed her eyes and pictured Stone behind her, covering his engorged cock with *ponga* and slowly sliding inside her, stretching her, filling her.

Sasha moaned and her nipples pebbled against Alyssa's sensitive skin shooting several jolts of power straight to her aching pussy. Her hips began a slow grind against the maid's bare mons as she pictured Stone pumping into her, harder and faster until her breath came in short quick gasps. When Sasha reached down between them and rolled Alyssa's swollen clit between two fingers, she saw stars behind her closed lids as an orgasm slapped into her like an angry fist. Her entire body exploded with sudden sensations and large lightning bolts sizzled away from her, drawn out in every direction to strike stone, wood, water, and anything else in its path.

Sasha gasped as the energy hit her and then screamed as her resulting orgasm claimed her too.

Alyssa's energy drained away like water in a cracked cup and her knees buckled under her. Before she could right herself or even open her eyes, strong arms gripped her and curled her against a clothed and very muscular chest. "Stone . . ." The familiar sandalwood scent of him filled her senses and she buried her face against his chest.

He sat down at the edge of the bathing pool, still cradling her in his arms, his boots soaked and resting on the first step, still half covered in the warm water. "Had a little too much *ponga* I see." His voice wasn't angry, but sounded very strained. He turned toward the four royal guards. "One of you see to the maid. She needs to be thoroughly cleansed of the *ponga* and must have enough sustenance to clear it out of her system."

One of the guards nodded and waded in after Sasha.

Alyssa opened her mouth to tell Stone that the overdose had been her fault, but before she could form the words, his mouth crushed hers and his tongue demanded admittance. Sensations assaulted her as his soft linen shirt and breeches scratched against her overly sensitized bare skin and his wonderfully callused hands traced every inch of her.

She balled her hands in the cloth of his tunic and held on for dear life as she weathered the storm of his passion. He growled against her lips and lifted her so she straddled him, then he stood and walked down into the bathing pool and turned so he could sit her down on the first step.

The *balda* stone under her bare ass and swollen nether lips sparked and sizzled, and she rubbed against it seeking release. Before she could find it, Stone pinned her, bracketing his arms on either side of the step and thrusting against her, his hard cock rubbing her aching slit through his breeches.

"Witch!" His lips curved into a sensual smile as he continued his slow assault on her senses. "I was having breakfast with my parents when a sudden, extremely vivid vision of you, me, and your maid in the bathing pools popped into my head and couldn't be dislodged. I almost came in my breeches at the thought of fucking your tight ass while you pleasured your maid. Then I rush down here to find you and Sasha pleasuring each other—a scene that will live in my fantasies forever. I think my cock is about to burst."

Even though her body was on fire, smug satisfaction at pushing Stone beyond his normal limits filled her and she threw back her head and laughed, the sound echoing around her.

Freedom and exhilaration flowed through her and large sparks of electricity shot out from her to sizzle around her on every available surface. Stone took the opportunity to rain a row of open-mouthed kisses against her neck causing her to cry out as the now familiar wave of energy began its relentless path through her. He nipped her shoulder and then licked the spot to soothe away the pain, but it only served to spiral the maelstrom of energy even faster.

Stone continued pumping against her, pounding her against the stone steps until she thought she would go insane if he didn't plunge his thick cock inside her. Then, he reached between them to rub her clit and she spiraled suddenly higher, her breath backing up in her lungs, as small black dots danced before her eyes.

Stone pumped against her faster and then stiffened and cried out her name as he soaked his breeches for the second time in the last few days. The undone look in his lavender eyes pushed her over the edge and she shattered as power again spun outwards to sizzle along the pink seams of *balda* embedded in every wall, floor and counter.

Stone lifted her higher before he fell limp against her so his essence wouldn't touch her. She wrapped her arms around him, enjoying the closeness of his body and the way his clothes rasped over her still sensitive skin.

"Mmmm." The sound escaped from her throat and she smiled at the contentment of it. Something she'd never known before she'd met him.

Stone braced his forearms on either side of her and raised himself in a push-up motion to face her. His chiseled lips curved into a very self-satisfied grin. "I will never be bored keeping you well pleasured, Princess. But I may have to see about having several sets of replacement boots at the ready in case of any more *ponga* incidents."

She reached out to caress his freshly shaven cheek. "I'm sorry about the vision. It seemed the quickest way to get rid of the overdose of *ponga*. I didn't realize I'd shared it with you as well as Sasha. After what we saw in the garden, I seem to have a lot of fantasies centering around several variations on threesomes. But since you saved me today, I'll wait until later to scold you for the way you treated me this morning."

His eyes widened in shock. "What do you mean? I don't recall treating you badly this morning." He didn't meet her eyes, and she knew he was lying.

She snorted. "Of course you don't." Her irritation returned full force and she poked a finger against his broad chest, chasing the afterglow of her orgasm away. "I know you're hiding something from me about my vision, and you just ruined the effect of a really good orgasm." He opened his mouth to say something and she barreled over him. "Let's get something straight, Stone, I will *not* be treated like a child. Either we have a partnership or we have nothing—planet or not. Are we clear?"

After a moment more of stunned silence, Stone's lips curved. "I think I'm learning that women are much smarter than I give them credit for."

She bristled, anger flowing up to heat her cheeks. Before she could open her mouth to tell Stone exactly what he could do with his comments, he crushed his lips to hers, not relenting until Alyssa's bones had turned to jelly.

"As I was trying to say," Stone continued, "I'm sorry about this morning. But I'll make you a deal. We'll forget about the *ponga* incident and I'll make sure no one knows about it beyond the guards and Sasha and you let me keep this one secret for a few more days."

She didn't like the deal, but she didn't want to be remembered as the queen who OD'd on *ponga*, so she finally nodded. "Deal. But I'm only giving you a few days before I expect full disclosure."

"Deal." He brushed a kiss across her frowning lips. "Anyway, I'm intrigued that you were able to share your vision, and not sure how I'll face all of Sasha's smirks for the next few days." He kissed the tip of her nose. "Why don't we make sure to explore that whole scenario in more detail right after the ceremony? As well as all manner of threesomes." He nipped her bottom lip before standing and signaling for one of the guards to bring him fresh clothes.

"My control is weak, Alyssandra. I've waited too long for you." He turned back to her and smiled. "Mark my words, when we are well and truly mated, I intend to tie you to the bed, cover you in *ponga,* scented oils, and anything else I can find, and fulfill every one of our fantasies."

Her sex clenched at his erotic promise and she licked her lips. The way he stared down at her swelled her heart with emotions she wasn't yet ready to name. This man studied her as if she were something infinitely precious—something to be treasured. Before she knew it, she'd opened her mouth to speak. "I intend to fully hold you to that promise, my prince. But I think you'd better be careful, or it will be *you* who finds himself tied to the bed."

Stone's eyes darkened with desire and he started forward toward her until the soft scrape of a boot on stone told him the guard had returned with his clothes. "Soon, beloved. Very soon." He knelt on the wet *balda* to brush a tender kiss across her forehead. "For now, you'd better finish your bathing. I must go to the king's archives to ensure I have everything in order for the ceremony."

She caught and handful of his tunic in her hand. "There's a king's archive too?" She almost laughed at the excitement in her own voice.

He grabbed her hand and placed an open-mouthed kiss in the center of her palm. "Yes, my curious witch. All are welcome to the archives of both the king and queen. I'll be happy to escort you sometime, but Sasha advised me you already have plans to go to the queen's archive this morning." He caressed her cheek with his fingers before he stood. "I'll find you later for lunch . . . and whatever else you desire."

She nodded. Her quick fantasy picture of Stone flashed inside her mind and she sighed with regret as he winked over his shoulder before disappearing down the hall, his boots ringing against the stone.

A gentle touch feathered against Shawn's mind and he sighed and closed his eyes waiting patiently. The familiar presence had always brought comfort and peace ever since he could remember. In fact, when he was but a small boy, the soothing voice inside his head had kept him sane when he'd been locked away in dark rooms or beaten for some imagined transgression at the hands of the Cunts. He'd long since stopped questioning where the voice came from or why it had chosen him, and instead embraced it as a gift.

Throughout the years since he'd grown into a man, the voice had given him knowledge and allowed him to outmaneuver Sela and keep her on the offensive. He may have grown up under her "care," but that didn't mean he trusted her. Sela didn't do anything that wasn't for her own gain. If it hadn't been for the fact that his own people were even worse than the Cunts, he would've broken away from Sela's hold long ago. However, if he had a chance to redeem the name of Klatch, he would readily take it. He would ensure that the Klatch race could hold their heads high once again.

Watch and see your destiny . . . The voice beckoned.

A lovely face coalesced inside his mind's eye. She had similar olive skin to his own as well as lavender eyes and flowing mahogany hair that reached down past her rounded ass, almost to the floor. Her lovely oval face was set in a smile and her ripe lips fascinated him. He reached for her and she vanished like vapor on the wind.

Soon, the voice promised. *Trust only yourself, and you shall find your true destiny. Beware of lies and deceit that could steal her from you . . .*

He opened his eyes, but the memory of her burned into his mind. He'd seen her in his mind's eye many times. Yet tonight she seemed closer somehow, almost as if he could reach out and touch her golden skin. "I will find you," he promised the empty room. "I swear it."

Stone entered the king's archives and breathed deep as the familiar aroma of pine polish, hard wood, and wine filled his senses.

"I know what you mean. I've always loved the way this place smells."

Stone turned to look over his shoulder at Grayson. "It's one of my earliest memories. As soon as I was old enough to understand that I was betrothed to King Darius's daughter—not that I had any idea what that meant at the time—the king would bring me here and sit me on his knee while he read to me. He would drink wine and I would drink *salda* juice from a goblet." Stone smiled as the vivid memory flashed into his mind's eye. "I felt like I was privy to the inner men's sanctum. I was almost disappointed when I found out all were welcome in the king's archives."

Grayson laughed and stepped past Stone to flop down in an overstuffed chair and prop his booted feet on an equally overstuffed ottoman. He let his head fall back to rest against the top of the chair and looked up. "This is my favorite part. I'd come here with my father and sit and look up at the ten different levels. It was even better when I could see people on all the levels bustling around."

Stone chuckled and sat down on the footstool next to Grayson's feet. "It's amazing isn't it? In a few short days, the ascension will be complete, I'll be married and a father-to-be." He shook his head at the enormity of the changes that faced him. "It doesn't seem all that long ago that we were children ourselves, and now I'm about to have a daughter of my own. How is it possible that time has flown by so quickly?"

"Spoken like a man with too much responsibility on his shoulders." Gray pulled his feet from the ottoman and let them drop to the floor in front of the chair, and then leaned forward to look at Stone. "Don't forget to enjoy some of your life along the way, Stone. Your future looks much brighter than mine and Ryan's."

Guilt snaked through Stone's gut. "I'm sorry, Grayson. Here I am struggling with all of this, when your best prospect is the Eighth Princess who is two years older than your mother."

"It wouldn't be so bad if she didn't talk about the conquests she and my mother have while we are in bed."

Stone's eyes widened as shock slapped at him. "You and . . ."

Grayson threw back his head and laughed, the sound echoing back and forth against the round walls of the archives, making it sound as if a dozen men were laughing on various levels. "I'm just kidding, Stone. Bloody hell, the woman changed my diapers when I was a lad. It would be too close to some sort of warped Oedipus complex to even consider."

Stone's audible sigh of relief made them both laugh.

Grayson slapped Stone on the back. "It's good to shock you now and then, although I have a feeling your princess will do that often enough to keep you from getting too stodgy and old."

Alyssandra's sexy half smile popped into Stone's mind and he smiled to himself. "Yes, I'm sure she will." When Grayson rolled his eyes at Stone's reaction, he shrugged self-consciously. "Where's Ryan? I thought he was joining us?"

"The last time I saw him, he was having a water fight with six serving women in the garden waterfalls. Who was I to dissuade him?"

"Who indeed?" Stone pushed to standing and looked down at Grayson. "Well, we can start up on level four. I think that's where all the ascension documents are stored."

"What are you hoping to find?" Grayson unfolded his lanky frame from the chair and started toward the spiral staircase that wound upward for ten floors before ending at the basement door to the castle proper.

"I've heard bout the ascension my entire life, but I'd like to read past king's accounts, history, anything I can to ensure I'm making it as easy on Alyssandra as possible."

Gray's hand closed over Stone's shoulder and Stone stopped before he stepped up to the next step and turned to face his friend.

"Stone, Alyssandra isn't Lianna. You said yourself that she's already coming into her powers and that she would be fine.

Lianna couldn't even do a simple spell before the ascension, she should've known better. It wasn't your fault—you tried to warn her."

Familiar pain assaulted Stone and he closed his eyes against the onslaught. When he opened them, Grayson's lavender eyes studied him. "I know. But if there's anything I can do to ensure that Alyssandra is safe—anything at all—I have to know I did it."

A long slow sigh fell from Grayson's lips. "I wouldn't have expected anything else from you, Stone." He slapped him on the shoulder. "Let's get started, and as soon as Ryan's done getting sucked off by the half dozen, he can help. If I recall, the ascension section is only half the fourth level—right?"

Stone nodded. "True, only about ten thousand books and documents, if memory serves."

A strangled noise emanated from Grayson and Stone turned back to look at him with a smile. "I know . . . I've already ordered wine and food to be sent up while we read."

An hour and several goblets of wine later, Stone shut the dusty tome he'd been reading and rubbed his bleary eyes.

"Stone." Ryan leaned forward in his chair, having joined them only ten minutes ago. He rested the small black book he'd been reading on the ottoman they all shared.

Stone leaned forward and noticed Grayson did the same beside him. "Did you find something?"

Ryan pierced Stone with an intense gaze before answering. "You said Alyssandra was more powerful than any princess about to ascend the throne has ever been, correct?"

Stone's brow furrowed and he nodded to his friend.

"There's a legend here that tells of a powerful princess who even before the ascension has more power than the reigning queen."

"Go on." Icy dread trickled down Stone's spine. He wasn't

sure how he knew, but he knew this legend spoke directly of Alyssandra.

"It says that such a princess will come when Tador is in danger and she will wield so much power that it tends to be unstable and even dangerous. Then it alludes to something called the triangle, which is needed to allow full healing to come to Tador and to keep the new queen from destroying herself. It sounds almost as if this triangle, whatever it is, is the only thing that will keep the queen alive and thriving after the ascension." He shook his head. "You both know what that means for Tador if she's not."

Stone took the book from Ryan and stared down at the words. "We have to figure out what this triangle is before the ascension."

Grayson gestured to the half of the fourth level that held books pertaining to the ascension. "Any bright ideas on how to do that with just the three of us? We'll need to enlist more help."

Stone snapped the book shut and rested it against his forehead. "I get an eerie feeling that we need to be extremely careful who we ask to help." He looked at his two friends.

"Agreed." This from Ryan. "The council doesn't need any reason to question Alyssandra's right to the throne. After the way she embarrassed the Council Head, no matter how well-deserved, I think they would be happy to find any weakness to keep her from ascending, no matter the threat to the planet."

"Prince Stone!"

Stone turned to see an elderly servant on the spiral staircase. "Come quickly, it's the queen."

Chapter 10

The queen's archive turned out to be in the basement of the castle. Lovingly polished bookshelves stood floor to ceiling, overflowing with books, while sweeping spiral staircases and landings dotted with comfortable alcoves allowed access to any of the ten floors. The smell of beeswax and lemon made the room comforting and homey even though a hundred people could fit in the round chamber.

Alyssa stood at the bottom in between the overstuffed chairs and footstools and looked up, her mouth open in awe. "I can see all the way to the top."

Sasha laughed as she stepped up beside her. "The top you see there is actually the bottom floor of the castle proper."

"I can't believe I can read any of these books I want to at any time." She turned in a circle, her head still tilted back to study the view. She suddenly felt like a child at Christmas—or at least what she wished Christmas would've been.

"You'll soon be queen and will be writing a nightly journal which will someday grace this archive along with your mother's, and all the queens who ruled before you." The pride in Sasha's voice surprised her.

Alyssa stopped turning and looked over at her lady's maid. "Every time I think I'm getting used to the notion that I'm going to be queen, something comes along that makes it seem surreal again. There must be thousands of journals here." She trailed her fingers along a bookcase full of multicolored journals written by past queens, the history and the legacy contained in those pages her birthright.

"I can't imagine people wanting to read a journal full of my thoughts when they have all these to choose from. In fact, until Stone found me, my adoptive family convinced me that I wasn't smart enough to read anything but magazines." Her laugh was bitter and short. "But I've decided to take some good advice and decide for myself what I can and can't do." She smiled across at Sasha.

Alyssa closed her eyes and inhaled, imprinting the smells and ambience of this room into her memory. When she opened them, she was eye level with a journal that had been dyed a soft lavender. The color had faded a bit with time, but when she pulled the book from the shelf and opened the first page, the leather that folded inside the cover held the full rich color that reminded her of Stone's eyes when they were darkened with passion.

"That's the oldest queen's journal we have in the archive. I've never read them all, but when I asked why there were none before this one I was told that that queen started the tradition of journaling and has passed it down through the ages."

Alyssandra smiled and ran her hand over the soft leather of the cover. "At the beginning. That sounds like a good place for me to start learning how to be queen."

Sasha smiled. "I'll have some refreshments brought. Read at your leisure, Princess. I'll let you know when it's time to meet Prince Stone for lunch."

152 / Cassie Ryan

Alyssa nodded, taking her treasure and settling into a large overstuffed chair with a large leather ottoman in front. She turned her gaze toward the title page.

Queen Angelina de Klatch

Today is my first day as queen. I'm still terrified that I won't know what to do, that I'll let my people down. My darling William rules at my side, and I'm eternally grateful. But if not for Gwen, my faithful lady's maid, I would be lost.

Several have already questioned my decision to bring back traditions from the past. It has been many centuries since a queen employed the strength of the triangle, but to restore Tador, I will do what I must. I couldn't live with the destruction of the planet I love.

How past queens have managed to maintain the symbiosis without the triangle amazes me. I envy their strength and their persistence. May Tador forgive me if I've made the wrong decision.

I must prepare since the Seer's and Healer's coming-of-age happens over the next few weeks and soon after we must form the ancient bond if Tador is to be saved. I hope . . .

Alyssa held her breath as she turned the page, but the ink had faded until it was almost unintelligible. "Damn!" She vowed to read every journal in the archive if that's what it took to find out more about this triangle. The Klatch Council may not be open to listening to options, but Alyssa certainly was. She trusted her parent's judgment, and her gut told her whatever this triangle turned out to be, could very well be the saving grace of Tador.

"Alyssandra."

She turned to see Stone, his face set in hard lines of granite, his eyes shadowed. "What's wrong?"

"The queen has collapsed. Come quickly." He held out his

hand to her and she scrambled up, dropping the journal in the overstuffed chair and following Stone. Panic clawed inside her throat and her eyes burned with unshed tears. She'd spent so many years without her mother, she couldn't bear the thought of losing her now.

When they reached her parents' chambers, she ran ahead of Stone, shoving open the large wooden doors and rushing to her mother's bedside. Annalecia lay on her back, the rich purple blankets pulled up to her chest. Her face was drawn and pale, her eyes closed, her breathing shallow.

"Mother . . ." It came out a strained whisper, her voice carrying all the desperation and helplessness that swamped her. Her mother gave no indication that she heard.

"Alyssandra."

She turned at the sound of her father's voice and rushed forward into his comforting embrace. "What happened?" She murmured against his tunic while she squeezed her eyes shut against the words he would say.

Darius gently stroked her hair and rested his chin on the top of her head. "She and I were meeting privately with the leader of the council and she collapsed in a heap. She is weakening, as is her bond with the Tador."

Alyssa pulled back enough to look at her father. "We have to start the ceremony. I won't risk losing her!"

Stone started forward, but King Darius held up a hand that stopped him in his tracks and returned his gentle gaze to his Alyssa. "If we start the ceremony early, you both will die." His thumb swiped across her cheek to capture a tear that had escaped. "It is only another few days."

Protests lodged in her throat and she swallowed them back like bile, bitter and harsh. She knew her father's words were true, but she couldn't bear the thought of anything happening to her parents now that she'd finally found them.

A soft moan from the bed caught her attention and she turned to see Annalecia's eyes flutter open and focus. "Mother!" She rushed to her bedside and sat down beside her, careful not to jostle the frail woman.

Annalecia's hand reached out to close over Alyssa's. "Shhh. I'm fine, just a bit tired."

Stinging tears flowed freely down her face to fall in fat round drops onto the blankets. She took her mother's hand in her own and remembering what Stone had done for her many times, she concentrated and sent a steady flow of energy through their bond and into her mother.

Annalecia gasped and arched up on the bed, but Alyssa refused to stop. She pushed the energy through her mother and out to meet the tenuous bond with Tador. The planet responded like a cat wanting attention. Warm waves of energy flowed back and forth between them until she could sense almost an invisible sigh of contentment. But she didn't know if it came from the planet or her mother.

She slowly drew enough energy back inside her mother to ensure she was safe and then broke the mental connection and let go of her mother's hand. When she tried to stand, her legs buckled under her and Stone's concerned face loomed large in her vision as he swept her into his arms. She buried her face against his chest and allowed sleep to claim her.

Alyssa awoke to the wonderful sensation of a muscular and very male body spooned behind her. Stone's thick cock lay cradled against the crack of her ass and his springy chest hair tickled the sensitive skin on her back. She reached back to touch him and her seeking hand met the cloth of his breeches. She bit back a sigh of disappointment. For one glorious second she thought she had him entirely naked in her bed, but she knew that wasn't advisable before the ceremony. Stone would never put her in danger.

His index finger traced lazy circles around the fullness of her bare breast, a strangely possessive yet comfortable touch. "I'm glad you're awake, Princess. I was beginning to worry that you'd pushed yourself too far past your limits."

There was no censure in his tone, only deep concern. A flow of warm emotion curled around her heart. "Did it work?"

Vibrations from Stone's deep chuckle reverberated through her body, bringing with them a slow wave of mounting arousal. His finger tracing moved to her areola, the touch gentle but steady. "What you did was very brave, Alyssandra. You most likely saved her life, not to mention it stopped the deterioration of Tador . . . for now. The queen is feeling much better. She wanted to resume her normal duties, but Darius has confined her to bed and is most likely doing everything within his power to keep her there and well provided with energy."

His words pushed away the arousal his touch brought. Relief flowed through her followed by pure joy at Stone's words of praise. It was only the second time she could remember that someone actually sounded proud of her—the first was just a few days ago after the meeting with the Klatch Council when her father had expressed his pride in her. She was surprised to realize she was proud of herself, as well. "So is that your plan too? To keep me confined to bed and well provided with energy?" She arched back against him, grinding her ass against his cock.

He hissed and nipped her shoulder until she stopped, causing her to laugh aloud. Then he continued his slow feathery touches over her sensitive breast. His callused finger sent tiny jolts of awareness through her, igniting small fires all over her body.

"Definitely, witch." His breath feathered over her nape and he leaned down to place a gentle kiss against the spot. Gooseflesh marched over her skin and she gasped at the intensity of the sensation. Then he placed his lips against her sensitive nape and sucked softly, ripping a moan from her throat and whipping energy through her body like a sudden explosion.

All the while, his finger continued to trace, around and around, slowly moving up to tease the aching tip of her breast. "In fact, I plan on keeping you here all day, replenishing you with all the energy you need—even if practicing that much restraint kills me."

She moaned again as he switched his gentle ministrations to the other breast. "Let's hope it doesn't come to that." Her whispered words sounded husky and faint.

He laughed again, the vibrations zinging a path straight to each of her engorged nipples and then flowing in a wave of hot lava to her aching pussy. A long sigh escaped from her throat before she could stop it and her hips began a slow instinctive grind against his heated cock.

In a quick movement, Stone rolled forward, forcing her onto her stomach. She gasped at the sudden move and then relaxed as he straddled her and began his gentle tracing over every inch of her skin. He ran his fingertips down her arms and then linked his fingers with hers, and in another quick movement, lifted her arms so they lay palm down on the bed above her head. When she tried to lift them, she discovered that they were magically bound again. "Damn it, Stone. I hate it when you do that!"

Stone's weight shifted as he leaned over her and his hot breath feathered against her ear. "It's time for more energy lessons, Princess, and the bindings keep you from hurting yourself. Magical binding is an easy spell. I'll teach it to you sometime—after I've had my fill of you." He nipped her earlobe and fire speared through her straight to her womb. Moisture pooled between her swollen pussy lips and she groaned as her hips began their instinctive grind against the softness of the mattress.

"Be careful, my prince," she warned. "Paybacks will be absolutely my pleasure. And I happen to know Klatch Witches are a very vindictive breed."

His low rumbling laugh feathered across her neck and she tipped her head to the side to give him better access. "Really, Princess? What makes you say that?"

"Because I'm enjoying fantasizing about my revenge." She bit down on her bottom lip as he placed his lips against her neck and gently sucked, then soothed the site with a swipe of his tongue. Another gasp ripped from her unbidden, ending in a long sigh. "Just remember, revenge is exponential."

"Good, I'm always up for a challenge."

Alyssandra opened her mouth to continue the banter, but then Stone began to explore her body in earnest with seeking hands, lips, teeth, and tongue. He lavished each curve and dip with so many sensations that she thought her body would spontaneously combust. The hurricane of energy began its rushing flow through her, steadily building in intensity.

She couldn't form any coherent thoughts, she could only feel as Stone caressed and teased her. When he nipped her hip and began to slowly trace a finger deeper and deeper between her ass cheeks, she arched toward him as best she could since he straddled her knees. "Please, Stone. Please . . ."

"Shhhh." The soft hiss of air against her hip sent another wave of fire through her and her clit throbbed and ached.

Warm oil dripped against her ass, surprising her, and the scent of lavender and vanilla suddenly filled her senses. Stone's strong hands rubbed and caressed both her ass cheeks in turn before once again dipping down inside toward her openings. One blunt finger probed her tight rosebud and she shuddered and pushed up against him, silently begging him to enter her.

"I've been thinking about that day in the gardens when you ached for a cock inside your ass. The ceremony comes soon and I thought we should prepare your body to accept me, and give you more chances to get used to channeling energy."

Another rush of the warm oil against her skin, and she inhaled, letting the scents fill her. Stone slowly inserted the tip of his finger inside her ass, gently rotating until she relaxed to accept him. His finger slowly retreated until her body retightened behind him and then he slipped easily back inside her with the aid of the warm oil.

Alyssa shifted her legs farther apart to give him better access and moaned as his finger delved deeper with each slow thrust. She arched up to try to take more of him, but his other hand anchored on the small of her back inhibiting her movements as he continued to set an agonizingly steady pace that was driving her crazy. The energy inside her began to whirl faster and faster and her skin tingled and sizzled with the force of it.

"Stone . . ." she warned.

Her words caught in her throat as his thumb dipped lower to tease her slick slit and trace a path all the way down to the soft underside of her aching clit. All the while, his finger continued his erotic invasion of her ass.

Slowly, she became used to his width and relaxed to accommodate him. After another rush of warm oil, two fingers slowly stretched her opening until they could slide in together. The sudden invasion speared even more power through her, which sparked against her skin in tiny sizzling pops. Stone's fingers delved deeper and he increased his rhythm to match the seeking movement of her hips.

The only sounds in the room were the slippery slap of flesh sliding against heated flesh and her ragged breaths as her orgasm built until it was just out of reach. She closed her eyes and pictured Stone's engorged cock slowly pushing inside her tight ass, impossibly stretching her. His beautiful golden muscles flexing as he thrust fully inside, burying himself to the hilt.

Stone's answering groan made her smile. *Maybe I'm not the only one going crazy from this . . .*

He suddenly pushed his fingers deep, startling her and breaking her concentration on the vision, which dissolved like mist before a strong breeze. Then he slapped an open hand against her ass, the stinging sensation only adding to her tightening arousal. The hurricane of power howled in reaction, building to easily double what it had been in the garden. She prayed she could hold on before it broke her into a million pieces.

Stone's weight moved off her legs and he pushed her thighs apart until his other hand found her slit and followed its path to her swollen clit. When his fingertip caressed the swollen nub, she nearly came undone, bucking off the bed, but Stone only continued his slow even pace on both fronts.

"Concentrate on the power flowing through you, my love. Channel it where it's needed."

His breath feathered over the sensitive skin of her hip and she shuddered. She was about to explode and he wanted her to concentrate? *Is he fucking insane?*

"You can do this, Alyssandra. You're already coming into your powers. The way you handled the energy in the garden, visions that you can share, the way you shared energy with your mother, the power that explodes outward when you orgasm. This is your birthright, claim it. Direct the power. Concentrate."

She shook her head back and forth against the pillow in denial.

Stone smacked her ass again with an open hand, just hard enough to gain her attention. "Focus, Princess. Look inside yourself—your body will know where sustenance is needed. Channel your power there first. You must always nourish yourself first, before you nourish others—even the planet or those you love."

Frustration flowed through her and she shoved it aside. Closing her eyes, she concentrated, forming a picture of herself within her mind. Several areas of her body appeared shadowed.

She envisioned the channeled power flowing to those areas, re-plenishing, repairing, nourishing. Intense tingling in the areas of her body she'd seen as shadowed shocked her and she gasped.

"That's it, Alyssandra. You're doing it. Finish nourishing yourself and then gather your power and we'll go to the next step." Stone's voice seemed very distant, but his voice was gentle and comforting.

When her entire body buzzed with health and vigor, her awareness returned and she realized Stone still thrust in and out of her in a steady rhythm, his long blunt fingers delving deep inside. She had the sudden urge to flip Stone over onto his back and ride him until they were both satisfied and too tired to move. She pulled against her invisible bonds in frustration, but they refused to budge.

He laughed. "I see your visions are back. Good. Have you gathered your power?"

She closed her eyes and was surprised to find it curled inside her, like a sleeping predator just waiting for her direction. She nodded against the pillow to let Stone know she'd heard.

"Now, the same way you healed yourself, concentrate on everything around you—people, plants, trees, *balda,* and the entire planet as a whole. You won't be able to heal everything until you're queen, but there's no need to waste your leftover power. Flow it to where it's most needed. Don't forget to leave some for yourself."

A picture of Tador formed as if she were looking down at a globe she could reach out and hold in her hands. Large portions of the planet were shadowed, some deep inside the planet, even though the surface still looked bright and healthy. She frowned as she surveyed the damage. There was so much sickness to heal she wondered if she'd even be able to repair it all once she was queen. If only the Klatch Council could see this.

As if from a great distance, she felt Stone's hands still pleasuring her body, supplying her with a steady flow of energy.

Returning her attention to the planet, she chose the most inhabited places and watched in wonder as they slowly healed before her eyes. Trees that had been limp and discolored brightened and now shown with health and vigor. Grasses plumped with life and multicolored flowers lifted their faces to the sun.

When she neared the end of her energy reserves, she forced herself to stop before depleting herself and kept enough in reserve to make it through the rest of the day. As much as she hated to admit it, Stone was right. She had to ensure she kept herself nourished and healthy or there would be no hope for the planet and her people.

She sighed as she opened her eyes and realized she was staring at the ceiling. Stone shifted and his handsome face filled her vision. Dark shadows marred the skin under his eyes and strain was clearly etched in the hard lines of his chiseled face even as he smiled down at her. "I'm not quite done with you yet, Princess."

Guilt pricked at her. She'd funneled energy to herself and the planet around her, but she hadn't given a thought for the man who had saved her from her old life and brought her here. The man she loved . . .

She gasped as she realized the truth of her words. They'd shared a deep connection even beyond the physical ever since he'd invaded her dreams. But this caring, wonderful man before her had somewhere along the last few days, stolen her heart as well.

Alyssa opened her mouth to say the words and found that she couldn't force them past her lips. She closed her mouth and grinned as an idea formed. She might not be able to express her emotions yet, but she could definitely show him how much she cared until she worked up the courage to say the words.

She shifted and realized her hands were still bound over her head even though she lay on her back. Stone settled himself between her thighs and blew a hot breath over her swollen nether lips. Alyssa gasped at the sensation before closing her eyes and concentrating on gathering the energy as he'd taught her. She expanded her awareness and carefully formed a vision inside her head.

Extending a tendril of power, she carefully directed it toward Stone. If she could fine-tune her new skills, she could touch and tease him all she wanted. When Stone swiped his tongue over her aching slit, she directed her tendril of energy to close around the tip of his cock as she longed to do with her mouth.

He groaned against her clit, even as he continued to lave her. She let her thighs fall open to give him better access and returned her attention to directing her energy. It obediently teased the swollen head of his cock and swiped at the pearly white drop of pre come that glistened at its tip. Then the energy flowed over him, as if she took him into her mouth, all the way to the back of her throat.

She almost laughed aloud as she realized that while a large man like Stone may not have ever had anyone able to fully take him inside their mouths, her obedient tendril of power had no such limitations. She directed her energy to split and even as she continued her soft torture against the thick length of him, she directed the other wisp of power to caress and tease his balls and the soft stretch of skin that ran between his balls and his ass.

Stone's cock hardened impossibly further inside her stream of energy and she reveled in the burst of pure feminine power that flowed through her. Something that had everything to do with being a woman who could please the man she loved and nothing to do with her royal status and duties. This power was far more elemental and primitive.

Alyssa continued to stroke and tease him even as he pleasured her. She allowed Stone to set the pace and just enjoyed where he took her. When he intensified the rhythm between them, or increased pressure, so did she. The vortex of arousal between them continued to tighten until their harsh pants and moans filled the air around them, twining with the musky scent of sex, vanilla and lavender.

"Alyssandra, you must stop. I won't drain your power by bringing you to orgasm. You collapsed earlier today and I won't risk your health." He dropped his forehead to rest against her stomach as if gathering the frayed reigns of his control.

"You have to learn to trust me, Stone."

He raised his head and opened his mouth to retort when she directed her tendrils of energy to increase their efforts, cutting off his protest. His gaze met hers moments before Stone stiffened against her as his control shattered and his orgasm rocked him.

He sucked her clit hard in reaction to his own surprise orgasm, pushing Alyssa over the edge. A shimmery kaleidoscope of colors flashed behind her eyes as a maelstrom of energy burst outward from her body. The mirror over her dresser shattered and every inch of exposed *balda* sizzled and popped with bright pink sparks that rained down over them, tingling as they hit exposed skin.

Alyssa surveyed the damage with lidded eyes. Once she was sure there was no immediate threat, she used her tendril of power to snap her magical bindings and she lay her hands lightly against Stone's dark head, which had fallen limp against her mons. She let silence fall between them and enjoyed the sound of Stone's breathing and the occasional leftover sizzle or pop from the overcharged *balda*.

A few moments later when Stone's breathing returned to normal he glared up at her with amusement twinkling in his gaze. "That's cheating, Princess, and I think I liked it."

Chapter 11

After several more bouts of sustenance, Stone had called for two bathing tubs to be brought to Alyssandra's room. Even with as much sexual energy as they'd shared in the past few hours, his cock hardened again as he saw her slip into the warm water, a sigh escaping her ripe lips, her head thrown back in near ecstasy. He stepped into his own tub hoping his raging erection would take the hint if he ignored it. The information Ryan had found in the king's archive had haunted him and he'd decided to take Queen Annalecia's advice and stop treating the princess with kid gloves.

As he relaxed in the warm water, he sighed as overused muscles unknotted. He glanced over at Alyssandra, only to see her in the same position as when she'd first slipped into the bath. "You're not going to fall asleep over there and drown, are you, beloved?"

She smiled and managed an amused sound. "No. But it feels good to just soak here for a bit and enjoy the sensation."

Stone had never been big on bathing tubs, at least if they

didn't involve the co-ed baths. There used to be several different assortments of women who were more than happy to help
him complete his daily sustenance, but since he'd found Alyssandra, he'd bathed alone—usually stroking his cock while fantasizing about what he would do to his new bride as soon as the
ascension was complete. When he'd walked in on Alyssandra
and Sasha after the *ponga* incident earlier, he realized that he
may yet hold a certain fondness for the bathing pools. But there
would definitely be a more select set of participants than he'd
had in the past. His feisty princess would most likely keep him
occupied for quite a while before either of them decided they
needed to invite anyone else. His cock hardened again and
stubbornly poked its swollen head out of the water.

He firmly set his bathing pool fantasies about the princess
aside and decided he could no longer put off telling her what
he'd found. "Alyssandra."

"Mmmm?"

"I found something in the king's archives today that I
wanted to talk to you about."

She turned her head to look at him, but made no other
move, keeping her body submerged from the neck down in the
warm water.

Stone took a deep breath as he wrestled with his instinct to
protect her and keep her safe.

"Are you going to keep me in suspense?" She smiled, a slow
languid movement of her full ripe lips that sent a fresh surge of
arousal straight to his already aching balls.

He cleared his throat and wished that the water in the tub
would cool before his cock exploded from excess pressure. It
had to be her increased pheromones, but the logical explanation
did nothing for his uncomfortable aroused state. "Well, actually, Grayson found it. There was mention of a legend."

Curiosity sparked in her lavender eyes and she pushed up in

the tub so she could face him. "A legend?" Her voice filled with excitement, like a child who had been promised candy.

"Yes, it speaks of a princess who, even before the ascension, wields more power than the reigning queen." He studied her, waiting for her reaction.

Her face a mask, she countered with a question. "And why do I get the feeling you think this legend is referring to me?"

He pushed up in the tub, facing her, wincing when the cool air of the chamber hit his wet skin. "No princess about to ascend the throne has shown as much power as you already do. We won't know for sure until the presentation ceremony, but I wouldn't be surprised if you prove that you already wield more power than your mother."

"What's the rest of this legend, Stone? I get the distinct impression that this legend isn't a good thing, so get to the point."

"Damn, Alyssandra. I'm not handling this very well. I'm fighting against my natural instincts to even tell you. But the queen . . ."

"The queen what?" She raised her eyebrow and pierced him with a hard stare.

Stone sighed and realized he'd maneuvered himself into dangerous waters. "Let's just say that your mother gave me quite a lecture on keeping things from you for your own protection."

"You mean like why my vision about the ascension ceremony upset you?"

He closed his eyes. This woman was entirely too smart for her own good. "Yes, exactly like that." He held up a hand to stop her next question. "I have a day or so left on our deal and I still need that time. But this legend is something different. It speaks of a princess who will come when Tador is in danger and she will wield so much power that it tends to be unstable and even dangerous. Then it alludes to something called the triangle, which is needed to allow full healing to come to Tador and to keep the new queen from destroying herself."

The sudden splashing as she bolted upright in her tub surprised him. "The triangle! I almost forgot. When I was in the queen's archives, I was reading something about a triangle right before you came to tell me my mother had collapsed." Her brow creased and she chewed her bottom lip for a moment. "It was in a journal written by the first queen who had started journaling, and she mentioned that she was reinstating the triangle to fully heal Tador. There was also something about a Seer and a Healer and their coming-of-age, although it didn't mention a ceremony, so I'm not sure if they are royal or not." Her brow furrowed as she turned toward him. "Then, when I turned the page, all the ink was faded and illegible, but the rest of the journal was still clear and readable—almost as if that part was purposely obscured."

Stone's mood darkened and a sudden urgency beat inside his chest. "I think we need to call Sasha, Grayson, and Ryan and spend some more time in both of the archives. We have a lot of reading to do before the ascension."

After breakfast and bathing, Alyssa returned to the queen's archives and began to search in earnest for more information on the triangle Queen Angelina had spoken of in her journal. She enlisted Sasha's help as well as Grayson and Ryan's, while Stone had gone alone to the king's archives.

She'd had to promise the men lots of wine and refreshments, but they'd finally agreed to help her. She wasn't sure if they were more interested in finding options for saving Tador or just making the council look foolish, and as long as they helped her, she didn't care. They didn't have much time before the presentation ball tonight, but they wanted to use every spare minute they could.

"My lady, here are the rest of Queen Angelina's journals."

Sasha stacked them on the table next to her and then sat down in the opposite chair to begin reading her own stack.

Grayson snorted in disgust and tossed another journal into a growing pile on the floor in front of him. "Fuck! Whoever wanted to erase the information about the triangle did a damn good job of it. Every time we start to find more information, the following pages are illegible."

Ryan examined the latest addition to the pile and scowled. "It's some sort of blocking spell. I don't know of any Klatch today that have that type of specialized talent, do any of you?"

Sasha and Grayson shook their heads and Alyssa pursed her lips, remembering something her mother had told her. "I don't know what my talent is yet, maybe I can do something."

Ryan tossed her the journal. "Can't hurt to give it a try. If you're the all powerful princess in the legend, then most likely you can wield your energy to do several things that most normal Klatch can't."

She flipped the pages until she found the faded entry. She concentrated, reaching out with her tendril of energy. It brushed over the page and sizzled as it met with the ancient ink, but nothing happened. "I don't think I'm doing this right."

"Don't give up yet, Princess." Sasha picked up another journal and opened it to the first page. "We'll keep reading while you try to break the spell."

Break the spell . . . Alyssa had tried to make the ink reappear, but maybe she should try breaking the spell instead. After all, she didn't know what form her special talent would take, and she had nothing to lose by trying. Closing her eyes, she reached out once more with her tendril of power. In her mind's eye, she saw the journal and a faint glow emanated around the edges of the binding. Her power feathered against the glow, testing it. It tingled against her energy, but rebounded as soon as she pulled back.

Taking a deep breath, she sent a surge of power shooting toward the journal. A large popping sound echoed around the chamber as the glow disappeared and the journal burst into flames in her hands. She dropped it to the floor a second before a cold flood of liquid hit her in the chest and she opened her eyes to see Sasha holding an empty glass and looking down at her.

"Princess, are you all right? Did you burn your hands?"

Alyssa studied her hands, glad to see no burns or wounds, and then turned her attention back toward the charred journal on the floor in front of her. "Crap. I think I broke the spell, but I also destroyed the journal. So much for convincing myself that I've got my power under control and I'm not the one in the legend."

Grayson picked up the ruined journal and set it aside. "Well, the good news is that you found your special power—you can break spells. Sounds like a very useful skill for a future queen. The bad news is, you have to learn a little finesse or we'll barbeque all the journals before we find what you're looking for."

"Thanks for the tip. Any idea how I can accomplish that?" She sifted through a pile looking for a journal with the least amount of smudged writing and waved it in the air in front of her waiting for his answer.

"Picture exactly what you did last time and then try it again, more carefully." He shrugged and snatched a cookie off the table.

"You guys are just a font of information, you know that?"

The men laughed and everyone gathered around to watch her next attempt.

"Great, no pressure." She closed her eyes and once again reached out with her tendril of power, just enough to illuminate the glow around the journal. Taking a deep breath, she concentrated on breaking the spell. Her power feathered across the edges of the glow and it sizzled lightly against her touch. She kept the energy steady and gentle. After several seconds, the glow slowly faded until it was gone. Quickly, she retracted her energy before it could ignite the pages and then slitted one eye open to see if it had worked.

The previously smudged words were now crisp and clear against the page as if they'd just been written. She read them aloud. ... *powerful humans with special gifts must fulfill the other two points and undergo an ascension with a full-blooded Prince of Klatch.*

Ryan whistled long and low. "When you uncover a controversial mystery, you really go all the way. The Klatch Council will have a fit."

Dread flowed through her. Stone had told her that offspring between humans and Klatch were Cunts. No full-blooded royal Klatch would dilute the bloodline with a human. Talk about an uphill battle.

"Don't give up yet, love." Stone stood leaning against the doorframe watching her. "You don't know all the details until you've unlocked the mysteries in the rest of the spelled journals. The passages wouldn't have been hidden if there wasn't something to hide. It must not be as clear cut as it appears."

She had a sudden urge to push him down against one of the overstuffed chairs and lick every part of his body. A vivid vision of Stone with his hands bound behind him, his golden naked body helpless beneath her while she slicked his body with the lavender and vanilla scented oil and fulfilled her every whim flashed through her mind sending a sudden shudder through her. From the way Stone suddenly straightened, his breathing coming in short pants, she'd inadvertently shared her vision again.

She schooled her face to hide her smug smile. "Stone, I'm glad you're here. Did you find anything else useful in the king's archives?"

"Nothing for an entire morning's efforts except for one entry pointing me to the queen's archives for more information on the triangle." He sat down on the ottoman in front of her and took a small sip from her glass of wine. "Too bad we didn't find that book yesterday. I could've been here all morning."

She leaned forward and pressed her lips against Stone's, swiping a tongue across his lips and biting back a moan as she tasted the wine he'd just sampled. Closing her eyes, she forced herself to lean back a hairsbreadth, away from the temptation of Stone's body. "You're just in time to help." Stone shuddered as her breath feathered against his lips. "Why don't you three make some sense of these entries while I break the spells."

Stone brushed his lips over hers before putting enough distance between them that Alyssa could breath again without inhaling his scent. "Your wish is my command, Princess."

Four hours later, she slumped back against the chair, her head throbbing and her body screaming for sustenance. "So what have you guys pieced together while I've been breaking spells?" Her voice sounded raspy and dry, and she gratefully accepted a glass of wine from Sasha. The fruity liquid soothed the back of her throat and she swallowed it greedily, holding out her glass for a refill.

Stone finished writing down the last newly revealed paragraph and leaned back in the chair to rub at the bridge of his nose. "From what I can tell, Tador has been in dire straights before. Several times throughout our history, the triangle was employed to help bring it back from the brink of destruction. The three sides of the triangle are made up of the queen, a Seer and a Healer. The Seer and the Healer are humans, but not normal humans. They have special powers, which qualify them for their roles and most likely have some strong Klatch blood somewhere in their history."

"The council would paint any attempt at mating a human with a full-blooded Klatch Prince as some sort of blasphemy." Grayson's jaw hardened as he looked around the circle.

Stone lowered the paper and nodded. "However, that doesn't

mean it isn't what's required to restore the planet and to keep Alyssandra's power from destroying her. Listen to the rest." He raised the paper and continued to read. "The queen must assume the throne first and then the Seer and last, the Healer. The Seer and Healer must undergo a coming-of-age ceremony similar to the queen's, mated with a full-blooded Klatch Prince, but neither of them need to be virginal to assume their position. Once all three points of the triangle have ascended, then there is a ceremony with all six people—the queen, the Seer, the Healer and their respective mates. The fully functional triangle restores the planet and protects it until it can store up enough power to subsist purely on the queen's energy once more. Once it has enough, the offspring of the Seer and the Healer are no longer born with the requisite powers to hold their point of the triangle and we revert to a one point system of symbiosis with the planet."

Silence reigned as everyone digested Stone's words. Alyssa poured some more wine and sipped it as she thought through all the implications. "The Klatch Council is gonna freak if I suggest this. They are never going to believe it. Not to mention, where are we going to find two full-blooded princes willing to dilute the Klatch bloodline?"

Grayson cleared his throat. "I happen to see two princes sitting in front of you that have little or no prospects of mates in the near future. I'd have to wait twelve years just to have one of the younger princesses become old enough for the age of consent, or I can marry a woman who is of an age with my mother. I happen to know Ryan is in the same circumstances."

"What about your families? Would they approve of either of you mating with a human—no matter how special?"

Ryan shrugged. "Don't borrow more trouble than you need. Let's get you ascended and then when you explain this to the council, we'll back you up. I agree with what you said at the meeting—we need to do what's best for Tador, and this has obviously worked in the past. It's worth a shot. And besides, after four hours of reading the desperation various queens described in these journals and their reasons for bringing back the triangle—I don't think anyone has a choice. Especially if the volatility of your power can threaten your health as well as the health of Tador. We'd be fools not to try."

"Why do I think the council prefer to be fools?"

No one answered her rhetorical question. Thousands of doubts warred with just as many questions inside Alyssa's mind, but exhaustion won out and Stone picked her up and then turned to the group. "Can someone tidy up the archives and then put our notes in a safe place? I need to ensure our future queen has enough energy to complete the presentation ceremony later tonight. She needs all the support she can garner from the people if she's going to gain their agreement about the triangle."

Alyssa wrapped her arms around Stone's neck and buried her face against his tunic inhaling his scent. Woodsy and masculine and uniquely Stone.

She must've nodded off while he carried her, because suddenly, he laid her on her bed and pulled the covers over her. It took great effort, but she forced open her heavy eyelids to look for Stone. Before she could form the words to ask him to stay, he'd slipped off his tunic and boots and slid into bed next to her, assuming their normal spoon position—his arm draped over her, his hand cupping her breast.

"Sleep, beloved. We have a long evening ahead."

She sighed against the pillow as she let her eyelids fall.

Alyssa sat in front of her mirror while Sasha put the finishing touches on her hair. It frothed around her in a wavy mass, while tiny stones that reminded her of diamonds scattered through her tresses and winked strategically whenever one of them caught the light. "I'm terrified Sasha. What if they don't like me or if I throw up on someone important? Or even worse,

174 / Cassie Ryan

what if I prove tonight that I have more power than my mother, and this legend really is talking about me?"

Sasha's musical laugh lilted through the air. "Princess, you have a real obsession about vomiting on people. As for the legend, there's no use worrying about it—we'll all know soon enough. The Klatch people already love you. Even in your absence, you've been present in their thoughts and they were all confident you would return one day. Prince Stone promised them he would find you and they never doubted him. Besides, the entire population is still buzzing about what you said at the Klatch Council. Many think that the council no longer serves the needs of the people, and they welcome strong leadership from the queen." Sasha gasped and pressed her hands to her mouth. "I never meant to imply Queen Annalecia hasn't been a strong leader."

"Don't worry, Sasha. I know what you meant. My mother had several distractions, including taking on the needs of an entire planet." She smiled up at the maid, relieved when Sasha smiled back.

"I just hope I can live up to my own hype. I'm really nervous about the ceremony. I mean, what if it doesn't even work? What if I'm nothing but a fraud?" She glanced up at Sasha's calm features and huffed out a breath. "It's easy for you to be so calm. There won't be thousands of people looking you over like a lobster in a tank tonight."

"You'll be fine, and don't forget me, Stone, both sets of your parents, and even Grayson and Ryan will be right beside you if you need any of us." Sasha turned and walked toward the bed where Alyssa's outfit spread out looking like an explosion of see-through shimmery gauze covered in the same small twinkling stones that adorned her hair. "Come on, time to get you into your outfit for the celebration."

Alyssa stood and walked to the bed, studying her outfit skeptically. "How do you even know how to assemble this thing? It looks like a bolt of fabric and the Hope diamond exploded all over my bed."

Sasha clutched her chest in mock indignation. "You have to have more trust in your faithful lady's maid, Princess. Have I ever let you down before?"

Alyssandra couldn't help the giggle that escaped. "All right. I trust you." She stood in the middle of the floor with her arms held out at her side. "I'm all yours. Make me beautiful, Sasha."

Almost an hour later, when Sasha was done wrapping, tying, twisting and tucking, she stood back, a beaming smile lighting her lovely face. "It fits perfectly, Princess."

Alyssa turned toward the full-length mirror and gasped. She didn't recognize the stranger who stared back at her. She'd thought Sasha's last makeover—turning her into a Klatch woman—was a miracle, but this . . . this was beyond belief.

The shimmery silver fabric wrapped strategically under her breasts so they stood proud and perky, her beaded nipples and dusky areolas easily visible through the transparent cloth. The rest of the top lightly caressed her arms leaving her back bare almost down to her ass. The front waist of the dress ended in a soft flowing seam just below her smooth mons, then on the sides, the material veed outward and downward until it brushed the floor in a gauzy train. Her naked form was clearly visible through the filmy fabric, but as she moved the light caught the stones, causing an explosion of shimmery twinkling as they reflected off each other. Soft leather slippers, studded with more of the crystals, encased her feet.

Sasha had lined her eyes with a vibrant blue and stained her lips with the juice from a fruit that smelled like Parrot Bay rum, and turned her lips a ripe red color.

"Wow. Sasha, remind me to never doubt you again. Stone's going to swallow his tongue when he sees your handiwork. I can't quite believe it myself."

"Oh, believe me, Princess, I will definitely remind you. And

I think Stone isn't the only one who will be swallowing his tongue when he sees you. Prince Grayson and Prince Ryan drool whenever you're nearby normally, but this . . . this should make them all come in their breeches."

Alyssa barked a laugh at the sudden visual. "They do not drool around me."

"Actually they do, but you are too busy drooling after Prince Stone to notice, and that's as it should be."

Alyssa turned back toward the mirror and sighed. Sasha had only spoken the truth. "Stone is amazing. But the three of them standing in a line next to each other is enough to give any woman within a hundred miles a spontaneous orgasm so large she'll instantly combust."

A giggle escaped from the maid. "Most definitely. I hope you don't take offense, Princess, but I'm looking forward to seeing all three of them entirely naked."

Alyssa gasped and her eyes widened. "Grayson and Ryan are part of the twenty Klatch men that give me their . . . essence?"

Sasha nodded, amusement and mischief dancing in her large eyes.

A sudden vision of Stone, Grayson, and Ryan standing shoulder to shoulder wearing only their golden skin and a smile flashed through her mind. Each of them stroked their thick long cocks, with creamy pre come glistening from each swollen tip. Alyssa's mouth watered at the sight and moisture flooded her channel and she clenched her thighs together against the sudden sensation. She closed her eyes tight trying to dislodge the image from her mind. "Oh my. I think I might spontaneously combust just standing here thinking about it."

"Princess, I think I'm a very lucky lady's maid to have a mistress with such a vivid imagination who so freely shares her visions."

* * *

The celebration was in full swing by the time Stone made his way down the long white *balda* spiral staircase and into the sea of waiting Klatch. The sounds of laughter and revelry made him smile. They stood in groups around tables laden with rich food and drink while a dozen musicians played soft background music. The middle of the room remained clear in preparation for the presentation of the princess.

Stone waded into the crowd exchanging pleasantries with his people and trying to ignore the impatience that pricked at him. Where was Alyssandra? It had only been a few hours since he'd seen her, and yet he missed her with an almost physical craving. He wondered if it was an affect of their bond as betrothed or if it was purely the spell that Alyssandra had cast over his life ever since he could remember. He smiled as memories of his future mate flowed through him. His life with her would never be boring, and for that, he was thankful.

Grayson and Ryan waved at him from their post near the wine and he shook his head as he made his way to them. "Why am I not surprised to find you two near the refreshments?"

Grayson picked up an empty glass and filled it half full with wine before reaching into the pocket of his breeches and pulling out a small flask. "This should take the edge off. It's something called Everclear, imported from earth." He filled the glass with the clear liquid and stirred the drink before offering it to Stone.

"Do I look like I need a drink?" He took the glass to his nose and sniffed it cautiously.

"My parents said that when Darius brought Annalecia to her presentation ball, he injured several other Klatch men in possessive fits of jealousy. We just thought we'd help you through this without incident. What are friends for?"

Stone grinned at the two men before taking a sip of the offered drink. It had no taste other than the fruity wine, but the

178 / Cassie Ryan

familiar hot burn of hard liquor down his throat assured him it was there. "I don't think I'll need this, but I appreciate the gesture."

A collective gasp from the crowd caused him to turn toward the stairs. His breath backed up in his lungs as his gaze locked with Alyssandra's. The force of the sudden connection rocked him to the core and it took several seconds for him to allow his eyes to take in the full picture of her.

The traditional dress of the future queen shimmered around her like an erotic caress, the small *balda* crystals in her gown glimmering as they caught the light. Tantalizing glimpses of her supple body teased him and his cock swelled painfully against his breeches. He fisted his hands to fight off the sudden urge to drag her off to bed and drive himself inside her hot welcoming heat. He downed the entire contents of his glass and welcomed the searing burn, which he hoped would bring him to his senses. The glass lifted from his fingers, no doubt to be refilled with similar contents since smug chuckles sounded from behind him.

The strain must've shown clearly on his face because Alyssandra tipped her head to the side and smiled before holding out her hand—a silent offer for him to escort her the rest of the way. The movement pressed one dusky areola flush against the cloth and her nipple beaded at the contact. His mouth watered to take the stiff nub into his mouth, the creamy texture of her skin, smooth against his tongue.

When Grayson gave him a gentle push, he started forward, never taking his eyes off her. The crowd parted before him, oddly silent as if they waited with anticipation to watch this scene unfold.

When he reached her side, his hand settled possessively against the small of her back, her warm skin burning against his hand through the thin cloth. "You leave me speechless yet again, Alyssandra."

Her smile brightened and a sudden blush stained her cheeks. She leaned forward to whisper in his ear, her warm breath feathering against his skin, shooting hot arousal straight to his groin. "I think I'll make it my personal goal to ensure I continue to surprise you, my prince."

He clamped his jaws together as a sudden vision of Alyssandra riding him while still wearing the gauzy outfit flashed through his mind. He wasn't sure if it was a vision she sent, or his own rampant imagination, but he shoved it aside and returned his attention to his princess. "I sincerely hope so." Taking a deep breath and ruthlessly chaining his straining control, he offered her his hand. "Shall we?"

"Of course." She grabbed a handful of his tunic and brought his lips down to press against hers and his control strained to its limits. He crushed her against him, plundering her mouth, her musky arousal scenting the air around him. Her soft curves fit against him perfectly and he fought against the sudden desire to rip the dress from her body and impale her with his cock right here on the stairs.

A large cheer from the crowd cleared his head with the same efficiency as a bucket of cold water, and he slowly pulled back away from her, concentrating on pulling air into his burning lungs.

Alyssandra's lips, still swollen from his kiss, curved up into a sheepish grin and she studied him for a moment from under her long dark lashes. Then she squared her shoulders, and raised her chin defiantly. "Shall we?"

With some difficulty, since a majority of the blood in his body still firmly resided in his groin, Stone offered her his hand. She gently placed her hand in his as he led her forward into the crowd.

The next several hours he stayed by her side, relieved when after the first few introductions, her tense shoulders relaxed and she seemed to genuinely enjoy herself. His parents, Ryan, and Grayson made several appearances, but once they were assured Alyssandra was fine, they faded into the crowd again.

Everyone she met seemed utterly taken with her and he watched in awe as she listened to each person like there was nothing more important in the world than what they had to say. He wondered if she consciously realized what she did, or if it came naturally. He bet on the latter. She truly cared for people and it showed in her every word and movement.

Several stopped to talk with her about her words at the Klatch Council meeting. They echoed her sentiments and assured her they were behind her and believed in her as their future queen. Before his eyes, she blossomed into a confident, self-assured woman, and he began to feel superfluous. With or without him, this woman was a born queen.

Two hours more and Stone's patience began to ebb. The celebration was a success, the people of Klatch loved her, but he was ready to have her all to himself. Suddenly each smiling face vying for her time grated against his nerves and he had a sudden urge to throw her over his shoulder as he shouted, "Mine!" and steal her away to the closest bedroom. Maybe the effects of the drinks Grayson and Ryan had provided were wearing off.

He'd briefly spoken to King Darius who confirmed that his possessiveness would get worse as the ceremony neared. Apparently, it was Tador's way of ensuring the attachment between the future king and queen. There was no problem from that quarter, he was already quite attached. He just hadn't counted on the strength of the impulses. He had to lock his jaw to keep from warning everyone away from his mate.

He breathed a sigh of relief when a gong sounded from the back of the cavernous room, signaling the arrival of the king and queen. The crowd drifted away from them, ready to watch the presentation. He steered Alyssandra toward the center of the room and stood waiting for her parents to emerge and present their daughter as the future queen.

Chapter 12

Alyssandra took a deep breath as her mother emerged wearing a similar dress to her own. She was surprised to see that even though her mother had been ill, her body was shapely and firm below the transparent material. Her breasts just as pert as Alyssa's even though she'd given birth and had gone braless her entire life. *Looks like the Klatch women have something up on Earth's women.*

The queen's hair was pulled back away from her face and the transparent cloth of her gown glowed a rich purple. Stone had explained that the energy that constantly traveled between the queen and the planet would resonate with the *balda* crystals causing the dress to glow. Apparently, once Alyssandra ascended the throne she would have the same effect on any crystals nearby—especially the native *balda*.

When King Darius entered behind his wife in a dark purple tunic and trousers emblazoned with the royal crest—a curved sword crisscrossed with a red rose—the entire assemblage kneeled and bowed their heads in respect.

A lump formed in Alyssa's throat as she looked up at her

parents on the small dais. She still woke every morning afraid that the entire thing would be a dream and that these two wonderful people only existed in her fantasies. But with only one more day until the coming-of-age ceremony, her heart was beginning to believe this life was real and could really be hers.

"Welcome to all." The queen spoke, startling Alyssa out of her musings. "We have waited many years for this day, as have all of you. The king and I are proud to present your future queen, our daughter, Alyssandra de Klatch, the First Princess of Klatch."

Cheers rose in every throat and Alyssandra stiffened against Stone who squeezed her shoulder to reassure her before leading her forward toward her mother. They had explained the presentation to her over and over, answering all her questions, but Alyssa was afraid that it wouldn't work and her entire fantasy world would fall apart. Or, even worse, that she would prove the legend true and funnel more power than Annalecia. They hadn't yet told the king and queen about the legend. They'd opted to wait and see if it was even necessary before they added more worry to them both.

This ceremony would prove to the people that Annalecia had an affinity for the energy of the planet. If all went well, the crystals in her dress would begin to glow like Annalecia's when they linked hands. Stone had no doubts it would work perfectly. However, Alyssa wasn't so confident.

Annalecia held out her hand and Alyssa raised her chin and took a deep breath before she stepped up onto the dais. *You can do this, Alyssa. You are no longer the invisible nobody you used to be.* She looked down at her mother's outstretched hand and swallowed hard before reaching forward and grasping it. Immediately, energy whipped through her and she gasped in surprise at its intensity. Even in her energy lessons with Stone, she never knew this level of energy existed. She reminded herself to breathe deeply and relax as the power flowed through her. She glanced out at the crowd and noticed a proud smile on Stone's face, and only then did she realize her own dress glowed.

The sizzle of energy continued to flow through her faster and faster, the glow intensifying until she had to close her eyes against the blinding glare. Her mother's fingers tightened around her own and she mentally stepped back and allowed the power to flow through her. Every pore of her body pulsed with energy and every erogenous zone in her body buzzed just on the verge of overload. She said a silent prayer that she wouldn't either spontaneously combust or have a sudden orgasm in front of everyone. This may be a sexual society, but Alyssa didn't think she could face anyone in the crowd after an onstage orgasm.

Her hair whipped around her face in a stinging mass and joy welled up inside her so bright that it shoved its way out her throat in a bubbling laugh that echoed around the cavernous room. She'd never felt so alive. If this was anything like what it was to share energy with the planet as queen, it definitely wouldn't be an unpleasant job. Especially with Stone helping her build up that energy. The vision of Stone, Grayson, and Ryan naked flashed through her mind again, making the energy howl as it increased, and for a moment, Alyssa thought she'd be blown off the dais from the force of it.

Her mother squeezed her hand once more before breaking their contact. She kept her eyes screwed shut until the glow receded before risking a glance toward the crowd. Hushed murmurs spread throughout the room like fire, building in intensity until they were shouts of celebration. Alyssa let out a breath she hadn't realized she'd been holding and turned toward her mother.

"You are the true Princess of Klatch, Alyssandra. Do you have any more doubts?"

Her skin tingled with aftershocks and she brushed her hands

over her arms to chase them away. "I'm not sure, but damn! That was amazing." She laughed at the sound of stunned awe in her voice.

Darius enveloped her in his strong embrace and brushed a simple kiss against her forehead before relinquishing her to Stone's care and turning back to his wife to help her into a chair. The queen's skin still glowed with energy, but in her weakened state, she tired easily.

The cheers still rioted around them like a living thing, and she turned to Stone in awe. "Was that supposed to happen?"

He reached out to rub a strand of her hair between two fingers, as if he were imprinting the texture on his memory. His sculpted lips curved up into a smug grin as he studied her. "As far as I know, it has never happened like that. I'm not sure if you realized it, but you just proved you're the princess of the legend."

Shock slapped at her, but before she had a chance to ask any more questions, the crowd flowed up onto the dais to show their undying support to their future queen.

Shawn slammed his fist on the table in front of Sela, enjoying the quick look of surprise that twisted her features before she masked it with anger and arrogance. "The ascension is nearly here and you have yet to find the princess. Where is your little whore, minion?"

Her blue eyes glittered with malice as she slowly stood and returned his stare. "Watch your step, Klatch. We offered you a way to redeem your race, but my patience has its limits." She picked invisible lint off her skintight blue tank top and slowly raised her eyes to his. "Debbie has located the portal, but we have yet to find a way to get the princess to be near enough where we can take her."

Shawn raised one eyebrow in what he hoped appeared to be

mock surprise. He had assumed they had someone on the inside to help them recover the princess. How else would they know which portal to take? He'd never been through the *between* but he'd heard about it. Bone deep cold and the neck ruffling smell of dank mold combined with the sensation of walking through air as thick as honey.

"Time grows short and I'm no longer willing to wait for your underlings to carry out their tasks. Give me the location and leave the luring of the princess to me." *She'll feel me near and come out to meet me.*

Sela snorted and raised her chin, looking down her nose at him. "If I thought you could walk all over Tador until you found her, we'd have sent you through any portal and waited for you to bring her back long ago. You may look like a Klatch, but I won't risk our entire future because you manage to get caught."

"I won't have to venture away from the portal at all. Just give me the location." He stared her down, enjoying the battle of wills. He stood so close, he could see the small imperfections in her eyeliner.

She crossed her arms tapping one manicured nail against her forearm while she studied him. Silence fell between them until she let out a hostile sigh and pierced him with a steely gaze. "A contingent of Cunts must go with you to ensure both of you come back."

"Agreed, but no more than four. I'll not risk *my* future because you're paranoid." He watched impassively as Sela ground her teeth and her eyes sparked with fury. He knew she had no choice but to agree, but he truly enjoyed baiting her.

She grabbed her cell phone from the table and hit buttons with her knuckle since her manicured nails were too long to allow her to use her fingertips. Then she placed her phone against her ear. "Escort Shawn to the portal location and take three others with you to ensure his compliance and return." She flipped her silvery blond hair back over her shoulder and glared at him with open hatred.

"Don't worry, Sela, I'll be back. My destiny is here, I don't plan to waste it."

A soft brush of awareness teased at the edges of Shawn's mind and he sighed in his sleep. In the next instant, the woman who'd invaded his thoughts, his dreams and his fantasies formed inside his mind as if out of vapor.

Her ripe lips curved into an inviting smile and her lavender eyes were rife with mischief. She opened her arms to him and he willingly went, molding himself against her luscious curves.

She sighed as he threaded his fingers through her silky waterfall of hair and fused his lips with hers. She responded eagerly, her lips parting to grant him entrance, the fresh honeyed taste of her sweet on his tongue. When she gently nipped his bottom lip and then sucked it, hot arousal arrowed straight to his cock and he ground himself against her, enjoying the needy mewling sounds she made in the back of her throat while she clung to him.

He slipped his hand under her soft half top to cup the weight of her breast and gently pinch her nipple until it pebbled into a tight nub. He moved his attention to the other breast enjoying the way it fit perfectly in his large palm as if made just for him. In fact, every inch of this woman seemed to be tailor-made just for him. She was all lush curves, soft skin, and soft sighs and he swore he would make her his. This would be the woman who helped him redeem his race.

The inner voice that had protected him since childhood had decreed it to be so and he reveled in the knowledge that soon, very soon, he would be able to thrust himself deep inside this tempting seductress, claiming her as his own. She would bear him a son, the start of the rebirth of his race, and the redemption of the Klatch people.

She broke the kiss to nibble a path down his jaw and neck causing his already swollen cock to swell almost painfully inside his jeans. Her questing hands cupped him, rubbing his aching shaft through the rough denim, an exquisite friction that tightened his balls against his body and threatened to shatter him.

He caught her hand and guided it back up toward his chest. She chuckled deep in her throat and then dipped her petite hands under his tunic to trace the lines of his chest and tease his flat male nipples.

He threaded his hands through the hair at her nape and tipped her head back until he could fuse his lips with hers. She immediately opened for him, inviting him in to explore her lush mouth. Her tongue dueled with his and she pressed her full breasts against him, her pebbled nipples poking through the soft cloth of her top and begging for his touch.

His fingers dipped under her cotton top again to trace one dusky areola, and he enjoyed the way the soft skin puckered under his teasing touch. She moaned against his mouth, the erotic sound vibrating against his lips and causing his groin to tighten. When he slowly rolled her engorged nipple between his fingers she gasped, her head falling back, baring the long line of her creamy neck.

He gladly accepted her offering and laved his tongue over the smooth expanse of skin, nipping and licking as she shivered with reaction. He pulled on her nipple, enjoying the needy mewling sounds rising from the back of her throat.

"Please . . ."

He chuckled and continued to feast on her neck while he traced his hand down her ribs and lower to dip inside her bikini underwear. The smooth skin of her mons felt like silk under his questing fingers and he traced a slow line down to dip between her wet folds to find her swollen nub.

She gasped and ground her hips against his hand, silently begging for release, her petite hands digging into his shoulders.

He dipped inside her, gathering her juices to lubricate his movements as he massaged her swollen clit. Her breathing quickened, and her skin heated as he drove her toward her release. "Look at me. I want to watch you when you come against my fingers."

She slowly raised her head to meet his steady gaze. Her eyes were glazed with desire, her skin flushed and her full lips parted as she watched him.

He increased the speed and pressure on her clit, enjoying the mindless noises she made as her peak neared. "Let go, sweetheart, come for me." The pungent scent of her arousal rose around him and he knew he wouldn't be able to last much longer. Her clit pulsed under his fingers and her eyes widened with shock as the orgasm hit her. Her eyelids drifted closed and her brows furrowed as the contractions continued to flow through her. She bit down on her bottom lip as she rode out the tide of her ecstasy, and the red flesh pillowed around her perfect white teeth undid him.

Hot come spurted forward to soak the inside of his jeans as his balls continued to contract tight against his body. Pleasure rolled over him in waves so large they threatened to drown him. He held on to her lush body, to anchor him until his release flowed away, leaving him lightheaded in a languid haze. He leaned his forehead against hers, as he tried to relearn how to breathe. No other woman had ever held him like this one. Even in his dreams—he knew she was the only one for him.

When she spoke, her warm breath feathered against his skin causing him to shiver in reaction, her smoky voice tightening his groin once more.

"*When will I see you? My coming-of-age draws near. I want*

*you to be the one to take my virginity, to fill me, to spill your
essence inside me."*

Her erotic words hardened him further and he brushed his
lips lightly over hers, fighting for control before he found his
voice. *"Keep watch for me, I'm on my way, Princess."*

She stepped back as if he'd slapped her, her eyes wide, a
small crease forming between her dark brows as her ripe lips
parted in shock.

"What is it? Sweetheart, tell me . . ." He reached out to her
and his hands passed through as if she were no more than a
ghost.

Shawn sat up in bed, peeling his soiled sheets away from his
body and scrubbing his hands over his face as tendrils of the
dream grudgingly let go of him. "I have to find her soon.
Something is very wrong." He slammed his fist against the mattress as his frustration threatened to overwhelm him. "Damn it!
I won't lose her. She's mine."

Sasha gasped and bolted upright in bed as the dream shattered and freed her into waking. Her breasts and pussy still tingled with his touch, her lips still swollen with his kisses. If she
closed her eyes, she could still feel the sweet friction as he
rubbed her clit until she came against his hand.

She buried her face in her hands. He'd come to her in her
dreams for months, filling her nights with ecstasy, companion-
ship, and longing, his presence lingering inside her mind even
when she was awake. She hadn't realized it until now, but in all
that time, he'd never addressed her by name. It was always
"beautiful," "sweetheart," or "love."

They'd forged a bond between them these last months, and
she'd held hope that he would be the man to help her complete
her coming-of-age. She twisted the sheets in her hands. His last
word dissolved all her dreams and hopes in an instant.

"Princess . . ." A slow fat tear carved a path down her cheek as the pain and betrayal sliced deep. "He doesn't want me. He wants Alyssandra." She hugged her knees to her chest and slowly rocked against the pain of her heart splitting in two. "I wonder how he mistook me for her?"

Her body betrayed her, her breasts and pussy aching for his touch even now. She shook her head in denial, even though she knew the truth.

She loved the princess and couldn't even bring herself to be jealous. She understood how a man could fall in love with someone like her, but that didn't stop the pain or the tears. Sobs wracked her and she curled into a ball and let the piercing emotions riot over her in waves.

Alyssandra slipped out of bed and pulled on her clothes, careful not to wake Stone. A suffocating wave of despair had woken her and she'd recognized it immediately as belonging to her lady's maid. Since Stone had taught her to control her power, she'd learned to recognize and differentiate the energy signatures of those close to her.

She slipped into the hall, startled to find four royal guards posted in front of her door. She didn't remember having guards while she slept, but then again, she'd never gone out in the middle of the night. Stone had always either kept her busy or sated enough that she'd never been awake deep into the night.

"Good evening, Princess." The leader stepped forward and bowed her head in respect. "Would you like an escort somewhere?"

She smiled sheepishly, feeling like a child caught sneaking out after curfew. "No, thanks. I'm just going next door to see my lady's maid, but I appreciate the offer. Can you tell the prince where I am if he wakes up? I don't want him to worry."

"Yes, of course, Princess."

She knocked lightly on Sasha's door before pushing it open just in time to see her maid disappear through a door in the far wall that had been hidden by a large tapestry. If Sasha's rioting emotions weren't still chafing against her senses, Alyssa would be excited to find out the castle had secret passages. As it stood, she was worried why Sasha would slip away in the middle of the night in such a state.

She rushed forward to catch the passageway door before it closed. If there was some sort of secret latch to open it, Alyssa didn't want to waste time searching for it. Sasha was obviously distraught.

"Sasha," she called, her voice echoing down the dimly lit stairwell that descended into the gloomy dark below. When she received no answer, she reached out with her tendril of energy to brush against the maid's mind. Deep despair, heartbreak, and a sense of urgency were the only things she could sense clearly, but she received no sense that Sasha was fleeing from her, or was even aware she followed.

Alyssa rushed down the steps, the smooth *balda* stone cool against her bare feet, her fingers brushing over the walls on either side to ensure she didn't fall. She'd expected the dark stairwell to reek of mold and disuse, but no dirt or rubble scuffed beneath her feet and the air smelled faintly of the flowering trees so prevalent on the castle grounds. Obviously, Sasha used this passage often.

When she reached the bottom, her nose met painfully with an unforgiving wall and she staggered back until she could get her bearings. Her fingers traced the wall in front of her looking for a doorknob or latch, but she found none. She couldn't even detect the seam where the door sat. Surely she hadn't hit a dead end? She traced her fingers over the wall on either side, again finding no seams for a door or opening. There was nowhere else Sasha could have gone.

She turned her attention back toward the wall in front of her. She braced her shoulder against the stone and leveraging her feet against the bottom stair, pushed hard. With a soft grating noise, the wall swung outward, opening into a small clearing behind a copse of flowering trees next to the castle. No wonder Alyssa had never noticed the door, it was ingeniously hidden from view from outside the castle.

She almost laughed as disappointment arrowed through her that her own chambers didn't have a secret passage. Maybe Stone would have one put in for her. Her lips curved at the amusement she knew would shine in his eyes if she asked for such a thing.

Pushing aside the flowered branches of two trees, she slipped between them out into the courtyard. Weak moonlight filtered down through the thick clouds allowing her to see her maid leave the courtyard headed toward the road where she'd first entered the castle compound one short week ago with Stone.

She immediately hurried after Sasha, her only thoughts to ensure her maid was all right.

When Alyssa stepped out onto the road, she spotted the maid ahead standing in an open field dotted with a riot of blooming flowers, the colors clearly visible even in the silvery moonlight. She started forward again and stopped short as tingling energy flowed over her, raising every hair on her body.

A shimmery portal opened between her and Sasha, and one Klatch man and four Cunts stepped through, startling her.

Sasha turned and her eyes widened in shock. "No!" Her voice made faint by the breeze, carried toward Alyssa as she started toward them at a run.

The Klatch newcomer turned toward Sasha, and Alyssa saw his broad smile even from the side as he opened his arms while she ran toward him. *Was this the man Sasha had blushed over when asked about her coming-of-age?*

The four Cunts spared no glance for Sasha, but purposely stepped toward Alyssa, their hands raised with invisible threads of spells already cast. She raised her arms, flinging a shield of energy outward at the same time, deflecting their spells. Her haphazard bolts of pink power hit two of her attackers squarely in the chest and they dropped to the ground in boneless heaps. The other two continued forward, and all the air whooshed from her lungs as one of their draining spells hit her from the side.

"*Stone!*" She knew he'd never make it to her in time, but pain washed over her at the thought of never seeing him again.

Footsteps and shouts sounded from behind her and she knew reinforcements were on their way from the castle, but she also knew they were too late. Another draining spell hit her squarely in the chest and small black spots danced in front of her eyes. Her fuzzy gaze locked with Sasha's a split second before blackness closed in around her.

Stone paced his chamber, his anger warring with fear as his boots rang against the white *balda* floor with every step.

"Stone?" Annalecia's weak voice banked his anger and he turned, surprised when she hugged him tight. His reserve crumbled and he sunk into the comforting embrace, curling his arms around her and resting his chin on her head.

He met Darius's steady gaze over the queen's head, surprised to see only pain there and not judgment and accusation. "I'm so sorry I didn't protect her as I promised. I didn't even know she'd gone."

Annalecia pulled back and then, taking his hand, led him over to sit down on the bed before she settled into the overstuffed chair. Dark circles marred the pale skin under her eyes and her hair hung over her shoulders, lifeless and dull. Alyssa's sudden disappearance had put even more strain on the queen's weakened system.

Once his wife was settled, Darius took the chair beside her. "You thought she was safely asleep and the guards thought she was safely in Sasha's room. There was no way to know about that secret passage. Although apparently quite a few of the lady's maids and manservants' rooms have them, according to Sasha. If none of the royal families have known of them for centuries, you can't berate yourself for not factoring in that option."

Stone ran his hands through his hair in frustration. "You should've let me go after her." He gingerly touched his swollen cheekbone where he'd taken an elbow from one of the guards while they restrained him from jumping through the portal behind Alyssandra. If he were a few seconds quicker, he could've saved her.

It had taken almost the entire royal guard to subdue him and both they and he were worse for the wear. Once he'd calmed down and been locked into his chamber under heavy guard, the sergeant of the guard had reminded him that there could've well be an entire army of Cunts on the other side of the portal.

He knew he wasn't thinking rationally and yet he still didn't care, he would gladly give his life to save Alyssandra. However, the guards and the king and queen wouldn't allow him that opportunity.

The queen reached out toward Stone and he pulled back before she could touch him. "You need all the energy you have, my lady. Don't waste any on healing me."

Her wan smile widened. "I was just going to remind you that your duty is to Tador, and not just to Alyssandra, no matter how much we all wish it could be different. We can not afford to lose you too." Her chin lifted in a gesture so much like Alyssandra's it squeezed his heart painfully inside his chest. "If she . . . doesn't return, you must be mated with another royal princess. There are a few that have been widowed that are of age, even though they are quite a bit older than you. They are our last hope if Alyssandra doesn't return. Tador is waning, as am I." Her eyes glistened with unshed tears and she blinked them away.

Stone wondered if could ever put the planet's welfare over

that of his own child. Maybe he was the one who shouldn't be on the throne. Maybe he wasn't even worthy of Alyssandra. He had no doubt that she would do whatever was necessary in any circumstances. He closed his eyes and scrubbed his hands over his face, his beard stubble scratching against his palms. "I don't know if I can," he said honestly.

He looked up at both of them in turn. They were his godparents and if he had any power over the situation, his future in-laws. They'd known him his entire life and he loved them like second parents. He'd grown up instilled with a sense of duty to Tador and its people, but for the first time in his life, he balked at his duty—because to him, one woman's life was worth more than the entire planet.

"I can't imagine spending my life with anyone but Alyssandra. She is all I desire. You may have to find another prince to fill my role. If Alyssandra is not queen . . . then I cannot be king." Stone knew without a doubt that he was the strongest Klatch Prince of the sixteen houses, and yet, he knew he would not take the throne without her. She'd ruined him for any other— the consequences be damned.

Darius leaned forward to pierce Stone with a paternal gaze. Stone steeled himself for the king's words, but what he said surprised him. "All is not lost yet, boy."

Stone startled at the king referring to him as "boy." Darius hadn't used the term for him in many years and then only when he was disappointed in Stone's behavior. His curiosity piqued, he looked up to meet the king's gaze.

"Her powers are strong, as is her will and her love for you, us, and the planet that is her birthright. She grew up among those who have taken her, and that gives her a sizable advantage. Don't forget that."

Stone shot to his feet, fear for Alyssandra and helplessness that threatened to overwhelm him turning into white-hot anger. "An advantage? They know all her fears and insecurities, and they have her outnumbered. Who knows what they'll do to her?" Fear slowly rose above his anger, settling inside him like a heavy weight that caused his stomach to roil and pitch. "They will—"

Darius's voice continued calmly on. "They will underestimate her, as they have always done. They don't view her as a formidable princess coming into her rightful powers, but as the downtrodden woman they've conditioned for the past twenty-three years. Even in her short time here, she's blossomed into the woman she should've been. A woman who will be the next queen." He leaned back in his chair, his features proud, his voice clear. "Have faith in my daughter, Stone. I'm confident she won't disappoint you."

Stone thought back to all the times her resilience and strength had surprised even him. The king had a good point, but sitting here doing nothing while the woman he loved was alone and in danger grated against him. Helplessness flowed over him in a suffocating wave and he pushed it away before it overwhelmed him.

"Thank you, Darius. Forgive me for doubting her." He sat again, forcing his features to relax and his fists to open. "It's difficult for me to sit and wait, not being able to help her."

"That is a dilemma we both share. Inaction doesn't suit me either, but in this case, it's the best course."

Stone bit back a retort and reined in his fear and anger. He had to concentrate on the here and now and trust Alyssandra to find her way back. "What did Sasha say?" He'd demanded to speak to the maid several times over the last few hours and the guards had treated him with deference and respect, but on that count totally ignored him. He'd threatened to have them all beheaded and any other horrible retribution he could think of, and they'd all just nodded and said, "Yes, my lord."

He sighed. He would have a lot of apologizing to do once

Alyssandra was safely back in his bed, permanently tied down, where she belonged.

Annalecia laid a gentle hand on his knee and he steeled himself not to flinch away, but when no flow of healing power trickled against his skin, he relaxed. He hadn't been able to protect the princess, but he refused to weaken the queen further. "Sasha is devastated. She feels responsible for Alyssandra's capture."

Stone bit back his bitter retort. No wonder they hadn't let him talk to Sasha, he would've frightened the poor maid to death. His mind flashed back to the day he'd saved Sasha from being raped by Cunts. She'd been so young and vulnerable, and she'd looked at him with admiration shining in her eyes ever since. It was probably for the best the guards hadn't let him talk to her. In his anger, he would've most likely destroyed their friendship.

He took a few deep breaths to regain his composure and nodded for the queen to continue.

"Here's the interesting part. She's been visited in her dreams for several months by a very attractive Klatch man she's never seen before. He's been courting her in her dreams, much like you did with Alyssandra. She thought he was from an outlying village. Then last night, since her coming-of-age is near, she asked him when they would meet and he told her to keep watch for him as he was on his way."

The queen paused and unease snaked down Stone's spine. He'd known her his entire life, and knew from the guarded expression on her face he wouldn't like what she said next. "And then?" he prompted.

Annalecia met his determined gaze and then sighed. "And then . . . he called her 'Princess'." Silence hung heavy in the air for a few moments as the implications sucker punched Stone in the gut, making his stomach churn with nausea and fear. "When

Sasha sensed him near, she ran out to meet him to tell him she wasn't the princess in hopes he truly loved her and not just the title—regardless of the mistaken identity."

Stone shot to his feet again as puzzle pieces fitted together inside his mind. Alyssandra's vision of the Klatch man who wasn't him and men with blond pubic hair surrounding her at the ascension ceremony.

Then there was Sasha. He'd always liked the spunky little maid, and thought her a perfect companion for his fiery princess. How devastated must she have been? The man she thought in love with her had mistaken her for the princess and then betrayed them both.

He knew instinctively Sasha hadn't willingly led Alyssandra into a trap. His stubborn little betrothed had done that all on her own, he was sure. Her compassion for others was an admirable trait and one of the reasons he loved her, but she also had a knack for finding herself in trouble for it. This time was apparently no different.

Guilt flowed through him as he realized he should've heeded Annalecia's warning and told the princess the truth about her vision. Then at least she might have been more careful before running out at night straight into an open portal full of Cunts ready to take her back to fulfill a false ascension ceremony. He made a silent promise to himself that he wouldn't keep things from her in the future. For all his efforts to protect her, he had only endangered her.

"They are going to try to recreate the ascension so we'll be forced to allow them to return to Tador. Without a queen who has the symbiosis with the planet, we will all die." Stone shook his head. It was an ingenious and foolproof plan—if they could pull it off. Stone was sure every Klatch alive would do everything within their power to prevent it. They'd fought and won the war once; they would do so again. He just wished Alyssandra wasn't in danger. His gut twisted at the thought—especially since he held a large amount of the responsibility for putting her there.

Darius stood. "We must trust Alyssandra to find her way home. Even if they force her to submit to the ceremony, she would never do anything to harm Tador. It's too much a part of her."

Stone's heart twisted at the thought of Alyssandra being forced to submit to another man entering her body. He shoved the unthinkable vision away. He didn't disagree with Darius. In fact, that's what worried him. Alyssandra would rather die than be used in such a manner. He just hoped she found enough other options available to her that it didn't come to that. He knew Alyssandra wasn't helpless, but a few self-defense classes and her raw unbridled power were not enough to ease his sense of worry.

Hatred burned through him in a white-hot rush as he thought about the nameless Klatch man taking his beloved by force. "The traitor had better hope the false ascension does not complete or I'll hunt him down and make him wish for death."

Darius met his steady gaze and the men shared a look of complete understanding. Anyone who hurt Alyssandra would lead a very short and painful life.

Chapter 13

As awareness returned, Alyssa lay very still as she took stock. Her heart pounded so hard within her chest, she was surprised it didn't split in two. Every part of her body ached—even her hair, and the inside of her mouth tasted like she'd licked a freeway clean. The sound of her breathing grated against the pain in her head like jet engines. She recognized her symptoms as the effects of too many draining spells in a short period of time. Before her time on Tador, she'd lived this way almost every day, not realizing that Debbie continually drained her like she was a walking energy donor.

She debated the wisdom of opening her eyes—not only would it let anyone watching know she was awake, but she was sure the light she saw through her eyelids would pierce through her brain like branding irons. *Get a grip, Alyssa! You need to figure out where you are and find a way back to Stone before the ascension. Your mother and all of Tador hang in the balance.* The fear of losing her mother and condemning her home world were enough to make her force her eyelids open.

Pain blazed through her and she blinked and flung her arm over her face in an effort to let her eyes adjust slowly.

"She's awake." Debbie's voice from across the room sent chills down her spine. It was laced with pure evil and promised retribution. "Inform Sela and the Klatch bastard."

Anger flowed through Alyssa's veins like a wave of hot lava, forcing back the pain and the weakness. She opened her eyes and pushed herself up to sit on the edge of the cot. Debbie stood leaning against the wall, her arms crossed under her perky breasts, looking much like Alyssa remembered her—silvery blond hair, fair skin, and a condescending grin.

"Too busy off fucking a football team to have the balls to come after me yourself, Debbie?" She smiled when her voice sounded steady and confident, and bit back a laugh when Debbie's smug grin faltered for a moment before she replaced it.

"I had more important things to do than chase after a rodent." Debbie straightened and winced, favoring her side. "Besides, I'd done my job. I played nursemaid to you for far too long."

Alyssa briefly wondered what punishment Debbie had received for allowing her to escape with Stone.

An invisible tendril of power shot out from the Cunt, but before it connected with Alyssa, she instinctively held up her hand and called energy from all around her to counter it. The power rebounded on its maker with a sizzling zap. A feral cry ripped from Debbie's throat and she slumped to the floor in a boneless heap.

Slow applause from behind her had Alyssa pushing away from the cot to stand with her back against the wall.

Sela stood just inside the small room with a Klatch man and several Cunt guards ranged behind her. As usual, she wore a skintight outfit, her small breasts nearly spilling from the low-cut top, and leggings that looked almost painted on. The outfit served to accentuate the model-thin figure and lack of curves so prevalent in all the Cunts.

I can't believe I used to wish I looked like that. She started as she realized that for the first time in her life she was comfortable with who she was—not just physically, but as a woman. It was ironic that it took seeing her old "family" again to show her just how far she'd come. She swore it wouldn't be wasted.

Sela stepped forward into the room and tsked, "Debbie never was very competent. I should've gotten rid of her long ago. Apparently, she's served her purpose—I wondered if you'd come into your powers yet. It makes all those years of putting up with your sniveling worth it in the end. That means I calculated correctly, and you are the princess who will ascend the throne, and also the one the legend speaks of."

Alyssa hid her shock at Sela's observation and wondered how Sela thought she could twist that to benefit the Cunts.

Sela's laughter crept over her skin like roaches skittering over her flesh and Alyssa raised her hand to zap Sela as she had Debbie.

Before she could call her power, multiple blasts of energy hit her in the chest and stomach. Pain arrowed through every part of her body and her energy spiraled away, drained by the blasts.

She moaned and locked her legs to keep from sliding down the wall onto her butt. *Okay, note to self—have to use the blast spells strategically so I don't get my ass kicked!*

"I took the liberty of having several of the Cunt guards handy. I'm pleased you found your powers little mouse, now it's time to fulfill your destiny. Sundown is in two hours and then you will be mated to Shawn." She gestured behind her and Alyssandra recognized the man as the Klatch man in her vision. "Debbie was going to introduce you two anyway. You just ran off with that bastard prince before she had a chance." Sela stepped closer, her eyes narrowed in a look that used to make Alyssa cower, but no longer. "You'll finally get your wish to have someone happy to fuck you on a regular basis. Just don't mess it up. You've already wasted far too much of my time."

Shawn seemed to be studying her intently, almost as if angry she was there at all.

Alyssa forced herself upright and raised her chin defiantly as she glared at Sela, letting all her fury show clearly in her expression. "Fuck you, Sela. You stole my childhood, and you've endangered my home world. If you think you're going to get me to agree to a mating ceremony with anyone but my betrothed, you're fucking crazy."

The Klatch man's eyes narrowed but he remained silent. Sela's booming laugh rolled through the room causing gooseflesh to march across Alyssa's skin. "Whoever said anything about asking *you?*" She spat out the last word, something Alyssa remembered quite well growing up. "You will be tied to the altar and used as breeding stock, as your inferior race should be. And you'll be thankful I don't gut you where you stand for your disobedience. I've spent the past two decades waiting for my vengeance against Annalecia and Darius, and I swear I'll have it."

She stiffened as Sela's words sank in. They meant to rape her and complete the ceremony and then use her to hurt her parents and all of Tador. Her mind blanked as panic set in, and even though tears burned unshed in the back of her eyes, she furiously held them back. Showing Sela weakness would only invite more abuse. Her only hope now was to bide her time until she could escape.

Alyssa squared her shoulders and opened her mouth to protest, and was hit with another blast of power from the guards. Agonizing pain flowed down the same paths they had before, making her feel as if her bones would explode under the pressure. She crumpled to the floor curling into a fetal position and just concentrated on breathing in and out while black spots danced in front of her vision. Passing out didn't seem like a very good plan right now.

"Stop!" The Klatch man stepped forward, into the stream of the draining spell and turned to face Sela. Alyssa gasped when the pain suddenly stopped, surprised that the guards didn't continue to zap the man. "If you drain all her energy, she won't survive the ascension ceremony, Sela. Then where will all your grand plans be? Try to think with something besides your overused pussy and your temper for once before you endanger all our destinies."

Sela's cool blue eyes glittered with hatred, but she finally nodded toward the guards who dropped their hands and stepped back. She pointed her index finger at the Klatch she'd called Shawn. "Be very careful how you speak to me, Klatch. One of these days, your usefulness will run out. She *will* survive the ceremony and she *will* bear a child. If you need to provide her with enough energy to get her through, then make sure you do it. I won't have my years of sacrifice wasted."

She started to turn away and then hesitated. "Just remember, the honor of your people depends on this. No doubt they've filled her head with lies, so watch out for her sharp tongue." A quick gesture to her guards and they followed her out, slamming the door behind them.

Alyssa raised her chin as Shawn turned to look down at her. His jaw was chiseled like Stone's, but there was no fullness of the lips or softness around the eyes to make him seem approachable. This man seemed carved from solid granite, his eyes dark and guarded—even though they were the familiar lavender of the Klatch.

She tried to push to her feet, but her muscles still refused to cooperate. She held a hand out in front of her, realizing she didn't even have enough power to stun him if she needed to. "I warn you, if you lay one finger on me, I'll find a way to kill you." Her voice wavered a bit, ruining the tough girl perception she was trying to give.

He ignored her as if she were no threat at all. "Who was the other woman in the clearing where we found you?" It was more demand than question, as if he were used to giving orders. He stepped forward crowding into her personal space and she tensed in case she had to attack, while her energy was still low. "Who was she?"

It took a few minutes for the question to cut through the haze of pain and fear clouding Alyssa's brain. When it did, her brow furrowed in confusion and her senses sharpened. What did he want with Sasha? How did he even know her? She lifted her chin, raised her brow and pierced him with a steady gaze. "Why?" She held his gaze, waiting for an answer.

He seemed ready to argue, but then his lips softened from the harsh thin line and he almost seemed . . . vulnerable. "I have to know. Please, who is she?" Pain and loss laced his deep voice.

She studied him for several long moments, trying to decide if she should tell him or not. Her gut told her to give him the truth, and she'd learned not to ignore her intuition. "Sasha is my lady's maid."

His jaw clenched and he shook his head back and forth in denial, pain etched into his pale eyes. "No! She can't be." He paced to the door and back before returning to stare down at her. "The voice told me she was my destiny. She should be mine. *She* should be the princess."

Terrific, someone who hears voices. Just what I needed to make my day complete. "Then come back to Tador with me and I'll introduce you." *To the dungeon—if we even have one.*

His laugh was a bitter bark. He glared down at her, contempt curling his lip, any softness gone from his harsh features. "Unfortunately for you, Princess, a commoner can't give me what I need to fulfill my destiny, so we're stuck with each other. No matter how both of us wish it were otherwise." His last few words seemed sad—almost as if he wished he didn't have to go through with the ceremony.

That makes two of us.

"Prepare yourself, because the ceremony *will* be completed."
Then he turned and left, slamming the door behind him.

Alyssa closed her eyes and rested her head back against the
wall. Her energy was slowly returning, but if she was going to
find a way to escape, she needed to generate some in a hurry.
"Terrific," she muttered. "One fucking day back on earth and
I'm back to whacking off."

Natasha's eyes snapped open as Alyssandra's fear buzzed
against her mind. "Damn it! They've captured her." She sat up
on her thin cot and allowed her eyes to adjust to the dark room.
Only one guard stood against the far wall tonight, most likely
the rest were preparing for Sela's false ascension. There were
usually at least four guarding her in constant shifts, to keep her
from escaping. Even when they held Alyssandra as a bargaining
chip, they hadn't entirely trusted that to keep her in line.

Sela probably thought she was of little consequence now,
but Natasha planned to surprise her. She hadn't spent the last
twenty plus years in this dingy corner cell to watch Sela destroy
her son, the royal family, and her entire home world. She'd had
little choice but to wait all this time without risking the princess
and her son, but waiting time was definitely over.

She stood and slowly stretched, ensuring the tips of her
breasts pressed against her thin T-shirt. When her gaze slid toward the guard, he hadn't budged. *Great. I get the one Cunt
not interested in a show.* Sela had never allowed her any clothes
except for grungy T-shirts and sweatpants, but Natasha was
still a Klatch Witch with resources at her disposal.

She sighed dramatically and pulled her shirt over her head
before dropping it on her bed. Her nipples pebbled in the cool
air and she inhaled to display her breasts to their best advantage. She may be twenty years older than when she got here, but
she'd kept in shape—in spite of Sela not allowing her any activities save reading. She reached up to cup her full breasts and

lightly pinch the nipples, allowing a soft moan to escape from her parted lips.

A small rustling sound from across the room made her smile. *That's right. Come watch the show.* She hooked her thumbs into the waistband of her sweatpants and slowly slipped them down over her hips, inch by inch, until they pooled around her feet and she stepped out of them. She rubbed her hands over her breasts again, teasing the tight buds of her nipples with gentle strokes from the tips of her fingers. She rolled the engorged nipples between her thumbs and forefingers, enjoying the sharp intake of breath from her audience. She allowed a groan to escape her lips and she slowly trailed one hand down to her mound.

"You're certainly not being shy today, Klatch." The guard's blue eyes darkened and he licked his lips as he watched.

She sat down on her cot, leaning her back against the wall and propping one foot up, so the guard would have an unimpeded view of her slick folds. She reached down to trace them while she talked, slowly massaging her clit until her hips began their slow rhythm and her breathing deepened. She looked up at the guard and slowly licked her lips, silently noting when his eyes darkened.

"It's been twenty-three years since I've had a thick cock filling me. Twenty-three long years since I've felt hot come spurt deep inside my core, or even deep inside my throat. Masturbation can only take me so far. A woman has needs, you know. No matter what her home species."

Sela had always strictly forbidden any of the guards to come within twenty feet of Natasha's cell while guarding her. Food and any necessities were brought in and out twice a day by a Cunt who had been castrated for failing to pleasure Sela one night. Probably Sela's way of keeping her from tempting the man with sexual favors to help her. Natasha hoped since Sela had only left one guard, that he was more interested in sex than following orders. She needed the energy to escape and she would be more than happy to drain his in exchange for a few quick bouts of sex.

Natasha licked her fingers before tracing them down her slit and dipping them inside her hot pussy. She smiled as the guard's lips parted and his eyes riveted to her crotch. "Why don't you come over here and help me?"

Carefully, she sent out Klatch pheromones, her special gift, and watched in satisfaction as the bulge in his jeans swelled and his breath came in short panting gasps. Her pheromones were very subtle and would only work on one person at a time, but they seemed to be working overtime on this one.

"Sela has forbidden us to approach you." He took a few steps forward and then stopped, shifting uncomfortably at the erection straining at his jeans.

Natasha sighed and turned on her pheromones full force, silently praying they hadn't lost their potency with so many years of non-use. She'd been afraid to use them with the groups of guards. A gang bang would drain her of energy, not allow her to gain the upper hand. "I've been locked in this cell for two decades. Don't you think if I was as much a threat as Sela thinks I would've escaped long before now?"

The guard seemed to consider, his long silver-blond hair glinting in the florescent light. "We do have several hours before anyone will come down here." His pale features suddenly hardened and he pinned her with a steely gaze. "But if you try anything, I'll drain your power and then fuck you anyway before I throw you to all the other Cunt warriors as a play toy. Understood?"

She nodded, trying her best to look meek. "Understood. I just need a large cock filling me. You don't know what it's like to go so long without fucking." She continued to finger herself while he undressed and then unlocked her cell.

She smiled up at him and then allowed her eyes to travel downward toward the stiff cock straining from a nest of blond curls. *Not as impressive as a Klatch cock, but not too bad. It will have to do. Time to turn the tables on these Cunt parasites.*

His eyes devoured every inch of her as he looked her up and down appreciatively. "You know, for an old woman who's been locked up in here for as long as you have, you're still a nice piece of ass. I can't wait to fuck you until you scream and show you what a Cunt man can do."

She licked her lips slowly and turned on the pheromones as high as they would go, hiding a smirk when his cock turned red from the sudden rush of blood and his balls tightened against his body—painfully, if his grimace was any indication.

"Lie down." His words were strained and curt.

Natasha smiled and scooted down on the cot so she could lie flat. No sooner had she settled herself than he fell on top of her, pushing her legs open and plunging himself inside. Natasha was glad she'd made herself wet first, or his lack of finesse would've been very uncomfortable. Apparently, Cunts weren't much for foreplay. She was surprised at how tight a fit he was even though Shawn's father had a much larger cock. But then, she hadn't had sex in twenty-three years.

She wrapped her legs around his waist and allowed him to set the rhythm. She moved her hips, bucking against him until the first sizzle of energy shot through her—his pre come. Her muscles tightened and tingled as they absorbed the life-giving energy and cried out for more. It would've taken her a month of masturbation to gain as much energy as one ejaculation.

She kept her pheromones on high, which caused him to piston inside her, even while sweat trickled down his face and his breathing hitched.

"Come for me, Cunt. I need your energy."

As if her words triggered his release, a thousand volts of power shot though her body as he emptied himself inside her and collapsed against her breasts. She smiled and wrapped her arms around him even as he hardened inside her again.

He raised his head to look down at her, his eyes wide with shock. "No wonder Sela's been keeping you a secret. You're a tight little package and I think I could fuck you all night."

She laughed and swatted his ass playfully. "I'm ready for you. Show me what I've been missing, Cunt." *A few more of your orgasms and I'll turn off my pheromones and let you sleep off your energy hangover, big boy.*

By the time the Cunts returned to her room to fetch her for the ceremony, Alyssa thought her clit would fall off from all the masturbating she'd done over the past hour. She'd never realized how long it took to build up her energy while masturbating. She wished Stone were here to come inside her, then she'd have all the energy she needed. However, locked in this room alone, there didn't seem a lot of other options open to her.

She'd tried to visualize like she'd done back on Tador, but her throbbing head from all the energy drains had made it impossible for her to form her visions. Now she just needed to bide her time and wait for her chance.

Twenty rather large Cunt men roughly escorted her to the basement and then pushed her ahead of them to land in a heap at Sela's feet. Alyssa caught herself right before she smacked her teeth against Sela's perfectly pedicured feet encased in strappy sandals.

"Strip the bitch and tie her to the altar." Sela's voice boomed across the chamber before Alyssa could push herself to her feet.

Dozens of hands ripped the traditional Klatch clothing from her body and then lifted her. Before she'd visited Tador, she would've been mortified to be so exposed, but her time on her home world had taught her to be comfortable with her body as well as her sexuality. Maybe she could find a way to use her new confidence to her advantage.

She struggled, but even with her additional energy, there was no way she could break free of so many. They flipped her onto her back and she landed hard against the stone altar, her breath knocked out of her in a painful rush. When she finally caught her breath, her hands were tied securely over her head. *Great! So much for breaking out of here before I'm served up on an altar as a sex appetizer.*

She forced herself to take deep even breaths until her panic receded. She had to find a way out of this and back to Stone. She took a moment to study the room. Hundreds of different colored candles sat on every available surface burned down to varying lengths, their flames casting menacing shadows over the cement walls. The altar beneath her was rough stone against her bare back and short enough so it stopped midthigh, and dug into her skin painfully. But then she didn't think Sela and the rest of the Cunts were very concerned about her comfort.

"Shawn," Sela bellowed. "Get it done, now. Fuck the little bitch and breed me that heir."

The twenty Klatch men who had escorted her to the basement crowded around the altar, stroking their pale cocks and looking her over like she was the lone gazelle in the lion's den.

"Step away from her!" Shawn's voice echoed through the basement, his anger palpable in the air around them. "Don't let any of your essence touch her until the time is right. She's not any good to us dead." He turned his wrath toward Sela. "That's the last time you'll endanger this ceremony. My future depends on this and I'll not have your hot temper destroying it. If you give one more order, I swear I'll kill you myself."

Sela swallowed, but held her ground. "Just make sure you finish it." She nodded toward her guards.

The ring of pale cocks receded and Alyssa breathed a sigh of relief. She glared at Shawn. "If you lay a finger on me, I'll make sure you die a slow, painful death after I rip off your tiny cock and wear it for a necklace." When her voice came out sounding authoritative and sure this time, she said a silent prayer of thanks. She might not have a clue what to do, but at least she sounded confident. That had to count for something.

Shawn looked down at her from the foot of the altar, the gap in his dark blue robe revealing a muscular chest dusted with crispy black hairs. "I regret your wrath, Princess, but our destinies are set. I'll try to make this as painless as possible. It would help if you'd relax and cooperate."

It was on the tip of her tongue to tell him to fuck off, but seeing as fucking her was part of his plan, she amended it to, "Go to hell. You're a traitor to your people, you bastard!"

Ignoring her, Shawn dropped his robe, revealing broad shoulders and arms that proved he definitely had a gym membership. "I'm trying to rectify the evil the Klatch did and redeem our race. Our children will help ensure that."

He stepped to the side of the altar, giving her a bird's-eye view of his long, thick cock. He smirked down at her, as if he knew she was mentally recanting her tiny cock comment. He was only partially hard, but she could see he would be almost as impressive as Stone fully erect.

"Don't worry, Princess. I'll have you sufficiently aroused by the time I take your virginity. But for now, you need to take my essence into your mouth." He began to stroke himself as he looked down at her. "I'll pry your jaw open if I have to, but I'd rather not hurt you."

Aroused . . . She hid her smile as an idea formed inside her head. Her time learning to control energy would definitely not be wasted. She closed her eyes and concentrated on building a shield of energy around her—a dome to deflect any spells sent her way if they figured out what she was up to. When it pulsed around her settling into place, she split off several thin tendrils of energy and sent them carefully toward every person in the room. She concentrated on heightening their arousal, a talent her mother mentioned she had, but Alyssa had never tried. If anything would work, this had to.

Her power slipped silently inside them, insidiously, teasing their senses until she ignited small fires throughout their bodies. Then she increased her focus, fanning the flames until their arousal took on a life of its own, building steadily. Her energy whispered inside their minds describing the erotic slide of flesh against flesh and their bodies tingled and tightened in response. The pungent smell of arousal and sweat slowly filled the room.

When she opened her eyes, Shawn's cock had stiffened and his eyes had darkened with desire. *It's working!* She drew energy from the fresh arousal swimming around her in the room and pulled it back into herself, turning it to her will before sending it back out to continue building their arousal even higher.

Shawn stroked faster and faster, until his passion-glazed eyes lost their luster and they narrowed even as his jaw clenched. A grimace twisted his features as groans of discomfort sounded from around the room.

Alyssa increased her efforts until a few of the Cunt men fell to the floor, grasping their crotches. Shawn's face turned purple and he grasped the edge of the altar to keep from falling.

Several bolts of blue power sizzled against the shield she'd erected around her and were harmlessly absorbed, strengthening her protection with every strike. She increased her concentration, driving blood flow to erogenous zones and arousal hormones flowing on overdrive.

"Shawn! Do something." Sela's strained voice sounded from across the room and Alyssa increased her flow of power until Sela's words thinned and silenced.

Shawn's hand sizzled against her shield until the stench of burning flesh filled the chamber, almost choking Alyssa. He pulled his hand away cradling it against his body, while his other hand still held his now purple cock. His features twisted with pain, but he stared down at her with determination. "Don't fight me, Princess. This is our destiny," he said through gritted teeth as sweat dripped down the sides of his face.

"Let me up, Shawn. Let me up or I'll make sure you cock explodes in your hand!" She tried frantically to figure out a way to use her "break the spell" power on her bindings, but she couldn't do that and maintain the arousal spell at the same time, not to mention her shield. She'd reached the limits of her budding power. *Damn, why didn't I think to do that first?*

Shawn shook his head and swayed against the altar as the door banged open and a Klatch woman wearing oversized sweats and a T-shirt rushed into the room. "Let her go, Shawn. She's not meant for you."

Shawn's eyes widened in shock. "The voice . . . You're the voice."

The newcomer kicked Sela in the face and a sickening crunch echoed around the basement. Not that Alyssa wouldn't have gladly done the same thing, but the sudden violence of the action surprised her. "Sasha is your destiny. The princess is not for you. Come with me, and everything will be revealed." She didn't wait for his answer, but turned her attention to Alyssa. She reached through Alyssa's power shield, unharmed, and sliced the bonds tying her before turning to open a shimmering portal in the air just in front of the altar. "Don't stop your power until we're through the *between*. Help me with Shawn."

Alyssa's brow furrowed, but she didn't question this new voice of authority—besides, she didn't know how to open a portal by herself, especially one that would take her where she wanted to go. She wrapped her protective shield around her like a blanket before she opened it just enough to grab Shawn's arm and shove him through the portal. She took one last look around at the groaning Cunts before she jumped off the altar and into the shimmering portal behind him.

Her naked skin tingled inside the darkness of the *between* and she concentrated on walking in a straight line. She trudged forward, her movements becoming more sluggish as her energy waned. As the woman advised, she continued directing her power, to buy time so they wouldn't be followed before they were safely back on Tador. Her limbs moved in slow motion as though she were trying to walk through thick molasses and she used all her remaining strength to force each foot in front of the other.

Thoughts of Stone and her mother pushed her forward until she fell through the other side of the portal, at the feet of several of the Klatch royal guard. She blinked against the bright sunshine in confusion until she remembered that earth and Tador were always on opposite schedules.

She'd done it. She'd arrived back at Tador before night had fallen, before her ascension was scheduled to begin. She called her remaining power back and it returned in a small rush that sounded like a balloon popping. Laugher, full and rich, bubbled up inside her until it spilled out, even as tears streamed down her face. "I'm home!"

Chapter 14

Stone sensed Alyssandra's presence and immediately set out at a run toward the portal. He'd been on his way back after checking on the queen, whose condition was worsening at an alarming rate. When he burst outside and rounded the building, he ran out into the courtyard, the noise of a commotion pushing him faster.

Fear for Alyssandra rose up like bile in the back of his throat and he swallowed hard as the shimmery portal came into view. Several guards ringed the portal blocking his view and he shoved them aside hoping for a glimpse of the princess.

He stopped short as he saw her. She lay on the flower-covered ground totally naked and laughing while tears streamed down her face. He started forward, but stopped when two more people fell through the portal and were immediately set upon by the guards.

Alyssandra rolled out of the way as she was nearly trampled by the guards in their haste to subdue the Klatch man and woman who'd emerged behind her. Stone rushed forward lifting her into his arms and crushing her against his chest as he'd longed to do since she'd gone missing.

She threw her arms around his neck and buried her face against him. "Stone. I was so scared I wouldn't make it back in time."

"Alyssandra." He closed his eyes inhaling her scent, gripping her to him, almost afraid at any minute she'd dissolve away. "Are you all right? Did they hurt you? Did they . . ."

She pulled back far enough to look up at him, a weak smile curving her lips. "I'm back where I belong. That's all that matters."

He wanted to hear her say that no one had touched her, that no one had forced her to complete the ceremony, that she wasn't carrying another man's child. But when he looked deep into her eyes, and his heart swelled inside his chest, he knew nothing mattered except that she was back in his arms for good.

When she pulled him down for a kiss, he lost himself inside her plush mouth, reveling in the knowledge that she was once again safely back home.

"Prince Stone, should we take these two back to the castle?"

Stone reluctantly broke the kiss with his beloved and looked up at the guards. He opened his mouth to tell them just that when the woman cut in.

"I am Natasha, Princess Alyssandra's nanny, and this is my son, Shawn. We've been held captive by the Cunts for the past twenty-three years. I need to see Queen Annalecia immediately."

Alyssandra's head whipped around to stare at the woman and the Klatch man's mouth fell open as he stared at her while several emotions flowed over his face including anger, hurt, and disbelief.

Stone cleared his throat. Obviously, there was an interesting story behind all of this, but his first thoughts were only for

Alyssandra. "Bring them before the king. The queen is too sick to take visitors."

Alyssandra stiffened in his arms as the guards led the two Klatch away and she looked up at him with fear shadowing her eyes. "How bad is she?"

He took a deep breath before answering, but there was no way to hide the truth. "When you were taken, the brunt of the energy needs for the planet reverted to her. She was already weak and the sudden power drain nearly killed her. She's been abed since you left."

"I need to see her." She caressed his cheek with her fingers, even as her eyes were etched with guilt.

"This wasn't your fault, Princess. Your thoughts were purely for Sasha. You had no way of knowing the Cunts were coming for you."

"Of course I did, Stone. Even without you voicing your concerns about my vision, the conclusion was obvious—especially since I knew the Cunts wouldn't give me up without a fight. I should've been more careful."

Stone's brow furrowed as the queen's words came back to haunt him yet again. "I'm sorry, Alyssandra. I should've told you. There will be no more secrets between us, that I promise you."

She smiled up at him, caressing his cheek with her fingers. "It's a deal." She traced her fingertip over his lips. "I can walk, Stone. I just have to see my mother and make sure she's all right."

He brushed a gentle kiss against her forehead. "We'll go, but I'm not putting you down. I've spent every second since I found you gone swearing that when you returned, I'd never let you out of my sight again. You'll let me carry you everywhere for the next sixty years, and you'll like it."

She laughed, the sound twisting through him, filling his heart with hope and happiness.

* * *

Annalecia sat up in bed and leaned back against the headboard, a soft sigh escaping her lips. The draw of energy had lessened in a sudden surge and she knew Alyssandra was back, hopefully unscathed from her ordeal on earth. For the last few hours, she'd been worried that the planet would drain the last of her energy before her daughter could return and ascend. She wasn't sure exactly what would happen to the planet or its people if she died, but with a sudden loss of energy, she could see the inner core of the planet imploding—at least that's what her fevered dreams had shown her vividly every time she slipped into sleep since Alyssandra had been gone.

A few past queens had died before their daughters had ascended, but Tador had been at full health both times and had a reserve of energy to survive on until a hasty ascension could be arranged. This time they had no such reserve.

The door opened, pulling her from her thoughts, and she leaned forward in anticipation of seeing her daughter. Instead, the one face she thought she'd never see again peeked around the doorframe. "Natasha!"

The nanny, a longtime friend of Annalecia's growing up, was taken twenty-three years earlier while she'd been watching Alyssandra. When she'd not been heard from, everyone assumed she'd been killed by the Cunts along with all the others who had been captured.

Natasha rushed forward to envelop the queen in a crushing hug and tears pricked at the backs of Annalecia's eyes. "I thought you were dead!" She pulled away, holding her friend at arm's length and studying her. "I can't believe you're here. I never thought I'd see you again."

The queen smiled at her friend until a thought struck her. "Wait, what happened to the baby?" The very day she'd disappeared, Natasha had told Annalecia of her pregnancy, and they'd laughed and celebrated, imagining their children playing together.

"He apparently tried to rape our daughter." Darius's voice

boomed from the doorway and Annalecia recoiled as if she'd been slapped, while Natasha stiffened, her expression suddenly guarded.

Annalecia collapsed back against the pillows as Darius stepped aside so Stone could enter carrying a very naked Alyssandra.

"Is she hurt?" Panic rose until her daughter smiled at her.

"I'm fine, but Stone refused to let me walk. Although, I am a little cold."

"Stone, grab my robe for her and then tell us what happened."

Stone gently settled the princess on the bed next to her mother before pulling a robe from the queen's wardrobe and wrapping it around the naked girl. Annalecia gathered her into her arms, inhaling the scent of her daughter's hair and thanking the universe that she'd been restored to her again. Alyssandra returned the tight hug and for a moment they just held each other.

Finally, she pulled back studying the princess critically, but other than the dark circles under her eyes and a general lackluster appearance to her hair and skin, Alyssandra seemed fine. Once Stone restored her energy, she'd most likely be perfectly healthy. Although, depending on what happened while on earth, any emotional damage could take much longer to heal.

"Mother, I'm fine. I'm more worried about you."

Annalecia laughed. "I'm tough to keep down. I was just resting until your return." She kept her arm draped around her daughter and turned her attention to her friend. "Tasha, why don't you tell us what happened?"

Natasha looked at everyone around the room before taking a deep breath and letting it out slowly. "I never thought I'd find my way back to Tador. It's good to be home, Anna." She smiled sadly and studied her hands.

A fat tear escaped Annalecia's eye to carve a path down her cheek. No one but Natasha had ever called her Anna, and she'd thought to never hear it again. Her friend had aged, a few more wrinkles around the eyes and mouth and her hair a long mass that desperately needed a trim. Yet, even dressed in baggy sweats and an oversized T-shirt, Natasha looked lovely. She realized she'd missed her friend much more than she'd ever allowed herself to admit. She squeezed her hand in encouragement. "Tell us what happened, Tasha."

"When Alyssandra and I were taken, the Cunts didn't know I was pregnant. Once I gave birth, they took Shawn from me and raised him to believe that the Klatch were the cause of the war, and the only way he could redeem the honor of his people was to complete the ascension and father a new race." She closed her eyes as if holding back all the painful memories from overwhelming her.

"I spent the last twenty-three years locked in a cell trying to keep tabs on both Alyssandra and Shawn through mental links. Then, when the false ascension started, I knew I had to stop it. However, by the time I got there, the princess had overloaded everyone's arousal to the point they were all but incapacitated. I only had to cut her free and open the portal." She smiled weakly up at the queen. "I'm glad I still remembered how."

Alyssandra crossed her legs under her, and tucked the robe around her. "What's Sasha got to do with this? When they brought me back, Shawn was surprised I wasn't Sasha. In fact, he was almost angry that I wasn't."

Natasha smiled over at her. "Just like your dreams from Stone, Sasha received them from Shawn. Once I figured out who he'd contacted, I nurtured the relationship as much as I could. I had no idea he thought she was the princess. Apparently, all the lies Sela told him worked to our advantage."

Annalecia took a few minutes to digest the information before turning to her daughter with the question that burned on her tongue. "How much of the ceremony was completed?" She held her breath as she waited.

"None. I was able to . . . distract them before anything happened." Color rose high on her cheeks and she smiled gratefully at Natasha. "But I really appreciate the help with the portal. I wasn't sure how I was going to get back." She turned her attention to Annalecia, her brow furrowing in concern. "Seriously, how are you feeling? I was so scared I wouldn't arrive in time . . ."

She laughed as she realized what Alyssandra was trying not to say. "Don't write me off just yet, daughter. As soon as you returned, the drain from the planet lessened again. I'm all right, and can certainly last a few more hours. I'm well enough to escort my daughter to her ascension ceremony, as is my right."

Darius opened his mouth to object and she held up her hand to stop him. "Darius, I promise I won't overdo. I'll just escort her in and then relax until the ceremony is complete."

Darius didn't look happy, but finally he nodded. "You've won this round, but I'll be there to make sure you keep your promise." He glared down at her, his expression stern, and she resisted the urge to smile. It wouldn't do to gloat. Darius might get it into his head that he needed to fight harder to win their small skirmishes of will. Soon, they would lose the empathic link they shared when Alyssandra ascended the throne. But after sharing thoughts for so many years, they probably knew each other so well that the link wasn't even required anymore.

Natasha bowed her head before the king, staring at his boots, while her hands trembled in her lap. "What about my son, my lord? The guards confined him to a room when they brought us here." She swallowed hard before she continued. "He's not an evil man . . ."

Darius looked like a miser caught giving alms to the poor. He cleared his throat and shifted from foot to foot. "I sent his father to him." His brow furrowed and he glared around the room, defying anyone to contradict him. "The boy should hear the truth from his father. It will be a difficult transition for him."

Annalecia reached out and pulled her husband's hand into her own. "Thank you, Darius." She knew he must have known how hard it had been all these years without Natasha. It was for her that he showed kindness to the man who had almost hurt their beloved daughter.

His cheeks flushed and he cleared his throat again. "It's not the boy's fault. He's been raised on lies and he should be allowed to learn the truth about his culture before deciding his future. A few days spent with his mother and father, then perhaps Sasha can show him around."

Stone broke in, clearly rescuing the king from his discomfort. He placed a protective hand on the princess's shoulder. "There are only four hours until sunset. I think Alyssandra needs time to rest and recover before the ceremony."

The queen caught Stone's gaze and held it. "You're a good man, Stone. Take care of her for me. I'll see you both at sundown. On your way out, can you have the servants send up a bath, some fresh clothes and some food? I have some catching up to do with Tasha."

When Stone dropped Alyssandra off at her room, Sasha was waiting for her. The maid's eyes and nose were puffy and red from crying, while dark circles marred the delicate skin under her eyes and her face was drawn with grief.

Sasha dropped to her knees before Alyssa, her head bowed submissively. "Princess, I'm so sorry. I never meant for anything to happen to you. Please believe that I would never willingly put you in danger."

Stone had filled in the gaps for her while he'd carried her back to her room, so she knew now the full story on everything that had happened with her maid. Had it just been a few hours ago that she'd been on an altar on earth about to be raped and forced into an ascension? She sighed. *Talk about a long fucking day . . .*

"Sasha." She knelt and hugged the maid. "It wasn't your fault. You didn't know what he planned to do, or even that I'd followed you."

The maid sniffled and raised her gaze to Alyssa's. "Regardless, I put you in danger. I'm so sorry."

Alyssa grabbed Sasha's hand and pulled her up to stand in front of her. "Sasha, I need your help for the ceremony. I'm counting on you." She took the girl firmly by the shoulders. "Will you be there for me?"

Hope lit Sasha's eyes for the first time. "You . . . aren't going to dismiss me?"

"No. Of course not. You've been nothing but kind to me. I need your help if I'm going to become queen."

Sasha swallowed hard before speaking. "Thank you, Princess. I'm so sorry."

Alyssa's blinked her gritty eyes and prayed for a bath. She resisted the urge to shake Sasha if she apologized one more time. *I suppose in her place, I'd be doing the same thing.*

She sighed and crossed to the bed, flopping down and sighing in near ecstasy when the soft mattress cradled her ass. "Sasha, why didn't you tell me about Shawn?" Alyssa pulled the maid down onto the bed to sit next to her.

Sasha closed her swollen eyes and took a deep breath before continuing. "I thought he was from an outlying village, and that he'd seen me, but I'd not seen him. I wanted him to be the one to help me with my coming-of-age. I thought it was all very romantic the way he visited me in my dreams like Stone did with you . . ." She raised her chin, meeting Alyssa's gaze. "It sounds stupid now."

She laid a comforting hand on top of the maid's. "No, it

doesn't. I remember when Stone visited my dreams. They gave me something to look forward to, a place to feel like I belonged. A place where the Cunts couldn't take my hope away from me. I understand exactly how you felt."

Sasha's lips curved into a brittle smile. "When he called me Princess, I was devastated." She looked down at her hands. "Not that I could ever blame him for desiring you, but when I went to meet him . . ."

"You hoped the title didn't matter and he wanted you anyway."

Fresh tears welled and Sasha sobbed into her hands. Alyssa pulled the maid into a hug and let her cry. She made soft "shhh" sounds until Sasha's tears ran out and the maid pulled away to wipe at her eyes and nose with a handkerchief Alyssa took from her nightstand.

Alyssa pulled the robe tighter around her. "Shawn asked me who you were, when they took me to earth. He seemed angry that I wasn't you."

Sasha's tear-stained face tipped up. "Really?"

"They convinced him that he had to father a new race because of the supposed atrocities past Klatch had committed against the Cunts. He grew up believing their lies. When he tried to go forward with the ceremony with me, it was because he was doing what he saw as his duty." She squeezed the maid's hand. "But he made it clear, he'd rather have you."

Sasha's brow furrowed and she fisted the handkerchief. "He almost . . . The king would never let him live . . . They . . ."

Alyssa held up her hand. "My father understands that he was raised among our enemies and raised on lies. He also loves you and wants you to be happy. He's agreed to let you start showing Shawn around, once his parents have spent some time with him and ensured he understands the truth. Then it will be up to him if he wants to return to earth to stay, or to remain here on Tador."

"Do you think he still wants to see me after everything that happened?

Alyssa grabbed her pillow and hit the maid in the shoulder with it. "Sasha, I've never seen you so insecure. And to think, when I got here, I was the timid one." She smiled to remove any sting from the comment, breathing a sigh of relief when the maid laughed.

"Thank you, Princess. For everything." She stood, wiping her face one last time. "Now, why don't I have a bathing tub brought up so we can get you cleaned up and then you can take a nap until the ceremony?"

An erotic moan escaped Alyssa's throat at the thought of a nice hot bath, and both women laughed.

Sasha put her hands on her hips and winked. "I'll take that as a definite yes."

Chapter 15

Alyssa's nerves thrummed. *This is it!* She placed her hand against her stomach hoping to quiet the herd of butterflies that had taken up residence and threatened to make her lose what meager dinner she'd been able to force past her lips.

"Are you ready for this, my daughter?"

She glanced over at the smiling face of her mother. *Sure, I'm totally ready to lose my virginity while twenty naked men whack off around me, so I can "absorb their essence" and save the planet.* She returned her mother's smile. "I hope so. It can't be harder than the ceremony earlier today on earth." She took several deep breaths, hoping to drown the jitters with oxygen. Turning to look into the full-length mirror, she shook her head, still not quite believing.

"You're stunning." Her mother hugged her from behind, ignoring the reference to the false ascension.

The woman staring back at her in the mirror *was* stunning. *I just still can't believe it's me!* She wore an almost transparent shimmering white floor-length robe. High necked with long sleeves and covering her from neck to toe, the flowing fabric moved with her giving erotic views of everything she had to offer.

Her hair fell over her shoulders in the style of the Klatch, braids sprinkled throughout with snow-white beads worked in here and there. Her lips were full and red and her kohl-lined eyes appeared luminous and exotic. Tears burned at the backs of her eyes as she realized she looked like a healthier version of her mother. Her lips curved at the thought.

"You'll make a wonderful queen, my daughter. Don't worry, you'll do fine. I have to get back before your father decides to confine me to my room." The queen kissed her cheek and then quickly turned to go.

"Mother . . ."

The queen paused and turned back.

"I love you." She caressed her mother's slightly sunken cheek with her fingers. "Thank you both for not giving up on me—both times I was taken from you."

Annalecia's smile lit her face, and her eyes misted. "We will always be here for you, my daughter. Always. There will always be a connection between us that the Cunts can never steal from us." The queen brushed a kiss against Alyssa's cheek and turned to disappear through the door. Alyssa watched her go, blinking back the tears that threatened as thick emotions welled up inside her chest.

Sasha stepped inside the room. "All is ready, Princess."

Alyssa turned toward her lady's maid, fighting a last-minute urge to flee. Instead, she forced herself to say, "Let's do it." She stepped through the doors after Sasha and into a large open chamber lit by thousands of flickering white candles. The tiny waving flames threw shadows over the large altar dominating the middle of the room. *At least this time, the shadows are intimate and not scary!*

The altar, covered with layers of deep purple fabric spilling over the sides, made her think of a royal throne, only in bed form. A large half circle indent cut into one end of the throne, she knew to allow Stone access between her legs for the final stage of the ceremony. *Wow, much nicer than the Cunt altar.* She bit back a laugh as she realized most women were never on an altar in their entire lives and in a few more minutes, she'd be able to say she'd tried out two in less than a day.

The flock of butterflies increased their rhythm and she swallowed hard against the lump of nervousness and curiosity inside her throat. More memories of the false ascension room on earth assaulted her and she shivered.

Holding her chin high, she walked forward into the room and took her place beside the altar. The door on the opposite side of the room immediately opened and Stone emerged looking dark, dangerous and sexy. He wore a robe similar to hers, but black and knee length. She found herself mesmerized by the tantalizing glimpses of his wonderful anatomy as the fabric shifted with his movements.

"The ceremony may now begin."

The gravelly sound of a woman's voice startled her from her perusal of Stone. An elderly woman dressed in the normal Klatch gauzy clothes, braids sprinkled throughout her long gray hair, stood at the head of the room.

"I am Annara and as the eldest Princess of the second house of Klatch, it falls to me to officiate." She held her hands out to both Alyssa and Stone. Alyssa stepped forward to take the offered hand while Stone mirrored her movements. Annara brought her hands together, keeping her hands cupped over Stone's and Alyssa's.

"Princess Alyssandra, do you willingly come forward to assume the throne? To be responsible for the sustenance of the people of Klatch and for maintaining a symbiotic relationship with the land of Tador which sustains your people?"

Emotions swirled through Alyssa as the importance of this moment and this ceremony fully registered. She swallowed hard before she spoke, placing a firm hand over her stomach to calm her herd of butterflies turned into bats. "I do." The words made her think of a wedding ceremony. Something she thought she'd never have. However, in the Klatch culture, the wedding was a small part that happened after the ascension. A quick glance at Stone's charming grin reassured her.

Annara turned to Stone. "Prince Stone, do you willingly come forward to support the future queen, safeguard her well-being and supply her with replacement energy so she can provide sustenance to all her people?"

Stone turned to smile down at Alyssa, love and determination shining in his eyes. "I do." The seductive rumble of his voice sent gooseflesh spilling over her—a promise of things to come.

"The vows have been affirmed, let the ascension begin." Anna clapped her hands together twice. In response, a side door opened admitting a line of twenty of the most virile Klatch men on Tador. They were any woman's erotic fantasy come true and she instantly thought of them of as "the Adonises." But in her mind, none of them could come close to Stone.

It took her a moment to realize they were all entirely nude . . . and just as well-endowed as her betrothed. A chuckle from Stone made her realize he'd caught her staring. Then when she finally traced her gaze up from their swollen cocks to their faces, she realized that the two best-endowed Adonises were Ryan and Grayson. *Wow, my vision of them naked was pretty damned accurate.* She swallowed hard as the vision of one of their cocks stretching her ass while Stone fucked her flashed through her mind. *I really have to find a way to limit my vivid sexual imagination!*

Annara stepped back against the wall and then gestured toward Sasha. The lady's maid stepped in front of Alyssa and immediately dropped her robe. And even though Alyssa had already seen Sasha naked many times, her eyes were drawn to the luscious curves of her breasts and hips and memories of their time together in the baths brought a rush of dampness flowing between her thighs.

"Princess, I offer myself to ready your body for the ceremony, to be your protector and companion for the duration of your reign and beyond. Will you accept me?" Sasha bowed her head awaiting Alyssa's acceptance.

The many eyes watching her from around the room bored into her like lasers and she tried hard to ignore the self-consciousness that came with that knowledge. They'd be doing more than watching in a few minutes and she had to keep moving if she was going to get through this ceremony without dying of mortification and embarrassment. *Besides, it is kind of erotic to have all of these men standing here naked watching me. Might as well enjoy the fantasy while it's here!*

She took a fortifying breath, loosened her robe and slipped it off, letting it fall into a silky puddle at her feet. She tipped Sasha's chin up to meet her gaze. "I accept you Sasha as my protector and companion for the duration of my reign and beyond." Cool air assaulted her bare skin causing her nipples to pebble into tight peaks. She shuddered as more gooseflesh marched over her.

Stone cleared his throat, reminding her to turn and take his hand so he could help her up to sit on the edge of the altar.

She flushed at her breach of protocol and took Stone's hand, allowing herself to settle atop the altar with her legs straddling the half circle indent in the edge of the table.

Sasha stepped forward into the indent, before dropping to her knees and spreading Alyssa's pussy lips wide.

A quick glance around the room showed dark desire sparking in every eye. With that knowledge came the heady flow of pure feminine power. A small smile curved her lips as she leaned back on her hands and tried to relax.

The first swipe of Sasha's talented tongue made her gasp as a trickle of power traveled from the point of contact to both breasts. Before she had time to recover, Sasha laved her cleft again, setting a steady rhythm.

Creamy wetness pooled between her thighs and she glanced down to watch Sasha's small pink tongue dart out to caress her aching clit. She moaned at the sight, but Sasha only smiled and sucked the swollen nub between her lips, reaching around Alyssa's thighs to cup her bare ass. The delicious friction started a thrum of energy low in her belly. As Sasha sucked harder, the power coiled tighter and tighter until Alyssa's breath came in choppy pants and she wantonly thrust her hips forward to give the lady's maid better access.

Movement caught her attention and she looked up in time to see Stone drop his robe, revealing corded muscles and sculpted planes to her hungry gaze. His cock, fully erect, jutted toward her, a pearl of wetness beaded on the engorged tip. His eyes blazed with desire as he stepped forward behind Sasha, leaning over her to brush his lips lightly across Alyssa's. She opened for him and he needed no further encouragement—he thrust his tongue inside her mouth in a similar motion to what Sasha did inside her swollen pussy.

The combination of sensations, Stone's rough tongue mating with hers and Sasha's soft sensual assault on her swollen clit, pushed her past all reason. Power flowed through her along with her orgasm, blanking her thoughts. Instead of relaxing her, the release only heightened her senses and her arousal. Every inch of her skin felt like an expanse of exposed nerve endings and her breasts and pussy were heavy with need.

A crackling noise startled her. She opened her eyes and noted small pink sparks of energy sizzled over every inch of the room. Each of the twenty Adonises were so erect, they looked almost uncomfortable. But each of them nodded and murmured to each other. It seemed they already had faith she would succeed where many others had failed. Grayson and Ryan both smiled as they watched her.

Returning her attention to Sasha, she noticed a smug smile creep across the woman's lips before the maid bowed her head as she allowed Stone to help her to her feet.

Before stepping away, Sasha met Alyssa's gaze and whispered, "Blessings on you, Princess. You will be the one to save us all. I know it." At any other time, Alyssa would have appreciated the sentiment, but her body's demands were making it difficult to think.

Stone stepped forward into the circle indent in the table Sasha had just vacated, the heat of his body in close proximity sending shivers over her entire body. "It is time, Alyssandra."

Her mind whirled, her breath coming in small pants. Her body ached for Stone and he stood so close that his proud cock jutted against her belly. "Tell me what to do. I'm ready. Just please, do it now. I need you inside me." Her voice sounded pleading in her own ears, but she didn't care. If Stone didn't bury his cock inside her right now, she couldn't bear it.

"You need to take in my essence three times, the last time in tandem with the other Klatch men's contribution."

She shook her head, past the ability to think enough to form words. *Don't give me words, damn it, just show me!* Stone must have understood, because he lifted her gently down from the platform helping her kneel before him.

Like a homing beacon, his erect cock arched toward her. Her pussy ached for him, but seeing his beautiful erection in front of her, she knew she had to touch him. To taste him. A fleeting thought ran through her mind that several other people were in the room watching her, but the pull of Stone's body overrode any reservations she had.

She wrapped her fingers around the velvety length of him, his gasp echoed through the room. His cock was rock hard and jumped as she stroked him. Power flowed from her hand and into Stone at the point of their contact, breaking a long moan from deep inside his throat.

The milky dew glistening on the swollen tip of his cock called to her, begging her to taste, to pull his essence inside herself, to make it her own. She slowly lowered her head and licked a quick line over the tip, capturing the salty treat. Stone's hiss of pleasure made her smile. As soon as the pre come dissolved on her tongue, a steady flow of energy poured through her body, energizing her, driving her, making her crave more.

She took the head of his cock into her mouth and swirled her tongue over the swollen tip. His breath exploded out over her and she hummed in smug female satisfaction. With one hand, she grabbed his muscular ass and pulled him deeper inside her mouth, enjoying the way his ass muscles flexed as he thrust forward.

"Suck me hard. Drink my essence into your body." Stone's words sounded strained and she complied with his request, the thought of finally being able to do anything she wanted with him giving her power. He thrust deeper and the swollen tip bumped against the back of her throat, swelling impossibly, letting her know he was close.

She concentrated all her energy on Stone's beautiful cock. Her world narrowed until nothing mattered but bringing Stone to release and having his hot come explode deep inside her throat. Without breaking her rhythm, she reached up to cup his balls and gently roll them between her fingers. They were pulled tight against his body, his breath a series of small urgent gasps. She increased her rhythm, enjoying the way his cock swelled even harder inside her mouth. She ran a finger along the silky seam between his ass and his balls and he exploded inside her mouth just as she'd imagined. Stone's roar of release filled the chamber.

Power flared between them, and seared through her veins like lava. She continued to suck Stone's cock until she'd taken every drop.

Two of the Klatch men stepped forward, picked her up and placed her gently on the altar so she was lying on her back, her legs bent resting in the indents around the circular cutout in the altar.

She murmured her thanks knowing she wouldn't have been able to stand right now on her own. Too many small explosions of power still pounded throughout her body.

Stone stepped forward and placed a gentle hand against the inside of her thigh causing her to jump. "Relax, beloved. Let me tend you."

Before she could think, he lowered his head and laved a hot line over her swollen pussy lips. She arched against his mouth, shaking her head back and forth, silently begging him never to stop. He thrust his tongue inside her, teasing, but never touching her swollen clit. Before she could think to protest, he dipped one long finger deep inside her and then traced a slow line down to her ass.

Memories assaulted her of their last dream joining where he'd inserted his fingers inside her ass and promised her that someday he'd enjoy stretching her tight ass with his cock. Excitement arrowed through her causing another rush of moisture to pool between her thighs.

Stone's smug chuckle let her know he'd noticed her reaction. He scrambled her thoughts when he slowly inserted a single finger into her ass. While allowing her a moment to get used to the invasion, his tongue continued its steady assault against her clit. When she relaxed, he began to slowly finger fuck her with the entire room watching them. The sensations slammed into her, erotic and forbidden. Her nipples tightened impossibly until they ached and she arched her hips against Stone's hand wanting more—needing more.

His tongue finally moved up to caress the sensitive underside of her clit, pushing her closer to the release she craved. Her

236 / *Cassie Ryan*

inner walls tightened, ever tighter until he pulled her swollen clit between his lips and sucked hard. Her world shattered, power flowing outward in every direction and her screams echoing around her.

It took several minutes for her mind to float back to earth, and impossibly, her body still craved more. *What the hell is happening to me?* Her hips still ground against Stone's hand and she noticed he'd now inserted two fingers, her ass slowly stretching to meet this new demand. She moaned against the sensation, wishing he would make good on his promise to fill her tight ass.

"Soon, beloved. Soon . . ."

She startled at Stone's deep voice inside her mind. She knew once the joining was complete they would have an empathic link. It seemed they already did. And if he could talk to her, she could talk to him too! *"I want you inside me, Stone. I have to have you filling me. Now!"*

Without a word, he picked her up off the altar and slid her down the length of his body until her feet touched the floor. His hard cock dug into her stomach and he slanted his mouth over hers, dipping his tongue inside to tease her. She could taste herself on his tongue and threaded her fingers through his hair trying to pull him closer. He gently pulled her away shaking his head with a small smile.

"It's time for you to take my essence again." His voice was a husky whisper, meant only for her. He gently turned her toward the altar and bent her over it until her upper body lay flat, her breasts pressed against the soft purple cloth, giving him access to her from behind. Something slippery and cool spread over her ass and she realized it was some type of lubricant. When the tingling began, she knew it had to be *ponga*.

Then Stone's cock brushed between her ass cheeks a second before he slowly pushed forward, just the very tip stretching her virgin ass impossibly wide. Alyssa gasped. It hurt a little, but her entire body was so aroused, it rode the razor's edge between pleasure and pain and she wanted more.

Like a sudden switch turned on, the hurricane of power began its steady path through her body and she consciously relaxed and let the energy flow through her.

Stone reached around to rub her clit, the combination of sensations zinging raw pleasure through her body that exploded into power and joined the hurricane flow. Slowly, her body relaxed against the invasion of Stone's thick cock and she pressed back against him, taking just a little more of him inside her. Again, she took a moment to adjust and when she was ready, she moved her hips against him, sliding the tip of his cock slowly in and out until her body screamed for more.

Stone growled behind her as if unable to be still any longer. He began to move inside her, slow long strokes, entering her farther with each thrust. When the sound of skin slapping against skin filled the air and his balls slapped against her ass cheeks, she knew she'd taken him entirely. She spread her legs wider, giving him better access and braced her upper body on her forearms. *"Fuck me, Stone. Like I've always wanted you to!"*

As if her words broke the last chains of his careful control, he pistoned his hips, driving himself into her until the tip slammed repeatedly against the center of her being, bringing an ecstasy she'd never known. She watched in fascination as small sparks of power flared over her skin as Stone pushed her closer to the precipice. She looked up into the eyes of one of the Klatch men, thankfully not Grayson or Ryan, only then realizing they had the altar surrounded. From the Adonis's thatch of curly mahogany hair, his cock jutted out pointing straight toward her. While she watched, he reached down to wrap his long blunt fingers around it, making long, sure strokes.

Arousal threatened to overwhelm her and the air backed up in her lungs making it difficult to breathe. "Please . . ." she whispered, though she wasn't sure what she begged for. She only knew that the exquisite feeling of Stone buried in her ass while watching this gorgeous man in front of her stroke himself was killing her. If she didn't come soon, she knew she would explode. The rush of power continued to increase exponentially with every thrust until fear pricked at the edges of her mind. There had never been this much—even when she'd held her mother's hand and channeled the power of the queen. What if she didn't survive?

Stone rubbed one callused finger over her clit and she did explode, waves of pleasure and power flowed outward, bathing the room in pink sparks. Distantly, through a haze of sensations, Stone's hot come spilled deep inside her, and she knew the instant his essence touched her. The lights inside the room flickered like lightning and her body exploded again. The orgasm hit her like a fist, making her gasp for air. The surprised gasps of everyone else in the room drowned out everything else.

Alyssa collapsed against the altar, the side of her face pressed against the purple cloth, her limp arms resting on either side of her head. For a moment, Stone relaxed against her, leaning his forehead against her back, keeping himself buried deep inside her while little aftershocks flowed through them both. Finally, he slid slowly out, leaving her empty and bereft.

A cool wet cloth sliding over her backside startled her. Sasha laid a comforting hand against her back. "It's just me, Princess. There is still more to come, but we must wash the prince's member so he doesn't bring bacteria into your womb and endanger your heir. This warm cloth and salve will help you heal quickly and keep you from being too sore tomorrow."

Alyssa only nodded weakly and left the maid to her ministrations. Her entire body felt like jelly and she was exhausted, but she slowly realized that the enormous rush of power continued to flow through her. It lurked in the background like a spark waiting for dry tinder to unleash its power.

What if I can't finish the ceremony? She knew she had to for her mother, for Tador and for Stone, but she didn't know if her body would cooperate. Then another thought hit her. *"What about you, Stone? You've just come twice in a short period of time. Are you going to be able to . . . you know."*

His deep chuckled flowed across her skin leaving gooseflesh in its wake. "Don't worry about me, beloved. I'll be ready for you."

The cool salve Sasha spread over her ass felt divine and Alyssa sighed. The small soothing circles made by Sasha's fingers moved lower to tease her slick folds. Drowsy with sensation, Alyssa had been sure that nothing could arouse her again, but slowly, impossibly, arousal seeped through her like a sleeping dragon awakened.

A moment later, Stone took Sasha's place and picked Alyssa up to set her on top of the altar. He stepped forward to brush a tender kiss across her lips. "You are amazing, Alyssandra. There is only one part of the ceremony left."

Her apprehension immediately returned. She'd already done things in front of a room full of strangers she'd never done in private. *Can I really go through with this?*

Stone's large hand smoothed over her hair. "You can do this, Alyssandra. I'll be right here with you the whole time. And once this is complete, we can spend some time alone, just the two of us."

Her apprehension spiraled up another notch, but she forced a smile for Stone's sake and nodded.

He tipped his head to Sasha, who helped her lie back on the altar before magically binding her hands over her head.

When she opened her mouth to protest, Sasha explained. "The amount of essence you will absorb will be a shock to your system. This will protect you and Stone from harm."

Too weak to argue, she nodded in reply. But her mind frantically sifted through the possibilities. Stone had told her that all the others who attempted the coming-of-age ceremony since the last successful ascension had died. She was fairly certain she'd survived further than the others from the murmurs and nods from the Adonises, but if the last part required she be tied down for her own safety, somehow that didn't boost her confidence.

Stone stroked a long line down the inside of her thigh, igniting her arousal once more and the hurricane of sleeping power flared to life. As if on cue, the group of Klatch men surrounding them closed their formation, blocking them in. All of them rock-hard and aroused, their eyes burning with unbridled desire. She couldn't help but openly study some of their equipment, as if they were held out specifically for her inspection. Before Stone, she'd never seen a man's dick up close and personal and now she had the bird's-eye view of the Klatch's finest. Each engorged cock was a thing of impressive beauty even in their differences—long and thick with several glistening with pre come. She licked her lips as she remembered the taste of Stone's essence as it had dissolved on her tongue.

"It is time for the final joining." Stone's voice startled her out of her intense anatomy study and she turned to face him— suddenly embarrassed as she realized he'd heard her thoughts.

He winked at her and then gestured to the Klatch men. "With my claiming of the new queen, your essence will give her enough power to ascend the throne and release the current queen from her symbiotic joining with Tador."

"Long live Queen Alyssandra," they chanted in unison, giving Alyssa the creeps. *I feel like I'm about to be the virgin human sacrifice in a bad B movie!*

Then Stone's hands were on her body, erasing any thoughts that had been trying to form. He traced the seam of her pussy lips with his fingers, sending shudders, tendrils of arousal and a pure spike of power shooting through her to feed the awakened rush of power.

Every erogenous zone in her body was suddenly connected by an invisible thread of hot lava, thrumming just under her skin, making her feel as if she would explode outward at any moment. Judging by what had happened so far, she couldn't be sure that was very far from the truth.

Stone traced the head of his cock over her slick folds and the power howled like a hungry predator before doubling and then tripling inside her every few seconds. She tried to fight the sensations, to gain control over what was happening to her body. Her skin began to burn and heat until shooting pain flowed over her like a thousand ants eating her flesh.

"Relax, beloved." Stone soothed his hand over her bare skin. "Relax and let the power flow through you. Fighting it will only cause you pain. You were made to channel this power. You will control it, but you have to accept it first."

"It's never been this much!" she protested. Fear flowed through her in a burning rush, fear that her entire body would incinerate with that much power channeling through her at once. "I can't take it all."

"Trust me, my love. You can do this. Relax . . ."

She closed her eyes and after a moment of doubt, gave herself up to the sensations assaulting her. In her mind's eye, she saw the tendrils of power, pink and sparkling. She pictured them flowing into her body from the sexual energy in the air and in Stone's touch and then flowing out of her skin in every direction, feeding the land of Tador, healing it, sustaining it.

Stone's murmur of approval sounded from between her spread thighs and then the swollen tip of his cock caressed her folds once more. Another spike of energy shot through her, but she channeled it harmlessly away and opened her eyes to meet Stone's hungry gaze.

"I want you inside me, Stone. I've waited a lifetime for you.

Fuck me. Now." Her voice sounded calm and matter-of-fact, surprising her.

Stone leaned over her, and slid inside her aching core one slow inch at a time. She relished the delicious internal friction and arched her hips toward him, offering herself, begging for more.

The men around her began to stroke themselves in earnest, the sounds of flesh slapping against flesh and heavy breathing filling the room, imbuing her with more energy.

Stone rolled both her nipples between his thumb and forefingers while he surged forward, taking her virginity and burying himself deep.

A gasp wrenched from her dry throat. A sharp stinging sensation startled her out of the haze of her arousal and she took a moment to get used to Stone's invasion into her flesh, as she'd done when he filled her ass.

When he sensed she was ready, he began to move, and exquisite pleasure flowed through her in warm, tingling waves. *"So this is what making love is like!"*

"This is only the beginning, my love."

Arching her hips against him with every thrust, she spiraled higher and higher. She wished her hands were free, so she could touch him, could run her hands over the hard planes of his chest and through his thick dark hair to pull him down to her.

To her right, Grayson cried out, and she turned just as his chiseled features twisted with the strength of his sudden release, pearly come spurting out of his straining cock. As if in slow motion, he continued to pump his shaft until all his essence was spent. The hot come spattered against her breast, shooting an explosion of power through her. She arched off the altar as her body struggled to contain the new fission of power.

Her mouth fell open as the come disappeared as if her pores drank the essence in. Flashing white lights assaulted her vision and she felt like she was trapped in a room full of continuous flashing light bulbs. Dizziness threatened and her body bucked against this new overload of power.

After a few minutes of fighting it, she remembered to relax and funnel the power away, back toward Tador.

No sooner had she cleared her vision than another shot of come sizzled against her bare stomach, this time from Ryan. The thick liquid seeped into her skin like molasses through cloth, the power of the life contained inside, turning quickly to another surge of power inside her already overtaxed system.

She breathed deeply and let it flow through her and out into the land. A strong rope of power formed between her and the planet that was Tador, the world that sustained them all. With each new influx of essence, the connection of power between them strengthened.

Now that she controlled the power, she opened her eyes, bringing herself back to the present. Stone still thrust into her in a continual steady rhythm and as each Adonis spent his load, he stepped back, letting another one toward the front for his turn.

Her arousal continued to tighten in a leisurely burn against her senses. Another batch of come landed hot and erotic against her belly and she realized that all twenty Klatch men had given their contribution. She wrapped her legs around Stone's waist, pulling him in tighter with every thrust.

"Come for me, Stone. I need your essence inside me."

He growled in response and with three final pumps, emptied himself into her. His release deep against her core pushed her over the precipice and her body flowed with endless waves of pleasure.

As the final spasms of her orgasm drained away, Tador's link to her mother loosened and fell away. Instead, the steady thrum of energy it needed to survive, to thrive, now flowed from her. She felt like a mother breastfeeding her newborn, an exquisite pleasure totally unlike anything she'd ever known. Then she became aware of another entity slowly pulling power and nourishment from her.

A child. Stone's child, deep inside her womb where he'd planted it. No, she corrected—*her*, not *it*. "Stone's daughter," she whispered in wonder. "I'm carrying Stone's daughter."

Self-satisfied male laughter rang out over the room. But she knew him well enough to recognize the relief in his tone.

Sasha released her bonds and Stone picked her up, cradling her in his strong arms.

Curling against him, she whispered against his chest. "Where are we going?"

"I'm going to take you to the baths to get you cleaned up and soothe your sore body. Then I'm taking you to bed . . . to sleep," he added firmly before kissing her on top of the head.

Chapter 16

Alyssa lay limp in Stone's arms unable to summon enough energy to even open her heavy eyelids.

Shhh, my beautiful witch. Relax and let me tend you. You've had a long night. A gentle kiss brushed across her forehead as he slowly lowered her into the warm waters of the baths. The sensation of the gently frothing waters against her over-sensitized skin ripped a cry from her parched throat and she clutched at Stone's shoulders. Tremors ran through her entire body and she clamped her teeth together to keep from biting her tongue.

Stone sat, and cradled her in his arms, rocking her until her body slowly acclimated and she relaxed against him again.

Drink, my love. He held a goblet to her lips and she gladly swallowed the cool water, which helped soothe the aftermath of the fire that had raged within her. Stone's naked skin slid over hers in the warm water and she wanted to nuzzle against him like a cat and lick the moisture from his golden skin. He chuckled and she remembered that now he could hear her thoughts. Just as well since she didn't have the energy to speak, let alone make good on her erotic thoughts.

There will be time enough for that when you've recovered. I'm going to lay you on the bathing platform so I can wash you. Just relax, beloved.

The gel-like substance of the platform soothed her back and for a moment, Stone's touch disappeared, leaving her bereft and alone. Panic whipped through her and she fought to open her eyes, to find him, to beg him not to leave her. But then his warm hand settled against her scalp, calming her. *What the hell is wrong with me? I've never been so clingy and panicked.*

I'm here, Alyssandra. Don't worry, I'll never leave you. I'll always be close by. He brushed a kiss over her lips. *This is a normal reaction to the ceremony. Don't worry, it's temporary.*

She lay like the dead against the bathing platform as Stone carefully soaped her body—her hands, arms, and shoulders and then carefully rinsed them. He massaged her skin and aching muscles as he rinsed her clean. She wanted to moan in ecstasy when he massaged the palms of her hands and her fingers. She was amazed at how non-sexual touching could be so comforting and erotic at the same time.

Then slowly, deliberately, he soaped her breasts, stomach, legs and feet, again following each rinsing with a very thorough massage. Each time Alyssa thought there was no more tension in her entire body, Stone's careful massage would banish even more and she would sink against the platform farther.

He slowly spread her legs and took special care around her ass and slit, but rather than his touch being sexual, it was caring and nurturing and her heart swelled inside her chest. He rinsed her thoroughly and then placed a small kiss against her gently rounded stomach. *I can't believe our daughter is growing inside you.* He smiled, his lips still against her skin and she wished she had the energy to reach up and run her fingers through his hair.

He trailed his fingers against her skin as he walked around the platform toward her head. Warm water flowed over her hair and then something cool touched her scalp as Stone began to lather her hair. The shampoo filled the chamber with the scents of vanilla and lavender, reminding her of the oil he'd used with her just a few short days ago. He slowly massaged her scalp and she knew if she had any energy left at all, she'd be purring like a kitten under his attentive hands. When every inch of her scalp had been thoroughly massaged, he carefully rinsed her hair, ensuring no water got into her eyes or ears.

Alyssandra, I'm right here. I need to wash, but I don't want you to think I've left you. His presence stayed inside her mind, comforting her as the sounds of him washing his body reached her. When he was finished, he slowly lifted her, carrying her out of the baths and into the dressing rooms where she'd first met Sasha.

He took his time, carefully toweling her dry and reapplying the salve he'd washed from her ass. He bundled her hair into a towel and wrapped her in a fluffy robe before carrying her out of the bathing chamber and up toward her room.

What seemed like only seconds later, the soft mattress in her room cushioned her and Stone's naked form pressed behind her, his arm coming over her waist, his large hand cupping her breast. She gathered enough energy to place her hand over his before letting sleep take her.

Alyssa woke to Stone's strong arms around her and his hard cock nestled in the crack of her ass. She smiled and stretched back against him like a cat. Apparently, her energy had returned in force. She'd never felt better in her entire life. "Can we wake up like this every morning for the rest of our lives?"

His deep chuckling against her neck reverberated through her, making her nipples pebble and her clit swell. "As you wish, my queen."

Alyssa started at Stone referring to her as "queen," and then laughed. "You know, I guess I just realized that we are now the king and queen. Isn't it rather surreal?"

Stone rolled her over onto her back, immediately covering her as he slid his cock deep inside her slick channel, ripping a surprised moan from her throat. "I'll admit, the new titles will take a while to get used to. But my duties to my new queen will be no hardship. Especially since there are no longer any barriers between us." He pulled out slowly until the swollen tip of his cock teased the soft underside of her clit, and then he surged forward again, filling her.

Alyssa gasped at the intense pleasure and power that flowed through her body as her hips instinctively rose to meet his thrusts. It took her a moment to realize that she could feel everything Stone did through their empathic link. She wriggled under him and gasped as she was hit by double simultaneous sensations.

Stone laughed. "This might take some getting used to. I had no idea women were so sensitive to every movement."

Alyssa swallowed, her throat suddenly dry. "I had no idea how exquisite if felt to push your cock inside a hot wet woman."

She wrapped her legs around his trim waist, and pulled him farther inside with every thrust. The crisp hairs surrounding his cock brushed against her swollen clit each time he filled her, and they both moaned as her nails dug into his back. The now familiar rush of energy flowed through her body, increasing with Stone's every movement.

She looked up into Stone's eyes, surprised to see a gentleness and vulnerability there she'd never seen before during any of their sex play. He cradled her face in his hands, his movements inside her suddenly tender as his emotions swelled around her. He ran a callused thumb over her cheek before slowly lowering his lips to hers.

He dipped his tongue inside and caressed every inch of her mouth, exploring, tasting, memorizing. He tasted spicy and male and each caress made her heart swell inside her chest even as her arousal tightened deep inside her.

I finally have you all to myself, my lovely Alyssandra. He waited for no reply, but brushed a soft kiss over her lips and then pulled back to look at her while he continued the slow steady rhythm.

The moment was too tender for words and Alyssa found it erotic to look into his eyes while his cock filled her over and over. "Stone . . ."

Her muscles gripped around him, causing an exquisite friction between them and in unspoken agreement, they continued the slow smooth rhythm until Stone's hot come spurted inside her, triggering her own blinding release.

When her vision cleared, she threaded her fingers through his hair and pulled his lips down to hers. As their tongues dueled and played, his cock hardened inside her once more.

Did I mention I love Klatch men's recharge time?

He nipped at her lips and began to move inside her once more. "It's due to the energy of the queen, but I'll take credit if you like."

She chuckled against his neck. "Fuck me, Stone. Fuck me like you've always imagined."

A surge of all-male triumph flowed through their emphatic connection as she broke through his chains of control. He lifted her leg, changing the angle, before he pistoned inside her as deep as he'd ever been. With each powerful thrust, energy surged through her to spiral out of her body and into the air around them. Soon it became difficult to breathe and yet Stone didn't slow or stop.

He lowered his face next to her ear, his morning stubble gently abrading her cheek. "Nourish the land, my love, then I will make you scream my name while you come."

His whispered promise caused her inner muscles to clench

harder around his cock, milking him, and he groaned. "Witch . . ." he panted against her neck.

Alyssa closed her eyes and allowed the power to flow freely through her. She pictured the planet in her mind and carefully funneled her power toward the dark spots of decay. Each slowly brightened until they glittered with health and vitality before she moved on to the next.

When she neared the ends of her reserve of power, she opened her eyes, surprised to find Stone watching her, while he fucked her hard. "Welcome back, my queen." He lowered his lips to hers and thrust his tongue inside her mouth, where she met him with heated frenzy. She nipped his bottom lip as she threaded her fingers through his silky hair.

Wanting him deeper, she rolled over until he was beneath her and she could ride him. She placed a hand on either side of his head and impaled herself fully against him, the swollen head of his cock pounding deep against her inner core with each thrust. Her nipples bobbed in front of his face and Stone surprised her by taking one of the aching buds into his mouth, sucking hard while she rode him.

She could hardly breathe as her internal muscles tightened around him, her climax just out of reach. The rhythm between them increased and the sounds of flesh slapping against flesh filled the air along with the tangy fragrance of sex. When Stone scraped his teeth over her nipple and pinched the other between his thumb and forefinger, she exploded. Power burst outward to sizzle along every wall as her muscles convulsed around him. A second later, his hot come shot inside her, causing another surge of pure power that rushed outward to sizzle along the still smoking walls.

Alyssa collapsed on top of him, burrowing against his warmth as his arms enveloped her. "I love you, Stone."

He quickly rolled her beneath him again, without pulling

out of her body, his lavender eyes boring into hers. "What did you say?"

She smiled, as she realized it was the first time she'd actually said the words out loud. "I love you."

Stone's smug smile made her want to hit him, but she laughed instead when he said, "It's about damn time, witch."

That afternoon, in the time-honored tradition of the Klatch, Alyssandra walked up the front steps of the castle and stood facing the Klatch people who had gathered to see her wed Stone. The Klatch wedding ceremony was nothing like the earth ceremonies she'd seen, and thankfully a bit less intimate than the ascension ceremony—but only a bit. Not that Alyssa hadn't enjoyed the dark erotic ritual, but for now, she preferred to have her sex life with Stone be a little less public. However, that wish would have to wait for one more day.

Annara, the same princess who officiated the ascension, stepped forward and nodded for the wedding ceremony to begin.

"Welcome, people of Klatch." Her voice magically carried to the thousands of citizens who gathered to watch. "Princes, if you please?"

Ryan and Grayson, as the next two princes in line for the throne, stepped forward and each placed a chaste kiss on Alyssa's cheek. She held her arms wide as they literally ripped her soft cotton half top and skirt from her body, baring her to her subjects. Even though she knew what to expect, a small gasp ripped from her throat and her nipples pebbled against the cool fragrant breeze.

Celebratory murmurs arose from the crowd along with several appreciative comments about the vitality of the new queen. Alyssa was suddenly thankful she'd gotten past her insecurities about her body. If this were a few weeks ago, she'd

252 / Cassie Ryan

have never made it through the ascension, let alone the wedding ceremony.

Annara held up her hand and the crowd fell silent. "Queen Alyssandra appears before you today, stripped of pride and material barriers, carrying the future queen deep inside her womb. She has successfully ascended the throne and released Annalecia from her vows to Tador and its people."

Cheers rose from the crowd as the cool breeze fluttered over Alyssa's skin, bringing a march of gooseflesh and a rush of moisture between her thighs. Thousands of people seeing her naked still had a decidedly erotic air to it—especially since everywhere she looked, both women and men were eyeing her as if she were a decadent dessert. Finally, she looked at a point over the crowd's heads and prayed for it to be over soon.

"Will the king step forward?" Annara's voice rang out over the crowd.

The crowd parted and she found her eyes glued to Stone's muscular form. He walked forward, wearing a deep purple tunic and trousers. He slowly took the steps one by one and as he neared, Alyssandra's clit swelled with anticipation. Her traitorous body had turned into one of Pavlov's dogs when it came to Stone. Any time he was near, her body craved sustenance and demanded it now, even though they had the entire population of Klatch as witnesses.

Stone dropped to his knees in front of her and bowed his head, which only increased Alyssa's arousal as her overactive imagination found several interesting things they could do in their present position.

Annara turned toward Alyssa. "Queen of the Klatch, will you please ready your mate for the ceremony to come?"

Alyssa smirked as she took the proffered knife from Annara and sliced the tunic from Stone's muscled chest. "Rise, King Stone, so I may continue our preparations."

Just be careful with that knife, my love, or your sustenance could be severely curtailed.

When Stone stood, she carefully slipped the knife inside the waistband of his breeches and sliced the cloth just enough so she could rip it the rest of the way.

You dare blackmail the queen? For that, it's my turn to tie you up and make good on my promise. She tried and failed hiding a mischievous smile.

Her pussy clenched as she envisioned all the things she would do to her husband as soon as she got him alone and she licked her lips as his swollen cock sprang free from his ripped pants. It jutted out proudly from his body and another appreciative murmur rose from several throats in the crowd.

Witch!

Annara tried unsuccessfully to hide her open perusal of Stone's cock and smiled up at Alyssa, then shrugged before gesturing for them to step forward, now that Stone was naked as well. "King Stone appears before you today, stripped of pride and material barriers. He has successfully proven his ability to amply supply the queen with energy and to impregnate her with an heir." Annara turned back toward Alyssa and Stone. "Turn and face your people as you receive the wedding mark."

A quick sizzling jolt against her hip told her it was complete. *Wow, if getting a tattoo on earth were this easy, everyone would have several.*

She and Stone turned an about-face so everyone could see the tiny curved sword crisscrossed with a red rose emblazoned against their hips. The Klatch didn't do something so temporary as wedding rings, but something permanent and lasting. Just like her love for Stone and her home.

Annara stepped forward again. "I officially declare the king and queen wed. Let the celebrations begin!"

Alyssa threaded her fingers with Stone's and they walked

down the steps together toward a special tub that had been set up just for this purpose. The tub was a full head taller than Stone, large enough to hold four people and made of solid *balda*, so no one could see inside. Apparently, now that they were officially married, they were afforded at least the illusion of privacy. Wooden steps led up the side of the tub to allow entry.

Immediately surrounding the large tub were hundreds of tables also made of pure *balda*. Every table was laden with food and drink to allow all assembled to celebrate while the king and queen prepared to share their energy with the people.

Heat suffused Alyssa's face at the thought of what they were about to do. Sasha had explained that the tub and all the tables were *balda*, so all the energy she and Stone generated during the celebration would carry out to all the tables. No royal couple had ever supplied all the tables with energy, even though her parents had come close. However, due to their past history, Sasha was confident that Alyssa and Stone would be the first. *I'm extremely thankful the tub is made of solid balda, so no one can see us.*

Stone's amused chuckle sounded inside her head. *We've already shared energy in front of a roomful, surely a crowd of thousands can't be so different.*

Alyssa snorted as they reached the stairs, and didn't bother to answer. She started up the wooden steps with Stone close behind her. The scent of vanilla hung heavy in the air and she wondered briefly where it came from.

When they reached the top, she sat down on the wide edge of the tub, allowing her legs to dangle into the warm liquid, and then she stiffened as she realized exactly what the liquid was, as well as where the vanilla scent had originated. "No one told me this thing was going to be filled with oil!" She glared back at Stone and he only smiled. The possibilities intrigued her, but she wished someone would've told her.

"Did I forget to mention that, love? Oil is a great conductor of energy as well as wonderfully slippery." He sat next to her, dipping his legs down into the warm oil before pushing off the side and slipping down into the deep tub. When he landed, his lips were even with her crotch since he stood on one of the several different levels of seats cut into the side of the tub. He grinned up at her. "Are you going to come join me, or are you going to be the first queen in history to let the entire population watch the king bring you to orgasm?"

Heat flowed into her face and she slipped down into the pool, trusting Stone to catch her. He didn't disappoint her, and her breasts rubbed against every oily muscled inch of him as she slid down in front of him. She anchored her arms around his neck and smiled. "Hmm, maybe all this oil does have some promising possibilities." She nipped Stone's bottom lip and laughed as his cock hardened against her stomach.

"I think you're absolutely right, my queen." Stone's eyes darkened with passion and promise. A shudder of anticipation flowed through her as he stepped down into the bottom of the tub, the warm oil teasing just under her breasts.

The sounds of revelry outside the tank carried to them on the wind, but cocooned in the *balda* tub, it seemed like they were in their own private room. Latticed sunlight glinted off the oil, as the branches of the towering trees overhead slowly swayed in the breeze.

Alyssa wriggled against Stone, enjoying the silky slide of skin against skin and the resulting awakening of her hurricane of energy. "I think we should generate so much power that every table lights up like a Christmas tree."

Stone's brow furrowed. "What kind of tree?"

She laughed. "Never mind. How about we generate so much power that every table lights up like a . . . lightning storm?"

Understanding dawned as his full lips curved up into a sexy

grin that melted her heart and fired her blood. "I think we'd better get started." Without warning he slanted his lips over hers, dipping inside her mouth to plunder and claim.

Alyssa tightened her grip around his neck, meeting his passion with fire of her own. Her tongue dueled with his and she pressed her body closer, rubbing herself against him with the help of the slick oil. Her hurricane of energy howled like a beast about to be fed and whipped through her body causing every hair to stand on end—even inside the thick oil.

When Stone grabbed her ass in his two large hands, she leveraged her grip on his neck and lifted herself until she could wrap her legs around his waist. The swollen tip of his cock touched against her core and thanks to the oil, he slipped easily inside her, impaling her and filling her completely. Stone backed her against the wall of the tub and thrust into her in long slick strokes.

She groaned into Stone's mouth and rhythmically flexed and loosened her grip around his waist, bringing him fully inside her hot core with every thrust. The thick oil sloshed between them, wetting the ends of her hair and slowing their movements. Alyssa rubbed against him, working harder to achieve the friction they both wanted.

Without breaking their rhythm, Stone lifted her and set her on one of the seats carved into the side of the tub. She leaned back, spreading her legs wide. He leaned over her, wrapping his arms around her thighs for leverage and plunged back inside her, deepening the angle and ripping a scream of pleasure from her throat. Power sizzled along her skin to flow up the side of the tub, bringing a chorus of cheers from the crowd and coursing even more power throughout her body.

He pulled out of her and she cried out from a sense of loss and emptiness. Stone firmly turned her on the ledge until she faced away from him, her legs braced apart. He pulled her back until her weight rested on her shins. Alyssa looked back over her shoulder and her eyes widened as his thick cock slipped easily inside her ass, filling her completely.

Even the *ponga* during the ascension ceremony didn't slide Stone's cock inside her this easily. The exquisite friction built inside her body in an ever-tightening spiral. Alyssa matched his rhythm, slamming back against with every thrust, groaning as her arousal arrowed higher and pink ribbons of energy whipped around them like a sudden electricity storm.

The sloshing oil teased against her swollen clit and nipples, adding to the erotic sensations arrowing through her. A sudden image flashed into her mind of being sandwiched in between Stone and a nameless Klatch Adonis while they fucked her from both sides while the warm vanilla oil sloshed around them.

Stone stiffened as his hot seed emptied deep inside her. He called out her name, the feral sound bouncing off the walls and echoing around them.

As soon as his essence touched her, a nuclear explosion of power flung outward, sizzling along the *balda* seams and shooting pink tendrils of power into the air over the tub. The remains of Alyssa's orgasm flowed through her in rolling waves of contractions until it released her to slump forward against the side of the tank.

When enough blood returned to Alyssa's brain, she realized that the only sound around them was her and Stone's harsh breathing.

"You and your visions are going to be the death of me, Alyssandra. But I have to say, that one may be worth trying out in reality—including the oil." His deep chuckle reverberated through her body and out into the oil. Stone slowly slipped his softening cock out of her and turned her on the ledge so he could gather her against his chest.

He brushed his lips against her forehead, the gentle warmth

causing her to burrow deeper against his chest. "Shall we go out and see our handiwork, Alyssandra?"

Heat burned into her cheeks and she buried her face against his neck. "Do we have to?" Her limbs were jelly and she wanted nothing more than to curl up against Stone and sleep. It had been an exhausting, although erotic, few days.

"The faster we get out of here, the faster we can go up to our room and be totally and blessedly alone."

She pulled back to look into his amused lavender eyes and sighed. "All right. Let's get this over with." She forced her lips into a small smile even though she was still caught in a golden languid haze.

Stone's lips curved causing the adorable dent next to his mouth to catch her attention. She traced it with her finger before she turned to stand and then lift herself up onto the highest seat cut into the tub. As soon as she peeked over the top of the tub, Ryan and Grayson stepped forward to grab her under her arms and lift her easily out and onto the top wooden step.

Ryan winked at her before going back to help Stone. She lifted her head, looking out at the array of tables assembled and for the first time realized why there was a sudden silence. The top of every table held the smoking remains of charred food, while a few stray pink sizzles popped and fizzed along *balda* seams. A few nearby trees were still smoking and had angry burn marks up the sides of their trunks. The Klatch stood clear of the cooling tables smiling up at her and waited for Stone to emerge.

Stone threaded his fingers through hers and held their joined hands high. As if they'd flipped a switch, a wave of cheering assaulted them.

Annara stepped forward and bowed her head toward both of them before holding up her hand to quiet the crowd. After several seconds, where Alyssa was sure they would ignore Annara's signal, the sound finally died away.

"An impressive display of power, Your Majesties. More food is on the way so the celebration can continue. Prince Ryan and Grayson will escort you both to the baths where you'll be attended by the queen's lady's maid." She stepped back and then raised her gaze to meet Alyssa's. "Congratulations on your very successful wedding, not to mention a very . . . attentive king."

Chapter 17

As soon as they were out of sight of the still-cheering crowds, Grayson slipped a robe around Alyssa's shoulders and she shot him a grateful smile. "Thanks, I think enough people have seen me naked for one day." The soft cotton cloth stuck to her oil-soaked body and she looked forward to a very thorough bath.

Mischief sparked in his lavender eyes and his lips curved in a lecherous grin. "And let me be the first to say how much all of us appreciated the very clear view of our new queen."

She punched him on the shoulder and he laughed and stepped quickly out of her reach. "What? No comments about the new king's muscular body?"

"Thanks, but I must admit, I didn't even glance at him. However, I'd be happy to take another look at you, if it's at all helpful."

She shook her fist at him, but couldn't help the giggle that escaped through her wide grin. "Don't mess with me today, Grayson. I've had a hard week and I'm covered in oil."

"Stone told us how dangerous you are when riled, my

queen. I'll make sure not to push my luck too far." As usual, his features showed only good-natured teasing, with no trace of remorse.

"I appreciate the escort, but if you two don't mind, I think Alyssandra and I would like some time alone." Stone glared at both his friends, neither of which seemed to take the not-so-subtle hint.

Ryan rubbed his thumb absently over the bottom of his scar and shrugged. "We promised the king and queen we wouldn't let you out of our sight until you were both safely tucked away in your bed chamber. I think Darius is still worried about the Cunts trying to take Alyssandra, now that she's tied to the planet. She would still make a valuable hostage."

Fear trickled down Alyssa's spine as she realized the truth of Ryan's statement. She and Stone would have little or no privacy in return for their continued safety. She sighed as they entered the bathing chamber where she and Sasha had their ill-fated *ponga* overdose.

"I remember this place," Stone said as he pulled her against him, both their robes an unwanted barrier between them. "Something to do with *ponga* and your lady's maid, wasn't it?"

Alyssa narrowed her eyes, shooting daggers at her new husband. "You promised not to tell anyone!"

He covered her mouth with his, even as his words echoed inside her mind through their empathic connection. "I haven't broken my promise. I was only sharing fond memories with my new wife."

She laughed as she pushed him away. "Semantics, husband." The word husband rolled off her tongue easily and she smiled.

"I would love to hear about this in more detail." Grayson's deep voice echoed around the room as he studied them.

"As would I," Ryan chimed in.

"Your Majesties?" Sasha stood just inside the large bathing

chamber, her head bowed, her half top and string bikini underwear sticking to her skin from the humid air of the cavern. "I have news I think you should hear immediately."

Alyssa stepped forward toward her maid. "What is it, Sasha?" Her brow furrowed at the concern in Sasha's tone.

Sasha tipped her chin up to look at everyone around the room in turn before answering. "As you know, I have been spending some time with Shawn when you don't need me for my duties."

Stone stepped up beside Alyssa, placing a hand on her shoulder, which she immediately covered with her own.

"Has Shawn hurt you?" Stone demanded.

The maid's eyes widened with shock. "No, my king, of course not." She swallowed hard before continuing. "But he has news of the Cunt's plans that I think you should both hear—without the council's knowledge."

Unease snaked down Alyssa's spine like ice, chasing all her exhaustion away. "Bring him to us immediately."

Before Alyssa's last word echoed away inside the chamber, Sasha had ducked back through the dressing room and returned with Shawn, who was now dressed in the white tunic and breeches of the Klatch. He immediately bowed before them, carefully looking everywhere but at Alyssa.

Grayson and Ryan ranged beside her like overprotective guard dogs ready to pounce and Stone stiffened beside her. "*This had better be good, my love, or I'll kill him myself.*" Apparently, Stone still hadn't forgiven Shawn's part in the attempted false ascension.

"What information do you have for us, Shawn?" Looking at him, she waited to feel fear, unease or even anger from her ordeal, but none of those emotions came. Her eyes widened as she realized she actually pitied Shawn. They'd both been raised on the Cunt's lies, but his actions because of those lies had almost cost him and his entire race dearly. It would probably take him much longer to come to terms with his past than it had Alyssa.

After a long moment, he finally raised his gaze to hers, his shoulders squared, his manner proud. "Hello, my queen. It's good to see you again under better circumstances. I want to apologize for . . . everything." Shame etched across his expression.

Grayson took a menacing step forward and Alyssa held up a hand to stop his progress even as she noted Shawn hadn't moved an inch or shown any sign of flinching away. Maybe his spirit hadn't been broken after all. "Thank you, Shawn. Sasha said you had information for us."

He nodded and gripped Sasha's hand in his, a quick look of tenderness passing between them before he returned his gaze to Alyssa. "I overheard Sela speaking with someone several months before you were taken. I got a glimpse of them as they left through a portal and just saw them again this morning in the courtyard."

"Our traitor." Stone's hard voice could've cut granite.

Sasha nodded. "Shawn pointed them out to me. It's the Council Head."

Shock slapped at Alyssa and when she looked at Stone, Grayson, and Ryan, their stunned expressions mirrored her surprise. Tense silence filled the chamber as she assimilated the information. She'd known the council didn't see eye to eye with the throne, but she didn't think the Council Head would plot with the Cunts. "Are any of the other council members involved?"

"Not that I gathered from the conversation I overheard. She told Sela she'd erased all references she could find within the queen's archives to something called the triangle."

Alyssa exchanged a quick glance with Stone, his handsome features drawn and angry, before she gestured for Shawn to continue.

"Apparently, Sela was convinced you were the princess

mentioned in a legend and that due to the volatility and the intensity of your power, she had some way to harness it to her benefit. Although, I didn't hear any more details. I never trusted Sela. I'd planned on completing the ascension and then bringing my new bride back to Klatch to overthrow what I'd been told was a corrupt government." He shook his head. "I never planned for Sela to come into power. I'm sorry I almost . . ."

Alyssa shook her head. "You and I both have a lot to overcome from our past among the Cunts, Shawn. You can stop apologizing and repay me by taking good care of Sasha. She told me you asked her to marry you this morning. You do realize that only the royals are required to marry on Klatch?"

He smiled as he looked down at Sasha, his gaze tender and loving. "I think that's the one earth tradition that's stuck with me. I need no other woman besides Sasha. I want to make her my wife if she'll have me."

Stone stepped between Shawn and Alyssa and a long tense moment passed as the men simply stared at each other. Alyssa was a heartbeat away from calling off the testosterone pissing contest when Stone held out his hand to Shawn.

Surprise flashed in Shawn's eyes before he reached out to shake.

Stone kept a firm grip on Shawn's hand and pinned him with an intense stare. "Take good care of her, or you'll have one very unhappy king to answer to. Not to mention a queen I wouldn't want angry with me."

Shawn's lips curved into a smile and he gave a small nod to Stone. "Understood—on all counts." He turned to Sasha and brushed his fingers over her cheek in a tender gesture that made Alyssa smile. "When your duties are done, do you want to join my parents and me for dinner?"

Sasha nodded and watched him leave until he disappeared from sight before she turned back, a blush burning into her cheeks.

Figuring Sasha would welcome a subject change, she turned to Stone. "What do we do now? Is there any way to find out for sure if any of the rest of the council is involved?"

"I think we can leave that to Ryan and Grayson." He raised his eyebrows in question toward the two men.

"He's right," Ryan said. "We have a little more freedom than the two of you. We'll find out something before the scheduled council meeting next week."

"Anything you can find out will help." She puffed out a sigh and looked up at Stone. "Now I'd really like to wash off all this oil before this robe is permanently stuck to my skin."

One week later, Alyssa paced the throne room impatiently waiting for Grayson and Ryan to tell her the information they'd found. Her stomach roiled with a combination of morning sickness and nervous knots. She'd spent the past week scouring the queen's archives for any information they may have missed regarding the triangle. Nothing else had surfaced, but she'd read account after account of queens who had to be brave enough to make tough decisions for the well-being of Tador. Alyssa just hoped she could do the same when she met with the council.

"Alyssandra, you're going to wear a hole in the floor. They'll be here." Stone sat on one of the thrones, his long legs stretched out in front of him, crossed at the ankle. "They told us they'd be here, and they've never let me down."

"The council meeting is due to start in ten minutes."

"You're the queen, remember? They can't start without you." He leaned forward and smiled. "I say let them wait. It will keep them off balance for the discussions to come."

"Somehow I don't think what will be going on can be termed as 'discussions.' How the hell am I supposed to accuse the Council Head of treason without starting a riot?"

The large double doors opened and Ryan and Grayson strode

forward before the majordomo had a chance to announce them. Ryan startled her by brushing a quick kiss over her cheek as he walked by toward the council chambers. "I'll tell them you'll be a few minutes late," he tossed over his shoulder along with a cheeky smile.

Alyssa held her arms out at her sides, palm up. "What the hell's going on? Where's Ryan going?"

Grayson flopped down on the queen's throne as if it were his own. He poured himself a glass of wine and drank it down while Alyssa resisted the urge to shake him. She knew that would only make him draw out the suspense further, so she bit her tongue, crossed her arms under her breasts and waited.

Stone shook his head and glared at his friend as Grayson refilled the goblet before turning to face Alyssa. "Our little investigation has yielded some results. It seems there are two conspirators among the council. The Council Head and her son."

Alyssa remembered the Council Head's son. She'd never heard the man actually speak, he only stood behind his mother and nodded at everything she said. It didn't surprise her she'd dragged him into the conspiracy. "Do you know if there's any more to it than the meetings with Sela and the spells on the queen's journals?"

Grayson shook his head. "Unfortunately, without alerting them of our suspicions, we were unable to find out. Perhaps once we expose them in front of the citizens, the guards can question them further." He set down the goblet and held up his index finger in front of his face. "But beware, my queen. If they are in league with the Cunts, I would be ready for anything— even in front of the entire council and the population. Their lives won't be worth much on Klatch once they are exposed, and desperate witches often do take desperate measures."

Alyssa rubbed her hands over both arms against a sudden rush of goose bumps at what she was about to do. "Thanks, Grayson. Thank Ryan for me too. Don't worry, I'll be careful."

She looked up at Stone, his strong presence lending comfort. "Can you tell them the king and I will be a few more minutes?"

Grayson unfolded his lanky form from her throne and stepped forward to put his finger under her chin and tip her face up to meet his gaze. "You can do this, Alyssandra. It's time to bring out that woman who is comfortable being queen. Think about what they almost stole from you—not only Stone and your parents, but Tador as well. Don't let them get away with it." He leaned down and brushed a tender kiss across her forehead.

When he turned to walk away toward the council chamber, Alyssa's gaze met Stone's. A flood of emotions ran through her, reminding her of the torrential flow of energy that constantly flowed through her body and awakened like a sleeping dragon every time Stone provided her with sustenance. She placed a hand over their growing daughter and took a deep breath. *I won't let you down, little one. When you ascend, the council will be there to help you, not fight you!*

Two trusted Klatch Council members had betrayed their own people and even more personally, endangered people Alyssa loved. Her anger opened like a flower blooming in direct sunlight and she squared her shoulders and lifted her chin. Grayson was right, it was definitely time to become the woman who was queen. Tador deserved nothing less.

"I need a minute to erect my energy shield and then I think I'm ready to take on the council." She heard her words, strong and almost regal and when Stone's smile widened, new confidence surged through her.

"*We* are ready to take them on. You're not in this alone, Alyssandra."

She brushed a kiss over his lips and then stood back and closed her eyes, concentrating on awakening her power. The sleeping dragon of energy surged to life inside her and she directed it to form a barrier around her, especially around her stomach to protect their daughter. As her energy shield snapped into place around her, she opened her eyes and held out her hand to Stone.

He rose gracefully and closed the few steps between them to take her hand.

"I know I'm not alone. I'm counting on it. I just wish I took acting classes in school, because I'm going to need to give the performance of a lifetime in the next few minutes."

Stone chuckled and pulled her against the long line of his hard body. She sighed as she fitted herself perfectly against her husband and he kissed her hair. "Alyssandra, you should've seen yourself when you last spoke to the council. You weren't playing a part. You *were* queen. It's inside you. Just let it come out and take its rightful place."

Alyssandra stepped through the door to the council chamber, her steps unhurried and leisurely. When she'd taken no more than three steps, the Council Head banged her *balda* gavel against the council table and turned to scowl at her and Stone.

Alyssa ignored her, continuing her slow walk across the council chamber, stopping along the way to greet citizens she'd met at the presentation ball or family and friends.

The Council Head cleared her throat, and Alyssa had to bite back a laugh. There were a few parts of this she would probably enjoy, and baiting the Council Head after the way the woman had spoken to Alyssa's parents, was definitely one of them. She deserved much more than that for committing treason, but one thing at a time.

When Alyssa turned to greet her father and mother, she noticed Stone taking the same deliberate path behind her, slowly navigating his way through the crowd. His steady gaze met hers and she caught her breath against a sudden rush of arousal and love. She hoped there was never a day when she looked at

Stone and didn't feel those same wonderful emotions and sensations.

Darius brushed a kiss over her cheek and whispered against her ear. "I'm enjoying the show, daughter. And you look lovely." He placed a gentle hand over her stomach. "Take care with my granddaughter. It's a dangerous game you're playing—but necessary."

She smiled and moved away, finally stepping up onto the dais and settled herself in the chair appointed for the queen. She continued to ignore the murderous glare aimed at her from the Council Head, and instead watched Stone finish wending his way through the crowd until he took the stairs up the dais and then settled himself beside her.

The *balda* gavel pounded against the table in impatient bursts before the Council Head spoke. "Now that the new king and queen have seen fit to join us, we may begin with—"

"Actually, under the laws of Tador, the queen runs the Klatch Council meetings." Alyssa stood and faced the audience of Klatch, turning her back on the council. She smiled as she noticed her guards strategically placed around the dais in case they were needed. *Probably Grayson and Ryan's doing.*

"I know from the last council meeting I attended that the Council Head graciously ran these meetings while my mother was ill." Alyssa smiled down at her mother, who seemed to be trying to hide a smirk. "However, now that I've ascended, and am perfectly healthy, I'm ready to take on my full role as your queen."

Cheers and applause rose around the chamber until the pounding of the *balda* gavel finally calmed them down.

"Perhaps," the Council Head stepped forward into Alyssa's line of sight, "until you get used to keeping order during the meetings, you will allow the council to continue as it has done successfully for many generations, my queen."

Lady, you are such an amateur when it comes to intimidation. I've lived through the best and you're not even in the same league.

Alyssa did her best impression of Sela and raised one brow, glaring down her nose at the Council Head. "Perhaps not. Thank you Council Head, that will be all."

The woman's eyes narrowed and her eyes sparked with barely concealed fury while her lips thinned into a hard line. Alyssa kept her eye contact for a moment longer and when the woman made no move to return to her seat, Alyssa cocked her head to one side and frowned down at her. "You may return to your seat, Council Head. That way if I require advice from the council, I'll know just where to find you."

Tense silence filled the chamber, but when Alyssa surveyed the faces of the Klatch citizens, most of them seemed to be trying to hide their smiles. Apparently, the Klatch Council was even more unpopular than she'd thought.

Finally, the Council Head gave the barest of nods, just skirting the line of being disrespectful and returned to her seat.

Alyssa ensured her energy shield was firmly in place and turned to address the citizens. "My fellow Klatch, I've come today to discuss an urgent issue with you that concerns the continued health and survival of Tador. As you all know, my mother, Queen Annalecia, fought a losing battle to keep the planet healthy and whole since I'd been abducted by our enemies, the Cunts." Alyssa nodded toward her mother and several turned to look at her and smile, offering their silent support.

Over the past week, Annalecia's health and vigor had slowly returned. In fact, when they stood side by side, it was difficult for people to tell them apart—even with the age difference. The fact that her mother was healthy and whole once more was the only reason that the Council Head was still alive and well and on Tador. Alyssa wasn't sure she would've been so hospitable if the damage to her mother had been permanent.

"Now that I've ascended the throne, I've used the considerable power at my disposal to heal the planet. However, Tador has no reserves of power, and if we don't change something, before long, I'll be fighting the same losing battle as my mother." She placed a hand against her stomach. "And we don't have the luxury of waiting another twenty-four years for the next queen to ascend."

Quiet murmurs through the crowd assured her she'd hit a nerve.

"The king and I have spent many hours researching and looking for a solution and we've found one. If we are to save the planet and our way of life, we need to be creative in our thinking and look at the best long-term solution, so that our children don't bear the brunt of this issue once more. In fact, I was surprised to find that Tador has been in similar circumstances before and has survived because the reigning queen put aside her pride and instituted what's known as the triangle."

An urgent buzz of hushed voices traveled through the crowd and the air of fear and uncertainty scented the room for the first time since she'd spoken. She held up her hands and the crowd instantly quieted. "Hear me out. The purpose of the triangle is to stabilize the power base and to allow three individuals to lend their power to the planet rather than just one. It consists of the queen, a Seer and a Healer. The last two are humans with special gifts who mate with full-blooded Klatch princes and help the queen harness her power and heal the planet."

Outraged gasps of shock met her announcement and Alyssa mentally readied herself for a long battle. She had to make them see that this was the right course for everyone.

"My queen, you are too new to understand what you're suggesting."

Alyssa turned toward the voice in time to see the Council Head smile gently as if she were talking to a child. The woman's eyes sparkled with amusement and she gestured toward the crowd. "There's no need to concern the people with such outlandish ideas. You'll only cause fear and uncertainty."

Alyssa kept her stance relaxed and stared the woman down. "On the contrary, I used my time before the ascension well. I've read through all the queens' journals I could find in the archive pertaining to the triangle and I'm convinced that its time has come again. The Klatch people need to hear the truth, not lies that make them feel better. Anyone who hides that truth is doing them a disservice."

A quick flicker of fear flashed through the Council Head's eyes before she hid it.

"She knows we discovered that she spelled the journals in the queens' archives, Stone. Be careful."

"I was about to say the same thing to you, love."

Alyssa took a breath and continued. "Each queen who invoked the triangle was in a similar circumstance as we are in now. We can't wait until the planet deteriorates too fast for us to save it. If the council were truly students of Klatch history, they would've been able to suggest it to me rather than me having to find it on my own."

The Council Head stood and walked around the table to stand in front of Alyssa. She crossed her arms before pinning Alyssa with a glare worthy of any high school principal. "Perhaps your powers are not as advanced as we thought. Perhaps you aren't capable of holding the throne without help, and this is your way to cover up that weakness."

Stone stood behind her and his anger flowed through their empathic link. "Do you dare insult your queen in that manner? You forget yourself." He took a menacing step forward and the Council Head blanched.

Stone took a deep breath before continuing, struggling to control his temper. "With all due respect to the many past queens of Tador, only a fool would not realize that a queen as powerful as Alyssandra has never been in symbiosis with the planet before. She's proven many times over the extent of her power. Or were you not at our wedding ceremony, Council Head?"

The woman lowered her eyes and bowed her head before Stone's wrath. "My apologies, my liege, I meant no disrespect for the queen or yourself." She raised her chin to meet his gaze again. "I merely inquire as to the queen's experience. You must admit that being raised by Cunts, serving alcoholic drinks in a bar on earth, and then watching the former queen in her duties for only a week hardly qualifies her to make lasting decisions for the planet."

Stone's anger turned white hot and sizzled against their link.

Alyssa placed a gentle hand on his arm. *Stone, it's all right. If I can stand up to Sela, this woman is a piece of cake.*

His muscles flexed under her fingers, but he nodded. "You're lucky, Council Head, that my wife prefers to speak for herself. I am not quite as forgiving." He glowered at the woman before resuming his seat.

Alyssa pursed her lips trying to hide her smile at the discomfort on the many faces of the council. "I can speak for my experience." She stepped forward, invading the council leader's space. "You're absolutely right, I've held no leadership positions that would uniquely qualify me for this job. And yet, all of you trust me to maintain the planet. There was never any talk of my qualifications when the choices were to have me ascend the throne or let the planet and all of you die. Purely because I was a blood descendant of the reigning queen, you willingly handed over the reigns to your planet, your survival and your way of life to me—a woman without experience. I wonder who is the more foolish of the two of us, Council Head?"

Whispers from the crowd rose in a low hum.

Alyssa continued before the woman could retort. "From what I've read in the archives, all of you were born to the positions you now hold. None of you were elected or had to show any special talents to retain your jobs. Only an accident of birth keeps you serving on this council. An accident of birth, and the support of the reigning queen."

Outraged gasps sounded from the entire council, but she ignored them and pushed forward. "The law says the council's purpose is to advise the queen, to support her and to help her in matters of law and precedent. However, apparently, none of you have read the law because it also states that the queen has no obligation to accept your advice and that she can replace the council at will—either individual members or the entire council."

"How dare you!" The council leader's hands balled into fists and her eyes narrowed to slits. "This ruling body has served the people and their queen faithfully for thousands of years."

Alyssa crossed her arms under her breasts and stared across at the Council Head. "Actually, according to the queens' journals in the archives, this council served faithfully until my grandmother's reign. It was then the council took much of the queen's power and convinced her into a position of a mere figurehead."

She waited until the Council Head took a breath to speak before she barreled on, cutting her off. "From what I read of my grandmother, she was a shy woman and welcomed the council's help, and my mother was ill for much of her reign because of grief and then from the toll of keeping a deteriorating planet supplied with energy. But now . . . now you're all stuck with me. I'm not ill and I'm certainly not shy. I'm a woman perfectly capable of ruling this world and ensuring its longevity and that's what I intend to do."

Alyssa took another step forward as the swirling energy inside her increased, howling in outrage as her anger fueled it to dangerous heights. She was dimly aware that the Council Head's hair stood on end as if static electricity flowed around her. The woman's eyes widened in shock. "Today, I take all the queen's power back. I'm the one who maintains the symbiosis with the planet. The king and I researched the law and I'm the one who carries the heir."

She turned and stepped away from the Council Head, allowing her temper to cool before energy exploded in all directions—being pregnant had also increased the volatility of her power, but not its intensity. "Over the next few weeks, the king and I will meet with each council member to evaluate if they will continue on the council or be replaced by someone willing to do the job as stated in the Klatch laws."

Alyssa turned back toward the Council Head. "I already know there will be an opening for Council Head at the very least."

The woman's mouth dropped open in surprise and outrage. Then suddenly, she raised her hand and blue lightning zinged toward Alyssa. Alyssa flinched, but the energy bounced harmlessly off her energy shield and rebounded on the woman.

The Council Head's scream reverberated through the chamber as her flesh slowly burned from her bones as if she'd been hit by toxic acid like an old movie Alyssa remembered from the Sci-fi channel. The charred body collapsed onto the dais in a smoking heap, the smell of burning flesh filled Alyssa's lungs.

Another blue bolt sizzled from behind the council table, but before it even reached Alyssa, dozens of answering bolts of energy hit the Council Head's son squarely in the chest, knocking him off the back of the dais to fall with a loud thud to the *balda* floor below.

Chaos ensued and the guards swarmed the dais to fan out around the king and queen. Alyssa stood stunned, her hand resting protectively over her stomach. "She didn't just want to hurt me. She wanted to kill me . . ." Her words were lost in the chaos, but Stone must have heard them through their empathic link because he threaded his arm around her waist and pulled her back against him. A surge of comfort and borrowed energy flowed through her and she leaned back against him absorbing the wonderful sensations.

When she'd steadied her trembling nerves, she patted Stone's hand and he dropped his arm from around her. Alyssa turned toward the remaining council members who all looked as shaken and stunned as she felt. She stepped forward, reached for the *balda* gavel with shaking hands, and banged it against the table until the crowd quieted.

Alyssa motioned her guards aside so she could face the audience of Klatch. "You accepted me as your queen, and now you have to trust me to see you safely through. Everyone is welcome to visit the queen's archives to see the journals that explain the triangle for themselves. They explain not only how it works but also its purpose. In the meantime, Prince Grayson, the Seventh Prince of Klatch, will begin his search for the Seer, his future mate."

Silence met her declaration, but she could tell from the mixed expressions that not everyone supported this decision and several were still reeling with shock from the betrayal and death of the Council Head and her son.

"There will be weekly council meetings to answer questions and give everyone any updates we have."

Not sure what else to say before her legs gave out under her, she turned, carefully avoiding looking down at the smoking corpse of the Council Head, and walked toward Stone. When his arms closed around her, she leaned into the comfort of his embrace and allowed him to lead her from the room.

Epilogue

Alyssa reclined inside the baths, enjoying the froth of the warm water around her body as she waited for Stone to join her. Over the last few weeks, her increasing morning sickness had driven her to take more naps, soak in the baths a few times a day, and allow her very attentive husband to dote on her.

"Allow me to dote on you, beloved. I think you enjoy it and have become spoiled."

She laughed and looked up to see Stone standing just outside the baths, his naked body a study in fascinating textures, sculpted muscles and dusky olive skin. "You're right, I do and I am. But, since I'm the one who has to go through labor, I think it's only fair for you to spoil me while I'm pregnant. Although I intend to fully share the experience of labor through our empathic link."

Stone paled and his eyes widened as his unease beat against their empathic link.

A laugh bubbled up from deep inside Alyssa's throat to echo around the chamber. She traced her gaze over every well-muscled inch of her husband, following the arrow of dark hair that feathered down his chest and continued south, bringing her gaze to his cock, which was currently soft and nestled among an equally dark thatch of hair. She licked her lips at the thought of pulling him between her lips and teasing him with her tongue while he hardened inside her mouth. When her eyes traveled back up to his stricken expression, she laughed again. "Sorry, didn't mean to scare you. I was only teasing—mostly, anyway." At his weak smile, she crooked her finger at him, beckoning him to join her. "So, let's talk more about you spoiling me . . ."

He laughed as he descended the four steps down into the fizzing water to stand in front of her. "I suppose you're right, my queen. So, what spoiling do you require today?" He leaned over her and nipped at the sensitive skin just under her ear causing her to gasp as the sleeping energy awakened inside her, roaring to life like a sudden volcanic eruption. Her hair stood on end, flowing around her from the breeze caused by the river of power inside her.

He licked and nipped a line along her neck, causing her bones to soften in his arms as moisture rushed between her swollen pussy lips and her heavy breasts tingled inside the frothing water. Stone traced a path back up toward her ear and his words whispered against her skin, causing an avalanche of shivers and energy. "I think our little one is just as spoiled as her mother. Ever since your morning sickness started, you're insatiable . . . in all things." Stone nipped and licked a path around toward her lips.

Alyssa's lips curved as Stone covered her mouth with his, dipping inside until she tasted a combination of the wine he'd had for breakfast and the spicy taste that was uniquely Stone. She nipped his bottom lip even as she reached out to trace the hard ridges of his six-pack abs. He shuddered under her fingertips and straightened, leaving her eye level with his semi-hard cock.

She grabbed his hips, pulling him closer, until she could lean forward and pull his member between her lips. As her mouth closed around him, she kept a firm suction and laved her tongue over the tip before sucking him again. He hardened inside her mouth, lengthening and thickening, as she gently cupped his balls in her hand.

Stone threaded his fingers through her hair as a long moan escaped him. "Alyssandra, what are you doing to me?"

She chuckled, knowing the vibrations would tease him further. "*If you can't figure out what I'm doing, then I must not be doing it right.*"

She rolled his balls gently between her fingers and stroked his cock in a steady rhythm with her lips and her tongue. When her lips bumped against the underside of the sensitive head, she swallowed him again until he pressed deep against the back of her throat.

Stone's hips began a slow motion, fucking her mouth in long sure strokes until a salty drop of pre come dissolved against her tongue, exploding flavor through her mouth and energy through her body.

Alyssa pulled back, careful not to scrape Stone with her teeth as the spasm of pure power sizzled through her.

Stone sat next to her and pulled her across his body and into his lap. "Not that I don't love coming in your throat, Alyssandra, but I want to be buried inside you when you scream my name."

Her clit throbbed at his dark promise and she buried her fingers in his thick silky hair, pulling his mouth down to hers. Her bare breasts pressed against the muscles of his chest, and she enjoyed the smooth slide of her wet skin over his and the way his crispy hairs brushed over her engorged nipples.

Stone's cock swelled to life against her hip, shooting a fresh surge of fire through her veins and causing her flow of energy to howl in anticipation. Alyssa wrapped her fingers around Stone's thickness, enjoying the way his member jumped in her hand. She stroked his shaft slowly from the base all the way to the swollen head, enjoying the way the water lubricated her movements.

Stone hissed against the sensation and deepened their kiss, plundering her mouth even as she continued to tease him with her busy fingers. She met his frenzied passion with her own, letting him experience the overwhelming rush of the power surging inside her through their empathic link. He growled against lips and lifted her to straddle him, trapping his hard cock between them.

Alyssa wiggled on his lap, fighting against the pull of the water to press herself against him and grind her stomach against his cock. She wrapped her legs around his waist to anchor herself. The new position pressed her swollen pussy lips against the smooth skin of his cock and allowed her to plaster her breasts against his wet chest as she rubbed herself shamelessly against him.

The vortex of energy howled again, stealing the breath from her lungs and increasing her urgency. Her mouth still fused with Stone's, she unwrapped her legs from around his waist and bent them under her to rest on either side of his thighs. She rose on her shins, changing the angle of their kiss and allowing the head of his cock to slip down her stomach to trace a path past her clit to lodge against her aching opening.

Stone's large hands captured her hips and steadied her as she slowly impaled herself on his thick member. A moan ripped from Alyssa's throat at the sensation of Stone filling her. She leaned back as her eyes closed as she began to move. An exquisite friction built between them as the warm water sloshed around them. The only sound filling Alyssa's awareness was the rushing of the insatiable energy through her body and the steady thump of her heartbeat, which had increased to match the rhythm set by their bodies.

Stone's lips closed over one engorged nipple and her eyes

flew open at the intensity of the sensation. He nipped her sensitive peak and then soothed it with his tongue before he sucked hard, the sensation sending more moisture between her thighs to lubricate their movements.

Arousal curled tighter inside her belly as she neared her orgasm and the energy tightened inside her body almost painfully. Stone must've sensed her sudden urgency through their link because using his grip on her hips, he leaned her backwards, changing the angle and piercing her impossibly deep until she wasn't sure where Stone ended and she began. She gave herself up to his strength and he guided her again and again to take him deep, his swollen head probing her core, spiraling her higher and higher until the energy screamed out for release and so did she.

"Stone!" His name ripped from her lips as his hot come shot against her inner core, acting as a match to gasoline. Alyssa exploded, and for a split second, she saw nothing but pink lightning and knew nothing but the sea of pleasure that washed over her. In the next instant, her consciousness flew over the planet, bringing healing and energy where it needed, filling in the shadows and strengthening her bond with the land. Time lost all meaning as she nourished the land as if it were her child.

When her awareness reunited with her body, she found herself slumped forward onto Stone, his cock still snugly inside her, even as it softened. The sound of sizzling and the smell of something burning assaulted her senses.

He kissed the top of her hair as he feathered caresses over her bare back. "Welcome back, my queen." He glanced up at the still smoking walls. "I think your power is becoming a bit more volatile." He chuckled. "How does Tador fare today?"

Alyssa sighed and stretched with contentment before leaning back to look at her husband. "Doesn't it ever bother you to lose me like that right after an orgasm? I mean, it's got to be a bit disconcerting to have this amazing orgasm and then be left with this limp woman for several minutes until her brain snaps back inside her body."

Stone's full lips curved and he brushed his thumb over her bottom lip. "Not as long as you always come back to me, my love. Besides, if you stay away too long, I'll just start pleasuring you all over again until you're back."

She watched his eyes spark with erotic amusement, while she basked in the sharing of their empathic link. She knew he'd told her the truth, after all, it was a waste of time to try to lie or even omit things when you shared thoughts and feelings with each other every second of every day. She wasn't so sure she'd like it so much if she was the one left with the shell of a body for several minutes after each orgasm.

She brushed a kiss over his lips and then curled against him again. "It's about the same. The planet I mean."

Stone laughed at her roundabout return to his earlier question. "Is that good or bad?"

"Each time, I have to do more healing. It's never just as I left it and I never seem to make any headway so it can start storing away some energy for the future. I'm not sure how my mother held on so long with such widespread deterioration." Her thoughts turned to the triangle and she wished Grayson would contact them and give them an update soon.

Stone pulled her close, resting his chin on the top of her head. "He will, when he has found the Seer. We don't know how long it may take. Even then, he has to convince her to come back with him and take her place within the triangle. Not everyone will be as excited to leave their lives on earth as you were, love."

She huffed out a laugh. "True. Maybe they'll welcome a change as well. We need someone who is willing to become one of us."

Silence fell between them, even as her thoughts continued to churn. "I just hope I'm doing the right thing, Stone." She pulled back to look into his eyes. "Not only for the planet and the people, but what about our daughter?" She placed a hand over her stomach, silently reaching out to the life growing within her. "I'm making choices that will affect her and her children for generations to come." She closed her eyes and dropped her chin to her chest, as responsibility suddenly weighed heavy on her shoulders.

Stone placed his finger under her chin, tipping it up so he could brush a kiss over her lips. "Even if I gave you energy and sustenance twenty-four hours a day, you can not keep the entire planet healed forever. You've said yourself that even though it's much recovered since you've assumed the throne, the deterioration has begun again. We continue to search in both archives, but so far that's the best solution we've found."

She sighed and studied his handsome face as she reached out to trace the adorable dimple just next to his mouth. "I know. I think I just need to be reminded now and then. You'll have to continue to be my voice of logic."

He reached down to cup her breast and he grinned as her nipple pebbled against his hand and he hardened inside her. "I plan on reminding you how to control energy all afternoon." His eyes darkened with desire and he pinched her nipple, causing her to moan as her eyelids drifted closed.

"It's times like this I remember . . ."

He kissed her neck and whispered against her ear. "Remember what, my love?"

"It's good to be the queen."

Stone's chuckle sounded inside her mind as he began to move inside her again.

Here's a hot sneak peek at Elizabeth Amber's
NICHOLAS: THE LORDS OF SATYR,
available now from Aphrodisia . . .

1

Lord Nicholas Satyr lifted the dagger from the desk before him, anxious to have the task ahead complete. The blade flashed, reflecting the intensity of his strange pale gaze, before twisting to slice through the tasseled cord encircling the roll of parchment.

The missive's arrival that morning had been both unexpected and unwelcome. Dispatches from ElseWorld were infrequent and usually portended mischief of some kind. Trouble was already threatening the vineyards, which lay at the heart of Satyr lands. He could spare little time for any nonsense.

As the cord fell away, the coiled document unrolled with a will of its own, releasing a faint hint of magic into the room. Nick spared a quick glance for his younger brothers, Raine and Lyon, whom he'd summoned an hour ago from their adjacent estates within the Satyr compound. They would have sensed it, too.

Raine stood at the window, hands clasped at his back as he surveyed Nick's manicured gardens. Whirls of fog obscured the tangled forest and grapevine-covered hillsides beyond. He was, as usual, meticulously outfitted in gray, his cropped hair and garb as restrained as the late winter morning he observed.

Restless energy crackled from Lyon as he prowled Nick's salon, wending his brawny frame among elegant furnishings and curious artifacts. Occasionally he paused to examine one of his brother's newer acquisitions in his pawlike grasp, but he didn't linger. He was impatient to learn the document's contents and return to the business of overseeing his property.

Nick's fingertips tingled from the hum of ElseWorld magic caught in the parchment, but nothing in his face revealed his thoughts as he read. Over the course of three decades, he'd learned to disguise his emotions. They'd all found it necessary to hide their true natures, having grown up half Human, half Satyr in an EarthWorld intolerant of their kind.

Turning from the window, Raine glanced toward the parchment. "Is it from an Elder?"

Nick nodded, a curt inclination of his dark head. "King Feydon himself."

Lyon halted midstride and whipped around. "What the devil does *he* want?"

The leather of Nick's chair creaked subtly as he shifted all six and a half feet of his well-muscled form. "It seems he has managed to sire three Earth daughters."

Raine digested this news in silence, a slight stiffening of his shoulders the only indication that he'd heard.

Lyon snorted in amusement. "That randy old goat of a Faerie Elder sent us a birth announcement? From his deathbed, no less."

Not fully grasping the importance of the news, he blithely twirled a globe of EarthWorld upon the tip of one finger. Jeweled continents, sapphire oceans, and an emerald dragon or two sparkled in the candlelight.

"His announcement is somewhat belated," Nick clarified.

"The birthings occurred some twenty years ago. Apparently he's had an attack of conscience at this late date. And it's his dying wish that we remedy the situation he leaves behind."

Raine folded his arms, suspicion coloring his eyes a stormy gray. "And how precisely are we to do that?"

"According to his instructions, we are to locate his progeny and marry them," said Nick.

A bark of astonished laughter escaped Lyon. "What?!"

Nick tossed the parchment on the desk. "Read it yourselves if you doubt me. And have a care with my orb, Lyon."

Lyon looked down at his broad hands and saw they were very nearly crushing one of Nick's precious objects. His strength belonged to the outdoors and served him well in the Satyr vineyards. However, it didn't suit Nick's fashionable rooms, and he constantly had to be on guard lest he fatally upset something.

Grimacing, he set the globe back to rest in its cradle and headed for the letter on Nick's desk. He snatched it up and read aloud.

Lords of Satyr, Sons of Bacchus,
Be it known that I lie dying and naught may be done. As my time draws near, the weight of past indiscretions haunts me. I must tell of them.

Nineteen summers ago, I fathered daughters upon three highborn Human females of EarthWorld. I sowed my childseed whilst these females slumbered, leaving each unaware of my nocturnal visit.

My three grown daughters are now vulnerable and must be shielded from Forces that would harm them. 'Tis my dying wish you will find it your duty to husband them and bring them under your protection. You may search them out among the society of Rome, Venice, and Paris.

Thus is my Will.

"This is absurd," Lyon muttered in disgust. He slapped the letter to Nick's desk, causing the crystal bottles in the inkstand to rattle. The small act of violence did little to mollify him, and he turned to prowl the room again as though he were a caged animal seeking escape.

Raine took up the parchment and silently scanned its contents, assessing each phrase, searching for nuances of meaning. When he finally set it aside, his expression was grim.

He'd been wed before, three years earlier, but the marriage had ended in disaster within months. He had no plans to marry again. But he didn't speak of that now.

"Interesting that Feydon chose to produce three *female* offspring, and in locations so obligingly convenient to us," he remarked.

Nick slanted him a considering glance. "Almost as though he intended his daughters for us from the beginning."

Lyon swung around. "Seven hells! Do you suppose he spawned them on purpose in some misguided attempt to saddle us with wives?"

"Now that he has slipped into the shadows between life and death, we can only guess at his motives," said Raine.

Nick leaned back, causing his chair to protest once more. Candlelight flickered, glancing blue highlights off the jet black of his hair.

"It would be like him, however. We're the only of our kind left in EarthWorld, and he has long made clear he felt it our duty to procreate so Satyr lands won't fall into Human hands. Our properties need heirs, yet we have shown ourselves reluctant to sire them. He may have felt such an action justified."

"'Forces that would harm them,'" Lyon quoted from the parchment. "Do you think he means forces from his World or ours?"

"Or could it simply be a ruse to ensure our involvement?" asked Raine.

"If so, it's an effective tactic," said Nick. "Feydon knows our protective instincts would cause us to act if his children are in danger."

"It's an unfair obligation to thrust upon us," said Raine.

"Damn right, O Master of Understatement," said Lyon. "It's blatant manipulation."

"Manipulation or not, it makes our decision regarding a course of action or inaction a rather pressing matter," said Raine.

"Surely we must take some action," Lyon said, voicing reluctant concern. "These FaerieBlend females can't be left to fend for themselves. Can they?"

He and Raine looked to Nick.

"If we're to believe Feydon's missive, the females he mated were unaware he bedded them," said Nick. "That being the case, both mothers and daughters are innocent of any deceit directed our way."

"It's likely the daughters don't realize they're of ElseWorld," said Raine.

"Though they must be feeling the quickening pulse of Faerie blood," said Lyon.

"And misunderstanding its meaning if there's no one to guide them," said Nick. "'Tis a troubling notion."

"But not at all tempting," Raine stated baldly. "I've no interest in marrying again."

Nick and Lyon exchanged glances.

"Marriage to a half-Faerie creature could succeed where one to a Human failed," said Nick.

Raine shrugged. "Nevertheless, I'm unwilling to experiment."

Lyon ran blunt fingertips through the tangle of his thick tawny hair. "I find myself in agreement with Raine. I've no interest in tying myself to a woman not of my choosing, be she Faerie or Human. Isn't there some way to protect Feydon's daughters short of marriage?"

"How? Shall we hound their footsteps over the years to

come in order to guard them against trouble?" asked Nick. "They will have us arrested."

"I still say marriage can be avoided. Why not simply bring them to Satyr land and let them roam about as they please?" suggested Lyon.

Nick laughed, and Raine shot him a pitying glance.

Lyon looked affronted. "What? They will be safe here under our protection."

"Like your other pets?" asked Raine, referring to Lyon's menagerie of exotic animals that ranged freely on Satyr lands.

"They're females, not livestock," said Nick. "They will never agree to so ridiculous an arrangement. We must husband them and bring them under our protection. I see no other way."

Raine eyed his older brother. "You seem strangely committed to the idea of marriage after so little consideration."

Nick flexed his wide shoulders, straining the seams of his waistcoat and causing the subtle design in the dark teal brocade to shimmer. It was an unusual coat selected from among the treasures of his ancestors. Something about it pleased him. But then, he relished the unusual.

"Granted, the notion of marriage was unlooked for," he said. "But as I reflect on Feydon's edict I realize it provides a certain . . . opportunity."

Lyon gave him a look of false commiseration. "Poor Nick. Have you lacked for the attentions of a sufficient bounty of females all these years? You should have spoken sooner. Raine and I would be glad to share with you some of the legions angling for our portion of the Satyr coffers."

Raine smiled, a fleeting lift of one corner of his mouth. "He makes a point, big brother. We've all had more than a few opportunities to shackle ourselves over the years."

"We need heirs," said Nick.

Raine and Lyon stared at him in surprise.

"My thirtieth year approaches. You trail me by only two

years, Raine. And you by merely four, Lyon. Who else are we to sire sons and daughters on if not these FaerieBlends?" Nick demanded, gesturing toward the parchment. "They are by nature half breeds, a blend of EarthWorld and ElseWorld, like us."

"But unlike us, Feydon's daughters have Faerie blood in their veins," Raine reminded him.

"And the Faerie are volatile," added Lyon. "Who knows what diverse bag of tricks they may possess?" He shuddered.

"My material point is that while Human women might find certain of our ways strange or distasteful, a Fey wife would be less apt to present any objection to the manner in which we might presume to quest for heirs," said Nick.

"But what sort of heirs will they provide?" Raine asked, shaking his head. "A half-Satyr husband mating a half-Faerie wife? What kind of children can come of it?"

"If we don't intervene, it's probable the FaerieBlends will marry and mate with Humans. What offspring do you imagine might come of that?" Nick asked pointedly.

Lyon rammed his hands into the pockets of his sturdy trousers and sighed. He dressed the part of a vintner, wearing rumpled trousers, a nubby cotton tunic, and greatboots. "You're right. Neither they nor their children will know what to make of their abilities. That could prove disastrous."

A brittle tension settled over the room.

"The Satyr have always looked after the Faerie," Nick said decisively.

Lyon sighed. "It appears settled we must marry them. Bacchus, what if mine is stupid? Or offensive? How will I stand to bed her?"

"As I understand it, marriage and protection are our only obligations," said Raine. "Feydon's missive stated no requirement to mate or sire offspring."

Nick's eyes sharpened on him. "True."

"You would bind your wife to a childless marriage?" asked Lyon. "Bind yourself to one?"

"The choice will be hers, the facts put to her before we marry," said Raine. "I want no Blended children who will suffer the alienation of finding one foot in EarthWorld and one in ElseWorld while not properly fitting in either."

"What of the wine?" asked Lyon. "Our heirs must carry on our work in the vineyards when we're gone."

The vine-covered hills at the center of the Satyr compound produced grapes, which were made into wine each season. Labeled *Lords of Satyr,* it was hotly sought by the wealthy and titled throughout Europe and beyond. Some whispered that Satyr wine possessed magical properties, which it in fact did.

The brothers' trio of estates was strategically placed at triangulated points along the borders of an ancient forest, like guard towers at three corners of a fortress. At the center of each estate stood an ancient castle with extensive gardens and grounds that met and eventually mingled with the trees of the magnificent old-growth forest. The forest in turn ringed the base of the sloping hills of the vineyards, which formed the central core of their lands.

Theirs was ancient ground chosen by their ancestors for a special purpose—to serve as a sacred joining place for ElseWorld and EarthWorld. In centuries past, many Satyr had secretly dwelled here, protecting the portal that led between worlds. Now there were but three.

Raine flicked a speck of dust from his immaculate jacket, the expression in his gray eyes opaque. "Your offspring are welcome to my share. Let that settle the matter."

"For now," Nick relented.

Raine shrugged.

"Then it's only left to determine which daughter we select," said Lyon.

"Rome is most convenient for me," said Nick. "Any objections?"

"None. I'll take Paris," said Raine. "Damn, I abhor traveling."

"Traveling? To Paris? I'll remind you I'm left with Venice," said Lyon. "The journey there will be excruciating after the rains."

Raine quirked an eyebrow. "It should be no hardship since you travel there to meet buyers with regularity."

"Still, it's a bad time to be away. Many of my animals are in foal," said Lyon. "And the vineyards need watching."

"We can exert enough of our combined Will to bolster the forcewall around Satyr lands for weeks," said Raine.

"Why take unnecessary risk? It's my opinion some of us should stay," said Lyon.

"Agreed," said Nick. "I will go first. Once I secure my bride, your searches can follow."

Raine and Lyon assented, and soon thereafter, all three turned to the door.

Once outside, Nick breathed deeply. "The vines begin to awaken. I will make haste."

Eyes of sapphire blue, ashen gray, and tawny gold locked for a potent moment and then slid apart as the three Lords of Satyr were dispatched into the late morning mist.